D1082493

NICKEL CITY CROSSFIRE

GIDEON RIMES BOOK TWO

GARY EARL ROSS

GIDEON RIMES SERIES

Nickel City Blues
Nickel City Crossfire
Nickel City Storm Warning

∾

SEG Publishing invites you to visit our site!
Join our newsletter and receive a free short story in the Gideon Rimes
Series.

Copyright © Gary Earl Ross 2020

The right of Gary Earl Ross to be identified as the author of this work has been
asserted per the Copyright, Designs and Patents Act 1976. All rights reserved. No part
of this publication may be reproduced, transmitted, or stored in a retrieval system, in
any form or by any means, without permission in writing from the publisher, nor be
otherwise circulated in any form of binding or cover other than that in which it is
published and without a similar condition being imposed on the subsequent
purchaser. All characters in this publication are fictitious and any resemblance to
real people, alive or dead, is purely coincidental.

Cover design by Steven Novak

Published by SEG Publishing

For
Colleen, Timothy (Robin), David (Rebecca), Cody,
and Madelynne (Brian)
From Dad with Love
and
In Memory of Amrom Chodos,
supportive early reader, honest critic, wonderful friend.

1

Balding and brown-skinned, the Reverend Oscar Edgerton was a big man who dwarfed the client chair facing my desk. A chaplain twice retired, once from the army and once from the Georgia department of corrections, he had massive hands with well-kept nails. Beneath his thick salty mustache was a genial smile born of self-assurance. I had met him in October through Phoenix Trinidad, before Phoenix and I became lovers. The Friday before Thanksgiving we had seen him and his wife Louisa at a fund-raiser for Hope's Haven, the women's center where Oscar worked part-time as a security guard and where Phoenix served as legal counsel. She had called me last night—Wednesday—to tell me that Oscar would be bringing a friend in need of help to my office in the Elmwood Village this afternoon.

"I don't know what his friend needs," Phoenix said, "but Oscar thinks you're good people so be nice if you have to turn them down."

The man in my other client's chair was half Oscar's size but appeared to be around the same age, in his early to mid-sixties. His name was Winslow Simpkins. He was caramel-colored, with loose skin below his chin and thick gray hair in an arc above his forehead. He wore horn-rimmed glasses that did nothing to hide the sadness in his eyes and a topcoat that looked decades old. He had begun to tell me about his daughter Keisha, thirty-four, a nurse who served as the secretary for Sermon on the Mount, one of the city's most prominent black churches. Lower lip trembling, he had stopped when he came to the event that led to her disappearance. For a time, the only sound was the distant hum of washers and dryers in the laundromat downstairs.

"It's okay, Win," Oscar said finally, patting his friend's arm, trying to smooth the gravel in his own voice. "Take your time. Better you tell it, the better Brother Rimes can help you."

Winslow nodded, his eyes filling. "I didn't even know she was usin' drugs. I mean, I wouldn'ta been surprised if she smoked a little weed now and then. Lot of us did that back in the day, y'know." He glanced at Oscar, who nodded. "But me and Mona—that's her mama —we never seen nothin' to say she was even doin' that." He dropped his right foot to the carpet and tilted his head. "Her supervisin' nurses and all, the last thing we woulda expected was heroin."

"Heroin," I said, no surprise in my voice. As I took notes in my small leather-covered notebook, I leaned forward on my left elbow to relieve my right shoulder from the pressure of the chair's back. I'd had a small-caliber bullet removed six weeks earlier and was nearing the end of physical therapy. My shoulder still throbbed from time to time. "You had no idea?"

He shook his head. "Didn't know nothin' 'bout it till they called from the hospital in the middle of the night." Winslow closed his eyes and was quiet for a time, maybe trying to organize his memories of that night, maybe just reliving it. "Friday after Thanksgiving. She was out with the man she been seein' for almost a year, Odell Williamson. Nice fella, I thought. Taught sixth grade. Somebody found them in a car on Jefferson, outside Wylie. Tried to get high together and they both OD'd. The cops used that nasal spray—"

"Narcan," I said, recalling a *Buffalo News* photo of a Mazda SUV at the edge of the Johnnie B. Wiley Pavilion. At the corner of Jefferson and Best, Wylie was the inner-city high school athletic field built over the remains of the Rockpile—War Memorial Stadium—where the early Bills and Bisons had played and where Robert Redford had filmed *The Natural*. I had read about the double overdose over breakfast one morning. Over several days, the initial surprise that a much-loved teacher had died of a heroin overdose was gradually replaced by outrage and calls for greater scrutiny in the hiring of teachers after three informants stepped forward to reveal that Odell Williamson had been a mid-level dealer who laced his product with fentanyl.

"Narcan," Winslow said, nodding. "Yeah. It worked on her, thank God, but it was too late for him. She went to the ER at ECMC. He went to the morgue." He swallowed audibly and tried to steady himself. "He was the one got my Keisha into that shit, I can't say I'm sorry he gone."

"Easy, Win," Oscar said.

"I understand," I said, continuing to take notes. "What happened to Keisha when she got out of the hospital? Did police file charges against her? That's happening more and more to the surviving partner of a double overdose."

He shook his head. "The DA said he was the dealer, so she came home to us. We got a double on Orange Street. Keisha live upstairs, but Mona made up the guest room for her so we could keep her downstairs with us while she got better."

"What was she like?"

He snorted bitterly. "A total stranger, like the person who got out the hospital wasn't the same one who went in." For a moment he covered his mouth with his hand, as if afraid to let his next words out. "She was moody all the time, fidgety, like the least little noise would make her jump clean out her own skin. Her job made her take a leave of absence to go into rehab, and we thought that would help but it didn't."

"Where is she a nurse? ECMC or another hospital?"

"Neither. Keisha one of them itinerant nurses at the Humanitas Institute of Buffalo." His pronunciation of the final Latin syllable rhymed with ass. "They send her and her people all over the area—schools, clinics, homeless shelters, wherever they need her."

"So rehab didn't help?"

Another shake of his head. "It was a day treatment program because they didn't consider her hardcore enough, if you know what I mean. She went there for about a week and didn't talk much about it when she came home. Then one evenin'—" His voice cracked. "One evenin' not two weeks ago she just didn't come home. I mean, she was there long enough to leave her car in the garage, but she never came inside. Musta got a ride but we don't know from who. We went to the police but—"

"She wasn't gone long enough to be a missing person," I said. "Later, because of the overdose, no one took you seriously. Now she was hardcore enough."

He nodded and bit his lip. "Talked about her like she was a criminal and the word sure went 'round the local precinct. A few days later, when somebody tried to break in and the alarm scared 'em off, one of the cops said it might be our daughter trying to get money for drugs. Didn't listen when I said she knew the alarm code." He sucked his teeth. "Black folks do drugs a few blocks from they home, we got a crime wave. White folks from out in the suburbs come into town and overdose, we got a opioid epidemic and need all kinds of rehab and everyday folk supposed to carry that Narcan shit in they pocket."

"For black folks, it's a moral failure, not a disease," Oscar said. "Damn shame."

"So when we got her letter, they said there wasn't nothin' they could do."

"Tell me about the letter."

"Got it right here." His right hand slid inside his topcoat and returned with a white envelope. "She sent this to us after she took off." He leaned forward to pass it to me.

It was a business-size security envelope with a patterned interior to distort contents if held up to the light. The exterior had printed block letters and the same address in Orange in both the TO and FROM spaces, as well as a Buffalo postmark dated eight days earlier. Inside was a single sheet of lined paper half-filled with small, precise blue handwriting:

Dear Mom and Dad,

God knows what you must think of me right now. Whatever it is, I can't blame you. Know this, though. It can't be any worse than what I think of myself. You have loved me and cared for me my whole life and I have repaid you in unforgivable ways. I've put you through hell the past couple weeks and I am so sorry. I am sorry for being such a disappointment, to you and our family and our church family. But mostly I am sorry for disappointing myself. This shame wasn't what I planned for myself. I am going away for a while, to think and try to get control again of my once beautiful life. Right now my being with you will do you more harm than good, so please don't try to look for me. Just know that I love you both. Always.

K.

The writing was very tight, very controlled. I thought about that and took out my still new cell phone. I took a couple pictures of the letter before I returned it to Winslow.

"Do you have a recent cell phone picture of your daughter you can text to me?"

Winslow shook his head. "Just this." He handed me a wallet-sized headshot. "I ain't up on all the new stuff."

I straightened my stainless steel glasses and studied the woman in the photo: a wide smile, stylish eyeglasses, curled black hair framing a face made more attractive by the glint of playful intelligence in her eyes. *What made you inject heroin, Keisha?* I thought. *What made you run?* "If I take this case, there are lots of things I'll need to know."

"Anything," Winslow said. "Mona and me, we got no secrets we wouldn't trade for our baby girl."

I nodded. "First you need to know you're hiring me to find her, not bring her home. The police won't look for her because she's a grown woman who's chosen to cut ties to her parents. If I locate her and she doesn't want to see you, I will report on her condition and her temperament, but I will not try to bring her to you or give you her location. Can you live with knowing she's alive and well but that you may never see her again?"

Winslow pulled off his glasses and wiped his eyes with the back of his hand. Finally, he nodded. "More than anything we want to know she okay." There was a flutter of pain in his voice. "But what if she ain't okay? What if she in trouble, or worse? What then?"

"If she's in an environment where she's not okay or in danger, like a shooting gallery, I will remove her and get her whatever help she needs. I'll try to do so the safest and most reasonable way I can. Sometimes people get hurt in places like that, but I promise I'll do my best to make sure she's the last and least hurt that day. What I said stands. I'll report on her condition, but I won't reveal her whereabouts without her permission."

"She's grown, Win," Oscar said. "Legally, Rimes can't make her come home."

"I know," Winslow said. "What do you need from me?"

"First I need to interview you and your wife together. Then I'll need the names and addresses or phone numbers of her friends, coworkers, supervisors, old boyfriends, Odell Williamson's family—anybody you can think of."

"Done talked to her friends and people she work with. Nobody know where she at."

"Sometimes people know things they don't realize they know." I took a breath. "I'll need more than her picture. I have to spend time in Keisha's apartment. A lot of time. If she has a computer, I need to give it to my tech guy. Can you deal with all that?"

"If it means you'll look for my daughter, yes."

I took a couple of cell phone photos of Keisha's picture and slid the original back to her father. Then I closed my notebook and stuck it in my shirt pocket. "All right, Mr. Simpkins. I will do my level best to find her."

2

Winslow and Mona Simpkins lived in an old brown house with cream trim and a two-car garage in the heart of the Fruit Belt, a neighborhood on the edge of downtown. With streets named after fruits and trees—Grape, Cherry, Mulberry, Locust—the Fruit Belt had long been largely black and low income, but its proximity to the still-developing medical corridor had given birth to a new name to underscore its gentrification, the Medical Park Neighborhood. While upscale apartments had come to other areas of downtown, much of the development in the Belt was limited to a marked increase in parked cars as hospital, med school, and medical device manufacturing personnel chose not to ride the subway to work and sought free on-street parking three or four blocks away to avoid metered parking and exorbitant ramp fees.

The Simpkins home was on a stretch of Orange not close enough to medical sites to be a front in the parking wars. A two-story clapboard frame dwelling, it sat between a new vinyl-sided ranch with an attached garage and an overgrown lot. Having followed Oscar's old green Lincoln, I parked behind him as Winslow Simpkins got out on the passenger side and started up the front steps. I went to the driver's side, and the window hummed down.

"Thanks for doing this, Rimes," Oscar said. "Win is good people. Folks at church'll be more than willing to help with your fees."

"Don't sweat it."

"Your army pension can't be *that* good. Mine ain't." He was quiet for a moment, gloved fingers drumming the wheel. "If you need somebody to ride along with you—"

"Thanks," I said. "If the trail goes somewhere nasty, I'll call you for back-up." I meant it. I didn't know him well yet but from our first meeting, I had sensed Oscar was the kind of man who would have my back and cover it well, despite his age. "First let's see if I can find a trail. Judging by her letter, maybe her guilt makes facing the folks too hard."

He nodded. "Well, I'll be around if you need me, and the church will do what it can."

Outer door open, Simpkins was waiting for me on the porch. I joined him as Oscar drove away, and we wiped our feet on a thick brown mat. He left his boots on a plastic tray between the inside doors. I followed suit, stuffing my gloves and watch cap into my jacket pockets. Then he led me through the downstairs door into a living room with faded flowered wallpaper, a small fake fireplace, a pale brown sectional sofa, and beige carpeting so worn that fibers poked through my socks and irritated my soles.

"Make y'self at home," he said, draping his coat on a tree. "Lemme go find Mona."

As he disappeared toward the back of the house, I slipped off my leather coat and tugged my sweater down as far as I could. With my right shoulder still recovering, I kept my Glock 26 on my belt in a cross-draw holster instead of in a shoulder rig so I could reach it with my left hand. I didn't want Simpkins or his wife to focus on my gun. When I was sure it would remain covered, I gazed about to examine my surroundings more closely.

The walls were bare but framed photos stretched across the mantel displaying Simpkins and a heavyset woman at different ages, in different places. There were some of Keisha, at first all braces and glasses, then a pretty brown-skinned woman capped and gowned, then one showing her clad in scrubs. Shelves on the left held an old *Encyclopedia Americana* set and dozens of paperbacks. Shelves on the right displayed a mug commemorating Win's retirement from the gas company, snow globes from various cities, school awards and science medals, and framed BS and Doctor of Nursing Practice degrees. So Keisha was more than the registered nurse her father's description had suggested. I looked at her photos again, studied her flawless smile for a long time, and felt a twinge of sadness. Unlike parents proud of their child's achievements, I was not surprised drugs had entered her life. No profession was immune to substance abuse, and addiction among medical workers was often called a silent epidemic. But I did wonder what Keisha's tipping point had been.

I turned as voices drew near and saw Winslow and his wife step into the dining room. Mona was a full head shorter than her husband and clad in a dark maroon winter pantsuit that made her look wider than she likely was. She had a pleasant dark face and short permed hair. Her smile was a stark contrast to the grief in her eyes. Transferring a small notebook to her left hand, she extended her right as she came toward me. "Mr. Rimes, I am so grateful to meet you."

"The pleasure is mine, Mrs. Simpkins."

"Call me Mona," she said, shaking my hand and then holding it to lead me to the sectional. I laid my jacket on one end and sat in the middle. She didn't let go of my hand until she sat beside me. "Win says you agreed to help find my Keisha."

"Yes, ma'am," I said, as Winslow sank into the recliner on the opposite end. "I'll find her and let you know how she is. But I'll bring her home if and only if she wants me to."

She took a deep breath and nodded. "Win told me that too. I know you can't force her but long as I know she's okay, I'll be happy." She patted my hand. "Real happy."

I took out my notebook, a pen, two business cards, and my cell phone. "I want you to tell me about Keisha. Anything you can. You never know which details will prove helpful." I handed her the cards, and she passed one to her husband. Then I held up my phone with the picture Winslow had given me. "If you have any other pictures of your daughter on your cell phone, you can text them to the second number on the card." Returning the cell to my jacket pocket, I opened the notebook and uncapped my pen. "So?"

For a moment husband and wife looked at each other as if unsure what to say. Then the dam cracked. Leaked. Burst. For the next hour, as I took notes, the tension of the past month drained out of them in reminiscences that painted a portrait of a devoted honor student and daughter whose accomplishments were her parents' greatest delights. An early reader with limitless curiosity, Keisha had excelled at everything and had been drawn to medical studies by helping to care for her now-deceased great-grandmother.

"Couldn'ta asked for a better child," Winslow said. "When she skipped fifth grade, the teacher said she might grow up to be a doctor, but we kinda knew right then she'd wanna be close to folks she helped. She said bein' a nursing doctor was the best of both worlds."

"Even when she was only ten, she had a special understanding of how people hurt," Mona said. "The way she would help me with Granny. The way she would say things like, 'Mama, if we turn her this way instead of that, it won't cause her so much pain' or 'If we put it through the blender one more time, it won't hurt her throat so much going down.' It's like she knew without anybody having to tell her. Like her life's work was right out there for everybody to see."

Her father nodded. "She got scholarship offers from lots of schools, even Columbia in New York, but she decided to stay right here at home and go to UB. When she finished and started workin', we said she oughta get her own place. She did for a while but then moved in upstairs when our last tenant left."

"How long ago was that?"

"About five years," Mona said. "She doesn't make that much working for a non-profit but she pays us a little rent. We tore up our mortgage a long time ago so we got no house payments to make. Win and me, we don't need a lot, so we keep most of Keisha's money in the bank. You see, she said she was saving up to have a brand-new house built for all of us, and for the family she hoped to have one day. When the time was right, we planned to give it all back to her, to help." Briefly, Mona smiled, as if anticipating Keisha's reaction to their surprise or maybe the grandchildren she might now never see. Then her eyes welled and she made no effort to wipe them.

"But if we need that money to help her get through this..." Winslow began.

"Or to help you find her," Mona added.

For a moment I was quiet, wondering if the pressure to succeed had pushed Keisha off the straight and narrow. Or had it been her involvement with Odell Williamson? Her father thought the teacher was responsible for his daughter's undoing but was it likely the overdose had been their first time out of the gate together? Surely there had been some hint that things were not as they should have been.

"Tell me how she was when she was seeing Odell," I began as gently as I could. "Before she ended up in the hospital. Was she her usual self? Or was she somehow different? Maybe stressed or tired or distant?"

Without even glancing at each other, Winslow and Mona shook their heads in unison.

"She was fine," Mona said. "Working hard as ever but not at all bent out of shape about it. If anything, she was happier than usual. She'd been seeing Odell for ten months or so and liked him a lot. She didn't think much of most of the men who tried to get with her. Too many with no job, no prospects, nothing they could talk about. But Odell was different. A nice young man from a good family. A gentleman. A professional, she called him."

Winslow snorted. "Professional criminal."

"We didn't know, Win." Mona shook her head. "Truly we didn't, Mr. Rimes. We had no idea. I'm sure Keisha had no idea either."

"What about Odell's family? I wonder if they had an idea."

Winslow sucked his teeth.

"We wouldn't know," Mona said.

"Of course not," I said. "I'm just thinking out loud. Do you have his family's address and telephone number?"

Mona smiled. "Keisha keeps everything in her cell phone, but I'm old-fashioned. I have an address book." She handed me the wirebound notebook in her left hand. "Under W, Carl and Rhonda. He retired from the post office. She works at Penney's on the Boulevard."

I found two entries for Williamson and laid the address book on the coffee table so I could copy the particulars into my notebook. Odell had lived in an apartment on Main Street near Mercer. Carl and Rhonda Williamson lived about two miles away from their son, on University Avenue near the UB South Campus. Odell had no home number—no surprise, given his age—but Mona had his parents' home phone number and all three Williamson cell phones. That suggested a deeper level of acquaintance than people who had crossed paths because their children were dating. Keisha and Odell had moved beyond casual. I imagined both sets of parents were excited by the prospect of a good union. If Odell had been dealing drugs, his parents likely had no idea but they might provide me with enough scraps to lead me toward someone who would know.

"When was the last time either of you spoke to Carl or Rhonda?"

"Not since the funeral," Mona said. "Keisha was still in the hospital and couldn't come." Her eyes met her husband's. "Win and Carl had some words after the service." She turned back to me. "We didn't go to the cemetery or come back to the church for lunch."

I turned to Winslow. "What kind of words?"

"He want to know how Keisha was doin' and I told him she was alive, no thanks to his son." The bitterness of his tone sounded fresh as if the exchange with Carl had happened half an hour ago and not a few weeks earlier. The tension that had drained away over the past hour left ample space for anger.

"It wasn't the time, Win," Mona said. "Not with them standing by the family limo for the trip to Forest Lawn. They were about to put their only child in the ground."

Winslow leveled his eyes at Mona and shrugged. "I couldn't help it. I was pissed."

"How did he respond?" I asked.

"He said *Odell* wasn't the drug dealer, no matter what the news said."

"So he thought Keisha brought Odell to the party instead of the other way around."

"Yeah." Winslow crossed his arms tightly.

"Couldn't have," Mona said. "I helped her dress after the hospital. Her arms were smooth as glass, not a track mark in sight, except that one puncture."

Needles weren't the only way to take heroin but I said nothing.

"Shows what he knows," Winslow snorted. "Uppity post office motherfucker!"

"Winslow Simpkins!" Mona snapped her gaze toward her husband and her cheeks darkened as if she were embarrassed at his outburst. "There's no call for you to be rude or crude, especially when we have a guest." She drew in a deep breath as if gearing up for an argument, and Winslow tensed and pressed his lips together in a tight line as if awaiting the first salvo. "You apologize to Mr. Rimes for showing your ass in this house!"

"It's all right, ma'am," I said, placing my hand on her forearm. "Twenty years in the army, I heard a lot worse. And I understand how you feel, Win. If it were my daughter—" I shook my head. "But we can't let feelings get in the way here or keep you from doing what you have to do."

Winslow and Mona both looked at me—ashamed, angry, or confused, I could not say—and neither moved.

"You have to tell me about Keisha's friends, long-time and recent. Classmates, co-workers, old boyfriends. Anybody." I tapped the address book still open on the coffee table. "You have to give me any numbers you've got and take me upstairs so I can spend time going through her things. As I hunt for her I may come across something I need to know more about, so I'll call you, again and again if I have to. You have to keep your heads clear and focused at all times, both of you, to help me find your daughter. Can you do that?"

They exchanged a brief, apologetic glance and nodded. Then Keisha's mother and father both began to cry, loudly, chests heaving and shoulders shaking. Giving Winslow as much sympathy as I could with my face, I encircled Mona with my arms and held her.

3

K eisha's apartment was smaller than her parents' flat downstairs and painted in warm colors, mainly yellow and orange. Beside the entry door stood a wooden coat tree that held two coats and two jackets, one with a fur collar, one without. The vinyl storm door in her living room led to a front porch with wrought iron railings, outdoor furniture draped in heavy plastic, and an undisturbed layer of snow.

For a time after Mona left me in the apartment, I looked out the porch door and the window on either side of it. All the houses I saw up and down the street appeared lived in. Most had Christmas decorations and half-open shades or curtains to admit light. Sidewalks and driveways had been cleared of snow but a hardened crust clung to the pavement. A few driveways held cars. Most had iced-over tire tracks at least to the house, some as far back as the garage. Her parents considered Keisha a victim and believed she had been forced to write the letter they received. Near the end of our discussion, they wondered if she'd been snatched off the street and forced into a car or nearby dwelling, but they could not imagine who among their neighbors would do something like that. Nothing about any of the houses I could see suggested an urban fortress cut off from the world, like the Cleveland house where Ariel Castro had kept three women imprisoned for a decade. Sexual enslavement was, of course, still a possibility, but everything I had learned so far suggested Keisha had gone voluntarily.

First, she had left her car in the garage rather than take it with her. According to her parents, whenever she used the garage, she entered the house through the back door, just steps away. But on the day she disappeared she had parked in the garage and walked down the driveway to the front porch, where she dropped her keys, wallet, and cell phone through the mail slot. Then, presumably, she got into someone's car and rode away with nothing but the clothes on her back—and perhaps money and a credit card or two in her shoe. It was possible she had been forced into that car at gunpoint and later forced to write her letter, but a gun pressed against the temple makes the average person's hands shake. The handwriting in Keisha's letter —which both Mona and Winslow identified as hers—was so tight and fastidious it appeared not to have been done under duress. If anything, it suggested above-average self-control.

At last turning away from the window, I faced the interior of her home to see if I could determine why Keisha had left and how I could begin to look for her.

The living room was configured differently from her parents'— yellow paint instead of wallpaper, no fake fireplace with photos on the mantel, no knick-knacks or souvenirs in sight, a loveseat instead of a couch, a wooden rocker facing the LED TV on the outside wall, and a trio of packed three-shelf bookcases lining the interior wall. Above the bookcases hung three paintings—a coffee-colored nude and a street scene signed by artists whose names I didn't recognize and a print of the famous Paul Collins painting of Harriet Tubman, gun in hand, leading slaves through the forest.

Beyond the wall with the paintings was a dining room that appeared to double as Keisha's home office. It had bare orange walls and a square black table with four matching chairs. One side of the table held loose papers, file folders, and a pile of unopened mail. The other held a matching black Dell laptop and inkjet printer and a white iPhone, all plugged in. A quick check showed the phone and computer were password-protected. I'd have to take them to LJ to see if they held anything useful. Then I sifted through the mail—Christmas cards, junk, catalogs, and material from professional associations but no bills because Mona had already covered her daughter's utilities and credit cards. Their tabs labeled with a fine-point Sharpie, the file folders made it clear Keisha brought her work home. They were stuffed with newspaper clippings, magazine and journal articles, and internet printouts on a variety of topics related to public health, from methodologies for determining disease vectors to strategies for addressing vaccine-resistant parents to clinic protocols for dealing with the homeless. The loose papers consisted of unfiled articles, notes in Keisha's and other hands, and internal memos from Humanitas. I found an empty folder and slipped the notes, memos, and unfiled articles inside. Then I laid the folder and phone atop the closed computer.

Next, I went into the pale yellow kitchen, which had glass-doored wooden cupboards, a six-bottle wire wine rack on the counter, a stainless steel sink that dated from 1970, and a bistro-style dinette set with two chairs. The refrigerator had been cleaned out and held only a water pitcher and a few beers. The freezer above, however, was packed with meats, frozen vegetables, and plastic cans of concentrated juice. Mona had disposed of the perishables but left the freezer untouched for her daughter's return. Her optimism left a knot in my stomach.

I moved from the kitchen into a hallway with a closed door on either side and at the end. On the right was a guestroom with a neatly made full-sized bed and an empty dresser and closet. On the left was a clean white bathroom with a Mercator projection shower curtain that had brightly colored land masses and transparent oceans. The medicine cabinet held only over-the-counter products—pain relievers, cold medicines, antihistamines, toothpaste. There were no prescriptions and nothing stronger than Nyquil or Listerine. The linen closet beside the bathroom had towels and sheets on the two upper shelves and blankets on the bottom.

The bedroom at the end of the hall was Keisha's. It had a queen-sized bed with a bookcase headboard and matching dresser set. The closet was full of pants suits, skirt suits, and stackable shoe racks. One corner of the closet held a tennis racket, a volleyball, and two paintball guns, a rifle and a pistol. A door perpendicular to the bed led to a back porch with two plastic Adirondack chairs and a covered propane grill. I started with the nightstand and moved to the dresser and bureau. The drawers yielded clothing, from jeans to underwear to nightgowns. Atop the dresser were cosmetics, jewelry boxes, and a box of disposable contact lenses. More women's clothing was in the bureau but the top drawer had men's briefs and socks, a few shirts, and a pair of jeans. I didn't expect to find clues to Keisha's whereabouts in Odell's clothing but I went through it anyway. There was nothing special about any of it. No custom labels on the shirts, no silk in the underwear. If these were typical of the clothing in his home, and if Keisha's costume jewelry was any indication, Odell spent his drug money on something other than what he wore and precious stones for his girlfriend.

I thought about that as I went back to the dining room. I jotted a note that I must not only interview Odell's parents, but also see his apartment, and find a way into his financials. Then I pocketed the iPhone and charger, got the file folder and the laptop, and locked Keisha's front door with the key her parents had given me to use when they weren't home.

It was about six o'clock and dark. I had declined Mona's invitation to stay for dinner because I was meeting Phoenix at seven. In the mid-sized Nickel City, I had plenty of time to reach North Buffalo and deliver the phone and computer to LJ then get back downtown to Betty's Restaurant on Virginia Street. I went to my dark blue Ford Escape and climbed inside, putting everything in the front passenger footwell. I pressed the START button and punched in my favorite

satellite jazz station as I pulled away from the curb. With Sonny
Rollins as background, I pushed Keisha Simpkins and her parents
and Odell Williamson into a corner of my brain where they could
wait until I had enough information to immerse them all in a developer bath that would produce clearer pictures.

It wasn't until I turned onto Main Street that I suspected I was
being followed.

Ordinarily, I would have had to concentrate to distinguish one car
behind me from another at night. But the large SUV on my tail now
had a distinctive pattern of LED daytime running lights that half-
cupped the headlamps. I first saw the pattern in my rearview mirror
when I turned onto High Street and reached a stop sign. Because
LED running lights were increasingly common but still rare enough
to be noticed, I thought nothing of them at that moment. Eight blocks
later, however, when I made a right onto Main, the lights were still
with me, apparently matching my speed. I decided to find out if the
driver was tailing me.

A few blocks ahead I passed Sermon on the Mount, the Simpkins
family's church. Then I changed lanes and soon turned left into the
Delta Sonic complex across Main Street from Artspace Gallery and
Artists' Lofts. Between Barker and Bryant Streets, Delta Sonic was
more than a car wash. It had oil change and detail shops, twenty or so
gas pumps, and a convenience store with a Dunkin' Donuts inside. I
slid into an empty gas lane as if intending to fill up. The SUV behind
me eased into a well-lighted lane to my right and stopped behind a
Chevy Colorado. It was a black Lincoln Navigator with two men
obscured by smoked glass. I tried to get a look at the front plate but
my line of sight was blocked by waste bins between the pumps. I
counted to three. Then I shot forward and swung left past the store
and left again toward the driveway. I turned right on Main, right on
Barker, and right on Linwood. I parked as far as I could from a street-
light then got out and walked back. Left hand inside my jacket, I
peered around a wide tree trunk at Barker and waited.

After a few seconds, the Navigator rolled into view and paused at the intersection as if the occupants were gazing down the street. Then it moved on toward Delaware Avenue. I waited three or four minutes before I returned to my car. My pursuers didn't return.

Pulling away from the curb, I couldn't help wondering whether they were looking for me or looking for Keisha.

4

"They were probably looking for Keisha."

We were in the warm main dining room at Betty's, at a small table against an exterior wall that held the charcoal drawings of the artist currently on exhibit. The front windows and canopy framework outside were decorated with Christmas lights, and the night beyond them was clear after earlier sporadic snow. The Mediterranean cod had just been set in front of Phoenix, and her first bite was still on the fork in her hand. "Unless there's something you haven't told me, you've been doing only routine things the past few weeks."

"Mostly for your law firm." I cut into my grilled skirt steak and put a piece into my mouth. I worked on it slowly, savoring it, thinking.

"All of it low impact," she said as she chewed. "I can't see depositions, background checks, and process serving causing a covert tail. So the question is, why would somebody be looking for your client's daughter?"

"The first question I'll ask when I find her."

Oscar had told Phoenix nothing of what troubled the friend who wanted my help, so when I joined her in the restaurant and she asked how my day had gone, it was with more than casual curiosity.

Between the moment we placed our order and the moment the food arrived, I recounted my afternoon with Winslow and Mona Simpkins, and my examination of Keisha's apartment. There was no question of breaching confidentiality because Landsburgh, Falk, and Trinidad engaged Driftglass Investigations and agreed to represent me if the need arose. In fact, Phoenix had acted as my lawyer before we became lovers, having gotten me released from jail during my interrogation for a murder I hadn't committed.

In any case, I tried to explain the black Navigator as nonchalantly as I could. Our relationship was still in the probationary stage. We'd been together less than two months, and already she had spent a night sleeping beside my hospital bed as I recovered from gunshot wound surgery. I liked her a lot, perhaps more than I should have, for the limited time we'd been a couple, and didn't want fear to chase her away. Now I looked at her—oval face framed by medium-length dark hair she untied when she wasn't working, cinnamon skin glistening in the soft light, espresso eyeshadow and lipstick, tailored burgundy pantsuit—and wondered for the *nth* time what she saw in a rough-edged combat veteran and ex-Army detective who gazed at the world through lenses framed in stainless steel cynicism.

"Maybe Keisha owes somebody money for drugs and they tried to break in to get it," Phoenix said. "Maybe she knows too much about how her boyfriend moved his product and his crew wants to make sure she doesn't talk. Or the guys in the Navigator could be anything from rival dealers who see her as the gateway to Odell's operation to undercover cops who think she'll lead them to the next biggest mouth in the food chain."

"Maybe Odell's father is right, and she's a dealer on the run with her rainy day stash."

"You don't believe that." Phoenix's smile was one of her best qualities—wide and engaging, full of beautiful teeth. "It's possible but you'll be disappointed if it's true."

"You know that how?"

"The hint of a lilt in your voice when you talk about Keisha. You're impressed by all she's accomplished. Maybe you even have a bit of a crush. You'll understand if somehow she resorted to drugs because of career pressure or if recreational use got out of hand. Deep down you don't see her as a drug *dealer*. That would break your heart."

"A little. But it's not so much a crush as my being protective by nature."

"One of the qualities that makes you special and makes me care for you, but you have to realize it can also get you into trouble."

"I do. It has."

"She wouldn't be the first medical professional to go down that road. Lucas Tucker?"

Tucker was a suburban Buffalo dentist now languishing in a Nigerian prison. His story had stretched across three news cycles last summer and fall, before Phoenix and I had met. First, it was reported he'd been taken into custody without cause, and his wife made a tearful public appeal for his release. Then the State Department waded into the affair, only to find that in his semi-annual trips to provide free dental care to impoverished Ogoni villagers, Tucker transported sizable quantities of cocaine from Nigeria to London, where he always stopped on the way home to visit relatives. His arrest and that of the Colombian dentist who worked alongside him to treat the unsuspecting Ogoni barely made a dent in the Africa-to-Europe pipeline, but neither man would see the sun for many years to come.

"Tucker was a transporter, never a user," I said. "Keisha got a nose full of Narcan."

"She also wouldn't be the first to get high on her own supply."

"Lesson number two," I said, remembering *Scarface*. "But you're right. This woman did impress me, and not just with her achievements. I got a sense of how she lived and how she worked. Look, I know everybody's got secrets. I'm sure she's hiding more than the three emergency hundred dollar bills in the lining of her jewelry box and the vibrator in the back of her nightstand drawer. But nothing about her place indicated the type of personality that would be into dealing."

Phoenix put down her fork and looked at me for a long time. "You have good instincts about things like this. If you don't think she was dealing, most likely she wasn't." She reached across the table and took hold of my left hand. "Which takes us back to why someone would be looking for her—if they weren't looking for you." She smiled. "Maybe you can change the game and look for them. You have some good cred with the police right now. Maybe Rafael would do a vehicle search as a favor."

Long before we met, Phoenix had had a brief relationship with homicide detective Rafael Piñero. Recently, I had crossed paths with him and his partner Terry Chalmers at the start of an investigation that ended with their extending to me a grudging respect. "Too many possibilities," I said. "I couldn't get a look at the plate, not even the state. Black Navigators made in the last year or two and sold all over America? A longshot, not to mention Canada and Mexico, which compounds the complications."

She nodded. "But I know you'll figure it out. You're relentless like that, as long as you have a place to start."

I nodded. "The names of friends and co-workers."

"Anybody on the list you want to talk about?"

"Not yet." I drank some water. "We've talked enough about what I'm doing. Let's talk about something else."

"Bobby and Kayla get off okay?"

Almost two months ago, my godfather and landlord, Professor Emeritus Bobby Chance, had lost a bet to his lover, Judge Kayla Baker McQueen. The payment was a long theater weekend in New York City but my getting shot had delayed their departure. "I took them to the airport at six this morning," I said. "He texted me when they got in and reminded me that they get back Sunday night. But I'd rather hear about what you're up to."

For the rest of the meal we discussed her day—morning in court to finalize a divorce she felt could have been avoided with early counseling, an afternoon spent researching the particulars of an auto accident that had left a long-time client in a wheelchair, and a late-in-the-day partners' meeting to discuss the feasibility of a class-action lawsuit against a chain store whose policy of placing bulky items on high shelves had resulted in at least five serious injuries to customers in three area stores. "They cut back on staff to save money," Phoenix said. "Customers who don't want to wait for help jump and jiggle and try to pull these things down when other people are walking by and *bam!* Head injury. Facial reconstruction. In one case a lamp put a woman in a coma. In another, a guy tore off his finger when he jumped up and his wedding ring caught on the edge of a shelf."

"Ouch!"

"If we go class action, we'll need some serious investigating. A lot of billable hours."

"So when are we heading to Ponce? I can finally meet Tia Rosita."

Phoenix's aunt in Puerto Rico was her only living family. Some months earlier she had survived a major hurricane. Phoenix had offered to fly her to Buffalo, but with damage to her apartment minimal and electricity back on within a few days, Tia had declined. Buffalo was too cold year-round, she insisted, despite her niece's assurances to the contrary.

"They still need help with hurricane clean-up. You willing to put your back into that?"

"Of course," I said. "It's rough here in January and February. Last winter?" I shivered. "I wouldn't mind cleaning up debris in a warmer climate if the Weather Channel sniffs anything close to that one."

Phoenix chuckled. "The airfare won't come from this case. It's a long way off, but I think I can get away from things near the end of next month." She cocked her head and studied me a moment. Then she smiled. "Of course, I could be making a mistake. Tia Rosita likes younger men, especially dark, good-looking men with broad shoulders."

"A cougar," I said. "As long as you're with me I can be strong."

"More like a snow leopard since her hairstylist died." She leaned forward on her elbows and locked eyes with me. "But Tia's still pretty hot for a woman in her seventies."

"No surprise if she shares DNA with you."

"Think Rita Moreno."

"Oh." I shrugged. "That's different. Can she cook?"

Laughing, Phoenix kicked me under the table.

Later, after we had made love in the elevated queen-sized bed that occupied the front left corner of her Pearl Street loft, I lay awake, thinking. Naked, I was on my left side, facing the tall window that Phoenix seldom covered because she so enjoyed the eleventh-floor view and pulsing lights of downtown. Though I usually preferred total darkness for sleep, I'd come to appreciate the way outside lights played off the hues of our bodies during lovemaking, especially the way they caught the colors of Phoenix's mythical namesake rising from the ashes in the tattoo that masked her mastectomy scars. But tonight, as she drifted off to sleep while spooning me, her right arm around my torso, the lights were the last thing on my mind.

I remained still to keep from waking her, but my mind was bouncing off the walls of my skull. The more I thought about the men in the Navigator, the more convinced I was they were looking for Keisha—why, I thought I would learn soon enough. What Phoenix hadn't asked, and what I hadn't even wondered till I was lying there within spitting distance of sleep but unable to reach it, was why they had followed *me* in the hope of finding her. Whoever they were, they knew I had been hired to investigate her disappearance. Figuring out how they had come by *that* information might be the key to everything.

Minutes earlier Phoenix had jerked as if stumbling in her sleep and shifted onto her back. Now I felt her fingertips on my shoulder at the exact spot where scar tissue from my recent gunshot wound surgery was building layer upon layer.

"Is this still tender?" she asked, her voice barely a whisper.

"A bit, and it itches." Turning onto my back, I twisted to see her face in the light. Lower lip caught between her teeth, she looked distressed. I felt for her hand, squeezed it. "I didn't mean to wake you."

"You didn't. I was dreaming, about a man with a gun jumping out of the shadows."

"As if he were waiting for you to get close to him."

"Yes."

"So you thought about me getting shot."

"Yes."

"You're concerned it could happen again."

"Not concerned. Afraid. Afraid for you." The fingers of her free hand slid through my chest hair as if making sure I were real and not a trick of the outside lights.

"While Bobby's away, I'm in charge of the apartment building."

"Stop that." She twisted my nipple, lightly.

"Ow! Stop what?"

"You know." She took a breath. "So, those men in that SUV. How did they know you were looking for Keisha?"

"I was just wondering that myself. It's amazing how our minds—"

"Gideon, don't."

"What?"

"Don't deflect. A joke about Bobby being away. A cute comment about how alike we are. I know we're alike in a lot of ways and we're good together but that's not the issue."

"Sorry."

"Nothing to be sorry about, but I wonder if I should worry while you're looking for this woman." She swallowed audibly. "We're just starting, and I don't—"

"I worry about you all the time," I said.

"But I don't do the work you do."

"Doesn't matter. You've become a constant in my life. Life is full of unexpected kicks in the groin." I almost added *and nipple twists* but figured another try at humor would just fail. "Worry is part of the deal. But I'll be careful if you'll be careful. That's part of the deal too. I promise I'll look over my shoulder if you promise to stop talking on your cell when you cross the street."

She caught a few of my chest hairs between her fingers and pulled. "It's not the same."

"No, it's not. I think you stand a better chance of getting hit by a turning car than I do of getting shot again."

"Gideon, I look before crossing."

"I know you do. Just as you should know I always try to be aware of my surroundings and any people nearby. I'm not ready to clock out yet. I like breathing as much as the next guy, and I look forward to more nights like this with you. So trust me to be alert."

She was quiet for a few seconds. "I like how you breathe."

"Now who's being cute?"

She threw a leg over my legs, tightened her arm around my chest, and kissed me. "I am."

5

Friday morning we made love again and showered together before we took the elevator down to the underground parking garage, where our cars were side by side. Kissing me goodbye and opening the door of her white RAV4, Phoenix said she would see me Saturday night when I picked her up for the county bar association holiday party.

I got home a few minutes past eight and popped a K-cup into the Keurig on my kitchen counter. Then I set out the file folder I'd taken from Keisha's place and my pocket notebook. A few minutes later, seated on a bistro chair and sipping from a BuffaloPlace mug, I opened the notebook to the pages with the names of Keisha's friends and associates. The question was who to interview first. At the top of the list were Odell's parents, Carl and Rhonda Williamson, but I decided to save them for last in the first round. I needed space between visits with grieving parents. The next name was Ileana Tassiopulos, whose job title at Humanitas neither Winslow nor Mona knew. She was followed by Fatimah Howze-Kelly and Bianca Dawkins, Keisha's two best friends since sixth grade. Fatimah was a florist with a shop in the Kensington-Bailey area, and Bianca was a manager at Hunnicutt Jewelers in the Walden Galleria. The last two names were Sonny Tyler, a former boyfriend for whom Mona had only a cell number, and the Reverend Dr. Felton Markham of Sermon on the Mount Church.

I planned to call Tassiopulos, Tyler, the minister, and the Williamsons before I went to see them, but I would introduce myself unannounced to the two best friends. If Keisha had gathered her stash and fled, she might have been in contact with one or both of them. Caught in an unguarded moment, they might reveal something important. But it was too early for the flower shop or the mall to be open, too early even to begin making phone calls.

I opened the file folder and began to look through the papers I'd stuck inside. The articles and memos painted a picture of the Humanitas Institute as an independently funded agency that provided health and human services for the public good. Humanitas maintained both formal and informal partnerships with the public schools and selected charter schools, soup kitchens, homeless shelters, women's shelters, clinics, substance abuse treatment and counseling centers, immigrant and refugee assistance centers, housing assistance centers, daycare centers, senior citizen centers, and employment agencies. They offered supplementary vaccination services, home health visits and emergency room follow-up, after-school tutoring, individual and family counseling, and job placement.

One article noted that Keisha Simpkins, DNP, was in charge of community nursing. Another mentioned that Ileana Tassiopulos, MSW, was director of counseling. Some of the others, clipped from newspapers and magazines, made no mention of Humanitas but reported sharp declines in homelessness and a rise in employment in Western New York. The printed memos announced meetings or concerned internal matters I was in no position to evaluate. But they were on agency letterhead that noted both physical and online addresses and listed staff, including Keisha. The handwritten notes were out of context and even more confusing: inside jokes, happy faces, illegible scrawls, happy hour invites, phone numbers below only first names or initials. One pink post-it note, addressed to *K* and signed *I*, stood out: *Saw Veronica begging at Timmy Ho's. We have to help her.* Assuming *I* was short for Ileana and *K* for Keisha, I put the post-it in my notebook for later.

It was a few minutes past nine when I opened my Lenovo laptop and went to the Humanitas website. The home page had a photo montage that included shots of smiling children and their mothers, immigrants in various styles of dress, seniors and white-coated professionals engaged in discussion, and the agency headquarters, a refurbished mansion on Delaware near West Ferry. The *About* page confirmed the mission I had figured out from the other documents. The *Who We Are* page listed the names, pictures, and mini-bios of those in charge of the non-profit operation and the names of the board of directors, some of whom were prominent in business or politics. I skimmed all the bios but paid special attention to Keisha Simpkins and Ileana Tassiopulos, whose alphabetized listings appeared side-by-side. They had graduated from the University at Buffalo four years apart, but both had started at Humanitas at the same time, eight years earlier. Ileana's was the only Humanitas name Mona had in her address book. As I studied their adjacent smiles, it struck me that the director of community nursing and the director of counseling were more than workplace friends, which meant I would strike Ileana Tassiopulos off my call-first list.

After I shut down my computer, I looked again at one of the letterhead sheets that listed key Humanitas staff. I almost missed the name that appeared between Keisha and Ileana. The name had not been on the website: *Veronica Surowiec, MD, Medical Liaison.* Then I pulled the post-it out of my notebook: *Saw Veronica begging at Timmy Ho's. We have to help her.*

That settled the question of whom to interview first.

6

The Humanitas Institute was half a block past the Jesuit high school that sat on land once occupied by the Milburn Mansion, where in 1901 President William McKinley died eight days after being shot by an assassin at the Pan-American Exposition.

Unlike the Milburn home, many of the sprawling Delaware Avenue mansions once occupied by powerful Gilded Age families had been spared demolition. Over several blocks that stretched from the Gates Circle fountain to downtown, they had been repurposed as high-end law firms, foundation headquarters, charities, charter schools, social services agencies, a few architecture firms, and software companies. The two best known were the massive gray stone Clement mansion, which now housed the American Red Cross and a fundraising arm of the Buffalo Philharmonic, and the more compact Wilcox Mansion, now a national historic site because McKinley's vice president, Teddy Roosevelt, took the oath of office there. The Cardwell Mansion, which a prominent banker had inherited from his railroad magnate father, was a sandstone affair smaller than the Clement but larger than the Wilcox. Set well back from the curb of what was once called Millionaires' Row, the Cardwell bore a tasteful gold-lettered sign that read *Humanitas Institute of Buffalo*. With an entrance at one end and exit at the other, a long blacktop drive curved in front of the building but also looped behind it to a parking lot large enough for maybe thirty cars.

At nine-forty-five and with wipers on intermittent for a light snowfall, I drove into the lot, which was more than half full, and found a spot in front of a VISITOR sign. The main entrance was in the rear, at a point where flagstone steps and a hairpin-turn wheelchair ramp met. I climbed the steps to a door with pebbled plate glass and pushed the green button on a stainless steel intercom box.

"Yes?" a woman's voice crackled.

"I'm here to see Ms. Tassiopulos," I said, looking up at the white security camera mounted out of reach above the door.

"Do you have an appointment?"

"No." I was an ex-army cop but thought I still had a pretty authoritative cop voice. "I'm a detective. I'd like to talk to her about Dr. Simpkins." Still looking at the camera, I heard a flustered "Oh!" before the intercom went dead. A moment later the door buzzed. I pulled it and stepped into the vestibule to face another door with pebbled glass. I stuffed my watch cap into my jacket pocket, looked up at a second camera, and waited.

Momentarily, a blue shape neared the door, fractured by the glass but belonging to a woman in a pantsuit. The door opened, and I recognized Ileana Tassiopulos from her picture on the website—olive skin, large green eyes and high cheekbones in a patrician face, and curly brown tresses with blonde highlights. But the wide smile I had seen online was missing, the tense jaw signaling an anxiety that didn't surprise me.

"Ms. Tassiopulos," I said, extending my hand. "My name is Gideon Rimes."

Her hand was slender, fine-boned. When she shook mine I felt tension in her fingers.

"It's about time somebody considered this serious," she said, stepping aside to let me enter and closing the door behind me. "Is there word of Dr. Simpkins?"

The reception area was paneled, with two women and a man, all of whom seemed to be in their mid-twenties, seated at desktop computers. The woman nearest the door, probably the person who had spoken on the intercom, was a full-figured blonde in a blue sweater. The woman at the desk perpendicular to hers was brown-skinned and bald with hoop earrings and bright red lipstick. The small man at the back of the room had thick black hair and was about the same complexion as my foster sister Mira, whose biological parents had come from India. All three of them looked at me expectantly, as if awaiting my answer.

I turned back to Tassiopulos. "Is there somewhere I can speak to you privately?"

She looked at the others. Then she looked back at me and stiffened as if bracing herself. "If you have news, you can share it with all of us."

"I don't have any news yet," I said, "about Dr. Simpkins or Dr. Surowiec." I paused to let the second name register, and it did, on all four faces. The seated women exchanged a surprised glance, and the man's lips parted as he leaned forward. I was almost close enough to Tassiopulos to feel the pull of her sudden intake of breath. "I was hoping you could help me. Now, is there somewhere we can speak privately?"

"Of course."

Without looking at the others, Tassiopulos turned on her heel and led me past their desks. I followed her through a narrow corridor that opened into what once must have been a ballroom but had since been subdivided into cubicles with frosted glass partitions and offices along the far wall. She gestured me into one of the offices and closed the door as I sat in a black plastic shell chair facing the desk. Tassiopulos sat behind the desk and studied me.

"Detective Rimes, is it? I'm glad the police are finally paying attention to Keisha's disappearance."

I leaned forward to hand her a Driftglass Investigations card, and she slipped on a pair of drugstore reading glasses with a rhinestone-studded frame. She read the card, and I could see the corners of her mouth tightening.

"I used to be a cop," I said. "I've been hired to find her."

"Probably by her parents because the real police still aren't taking things seriously."

I said nothing.

Clearly annoyed—whether at me or the real police I couldn't say —she pulled off the reading glasses and set them on her desk. She studied me for a time, long enough for me to notice the flecks of gold in her green eyes, long enough for her to come up with a question that might determine whether the interview continued. "Mr. Rimes, how does Dr. Surowiec fit into your search for Keisha?"

"Call me Gideon." I hoped informality might tip things in my favor. I took out my notebook, peeled the pink post-it from one of the pages, and held it toward her. "Did you write this note to Keisha, Ms. Tassiopulos?"

She took the post-it and glanced at it. "Yes."

"I found it in Keisha's apartment. My clients are desperate to know what happened to their daughter, and I need a place to start looking. I noticed the name Veronica Surowiec on the letterhead of old memos but not on your website, so I came here first."

"Then the answer to my question is that there is no connection."

"The answer is, I don't know—yet. If Dr. Surowiec is the Veronica you meant, there must be a story behind how your medical liaison ends up begging outside a Tim Horton's. If that story involves drugs, Ms. Tassiopulos, and Keisha disappeared after a drug overdose, I think you should help me figure out if there is a connection, for both their sakes."

She was quiet for a long moment. "Call me Ileana." She folded her hands atop her desk. "How can I help, Gideon?"

"You're the only person from Humanitas that Mona Simpkins has in her address book." I took out my pen and held it above a blank notebook page. "That suggests your friendship with Keisha went beyond work."

"Goes. Don't bury her until we find her body." She gazed off for a moment and dragged the back of her hand across both eyes. "Yes. I have a few years on her but we were newbies together. We sat next to each other at orientation and struck up a friendship that helped us make sense of Humanitas and what was expected of us. Over lunches those first few weeks we talked a lot about the connections between physical and mental health and eventually we began doing site visits together."

"Site visits. What do those involve?"

"If you've been to our website, you know we offer comprehensive support services to a lot of other institutions, from schools to community centers. Sometimes site visits mean meeting with agency heads to review what they do for clients. For example, does this or that immigrant family have access to public transportation or health care? If not, we figure out how to make it possible. Sometimes we meet directly with clients themselves to offer face-to-face help. Is this Alzheimer's patient getting the support she needs to stay home as long as possible? How does this father's cancer impact his children's performance in school?"

"So you and Keisha were kind of a tag team on physical and mental health."

"Yes, on how the two worked together for an individual or family's quality of life. Sometimes she would do a routine physical and I would do a mental health assessment, and we'd compare notes and come up with a multifaceted treatment plan that worked beautifully. Yes, we were a team, a good one that got better the longer we worked together. Cassidy, the intercom receptionist, used to call us Batgirl and Robin but refused to say who was who." She smiled then, an almost bittersweet smile that brought color to her cheeks as if she'd remembered something else she was hesitant to share.

I set my pen aside. "Is there something you don't want me to write down?"

She sighed and her smile widened into the one I had seen online.

"I won't breach confidentiality by giving you names so you can write whatever you want. Anyway, I doubt this anecdote will help you find Keisha."

"But it will tell me something about her, something that will help me understand her better."

She nodded. "I was just thinking about one of the early visits that helped us bond with each other. We paid a home visit to an elderly couple in one of the assisted living facilities—I won't say which one. They were both in their early eighties and in pretty good shape. A lot of walking. Swimming in the pool. Nine holes of golf once a week for him. Yoga classes for her. That sort of thing." Even though we were in her office with the door closed, she leaned toward me and lowered her voice a bit. "We're sitting in their living room, doing a wellness check, when out of the blue the woman says, 'We don't screw like we used to. Two or three times a week for fifty years, and now he's tired all the time and won't come near me and sometimes I have to rely on BOB to go to sleep but I like to be kissed and BOB can't kiss me.'"

"No names," I said.

Ileana shook her head. "Not her husband. B-O-B. Battery-operated boyfriend."

"Oh," I said.

"I was brought up in a very proper Greek family." Ileana sat back, palms flat on her desktop. "I was nobody's prude and had graduate-level sexuality training and my own fair share of experiences before and after marriage, but the idea of elderly people having sex and actually talking about it and vibrators—well, yes, it caught *me* off guard. But not Keisha. She never blinked and eased right into a dialogue about variable hormone levels and possible physiological problems and ways they might approach communication. It was a couple's therapy session that gave the therapist in the room a moment to find her footing."

"Sounds like a smooth move."

"It was, and we got to the heart of the problem too, sort of. One of his golf buddies had died some months earlier, and the rumor that ran through the retirement community was that he had died *in flagrante* with his wife. Our guy didn't understand how much he'd taken the rumor to heart and withdrawn from his own sex life. Once everything was on the table and we got them talking, they got into a rhythm that made things better. Not three times a week but enough times a month the wife was happy." She looked off again, and her smile lessened but did not disappear. "That couple had this weird table lamp that looked like it was made out of that famous Remington horse sculpture."

"The Bronco Buster?"

"Yes, that's the one. For years, whenever things got dicey, one of us would look at the other and say, 'Ride her, cowboy!' and we'd almost fall off our chairs laughing." She wiped her eyes again.

"Thank you," I said.

"For what?"

"For cutting my fear of assisted living by ninety percent."

She laughed and sat forward, and I felt confident she would cooperate with me, not only in this interview but in any follow-ups.

"So Keisha was—is—quite good at what she does," I said. "Self-assured, sympathetic to the needs of others, and enough of a generalist to address those needs on many fronts."

"One of the smartest, kindest, most careful and balanced women I've ever known."

I locked eyes with Ileana and made no move to pick up my pen. "Therefore not at all the kind of person one would expect to have a drug problem she could keep secret, at least not secret from you."

"Exactly. If you used to be a cop, you must know something about drug use patterns. Sure, the desire to get high cuts across all ages, races, and classes, with alcohol and pot being the most common drugs of choice. But most users of illicit drugs begin in adolescence and drift into irregular and casual use by their late twenties. Younger users try opioids for a different kind of high but a lot of older users start with prescription painkillers."

"The road to heroin is often paved with oxy."

Ileana nodded. "Keisha is older but has had no accidents, surgery, or pain management issues that required a scrip. Now before you tell me about health professionals who find their maintenance levels and use for a long time, let me tell you about Veronica Surowiec. Yes, she was a medical doctor who worked here and developed a drug habit in the wake of her only child's death and her husband's abandonment. She lost everything, and her life spiraled out of control astonishingly fast."

"She never found her maintenance level."

"Not for lack of trying." Ileana took a deep breath. "Look, I'm a therapist trained to recognize the signs of addiction and indicators of addictive personalities. When Veronica's life started going off the rails, I saw it before anybody else because it fit her personality. Brilliance and persistence got her through medical school at the top of her class but these assets turned into something else after her losses. She turned to methamphetamines for the euphoria. She started with Desoxyn, which she prescribed for accomplices who gave the pills back to her."

"I take it this was in the days before New York required all scrips to be electronic?"

"Yes. Veronica resisted my help, and by the time everybody else noticed her dilated pupils and flushed skin it was too late. She had begun to cook her own and stopped coming to work regularly because she screwed up so much."

"Did she ever do time in rehab?"

"Not that I know of. When I reported her to our superiors, they took their own sweet time. When they finally got around to her she was too far gone. She was a liability. They had no choice but to let her go. Now she's homeless and snaggle-toothed from meth mouth and begging for drug money outside coffee shops."

"Your note said, 'We have to help her.' Did you try to help Veronica?"

"Yes. First, we looked for her in all the usual places."

"The usual places?"

"Various shelters. Homelessness is way down in the Buffalo area but still a big enough problem we have several places street people go, for two hots and a cot, especially this time of year. Keisha and I spent several nights looking for her this fall, waiting outside this or that shelter as people drifted in. Twice we saw her but she ran from us. Her sneakers against our high-heel boots? No contest there. The last time I saw her face to face was outside the Walgreen's two blocks from here, about three weeks ago. She was high then but she still recognized me. Breaks my heart to know she's out there somewhere, broken and alone—and invisible, because that's what the homeless are, people we choose not to see." For a moment Ileana's expression made me think she might wipe her eyes again but she didn't.

I let another second or two pass. "Do you have a list of shelters I can check out—in case Keisha shows up at one of them?"

"Yes, but if you're going to hang around any of them, take me with you. Shelter directors and most staff know I'm from Humanitas. They're very protective of the people they serve. Somebody has to be." She studied me, shaking her head. "Guy your size hanging around at night will probably scare them enough to make them call the cops." From one of the plastic organizers on her desktop, she produced a pamphlet, paper-clipped a business card to it, and handed it to me. "My cell number is circled. Promise you'll call me first."

I promised. "Mr. and Mrs. Simpkins told me Keisha had to go to rehab."

"A knee-jerk bureaucratic response intended to prevent her from becoming another Veronica. The truth is, the board doesn't know Keisha like I do. She never showed signs of instability or self-medication. Rehab was a waste of time. I've never even seen Keisha finish a second glass of wine."

I remembered the wine rack in Keisha's kitchen. "Do you think the drugs came from Odell Williamson?"

She was quiet a moment, then shook her head. "We double-dated several times. He always seemed intelligent and engaging. He talked a lot about his kids, about their progress and their science projects and the hilarious things they said in class." Her eyes brightened a bit, and she smiled. "He was playful as if being a kid at heart helped him connect with his students. But that side of him was infectious. It helped him connect with everybody and brought Keisha out in ways I'd never have imagined. She got him into trivia games and long walks but he got her into paintball and ziplining." She shook her head again. "I can imagine him smoking a joint now and then but can't buy him as a hard-core user or dealer."

I picked up my pen. "When was the last time you saw Keisha before she ended up in the hospital?"

"Here at work that very day. It was a Friday, and she was looking forward to her date with Odell that night. She'd had some bad experiences with men and kept her guard up. But Odell was different, and she appreciated him for it. From the way she'd been talking about him for the past few months, I got a sense her guard was coming down and she might even be thinking of a future with him."

For a long time, I said nothing as I compared Ileana's portrait of her friend to what I already knew. Both respected professionals, Keisha and Odell had overdosed in a car near an athletic center but only Keisha responded to the Narcan. Three informants had labeled Odell a dealer. After returning home from the hospital, Keisha was moody and different, but her arms showed no signs of prior drug use. Skipping out on rehab, she disappeared and sent her parents a letter that sounded a lot like an addict's apology. Logic said that either Keisha or Odell had gotten the other to inject heroin. Nothing else made sense. But two men in a black Navigator had followed me, perhaps hoping I'd lead them to her. That made no sense either. Unless...

"You have to be wondering what I tried to tell the police two weeks ago," Ileana said, breaking the silence, "when Keisha went missing. If she and Odell went from no sign of drug use, ever, to heroin in a matter of hours, what, or who made them overdose together?"

"Exactly what I was thinking."

"You're the detective. Figure it out. Then go find my friend and bring her home, one way or another."

7

With a digital photo of Veronica Surowiec now in my phone's image library, I followed Ileana back to the entrance. There I had a brief conversation with Cassidy, Yvonne, and Fareed—the three at desks near the door—but none offered anything that clarified what I had already learned. The conversation was Ileana's idea, and I understood after the first question it was an opportunity for her to short-circuit the rumor mill. If the three had been excluded, their speculations might have spread throughout the staff. By inviting them into an abridged version of our interview and making sure each one had a Driftglass card before she advised them to keep our conversation confidential, Ileana was making them co-conspirators. On the surface, it seemed a smart move motivated by office politics I did not understand. But I still would have put my money on Ben Franklin, who said that three can keep a secret if two are dead.

Outside, the snow had stopped and the sun, having climbed higher, promised a brighter day.

Sitting in my car as it warmed, I flipped through my notebook to decide my next move. Because my interview list wasn't long, I expected to clear round one by evening and hoped somebody would say something that pushed me toward the first step of round two. Three of those on the list I would have to call first: the Reverend Dr. Felton Markham, Carl and Rhonda Williamson, and Sonny Tyler, for whom I had only a cell number anyway. Ileana's blank reaction when I mentioned the names Fatimah and Bianca told me she had never met Keisha's childhood friends, which meant she wouldn't tip them off I was on my way to see them unannounced. Flowers by Fatimah was on Kensington Avenue near Bailey. Bianca worked at Hunnicutt Jewelers in the suburban Galleria. The Williamsons lived on University Avenue in Northeast Buffalo. It made sense to hit the florist first and take Route 33 to the mall. I could return to the city on Eggert Road and cut over to UB's Main Street campus, directly across from the Williamsons' street. If I saw Odell's parents last, I could swing over to the Doran house on Admiral Road and see what LJ had found on Keisha's computer and iPhone. At some point I would need to call my sister Mira, an assistant medical examiner, to see if she had access to Odell Williamson's autopsy report.

At the moment, however, I was closest to Dr. Markham, who lived near his Main Street church, close to downtown and just blocks away. I tapped in his cell number.

"Dr. Markham." The voice that answered was measured and resonant—and familiar to anyone who watched the local news. Felton Markham was a frequently interviewed mover and shaker not only in religious matters but also in politics, inner-city development, public education, job training, and community service.

"Dr. Markham, my name is Gideon Rimes. I'm a private investigator. Winslow and Mona Simpkins hired me to look for their daughter Keisha."

"Yes, I heard they planned to seek outside help. The police have been useless."

"I was wondering if you could spare me a few minutes this morning."

"Right now I'm in my office at the church. I won't be home till later this afternoon. I like to get my sermons done during the day on Friday so I can attend community events and spend time with my wife."

"I understand, sir. I'm close by, at Keisha's job, just on the other side of Main. I promise not to take much of your time."

For a moment he said nothing. "All right, Mr. Rimes. I'll give you ten or fifteen minutes. Come on over and ring the bell on the parking lot door."

I reached the sprawling sandstone Sermon on the Mount in less than five minutes and pulled into a blacktop parking lot that held only three vehicles: a new black Town Car in the MINISTER space by the door, a white Camry beside it, and a rusting blue F-150 four slots away. I parked beside the Camry, went up three steps, and pressed an electronic doorbell.

The man who answered the door was big, dressed in jeans and a navy pullover that contrasted with the pristine collar of his white shirt. The Reverend Dr. Felton Markham was bald, with a black mustache and salty stubble on his dark cheeks. He was likely in his mid-fifties—the time between the graying of the beard and the graying of the mustache—but he seemed younger and vibrant. The teeth revealed by his smile were startlingly white.

"Mr. Rimes, I presume." He offered me a large hand with thick fingers.

"Morning, Reverend," I said. "Thanks for seeing me on such short notice."

"Miss Simpkins is a cherished member of this congregation. Anything we can do in her time of need we will do without question or pause." He motioned me inside.

I didn't know if he intended to quote the song "The Impossible Dream" from *Man of La Mancha*, but as I put my watch cap in my jacket pocket and followed him around the corner to his office, the next line popped unbidden into my head: "To march into hell for a heavenly cause."

The office was a narrow, paneled rectangle. To the left of the door were two ceiling-high bookcases on either side of a small stained glass window and hissing steam radiator. To the right was a compact stainless steel coat rack that held a long black topcoat and a fur-collared green leather jacket. Beside it was an old cherry desk that faced three padded wooden chairs with their armrests touching and backs close to the radiator. The chair farthest from the door was occupied by a woman who turned to look at us as we entered. She appeared to be in her early forties, with an attractive amber face framed by short black hair. She had high cheekbones, a strong nose, sculpted lips barely parted, and peach-colored nails recently done.

"Honey, this is the investigator looking for Keisha," Dr. Markham said, closing the door. "Mr. Rimes, my wife Loni."

Loni Markham rose to her full height—she was almost as tall as her husband—and smoothed her russet pantsuit before shaking my hand. Bright and engaging even without makeup, her hazel eyes held mine for a heartbeat longer than I would have expected. "I am so pleased to meet you, Mr. Rimes." Her voice was deep but too smooth to be the by-product of cigarettes. Her smile was even more radiant than her husband's, though she offered it for barely an instant as if she were embarrassed by perfect teeth. For a moment I wondered whether they kept their dentist on retainer or chained in the basement.

"The pleasure is mine, Mrs. Markham."

Dr. Markham took the high-backed leather chair behind the desk and gestured to the armchair on his left. Mrs. Markham sat back down. Unzipping my jacket, I took out my pen and notebook before I took a seat.

Dr. Markham pushed aside a few file folders, closed the open laptop computer, and put his palms flat on his desktop. "Now, how may I—we—help you, Mr. Rimes?"

"At the moment I'm just gathering background information on Keisha, something to point me in the right direction. Her parents tell me she's the church secretary, so that's where I'd like to start."

"All right, but she resigned from that post a few months ago. I think it got to be too much with her job and her parents getting older."

"Maybe she was seeing more of that young man," Mrs. Markham said.

I considered the edge in her voice before I spoke. "How long was she the secretary?"

"About ten years, I think." Dr. Markham turned to his wife.

"Closer to eleven," she said. "I remember Mother Smith died in our ninth year here and we just celebrated your twentieth as pastor."

The minister nodded. "That's right. Keisha took Mother Smith's place."

Keisha had taken the position while in her early twenties. Relevant? Maybe, maybe not. I jotted a note before continuing. "What were her duties?"

"Mainly to type up and put out the weekly program and monthly newsletter. To keep minutes at major meetings like the quarterly congregation meeting, the monthly church board meeting, the monthly deacon board meeting, and sometimes the building committee."

"Was she good at fulfilling her duties?"

Dr. Markham shrugged. "Excellent, especially since she was a volunteer. I had no complaint with her work and I can't think of anybody who did." Again he looked at his wife.

Peripheral vision told me Mrs. Markham had been studying me across the chair that separated us, her expression a blend of curiosity and tension. Now she narrowed her eyes at me. "I don't understand how her secretarial duties are relevant to her disappearance."

"Loni, I think Mr. Rimes is just trying to get a feel for Miss Simpkins—a picture."

"The more pieces I have, the clearer the picture."

Mrs. Markham leaned forward, frowning. "Obviously, she fell in with the wrong crowd and was led astray." She paused as if gauging my reaction. "You're never too old to be led astray. Isn't that where you should start? Find those people and you'll find Keisha."

I almost asked her to identify someone in that crowd, but then I stopped and took a deep breath. "Ma'am, I don't mean to be difficult, but this is how investigations work. You start with nothing and build scraps into a pile. The bigger the pile, the better the chances of success. So far nobody has been able to point me toward people who might have got Keisha into drugs, which means I have to poke through the pile and hope I uncover a name."

"Williamson," she said, her lips pressed into a tight line.

"Odell Williamson is dead." I let that hang in the air for a moment. "His parents are as convinced Keisha led him off the straight and narrow as her parents—and, I presume, you—are convinced it was all his fault." I held her gaze as I softened my voice. "Even if it was, we know Keisha didn't run away with him, so I have to find someplace else to start. Did either of you know Odell?"

"Keisha brought him to Sunday service a few times. Said he was a teacher and might be willing to get involved in our academic summer camp for kids." The minister sighed and shook his head. "He seemed like such a nice young fella."

His wife sat back, her lips pursed. "Drug overdoses. Police. Keisha disappearing. This all casts the Mount in a very bad light."

"I don't recall any mention of your church in newspaper articles about the overdose," I said. "So far there's been no news story on Keisha's disappearance."

She swallowed hard. "Publicity or no publicity, *we* know, Mr. Rimes. *We* know. Our whole church family."

"Who are Keisha's closest friends in the congregation?"

"When she was a teenager it was Bianca. One of my first duties when my husband got this posting was to run the youth group. Bianca was like a sister to Keisha."

"Bianca Dawkins?"

"Yes. A strong-willed girl, as I recall. She hasn't been to church in years, not since her mother died and she went off to college. I have no idea where she is or what she's up to."

"What about Fatimah Howze?"

"I remember the name, not the face. Sometimes she came to

youth group but she went to a Catholic church. Keisha may have mentioned something about a flower shop?"

I scratched something into my notebook. "What about Sonny Tyler? Does that name mean anything to you?"

The Markhams exchanged looks as if each hoped the other might have an answer. Then Dr. Markham said, "We have a Tyler family in the congregation, Malik and Sherry. They're in their mid-twenties and have twin girls about two. We don't know a Sonny Tyler."

"Anybody else? It doesn't have to be somebody in her age group. Maybe somebody older who was like a mentor or somebody younger that she might have mentored."

"You mean somebody she might go to if she was in trouble," Mrs. Markham said.

"Yes."

She thought for a moment. "No. She wasn't especially close to anybody that I know of. I'd have thought she would go to her parents. But Brother and Sister Simpkins requested special prayers last Sunday and asked for help. If somebody knew something about Keisha, I expect they would have come forward then, to her parents if not to us." She huffed, as if exasperated. "This is all just too upsetting."

"This has been hard on all of us," Dr. Markham said. "My wife is very protective of the work we do here."

I lowered my pen to ease Mrs. Markham's agitation. "I know a few things about your church. You have an after school program, a food pantry, a job advocacy office. I've seen your wheelchair transportation vans. What other work do you do?"

"Saving souls is a complex business, Mr. Rimes, especially when we're born in the natural crossfire between heaven and hell." Dr. Markham smiled his dazzling smile. "Yes, we prepare for the afterlife. But we are called upon to help each other in this life as well."

Mrs. Markham managed another brief smile and leaned toward me. "Have you heard of the Sermon on the Mount Community Development Foundation?"

Though I had, I shook my head. I sensed talking about it might ease her tension.

"The SMCDF. It's a not-for-profit with a mission to elevate the neighborhood, make it a stronger presence in the city, all with grant funding and small donations. We have the programs you mentioned, but we also run a low-income family housing development two blocks from here and a senior apartment high rise on Virginia Street. We also co-sponsor the culinary arts program at the new GiGi's."

"Great!" I said. "I've missed their sweet potato pie since fire closed the old one."

The minister laughed. "I don't think truer words were ever spoken in this office."

His wife sat back, eyebrows arching. "If my husband will forgive me a moment of pride, I am happy to be the foundation's CEO."

"The Lord allows a sprinkling of pride tempered by modesty." Dr. Markham turned to me, his own face alight with pride. "What my wife didn't tell you is that she established the foundation. She's got a good head for business and an MBA. She organized the charter committee and went to the banks. She did the 501c3 paperwork herself and wrote the grants. She invited a real cross-section of the community to serve on the board. It's all her doing and she's helped too many people to count—without getting a lot of attention from the press." He reached across his desk to pat her hand. "Integrity is what you do when nobody's looking."

Mrs. Markham lowered her eyes as if embarrassed, and for a moment the only sound was the hiss of the radiator. Then I asked, "Did Keisha ever do any work for the foundation?"

"No."

"But at one point she was on the board," Dr. Markham said. "You see, the foundation has to have a board of directors who—"

"That was a good while ago, honey, but even then her job made her miss too many meetings. She stepped away from the board years ago."

"Seems like only yesterday." He shook his head. "Hard-working as she is, there are only so many hours in a day. Something my wife is constantly reminding me of." He got to his feet.

Taking that as his cue the interview was over, I pocketed my notebook and stood, noting the file tabs on his desk: BLDG FUND, NEWSLETTERS, HOMILIES. I tried to make my final question as non-invasive as I could: "Are you on the board, Dr. Markham?"

"Only as a non-voting member," he said. "Which is good because I spend so much time running here and there, I don't get to many meetings myself."

Someone in the hall knocked.

"Come in," Dr. Markham said.

The door creaked open. A light-skinned man in a gray hoodie and blue HOLLISTER sweat pants filled the doorway—literally. At well over six feet, he appeared to be in his late twenties with close-cut hair and a thin mustache. He looked as if he would clock in close to two-sixty on a digital scale—pounds that seemed less the result of donuts and soda than the by-product of an NFL weight room.

"Tito, this is Mr. Rimes. Tito Glenroy, our custodian."

He stepped inside, and my hand almost disappeared in his as we shook. His grip was gorilla powerful. He didn't crush my fingers but doing so would have been easy. Instead, he held them a few beats longer than he should have. I wondered why.

Turning, Tito nodded at the minister and looked at Mrs. Markham for a few seconds. "Reverend. Ma'am." He spoke in a voice that was half whisper, half crushed glass, in an almost apologetic tone. "I found where the water's coming from in the basement. Not the men's room but a wall in the kitchen. Had to pull the stove out to get to the source."

"We gonna need a plumber?"

"Yes, sir." He frowned and cocked his head to one side. "Probably work inside that wall too. Looks like it's been wet in there a long time. You got a minute; I can show you."

Sighing, Dr. Markham turned to his wife. "Looks like we're gonna go another month without getting the new organ in and the choir loft brought up to code."

"The choir's doing just fine in the front of the assembly," she said. "Nice for them to be seen as well as heard."

The minister looked at me. "These old buildings. If it isn't one thing—"

"Go," she said. "I'll show Mr. Rimes out. I gotta get going anyway." She stood and pushed the center chair forward to avoid touching the hot radiator. Then she sidled past me on the way to the coat rack, and I caught a whiff of her perfume.

Awkwardly smiling at her, Tito hesitated a moment before pulling the green leather jacket off its hanger and holding it for her.

"Thank you, Tito," Mrs. Markham said as she slid her arms into the sleeves. Then she turned to her husband. "I'll see you later."

Nodding, the minister shook my hand. "Old building like this..."

"I understand." I gave him a Driftglass card and passed one to his wife. "You remember something or hear something, either of you, please call me. Thank you for your time."

Dr. Markham followed Tito out as Mrs. Markham zipped up and tugged on a knit hat she pulled from a pocket. Then she worked her hands into a pair of thin leather gloves as she led me out of the office and toward the door.

As we emerged into sunlight, I glanced at the F-150 that must be Tito's and then looked again to memorize the plate. "Tito is a big guy," I said. "Looks like he played some serious ball in his day."

"He did for a little while," she said.

"I'm not surprised."

"About eight years ago he got a full ride to Eastern Michigan U— a real win for the son of a humble church janitor who never made it to eighth grade."

Zipping my jacket, I thought of my own father, a janitor who had finished only high school. A tireless reader, he had become best friends with the professor whose office he cleaned, who would raise me after my parents' deaths. When I was younger, Bobby made a point of telling me how much my mother and especially my father would have appreciated each milestone in my life. "His father must have been proud," I said now.

"We all were," Mrs. Markham said. "The congregation gave him a huge send-off party. There was talk he was a shoo-in for the NFL. But then—" She let out a long sigh. "Let's just say he was better at catching passes than passing classes."

I pulled my watch cap over my ears and adjusted the stems of my glasses as I thought about how easily that line had rolled off her tongue as if she had said it before. Often.

"He worked hard and scraped through freshman year only by the skin of his teeth," she continued. "When his father died at the start of sophomore year, he kind of lost the will to try. So he came home, settled into his father's job, and that was that."

She unlocked the Camry with her remote and got inside when I opened the door.

"Good luck, Mr. Rimes," she said. "Sorry if I seemed a little short with you before but this whole thing has been so very unsettling."

"I understand."

She looked at me for a long moment. "I believe you do," she said at last. "In the end, we all want the same thing, to find Keisha."

Alive, I thought.

STILL IN THE church parking lot and waiting for my car to warm, I punched Sonny Tyler's cell number into the Bluetooth display. The call took an unusually long time to connect. I asked for him by name when a man answered.

"Speaking. Who's calling?" The voice was crisp and dispassionate.

"Mr. Tyler, my name is Rimes. I'm a detective working a missing persons case. I'd like to ask you a few questions about Keisha Simpkins."

"Keisha?" His voice faltered before rising with concern. "Keisha's missing?"

"Yes. When was the last time you saw her?"

"Last time I saw—what the fuck is this, man?"

"I understand you dated briefly."

"That was a long time ago. Years. I ain't seen Keisha since we broke up."

"Why'd you break up?"

"I was young and stupid and needed to straighten out. I talked to her a couple times since then. We didn't say all that much but we stayed on friendly terms." He took a breath, and his tone changed. "Where you get my name from?"

"Her apartment."

"She disappeared in Buffalo?"

"Yes."

"How the hell she get lost in her own back yard?"

"One day she just didn't come back home. I'm—"

"Look, detective, I ain't been to Buffalo in almost four years. I talked to Keisha maybe eight or nine times since I left. I don't know what else to tell you."

"So where are you?"

"Stuttgart, in Germany."

That explained why the call had taken so long to connect. "You at the USAG there?"

"Nine months in, with the five-fifty-fourth."

"You're an MP?"

"Yes, *sir*." He sounded surprised. "You know your company designations."

I had been an MP in Iraq before transferring into the Army's Criminal Investigation Division. I shook my head at the irony but said nothing about my service. "When was the last time you were stateside?"

"About six months ago, for my grandmother's funeral, in Dallas."

I glanced at my watch and did a quick calculation. "What time is it there?"

"Stuttgart? Seventeen hundred hours and change. What, you don't believe me?" As if annoyed, he rattled off a name and contact number for his commanding officer.

"I believe you," I said, without adding that I would call both his commander and friends I still had in the CID. "Sorry to have troubled you but your number was on my list and I have to check everything."

"I understand." He was quiet a moment. It sounded as though he swallowed a couple of times. "Detective, will you please call me back and let me know when you find her? Let me know she's okay? Better still, have *her* call me—if that's possible."

I promised I would.

8

The florist shop was a small green clapboard storefront on Kensington Avenue near Bailey. It had once been a two-family house, with an upstairs porch and big two-car garage, but now the downstairs had plate glass windows flanking a center entrance. Neon tubing in the left window said, in pink: *Flowers by Fatimah*. The window on the right said: *For All Occasions*.

I opened the front door and stepped inside. To my left was a solid steel security door that looked fresh out of the box—to the upstairs flat, I thought. An open wooden door was on my right. As I climbed three steps and went through the doorway, I heard an old-fashioned shop bell ring, likely triggered by the electric eye mounted at calf level. The pale blue wall to my left held shelves of floral arrangements, indoor plants, decorative pots, and a security panel. The opposite wall had three glass-doored floral refrigerators with motors humming and interiors full of color. Mounted above the center refrigerator was an opaque plastic security camera bubble. Ahead was a service counter. The woman behind it was of average height and in her mid-thirties. Clad in a tan pantsuit, she had cocoa skin and black hair teased into a small halo. Looking up from a computer screen, she pulled off her black-framed glasses and let them dangle from a neck chain.

"Good afternoon," she said.

"Hi," I said. "Are you Fatimah?"

"I am." She smiled. "How may I help you today?"

I smiled back and thought about Phoenix, whose smile I cherished. I wondered if maybe the best way to go about my business was to help this woman go about hers.

"I'd like to send flowers." I unzipped my jacket because the air was so warm.

"Special occasion?"

"Special person." I let that hang a moment. "Just because."

Fatimah's smile widened. "You've come to the right place. We even have *Just Because* cards you can use to personalize your message." She rotated the countertop display rack and selected three cards, which she spread before me. "Is this special person a woman?"

"Yes, but not my mother or my sister."

She glanced at my ring-free left hand. "Not a wife but much more than a friend?"

"Yes." I examined the cards and looked up. "Which would you recommend?"

With an aqua-lacquered nail, she tapped the center card, which depicted two brown hands, fingers interlaced, in the glow of a lit candle. "May I suggest roses?"

"I don't want her to think I'm too conventional. This is kind of an impulse."

"Then what about a bouquet of orange and yellow roses? A spontaneous burst of warmth in a cold December—if this is a local order."

"It is. Can they be delivered today?"

"Our van is out on a funeral run right now but should be back before too long. Same day delivery for an order past noon does cost a little extra though."

"Fine. I'd like it to reach her office between four-thirty and five. Is that possible?"

"Just late enough for her co-workers to see them but not spend the afternoon gushing over them." Nodding, Fatimah consulted the computer screen, tapped something in, and tore an order form off the pad to her right. "We can make that happen."

After I gave the office address and inserted my MasterCard into the chip reader on the counter, I wrote *I'm Thinking of You* after the elegant *Just Because* inside the card. I signed *G*, wrote *Phoenix* on the envelope, and used the stylus to sign the chip reader screen.

"Is there anything else we can do for you today?"

I handed Fatimah a Driftglass card and took out my notebook. "I wonder if you've seen or heard from Keisha Simpkins lately."

The smile disappeared. She watched me for a long moment, saying nothing, not even blinking. Then she pulled on her glasses to read my card. "You're a private detective?"

I nodded.

"So somebody's paying you to look for her. Who?"

"Ordinarily, I don't give out that information but since I got your name from her parents, I don't think they'll mind." I gazed at her for a long moment, hard. "Who did *you* think was paying me?"

Fatimah looked away and pulled off her glasses again and took a deep breath before finding her footing. "I don't know." She turned back to me, and her voice climbed an unsteady notch. "But if she was into drugs so much that she OD'd, maybe she owes somebody money, so much they'd look for her. Hurt her. Or maybe it was that boyfriend of hers that owed them money. Now that he's gone, they want her to pay."

"So you think I'm looking for her to collect?"

"Might could be. You're big enough to be somebody's thug nasty." She swallowed as the weight of what she said sank into her gut. "Now that I'm looking at you, I guess that bulge under your sweater isn't a cell phone clipped to your belt." For a few seconds, she didn't breathe and didn't move as she considered the possibility I might hurt her in my quest for her friend. "Look, I don't want no trouble. I don't know about Keisha and I don't want her drugs around my kids."

"I'm a retired army cop," I said. "You just ran my credit card through your system so if I'm here to do you harm, I'm stupid." I kept my voice calm to ease the fear and uncertainty in her eyes. "A mutual friend put me in touch with Keisha's parents. I'm just trying to help. I'm looking for her because her folks are worried sick. Even if she doesn't ever want to see them again, they just want to know she's okay." I paused but never broke eye contact. "Phoenix Trinidad is very real and more than special to me. I know you need to put that bouquet together, and I want you to, so it's in my best interest to take up as little of your time as possible." I chanced a smile, a sliver of which she returned. "So, have you seen or heard from Keisha lately?"

She hesitated a fraction of a second, shook her head, and said, "No."

The eye shift. Was she lying or simply still afraid?

"But you knew she disappeared recently."

"Yes. Her mother called to ask if I'd seen her. But I hadn't."

"Mrs. Simpkins says you and Keisha and Bianca were like sisters growing up. You always had each other's backs."

Half-smiling, Fatimah nodded. "My mother used to call us the Three Mouseketeers, which I didn't understand until I was much older."

"That's why I'm here," I said. "I thought Keisha might reach out to you or Bianca if she was in trouble and needed help."

"I haven't talked to Keisha in months. At least three. Been busy with the shop and my kids. She's always working herself."

I decided against asking her about her children because I didn't want her to take it as a subtle threat. "What about Bianca? Think Keisha might have gone to her for help?"

"Bianca and me—we don't keep in touch much anymore, but I think Keisha still sees her—saw her—from time to time. So, maybe. Yeah, Keisha might've got in touch with her. Are you gonna talk to her too?"

"She's next on my list."

"Will you tell her I said hi?"

Somewhere outside a car door slammed, hard.

"I will." I put away my notebook without having opened it. "Thanks for your time, Fatimah. If Keisha does contact you, please give her my number and tell her I'd like to help her. The address for the flowers? It's a law office. Phoenix Trinidad is a lawyer, a good one. She's willing to help too. Whatever Keisha's going through, she doesn't have to face it alone. If you see her, tell her that."

Just then there was movement in the back of the shop. A burly brown man with short hair and a close-cut beard stepped into the room. He was clad in khaki work clothes with a *Flowers by Fatimah* patch on his shirt pocket. Only glancing at me, he moved to the counter and handed Fatimah a small clipboard full of papers. "What's next?"

"Only six this afternoon," she said. "Four are ready to go." She handed him another small clipboard. "I still gotta prep two. But I want you to take extra care with the last one."

His brow furrowed. "I don't understand."

"Mr. Rimes here just ordered flowers for his special lady, and we want him to come back to us when it's time for the wedding."

The delivery man looked at me and smiled and stuck out his hand. "Congratulations!"

"Mr. Rimes," Fatimah said, "I'd like you to meet my husband Isaiah."

"Ike," he said as we shook.

9

"If you see Fatimah again, tell her I said hi. But don't do it if she's with her husband. Ike Kelly is the reason she won't have much to do with me these days."

An imposing copper-skinned woman who wore mocha lipstick and nail polish, a well-tailored blue skirt suit, a platinum necklace, and a diamond-studded white-gold wedding band, Bianca looked every inch the manager of a jewelry store. I had reached the Hunnicutt counter on the first floor of the Walden Galleria and asked for Ms. Dawkins just as she was authorizing the return of a gold locket. She read my card as I explained why I was there. When she saw my eyes go to the ring on her left hand, she reassured me that she did use the name Dawkins and agreed to talk about Keisha if I treated her to lunch. Now she sat across from me at a table in the mall's second-floor food court, ramrod straight and eating a salad and pita wedges from Souvlaki Brothers. I worked on a calzone from Sbarro.

"Isaiah doesn't like you?"

"He thinks I'm a bad influence."

"On Fatimah?"

"And their daughters." She sipped Diet Pepsi through a straw but that action did nothing to reduce the tightness of her jaw. She leveled her eyes at me as she set down the cup. "He doesn't like that I'm married to a cop."

"That's a bad influence?"

"A white cop."

"Oh."

"Named Jennifer."

"Three strikes with a single swing," I said. "From his point of view."

"But a home run from mine. We were together five years before equality and were almost at the front of the line at City Hall afterward." Then she retreated from the edge of her wistfulness. "Ike told Fatimah it was his Catholic upbringing. But I know better. It's because I said no to a threesome a long time ago and he begged me not to tell her he asked."

"You never told her?"

"That her husband is a lesbian fetishist who can't believe I wouldn't be interested in what he's packing?" Bianca shook her head. "I'm an only child. In fact, Fatimah and Keisha are too. It helped us bond. They're the closest thing I have to sisters. I'd slash a wrist before I hurt either one of them, even if we don't see each other as often as we used to. Better to be there for Fatimah when she hits the brick wall than to drive her into it myself."

"Back to Keisha." I opened my notebook, which lay beside my paper plate. "When was the last time you saw her?"

"About two months ago. We had her and Odell over for dinner and game night."

"Game night?"

Bianca smiled for the first time, and the tension in her shoulders began to lessen. "Jen is from this big Italian family. Game night started back in the Depression before her great-grandparents could afford a radio. Back then they had cards, checkers, chess, charades, maybe Monopoly."

"No Scene It or Trivial Pursuit."

"Or Cards Against Humanity." She chuckled. "Game night is a lot less frequent today with their family spread all over the country and everybody glued to phones but it still happens. When Jen and I were just *close friends*, as her parents liked to say, she took me to a couple game nights. I fit right in, thanks to countless winter Saturday afternoons where we played board games with Keisha's mom. It helped when Jen came out that I was already a fixture in her family and one of the top Scrabble players. They were more accepting of her, and us, than she expected. Of course, I can only imagine what Great-grandpa Spina would have thought of us. He might have preferred Cards Against Humanity."

Something clicked, and it took me a moment to speak. "Spina? Your wife's a cop named Spina?"

"Yes."

"A sergeant. Tall, dark-haired."

"Yes. Do you know her?"

"About six weeks ago I got shot. She was the one who took my statement in the hospital."

Bianca's eyes widened and the last filaments of her uneasiness slipped away. "Jesus Christ! The PI who got kidnapped after he brought in the cop-killer? That was you?"

I nodded.

"Talk about a small world." She let out a long breath. "You know, Jen isn't easily impressed but she liked you, called you tough, in a good way. Wait till I tell her I met you."

"Tell her I said hi, that I'm doing fine, and I'm back to work." I glanced at my notebook. "So you and Jen invited Keisha and Odell over for a game night. What did you think of Odell?"

"He was a monster at Guesstures but sucked at Catchphrase." She sighed. "We both liked him. Keisha looked the happiest I'd seen her in a long time. Jen even agreed to wear her uniform to speak to Odell's class sometime before the Christmas break. With black men being shot by police all over TV, he didn't want his kids to be afraid of cops." Bianca looked away as her eyes moistened. "Jen never got the chance to talk, and Keisha never got her happy ending."

"Did Jen ever say anything about the overdose or reports that Odell was dealing?"

"This wasn't the first time we'd spent an evening with them, just the last." Bianca wiped her eyes and leaned back. "We had dinner together three or four times before, at our place or Keisha's. Saw a couple movies together. We knew Odell more than casually. Jen wasn't part of the investigation but prides herself on being a good judge of people. She said she'd bet a week's pay the informants who dropped his name were liars with other agendas."

"What do you think?"

"I'm pretty good myself at scoping out secrets. After all, I had to keep my own for years—from family and friends, folks at church. I have to read people every day for my job. Keeping secrets means layers of hesitation in conversation, evasive verbal maneuvers, failure to make eye contact." She smiled again. "Like a married man buying jewelry for a girlfriend and constantly looking over his shoulder for a familiar face so he can step away from her. I saw none of that with Odell. In fact, he reminded me of myself when I finally came out and found out who loved me and who didn't."

"You felt free to be yourself, and to hell with anybody who couldn't deal."

"Exactly." She leaned toward me on her elbows. "Odell was just what he seemed, a good guy who loved teaching and adored Keisha. He would never put a needle in her arm."

"Even at gunpoint?"

Bianca sat back, frowning. "What do you mean?"

"Just thinking out loud. Something made this overdose happen. I wonder what. Or who." I chewed the last bite of my calzone and took a swig of iced tea. "Fatimah seemed to think somebody might be after Keisha, maybe for money."

"I wouldn't know anything about that."

"So, you haven't talked to Keisha since dinner that night?"

"No."

"Who would she turn to if she was in trouble?"

"Her parents. Fatimah. Me."

I took out my phone and pulled up Keisha's letter to her parents. I enlarged the image and pointed to the closing lines as I passed the phone to Bianca. *Right now my being with you will do you more harm than good, so please don't try to look for me. Just know that I love you both. Always.*

"What if somebody *is* after her and she's afraid turning to all of you would put you in danger? Who would she turn to then?"

Bianca answered without hesitation. "Herself."

10

Despite his green sweatsuit and brown corduroy slippers, Carl Williamson had the posture of a military man. Dark, broad-shouldered, with thinning hair and a full mustache, he led me to a country-style kitchen table and put on a pot of coffee as I draped my jacket over a white wooden chair. He took the seat across from mine.

We were quiet as he lit a Camel and pulled on it. Then I asked, "Were you in Nam?"

"Yeah, sixty-six to sixty-seven. Infantry." His voice was an octave higher than his size and his cigarette would have suggested. "How could you tell?"

"Soldiers can pick soldiers out of a crowd," I said. "Iraq. MP."

"No shit? Was it crazy as they say?"

"Was Nam?"

He laughed. "Yeah. Clusterfuck from the get-go." He shook his head, relaxed a bit, exhaled. "When I got back I didn't think I'd ever feel *real* again. Know what I mean?"

"I do."

"Like hearing the Eyewitness News traffic copter and starting to look for cover." He shook his head again. "Mama said a job would get my head straight. I went to the post office to make her happy but I was shocked to find a *brother* in personnel. Told me he started after World War II when he got out of the navy. Worked his way up. He explained the jobs they had, benefits, veterans' credits, the exam I had to take. In fact, he was the one who gave the exams. I did okay on the test and delivered mail for damn near forty years. Like I said, infantry."

We both laughed.

He got up and went to the counter to pour us coffee. He took his black, and I told him I would too. He set a white china cup in front of me.

"It's good you came while Rhonda's at work," he said, stubbing the Camel in a glass ashtray. "You know, she just went back this week. Losing Odell's been real hard on her."

"I'm sure it's been hard on both of you," I said. "I'm sorry for your loss."

"Don't be. I've heard all the sorry any man could ever want to hear. I'm just glad the case is still active. I thought the cops wrote my only child off as a junkie. So what I want to hear is news about who killed him."

Having introduced myself as Detective Rimes working the case involving Odell, I had not yet given him a Driftglass card or explained I was searching for Keisha. I wanted to be cautious because my clients told me Carl blamed Keisha as much as they blamed Odell, which meant he wouldn't care whether or how I found her. "I just caught this case yesterday. Officially, it's still an overdose but I thought it deserved a second look, so here I am."

"Is that what you do? Give things a second look?"

"More or less." I blew a stream of air across my cup and took a sip to find it good and strong. "The woman with your son that night, Keisha Simpkins. What can you tell me about her?"

Holding his cup with both hands, as if absorbing needed warmth, he looked down a moment. "A nice girl," he said. "Her father turned out to be a prick, but Rhonda and me, we liked Keisha a lot, and her mother." He sighed. "That girl was a doctor. Definite daughter-in-law material."

"I've spoken to her parents and they say the same things about your son."

"They thought Odell was great until some assholes said he dealt heroin. Then her daddy blamed my son for the whole thing."

"Did you ever think Keisha was responsible? That she was the dealer?"

"Not really. Maybe I said something like that when I was mad but I couldn't see that girl messing with drugs." He studied me a moment. "You from narcotics or homicide?"

"Second looks," I said. "That's my specialty."

"Like cold cases?"

"Close enough."

"I ask because I'd like the names of those informants so I can beat the panties off their sorry asses for lying on Odell." He took a swallow of coffee and chuckled. "See how much street cred they got left after a retired mailman beats 'em shitless."

"What they claimed would piss me off too," I said. "But even if I had them, I couldn't give up names of another detective's confidential informants. That's against the rules. But I can tell you this much. Something about their statements bothers me."

He nodded to show he understood. "That's why you're giving it a second look."

"One reason."

"I bet another is the autopsy."

"What do you mean?"

"No needle marks—except the one that killed him."

Nodding, I made a mental note to call Mira the instant I left.

"Odell wasn't nobody's junkie or dealer," Carl said through clenched teeth. His back stiffened again and he set down his cup. "We cleaned out his place the week after his funeral. Jeans, khakis, button-down shirts—real dealers' clothes. Books and DVDs everywhere but no weed, no pills, and not one gun, except his paintball rifle. All those stacks of drug money you see in movies? The only cash we found was a hundred-dollar bill folded inside his passport and twenty bucks in change in a damn cookie jar. The manager at our bank did some kind of search for a safe deposit box in his name. Know what he found?"

"I'm guessing no box in his name. Anywhere."

"Bingo." Carl's eyes began to fill. "What kind of dealer shops at Target and drives a ten-year-old Mazda?"

I gave him a moment to breathe. "You have the autopsy report?"

He wiped his eyes and shook his head. "Leon Starks, the undertaker, is a friend of mine. I asked him to look for needle marks." Carl swallowed audibly. "I saw my boy before Leon put on his suit. His arms and legs were clean and smooth as a baby's ass."

For a heartbeat or two I said nothing. "Did you know that Keisha's missing?"

His brow furrowed. "Missing? Like disappeared?"

"Yes, about two weeks ago."

"Jesus!" He narrowed his eyes at me. "*That's* why you're looking into this. You're missing persons and trying to connect the dots. I didn't hear anything about this on the news."

"Sometimes publicity is wrong for a case like this. We'd appreciate it if you and your wife didn't tell anyone till you hear about it from the media. Keisha's life may depend on it."

He nodded and raised his cup to his lips as if the coffee would fortify his assent. Before he drank, he asked, "Did she disappear on her own or did somebody snatch her?"

"Too early to know. That's why we're keeping things quiet. We need to determine if somebody is after her or if somebody caught her."

"Poor Keisha." He bit his lip before he sipped. "But this kinda makes sense. Say somebody tried to kill them both—why, I have no fucking idea. But she survived. Then she ran. Had to. If they took her, her body woulda turned up somewhere by now."

"Still could," I said and waited a breath or two before adding, "You said you cleaned out your son's apartment. It might help me find whoever was behind the overdose if I could look at his phone or computer or maybe his car."

Carl had started shaking his head before I finished. "Sorry. Like I said, my wife was really torn up about this. My next-door neighbor is a retired shrink from UB. He said the faster I got rid of Odell's stuff, the better it would be for Rhonda."

"So you sold it."

"Yeah. The police never showed much interest in it—till now." He glared at me, but only for a moment. "Couldn't stand the sight of that car so I sold it for a few hundred cash."

"Do you have his name, the buyer?"

"Her. Ellen something. Something with a T. Rented a room down the street. Finished grad school this semester. She's probably back in New York City by now."

And probably a dead end, I thought but said, "I'd still like her name."

"Terrio," he said, index finger pointing toward the ceiling. "Ellen Terrio, Brooklyn."

I wrote down the name. "What about your son's computer and phone?"

"Odell had this big machine that did everything. We don't have much use for a computer that fancy—Rhonda's Kindle is just fine—so I donated it to the community center around the corner. Last I saw it, they were loading math games for kids in their after school program."

For a few seconds, I said nothing, calculating the odds of getting a computer tower away from the community center and getting something useful out of a hard drive that may or may not have been reconfigured. At best a longshot. "What about his phone?"

"I put it in one of those electronic recycling bins at the mall," Carl said. "I never even tried to turn it on." He sighed. "Sorry, I'm not much help. You got a card?"

"Fresh out but I'll write down my cell number. Call me if you think of something."

"Take my number too," Carl said. "Call *me* when you catch the motherfuckers."

Someone else had told me the same thing a few weeks ago, just before I got shot.

11

G lad you called," Mira said, lowering the volume of what sounded like her favorite group, U2. "We have to talk about Christmas. What to get for Bobby, who's coming to my house. So far it's me and Shakti, Bobby and Kayla, you and Phoenix, Julie and her boyfriend. Do you think the Dorans will come this year or will they have family from out of town again?"

"I'll ask them," I said, turning right onto Main from University Avenue. "I'm on my way there now." I did a quick count in my head. "Are you sure you'll have room for eleven?" Last year I hadn't met Phoenix, and Julie Yang, the live-in math grad student who looked after Shakti while Mira worked, didn't have a boyfriend. The year before last there had been nine of us in Mira's small dining room, including Jimmy Doran's wheelchair, at a table designed to seat eight.

"We can make it work," she said. "So let me know."

"I will." I hesitated. "You're not in the middle of something, are you?"

"Like a post?" She laughed. "Just paperwork. There's more to my job than autopsies, you know. If I were at the dissection table, I'd be talking to the voice recorder, not you. What's up? Wait, let me guess.

You're working a case and want me to risk my job because you need a copy of an autopsy report."

"That you would say that means you're at home, not in the office."

She laughed again. "My brother the detective. Nothing gets by him."

"I don't want a copy of the report. I just need to know one thing."

"What?"

I told her about Odell and Keisha's overdose and her disappearance, that her parents had hired me to find her. I told her no one I had interviewed believed Odell was a user. "I just left his father. He thinks somebody forced heroin into his son. He said there were no tracks on the body, no punctures but the overdose injection site. I just want to verify that."

After a moment she said, "I'll get back to you. You get back to me about the Dorans."

"Will do," I said. "Give my nephew a hug for me."

A few minutes later I reached Admiral Road and parked two doors away from a brick house with a center entrance and a steel wheelchair ramp. The house belonged to my former campus police partner, Jimmy Doran, and his wife Peggy Ann. Jimmy had been paralyzed from the waist down a few years earlier in a shootout we had with two spree killers passing through the Buffalo State campus. His silver wheelchair van sat in the driveway, and Peggy Ann's blue Impala was parked in front of the house. For a moment I just sat in my Escape, looking at their home and collecting my thoughts.

The side of the van bore modest black letters that said Doran Security Consulting. A former state police officer forced into his second retirement by the shooting, Jimmy had developed the firm with his son Little Jimmy—LJ—who would soon graduate summa cum laude in computer science. They offered high tech security solutions for a diverse clientele, including Driftglass Investigations. LJ was especially adept at cracking codes, hacking into databases, and covering his tracks on the way out. I had no doubt he had gotten into both Keisha's Dell laptop and her iPhone by now. But as I climbed out of my car and moved toward the steps, I realized that discussing the case with his parents might be useful too. Jimmy had been a smart cop whose instincts sometimes made me look at things differently, and Peggy Ann was a nurse practitioner herself who had retired early to care for her husband.

Pulling off my watch cap and pocketing it, I rang the bell.

After a moment LJ opened the door and said softly, "Hey, G." Honey-skinned and thin, he was under six feet tall and had the sandy curls typical of many biracial children. He wore a loose blue sweater, slim gray chinos, and sneakers.

I stepped into the paneled living room, and he shut the door. His father's motorized wheelchair sat near the lift track along the stairs. The lift chair itself was out of sight, which meant it—and Jimmy— were upstairs, where he kept a manual wheelchair. "It's quiet."

"Dad's taking his nap. Mom's at the gym with her friend Leslie."

I nodded. As active as Jimmy forced himself to be—working irregular hours for his business, driving with manual controllers, swimming in his all-weather enclosed lap pool out back, curling dumbbells—he needed regular naps. It wasn't urgent that I wake him right this moment, so I resigned myself to discussing things with him and Peggy Ann another time. "Well, how'd you make out?"

"I got in," LJ said. "But next time you bring me something, wear latex gloves so I don't have to spend time isolating your fingerprints from the owner's."

"She used fingerprint access, and you lifted her prints to unlock her stuff?"

Grinning, he shrugged. "Too late to use that to get into the phone, so I figured out her passwords. But I wanted to practice making fake fingers anyway." He walked past me and started toward the office in a converted breakfast room at the back of the house.

"Superglue and Gummi bears," I said.

LJ shrugged. "Actually, surgical glue. Close to super glue, and Mom's got plenty."

It was late afternoon, but the office was still bright because three of the four walls were exteriors full of windows. We sat at one of the tech-cluttered worktables, and LJ pulled over Keisha's phone and laptop, as well as a large zip-lock plastic bag with printouts, a yellow DSC invoice, and three gelatine blobs—fake fingers.

"Okay, you can get her emails, texts, call logs, and computer files." He tapped the plastic bag. "With her ID you can pull down anything she has on the cloud. Oh, and I checked credit card activity. Nothing recent."

"Anything especially interesting in her files?"

"I didn't read much. Just enough to make sure I got into everything. Besides, exam week starts Monday and I have tons of work to do this weekend." He hesitated. "But based on what you told me about this lady, I did see something in one of her text messages that sounded kinda like a threat. I tracked the phone number—"

"A burner," I said.

He nodded. "I found where it was sold. A corner store on the east side."

"Thanks," I said. But that information would be useless to me because I had no way of obtaining or executing a search warrant for access to any video surveillance. The most I could do was sit on the store and see if anybody connected to Keisha showed up there.

As if he'd read my mind, LJ added, "I tried to see if they had security cameras online but I couldn't find any. They may have a closed system or no cameras at all."

"Especially if they're a front." In recent years several neighborhood stores had been caught selling drugs, bootleg DVDs, and even handguns. "So what was the threat?"

LJ unzipped the bag and took out one of the fingers and pressed it against the phone's home button. The screen lit up—as did his face with a flash of pride. He called up the texts and turned the phone so I could see a single gray text bubble beneath a phone number: *Lucky once bitch but remember luck is like lightning.*

I looked at LJ.

"Lightning doesn't strike twice," he said.

12

P hoenix texted me hearts and kisses emojis to thank me for the flowers, but she was at a friend's bachelorette party, so I had Friday night to myself.

Before a light workout that included free weights and punching past shoulder pain on the heavy bag in my living room, I sent Mira a text that confirmed the Dorans would come to her house for Christmas. After the workout, I showered, toasted a ham and cheese panini on my tabletop George Foreman grill, and popped open a Corona. I ate at the dining counter in my kitchen as I examined Keisha's phone and computer.

I went through her iPhone first. Her home screen—which had a picture of earth from space—held the usual icons for the phone's features and half a dozen games that included Candy Crush and Words with Friends. I tapped Words and looked at the list of unfinished games and saw that Odell and Bianca were among Keisha's regular challengers. I returned to the home screen and jotted notes as I scrolled through her contacts, call logs, calendar, and texts. Her contact list had more than four hundred names—individuals identified by one name or two, businesses that ranged from Cora's Curlz salon to EM Tea Coffee Cup Café to pizzerias like LaNova, Bocce, and

Just Pizza, national and local professional associations, the Red Cross, more than thirty different medical offices, and two dozen social service agencies. I pulled up each entry, finding only a phone number for most, sometimes an address, and occasionally a birthday or office hours or a note indicating the best time to call.

Her call logs stretched back over two months and included calls to and from various states, as well as Canada. Most were brief, three or four minutes, just enough time to order food or answer a question or check a bank balance. Many, including three from the burner number LJ had shown me, lasted less than five seconds—just long enough for Keisha to hang up on robocalls or heavy breathers trying to intimidate her. The longest calls were between Keisha and those I already knew were closest to her—her parents, Ileana, Odell, Bianca, and Fatimah, whose frequency of contact with her missing friend was greater than I had been led to believe.

Why did you lie to me, Fatimah? I made a note to visit her again.

Keisha's calendar was mundane—meetings, appointments, reminders, even the date with Odell that ended with the overdose. The text messages ranged from the routine to the ridiculous—work matters, friendly chatter, comments on news stories, here and there jokes, confirmation of meeting times and lunch dates, playful banter and goofy emojis with Odell, some of it sexually suggestive. What emerged from most of the texts was a picture of the relationship Keisha had with each of her texting partners. With most co-workers she kept a professional tone: *Must postpone mtg till Fri* and *LED projector needs bulb before presentation tomorrow*. With her women friends there was a supportive sisterhood: *LMAO* and *usual spot, drinks on me* and *Ugly, don't buy!* under a picture of a dress. With Odell, there was a comfortable intimacy that included shorthand like *TOY*—thinking of you—and *ILY2*—I love you too. Other messages between the lovers included things like *Pick up wine & Ital bread* and *Feel like waking up at my place?* and *Hungry? I can order something.* So far there was nothing to suggest they wanted to try drugs together.

At first, my review of Keisha's information was clinical and detached. Then I listened to her voice mails, mostly voices I had never heard and names I had seen only on the contact list saying *Call me back* or *You'll never guess where I am* or *I just wanted to thank you*. I recognized the voices of those I had interviewed—her friends, Dr. Markham, her parents, who had left several worried messages before they realized she had disappeared without her phone. There were two heavy breathing recordings from the burner number that had made the text threat, and I felt a stirring of anger in my gut.

But it was hearing Odell for the first time that sent a wave of sadness washing over me. It was entirely possible that Carl Williamson had found nothing at his son's apartment because the organization had another site where product was prepared and money secured. But I doubted that as soon as I heard Odell speak. His voice was higher than his father's and rang with a joyful fluidity that reminded me of Bobby. Though retired from the classroom, my godfather retained the vocal range and cadences of the natural teacher, the person whose rightful place in the universe was among those who needed to learn something. Odell, I was sure, had the same intellectual DNA. That future students would never hear his voice only magnified his loss.

Carl's words rang in my head: *Call me when you catch the mother-fuckers.* I thought about the threatening text from a burner: *Lucky once bitch.*

I stood up and got another Corona from my refrigerator. As I popped the top, my phone buzzed. I pulled it out of my pocket and said, "Hello."

"Gideon Rimes?"

The voice was female, but its huskiness was familiar. "Yes."

"This is Jen Spina. You—"

"Sergeant Spina! This is a nice surprise."

"Call me Jen."

"All right, Jen. So, what can I do for you?"

"I know you talked to my wife today, about her friend who's missing."

"I did."

"We talked about it at dinner. She said it would be okay if I called." She hesitated. "Bianca is kind of reserved, so I'm guessing she didn't let you know how upset she is."

"She made it plain."

"Keisha's good people. So are her parents. They accepted me because Bianca was like another daughter, so I must be okay. I hate to see them left hanging. I hear you got friends in the department. For damn sure bringing in a cop-killer made your stock go up." She drew in a deep breath. "So if you need anything to help you find her, even on the down-low, please contact me. I'll run plates, check reports, dig up arrest records—whatever you need that won't get me shit-canned. If you gotta go somewhere you need back-up, call me. Not the number on the card I gave you in the hospital, but this one, my private cell."

I couldn't remember where I'd put her business card. "All right, Jen. I appreciate it."

"If you hear something, please let us know." Her voice caught. "If it's bad, tell me first so I can break it to Bianca."

Clicking off, I added her number to my directory. Then I sat down and forced my mind back into the case at the right point: *Lucky once bitch.* I remembered what Phoenix had said at dinner, that the botched break-in might have been Odell's crew looking for hidden drug money or rival dealers trying to learn how Odell moved product. Since I had begun to believe Odell had no crew, the break-in was either unrelated to Keisha's disappearance or an attempt to find something else. *Lucky once bitch.* Had that come from the would-be burglar? If so, what had he been trying to find? I took a hefty swallow of Corona as I thought about that. Then I turned on Keisha's laptop.

Her home screen background was a photo of a gleaming glacier shedding a chunk of ice. Against the brilliant white and stunning blue were assorted program icons, browser and email links, and several large folders labeled *Humanitas, Church, Pictures, Misc, Games,* and *Professional.* My first pass was through the folders. Most were like Russian nesting dolls, full of additional folders and files. *Humanitas* held Projects, Programs, Letters & Memos, Minutes, Staffing, Studies, Case Histories, Outreach, Outside Agencies, and at least twenty others that would take hours to examine. *Church* was home to Newsletters, Meeting Minutes, Cong Letters, Church History, Bldg Needs, and Memb Roll. *Pictures* had Family, Holidays, Vacations, Phone Pix, and Random. *Misc* was a nightmare of disconnected folders and files, a dumping ground to help keep the desktop uncluttered. Only *Games* and *Professional* had no other folders. The former had program icons for Scrabble, Trivial Pursuit, puzzles, several Sims games, and a handful of action games. The latter had only Word files, JPEGs, and PDFs of Keisha's resumes, degrees, and certifications.

There was nothing that, on the surface, would interest a thief.

Grateful that she was organized, I began opening Humanitas files and skimming through them, convinced I was going to be up for a long time. When I finished my Corona, I stood up to make coffee. At that moment my cell phone buzzed again.

"Hello."

The voice on the other end was breathless. "Gideon? Ileana. Are you free to join me at a homeless shelter right now?"

"Is Keisha there?"

"No, Veronica Surowiec. She says she saw Keisha earlier today. And bring money or she won't talk. She already got my last twenty."

13

Veronica Surowiec was hideous, the remnant of a once beautiful woman who had fallen into hell. Honey blonde hair now dry as broom straw stuck through holes in her old red watch cap. Her blue eyes were cloudy, the sallow skin of her face dotted with blisters. Behind her cracked full lips were the discolored, crumbling teeth of a long-time meth addict. If her hands were any indication, the body beneath her filthy mustard coat was skeletal and unwashed.

With her long charcoal coat open, Ileana Tassiopulos and I sat across from Veronica at a table in the back of a deconsecrated Bidwell Parkway church that now housed Sanctuary Nimbus, a ragtag social collective which had replaced church pews with folding cots and kept a soup kitchen in the basement. It was a cold night but only half the cots were occupied. Maybe homelessness was on the decline, but it was far from being a problem solved.

Sanctuary Nimbus, Ileana had explained as she led me from the front door, was the brainchild of an entrepreneur whose epiphany about asceticism and social responsibility would in another time have been called a nervous breakdown. Decades earlier, Paul Pollard had devised the Omicron Seven management system. For a time the rage in business schools and multinationals determined to humanize capitalism, Omicron Seven had made Pollard wealthy enough to squeak through the Great Recession with a third of his assets intact but less of his reason. Some years after his emotional collapse, he returned home to Buffalo and founded the collective, which offered food, shelter, and conversation to those in need, along with GED classes and workshops on the Seven Micromorphoses, the small changes that would sculpt individual and group identity into a more effective social personhood.

"So that was him," I'd said, glancing back at the elderly bald man enveloped in an oversized cloak that resembled a brown monk's robe. "The guy with the frozen smile who opened the door, Pastor Paul."

"Yes, but he's not ordained in any faith. Pastor Paul is a nickname."

Omicron Seven sounded like bullshit to me. Paul Pollard, now speaking to a wraith of a man seated on a cot, struck me as one who straddled the line between altruism and mental illness. But I said nothing as Ileana motioned me to a chair and introduced me to Veronica. I shook her hand—bony, chapped, with ragged nails and open cuts encrusted with dirt. I sat without reaching for the mini-bottle of hand sanitizer in my jacket pocket. Ileana spoke in tones intended to put Veronica at ease, repeating what she had explained before my arrival, that Keisha was in trouble and I was going to help her. My back to the room and the buzz of other voices, I took two tens and three fives from my wallet. I held them where Veronica could see them. Her dull eyes sharpened a bit. She looked at me with a faint leer, a mild kind of come-hither smile.

"Veronica, tell Mr. Rimes what you told me, and he'll give that money to you."

"One bill at a time." My need to find my clients' daughter struggled with my guilt for feeding a drug habit. "The more you tell, the more you get."

"Fuggin' real?" Veronica's voice was surprisingly deep but she slurred her words.

"Fucking real," I said. "I hear you saw Keisha Simpkins today. Where?"

"Here." She opened her hand, waiting for me to put a bill in it.

I moved a five toward her and lowered it slowly. "When? What time?"

"S'afternoon." Her fingers crumpled Lincoln's face, and the bill disappeared into a pocket quickly enough to impress a magician. Her hand returned to the table, her fingers uncurling in anticipation of my next question.

"But the Sanctuary doesn't open till evening," Ileana said.

"So why was she here today?" I said.

"I dunno." Veronica's hand made a *gimme* gesture.

I shook my head. "Just thinking out loud. I didn't expect you to answer that one." I held out the next bill. "But why were *you* here so early?"

She hesitated, looked off, and said, "Goin' to Elmwood."

Lie or truth? Her demeanor gave me pause but the stretch of Elmwood just a few blocks away was home to a dozen restaurants and coffee shops. She might have been on her way there to beg. I gave her the bill. "Do you know where she went or where she's staying?"

"No." Veronica wriggled her fingers, eager to close them around my last five.

I pulled it back when she reached for it. "If you don't know where Keisha is, I don't think you can help me find her." I made a show of reaching for my wallet to put away the rest of the money.

"I saw her someplace else, shithead."

"Where? Other shelters?"

Her hand was still open, "Me to know, ash-hole."

I put the five in her palm.

"Salvation Army, yesterday."

"Has to be the one on Main Street downtown but I called earlier and she's not there," Ileana said. "Veronica walks all over town but doesn't get out to the suburbs. Right, Vee?"

Veronica nodded without looking at her former colleague.

I leaned toward her, but her eyes were on the first ten. "Okay, this time I need more than one answer. In your walks all over town, have you seen Keisha at other places—and what places?"

Browning front teeth clamped over her lower lip, Veronica nodded again. "The Friary," she said after a moment. "Cornerstone. Gerard Place. Night People. Mercy House."

"Shelters that take women," Ileana said.

At that moment voices rose in anger some distance behind me —"Touch my shit I'll kill you, nigger!"—and as I turned around there was a loud crash.

"Who you callin' nigger, you muhfuckin' hillbilly!"

About thirty feet away from us, two full-bearded men, one black, one white, faced off amid overturned cots. They began to move in a tight circle as they prepared to engage. Those nearest them scrambled away, and no one produced a cell phone to capture a bum fight video for YouTube. In dirty camo and half-crouching, the gray-bearded white man held a tactical folding knife in his right hand—carbon steel, the black blade suggested. Taller and fatter, the other man was about my complexion. He wore a threadbare pea coat. His hands were balled into fists but his fighting stance was all wrong for defending himself against a knife attack.

I slid the pair of tens to Ileana and stood up, my legs beginning to move. My brain was already calculating how quickly I could reach the man in camo and how best to disarm him without drawing my Glock. Before I could get to them, however, another man darted in from my left—a sandy-haired man in jeans and a pile-lined suede jacket. He looked about thirty but moved like a teenager. In a quick, fluid motion he stepped between the combatants and caught the white man's wrist. He twisted hard and kicked the blade aside when it clattered to the floor. I bent to pick it up when I got there and closed it.

The younger man clutched the older by his jacket and pulled him up to his full height. "You know the rules, Norm. You can't stay here if you fight."

"Sorry, Brother Grace, but he touched my shit." He pointed to a black plastic garbage bag a few feet away.

"I ain't touch nothin', you crazy fool!" the black man said.

"I got this, Charlie," Brother Grace said, giving Norm a hard shake. "Charlie doesn't want anything you got. Now get your shit and go."

"Then I want my knife back," Norm whined, cocking his head toward me. "That other nigger picked it up. Make him give it back."

Brother Grace looked at me and grinned. Then he turned back to Norm. "You really are a dumb shit, aren't you? Can't you see that man is a cop?"

Everyone nearby began to cast sidelong glances in my direction, some to edge away. Charlie, who never thanked Brother Grace for saving him from a belly wound, started toward the other side of the room.

"I was you," Brother Grace said to Norm, "I'd grab my bag and go before he took me downtown and hooked me up to one of those machines."

Norm looked at me, his eyes widening in a panic that spoke volumes about his mental health. "Not the machines," he whispered.

"You still got time to get over to Night People," Brother Grace said.

"Occifer, I'm sorry," Norm said, hefting his garbage bag and backing toward the front door. "I'm real sorry." When he got to the exit, he turned on his heel, pushed the crash bar, and disappeared into the night. His exasperated "Niggers!" was audible as the door closed.

Handing Brother Grace the knife, I said, "I'm not a cop, not anymore."

Pocketing the knife, he smiled, his teeth strong and white. "But you still got the look, my man." He nodded as if congratulating himself on his perception. "You still got the look."

"Gideon Rimes." I stuck out my hand.

"Jeremiah Grace," he said, taking it. "I work here with Pastor Paul. So what brings you to Sanctuary Nimbus? You don't look like our typical volunteer."

"Just helping a friend."

He looked past me to Ileana and Veronica. "Miss Tassi-whassis, in the nice coat. She must be your friend." Turning back to me, he half-whispered, "Can't be Nasty Nica."

I tried to match his volume level. "Nasty Nica?"

Brother Grace glanced back at Veronica. "Don't know where it started but her street handle is Nasty Nica. Maybe 'cause she cusses like a biker—or maybe 'cause she'll give anybody a hummer for five bucks." After an impression of her throaty, slurred speech—"Blow job fi' dolluhs"—he shook his head. "I hear she can be haggled down to two. The microbes in *that* mouth have gotta be in their own version of World War III."

I looked back at Veronica and felt a stab of sadness anyone could have fallen so far. She wasn't close enough to hear what he had said about her but she watched Brother Grace intently, her expression somewhere between hunger and uncertainty. Just then the phone in my jacket pocket buzzed once. I didn't check the text because Pastor Paul joined us, his mild confusion tinged with concern: "Are you all right, brother?"

"Fine, Pastor." Brother Grace hooked a thumb toward me, and light glinted off the raised infinity symbol on the large stainless steel ring he wore. The print above and below the symbol was too small for me to read. "This guy had my back."

"Thank you, Mister—what was it again?" The old man appeared to concentrate but his unfaltering smile made the effort seem eerie. "I know you're a friend of Ileana's."

"Rimes. I met you when you let me in." *Not ten minutes ago*, I thought.

"Mr. Rimes. Thank you." He shook my hand, his grip feeble, liver spots south of his knuckles. "Brother Grace is one of my best helpers. We could not function without him."

"You're not gonna lose me, Pastor." Jeremiah Grace patted the old man's back. "I owe you too much. Why don't you finish your rounds and let me talk to Mr. Rimes and Miss Ileana for a minute." A hand on each shoulder, he began to steer Pastor Paul away from me.

But the pastor turned back as if attached to a resistant spring. "Maybe you can get this strapping young man to volunteer." As he studied me, I wondered if the flutter in his voice was from a neurological disorder like Parkinson's. "Latecomers will need a meal and conversation. Mr. Rimes, you look like a man who's seen lots of things to talk about."

Pastor Paul moved away and bent to speak to an oversized woman sitting on one of the cots. She wore layers of rags, three scarves on her head, and filthy fingerless gloves. Toothless, she smiled at the attention and slapped her knee when he said something funny. Watching him, I remembered an article I'd once read about mental illness among saints.

Brother Grace turned toward Ileana and Veronica as if ready to go to them but I asked him a question before he could move: "How long have you volunteered here?"

He grinned. "I don't serve food and launder sheets. I'm the shelter troubleshooter—kind of the operations manager. Only four of us get paychecks—Judy the cook, Marco the business guy, Drew the custodian, and me. Pastor and I are the only ones who live on site."

"You live here, in the building?"

"Not *here*, with the drop-ins." He shook his head. "I'm up all night. Volunteers clean the church after folks clear out in the morning. There's no place else in the building to sleep. The basement's too cold. The bell tower is locked because it's not safe. Our rooms are in the parsonage next door. I crash in the morning. Then I'm up by three for deliveries."

"Deliveries?"

"Food, blankets, linen, used clothing, cleaning supplies. Sometimes money."

"Pastor Paul gets a lot out of you for the roof over your head."

He laughed. "A roof that needs as much work as the rest of this joint. Pastor is rich but even he can't do all that needs to be done." Then Brother Grace started toward the table in the back. I followed him.

"Hi, Miss Tassi-whassis," he said when he got there. "I'm sorry but I always have trouble saying your name."

She looked at him without smiling. "I've told you to call me Ileana."

"*Miss* Ileana," he said, his tone ingratiating. "I truly respect what you do, so it's only right I show that respect." He shifted his gaze to Veronica—who looked down like a puppy caught standing over a shredded pillow—but he continued to speak to Ileana. "You try to help people. You're a good person." Then his voice sharpened a bit. "Nica, you haven't been taking advantage of Miss Ileana's kindness, have you?"

"No." Veronica's voice was flat but tight. "I'm tired, so I'm gonna go lay down now." She stood and pulled from under her chair a pair of bulging cloth shopping bags. Then she moved toward an empty cot at the center of the room.

"You know we worked together," Ileana said to Brother Grace. "She was—is—a doctor. She'll never practice again but I'd like to get her back into rehab. Maybe then—"

"Wish I could help," Brother Grace said. "I know what it's like to hit bottom and I know she needs more than a bed. But I got my hands full keeping this place together every night, and I never know who's gonna show up. The most I can say is, when she shows up here, she never tries to use."

Because she'd be afraid to, I thought.

14

Ileana's eyes were moist as she sipped her tea. "I hate seeing her like that, and I hate thinking Keisha might end up the same way."

With our coats on the backs of our chairs, we were sitting at a small corner table in Spot Coffee on Elmwood. We had retreated there to discuss our visit to Sanctuary Nimbus. Ileana had given Veronica one of the tens I'd slid to her. The other we had used to buy green tea for her and black coffee for me. Now I drank my coffee in silence as Ileana said whatever she needed to say. I wanted her to vent before I asked any questions, to get past the distress of seeing Veronica before I shared what I now knew about Keisha's drug overdose. Because it was almost closing time, few people were there, and no one was near us.

"I wish we could do something to help her. We tried before to reach out to her, several times—Keisha, me, other people at work. She pulled away every time and even ran when she saw us coming. But tonight she looked worse than ever. She didn't run when I came up on her. Her eyes were glazed but she knew who I was. Her skin and teeth are awful. She's lost so much weight, I don't see how she can go on much longer." Ileana finally wiped her eyes with the back of her hand. "Now it's starting all over again with Keisha. God, I don't know if I—if I'm strong enough to lose another friend to this shit."

She began to cry, quietly enough not to draw attention to us. I handed her my napkin because hers was already in shreds. I waited for her to finish. Finally, after dabbing her eyes, she blew her nose and let out a deep breath. Smiling awkwardly, she looked at me. "Sorry. I don't mean to be this way."

"No need to apologize." I placed my hand over hers. "I understand. We haven't lost Keisha yet. I promise to do everything I can to find her." I withdrew my hand, locked my fingers under my chin, and thought for a moment. I needed to talk, to get a reaction to all I had learned in round one of my investigation. But Ileana didn't know any of it. I would have to ease her into it, which meant I would have to trust her. My gut told me I could, that her concern for Keisha was genuine. "I'll need your help," I said finally.

"Anything."

"Your eyes and ears for one. But first, Veronica. Besides being wasted and wasting away, how did she seem to you?"

"Obscene." She half-chuckled. "Always did have a mouth on her. If something struck her as stupid or wrong, Veronica wouldn't hesitate to say so with language that used to get my mouth washed out with soap. She was persistent and stubborn enough never to back down."

"So she was pretty gutsy."

"Still is. I've heard from people she's approached for money that if you give her a dollar, she'll demand two. We must have seemed like a winning scratch-off tonight."

I nodded. "Drugs, drink, power, sex, religion—all those things don't change who you are. They just magnify it, right?"

"Yes." She sipped more tea. "So does being on the street. Homelessness doesn't make you less human. It underscores everything human about you, for better or worse. Got a drug problem? Now it's hopeless. If you're nice and fall on hard times, your kindness is a liability. Being homeless makes a happy person seem profoundly sad, a complainer a curmudgeon, a constant talker more annoying. Mental illness seems more pronounced—like Norm's."

"Did Veronica seem in any way less like herself tonight?"

"No, she was—" Ileana caught her lower lip between her teeth. "When it was just us with her, she was this bitter homeless Veronica that called everybody asshole. But toward the end she was different."

"How?"

"Skittish. Almost afraid when Brother Grace came over."

Feeling a stab of gratitude that she'd confirmed my perception, I said, "Tell me about Brother Grace."

Ileana looked down for a moment, perhaps collecting her thoughts. "Sanctuary Nimbus started maybe nine years ago, with Pastor Paul funding it out of pocket until it was established. For a few years, it had a good board that helped it get a 501c3 designation, grants, and other support. It had a bookkeeper, a lovely older woman named Betsy Kling, who lived in the parsonage and may or may not have shared Pastor Paul's bed. Whatever she was to him, she was the one who kept his quest organized and on track." Ileana sighed.

"What happened to her?"

"Cancer," she said. "Almost five years ago. Pastor Paul was devastated."

"Was that the beginning of his current decline?"

She nodded. "The Sanctuary foundered for several months until Marco Madden came on as business manager and Brother Grace began to help with day to day operations."

"Where did Brother Grace come from?"

"I'm not sure but I think the Southern Tier, maybe Jamestown. I heard him say something once about growing up not far from where they first put Scary Lucy."

I bit back a smile. Home to Lucille Ball and the National Comedy Center, Jamestown, near the New York border with Pennsylvania, had made the national news a few years earlier because a toothy bronze statue looked more like a short-haired bride of Frankenstein than the city's most famous daughter. Replaced by a more accurate rendering nicknamed Lovely Lucy, Scary Lucy was still on display in another part of the comedienne's memorial park.

"Also, he knows what it's like to hit bottom," I said. "Any idea what he meant?"

"No."

"Pastor Paul seems to depend on him for quite a bit."

"Paul Pollard is old, declining, as you said. He's likely in poor health, maybe showing signs of dementia. I think it's safe to say at this point he needs all the help he can get." Ileana shredded another corner of the napkin. "I don't know how well organized his operation is, but if something happens to him, Sanctuary Nimbus will fall apart, figuratively and literally."

"You don't think Jeremiah Grace can step in and save the day? I mean, he has the name for that kind of work."

"If that's his real name." She paused. "If he doesn't turn it into a cult."

"You don't trust him. Or like him."

"No." Lips pressed tight, she inhaled deeply through her nose. "There's something about him that's off. Unnerving. Even creepy."

"Maybe a little dangerous," I said.

"Maybe a lot."

"The way he treated Norm?"

"Yes. He almost seemed to enjoy the cruelty of it."

I nodded. "Did you and Keisha ever talk about him?"

Ileana shrugged. "Only in passing. She thought he was kind of a jerk too."

I drank more coffee and sat back, ready to trust her. "Now let's talk about Keisha. You called the Salvation Army and she wasn't there but Veronica saw her at several places."

"If she told the truth."

"There is that," I said. "But for now let's assume she did."

"All right."

"Let's assume she saw Keisha at several shelters, where people would know her from Humanitas."

"Some staff would know her but maybe not all the volunteers."

I thought about that a moment. "What if she went to the Salvation Army and the other places not as Dr. Keisha Simpkins but as someone else?"

"I don't understand."

"In ratty old clothes, her face hidden from those she knows. Essentially, in disguise."

Ileana wrinkled her brow. "Why would she do that?"

"Veronica's life spiraled out of control but Keisha's wasn't there yet, at the point of no return. Would you agree?"

"Yes."

"She had a drug overdose nobody thinks was her fault." I resisted the urge to count off my points on my fingers. "Even if it was, she had rehab and a job to come back to. She has a home, family, friends—none of which say they have seen her. So why did she leave without her car and cell phone? Why would a woman with a solid support system drop off the grid and mingle among those served by shelters?" I leveled my gaze at Ileana, hoping she would remember what she had told me about the homeless when we were in her office. "Why would Keisha make herself invisible?"

Ileana's mouth fell open and her eyes widened. "Because she doesn't want to be seen."

"Or found."

"You mean somebody's looking for her? Who?"

"Someone she believes will hurt her family and friends if she's anywhere near them."

"My God!" She sat up straighter. "Do you think Brother Grace has anything to do with this?"

"No idea. I just have a gut feeling he's bad news for people he's supposed to help."

"If he knows somebody's looking for Keisha, he'll sell her out in a heartbeat?"

"Right." Then I told her about the black Navigator, the attempted break-in at the Simpkins home, the absence of any evidence suggesting drug use or dealing on the part of either Keisha or Odell, Bianca's certainty that Keisha was self-reliant, Carl's belief someone had killed his son, and the threatening text on Keisha's phone. Finally, I said I had a friend in the medical examiner's office and showed her Mira's last text, which I had read in my car before driving to the coffee shop:

No trax. No bruising on arm. I pinpoint where you said.

"What does that mean?"

"One needle mark means it's murder," I said. "Lack of bruising means the M.E. concluded Odell injected himself without being forced. That's why I need your help, your eyes and ears—and maybe a couple of others to watch shelters and call me if they see Keisha. Maybe somebody in your outer office, if you feel you can trust them, but nobody else."

"Cassidy and Yvonne," she said. "I can trust them. Fareed has a wife and baby and probably can't get out at night. I'll set up a meeting with the girls tomorrow if you like." When I nodded, she swallowed, fear taking root in her eyes.

"I don't know yet which one was the intended victim," I said, "but Keisha and Odell were together when these people caught up with them so each one got a needle in the arm, probably at gunpoint. Keisha survived. That makes her a witness on the run."

15

I got home by ten-thirty and sat at the kitchen counter to research Sanctuary Nimbus.

Most of the information that popped up on my Lenovo confirmed what Ileana had told me about Pollard and Omicron Seven. There was no link to Keisha. I saved everything in a pdf. Then I logged into IntelliChexx to search for Jeremiah Grace. Three of the fifty-two hits were in New York, but only one address history included the right region: Jeremiah A. Grace, thirty-three, born and raised in Celoron, adjacent to Jamestown. Other addresses included two in Erie, PA, and three in Buffalo, but there was no listing for Bidwell Parkway or Sanctuary Nimbus. Never married. Sketchy credit history. Five speeding tickets but no current driver's license. Not listed on any sex offender registry. One DUI, at age twenty-two. Two arrests for possession, at twenty-three and twenty-six. Both drug cases dismissed. Six relatives and associates with names I didn't recognize. Nothing suggested he had hit rock bottom, but at least Jeremiah Grace was his real name. After compiling the information into another pdf and saving it, I ran a search of the F-150 license plate I had memorized in the church lot. The truck was registered to Titus Oliver Glenroy—Tito—and had nothing more serious than late-paid parking tickets. Further digging revealed Tito lived in a mortgage-free house on Masten Avenue near the armory, inherited from his parents, and had never been arrested. Also, he owned an old Cadillac that had belonged to his father. Disappointed his other ride wasn't a Lincoln Navigator, I closed my Lenovo and opened Keisha's Dell.

I started by searching for keywords like *drugs, money, shipment, delivery,* and *product,* among others, but the first twenty of the hundreds of hits led to documents in the *Humanitas* folder or to the church newsletter or to other appearances in text that had nothing to do with crime. Next, I tried *heroin, fentanyl,* and assorted street names for drugs. Again, nothing beyond professional articles and treatment summaries. After an hour I faced the fact that I would have to read or at least skim hundreds, if not thousands, of files and emails.

I was up till half-past three reviewing reports, letters, memos, proposals, meeting minutes, articles, alerts, real estate documents, supply lists, membership lists, spreadsheets, patient evaluations, newsletters, operating budgets, pictures, and even Turbo Tax files for Keisha and her parents going back nine or ten years. I skimmed to determine usefulness, reading till my vision blurred, and drank so much coffee my stomach burned. Every now and then I had a vague sense I was missing something but the sheer volume of material I faced kept me from stopping to ponder what it was. When I reached my limit for the night, I had plowed through perhaps a third of her files and found nothing that pointed toward Keisha's whereabouts or why someone would be after her.

Sore and tired, I stood up and stumbled to my bedroom.

Despite the coffee, I fell asleep quickly and stayed that way until someone knocked on my door around ten-thirty. It took a bit for the pounding to penetrate my coma. I called, "Just a minute!" as I pulled on sweatpants and stepped into my slippers. I went down the corridor and opened the door. There stood Dr. Lila Cook, who lived across the hall and taught literature at D'Youville College. Beside her was fifteen-year-old Andrea, whose dark hair and complexion must have come from her late father instead of her pale blonde mother. Both wore long coats and had large roller suitcases beside them. Lila

wore the customary half-smile that revealed her perpetual nervous-
ness. Andrea, like most kids her age—and cats—had a look of barely
disguised disdain.

"Morning, Lila," I said. "Andrea. Sorry it took me a bit, but I was
up late working." Unable to help myself, I yawned.

"Then I'm very sorry to bother you, Gideon." Lila handed me a
business envelope addressed to Bobby. "Dr. Chance isn't here. We're
on our way to the airport and won't be back until the middle of next
month. I wanted to leave the January rent check."

"Sure." In the few years since they had moved in, Lila Cook took
her daughter away every December, returning a week or so after the
charter school where Andrea was an honor student resumed classes.
Long ago Bobby told me that Lila's husband had died on Christmas
Eve and travel was her way of getting through the holidays. "Where
are you off to this year?"

"Ireland," Andrea said without emotion. "Mom's had me reading
Joyce, Wilde, and Shaw since the summer. Now I'm halfway through
Dracula. I'm supposed to be looking for subtext and the Irish imag-
ination."

"Don't sound so excited about it," Lila said.

"I was about your age when I read *Dracula*," I said. "I recall it as
pretty creepy."

Andrea smiled—but only while her mother was looking at me
instead of her.

I carried the suitcases down to the front vestibule and left the
Cooks there to wait for their taxi. Once back in my apartment, I
opened the envelope and took out the check, folded inside a full
sheet of paper. I had power of attorney and a card to Bobby's business
account, so I would deposit the check at an ATM later that day. But
before I could discard the paper, I noticed two handwritten words
near the top of the page: *January Rent*. The note struck me as unnecessary, especially since it was repeated on the memo line of the check.
The paper was unnecessary as well. The purpose of the untouched
white space had been to mask a check in a thin envelope. I suspected
it was Lila's custom to use the blank or near-blank page to hide her

checks, even those delivered by hand. Then I remembered the nagging feeling I'd missed something while scanning files last night. Putting the check on the counter, I booted up Keisha's computer.

Remembering that many of her Word files had a blank page or two at the end, now I wondered if she had changed the font color to white so the pages appeared blank to someone going through her computer. I began reopening documents I had examined last night. When I came across a blank page at the end of something, I selected it and clicked on the font button to make sure the color was black. For more than a dozen files, this produced nothing. I began to think my idea was silly. Just then random symbols appeared in the middle of the last page of a church membership list, a collection that looked like a mix of astrological signs and mathematical symbols. Realizing I had been right, I dragged the mouse over the symbols and watched the font name change from Times New Roman to Wingdings to Wingdings 2. I selected the block and clicked on Calibri. The symbols transformed into a short paragraph:

> It is clear from the data that this proposal provides a unique investment opportunity predicated on the belief that over time exponential growth will have such an impact on the surrounding area that everything will change to keep pace with similar projects underway nearby. Together, these will foster a broad economic development that will, quite simply, change the map. (40)

Ten minutes later, in another document, I found another paragraph:

> A chief advantage of the location under review is its proximity to other rapidly developing areas and a revitalized economic corridor. Beyond the national significance of such growth, it is also worth noting that no variances would be required to repurpose existing structures into configurations compatible with maximum marketability. (17)

Rereading the paragraphs, I surmised that they were part of a larger document that had been divided into at least forty sections, probably more. I opened both files' properties and saw that authorship and revision dates had been removed. There was no digital signature or company name. Wherever the paragraphs had come from, my clients' daughter had taken great pains to hide their source. Reconstructing such a document without a key—and doing so piece by piece from hundreds of files from both Humanitas and the church —would be a long undertaking.

I called LJ, explained what I had found, and asked when he was finished with his semester exams.

"Thursday," he said. "But the toughest two are on Monday. After that, I can squeeze in a couple of hours a day if you've got some more work for me."

"I do, but this could take a lot of time."

"Maybe, maybe not. Depends on whether I see a pattern. I can start Monday night, Tuesday morning at the latest. The usual hourly rate?"

When I said yes, I couldn't help picturing his smile.

16

By half past noon, I had compiled and emailed all of Keisha's documents to LJ in the hope that he could make a meaningful reconstruction. Also, I sent copies of everything to a cloud folder labeled KS. Then I shut down the Dell and took a quick shower so I could keep my one-thirty appointment with Ileana and the office workers she had enlisted to watch shelters.

I reached the Towne Restaurant at the corner of Allen and Elmwood before Ileana. I saw Cassidy and Yvonne seated at a round table in the center of the main dining room. They waved me over and stood to shake my hand when I reached them. Blonde hair in a ponytail, Cassidy wore an unzipped blue ski jacket and jeans. Bald head covered by a beret, Yvonne, several inches taller, wore a stylish mauve sweater and matching lipstick. I gestured them back into their seats and draped my jacket over the back of a chair facing the door.

"Thank you for coming," I said, sitting. "I don't know what Ileana told you—"

"That you need our help finding Keisha." Yvonne's voice was soft, slightly nasal. "She didn't say how but said we can't tell anybody and you would reimburse us for gas."

Cassidy nodded, pulling her arms out of her sleeves. "So what do you want us to do?"

"Let's wait for Ileana," I said. "Meantime, if you want coffee or lunch, it's on me."

A twentysomething server whose nameplate read MIA took our order—diet Pepsi and fruit for Cassidy, Greek salad and lemon water for Yvonne, spanakopita and iced tea for me. As we waited, I asked what each did for Humanitas. Cassidy was a receptionist-slash-typist who had come to the agency from a suburban training program. Yvonne was an IT specialist who shared duties with Fareed. They had attended Buff State together a few years earlier.

"I have a friend graduating from that program this spring," I said. "What LJ can do with a computer never ceases to amaze me."

"LJ?" Yvonne said. "As in LJ Doran?"

"Yes. Do you know him?"

She shook her head. "He came in after I finished but he's a legend. I keep reading about him in the newsletter. They make him sound like some kind of genius."

"He'd be embarrassed to hear that," I said. "But his parents would agree."

"I wouldn't mind meeting *him*. Picking his brain." She smiled. "He's cute too."

I thought about that for a moment. Most of the women LJ tried to date were students his age or younger. Some were intimidated by his computer talents. Others were uninterested because he could still pass for a high school junior, despite having reached drinking age last summer. I had zero interest in playing matchmaker, but LJ was a friend whose loneliness sometimes seemed to swallow him. Maybe meeting an attractive, slightly older woman in the same field was just what he needed. Our drinks came just then, and before I could offer to introduce Yvonne to LJ, Ileana walked through the door and started toward us.

"Sorry I'm late," she said, drawing near. Peeling off her charcoal coat and folding it over the back of a chair, she offered an explanation of her delay. I didn't hear it because I recognized the man who entered just a few paces behind her.

Dark brown-skinned and on the upper end of medium height, he wore a long leather coat, matching black gloves, and a leather Greek fisherman's cap. In October, when he had taken me at gunpoint to meet Lorenzo Quick, whose dry-cleaning chain fronted a complex criminal organization, he never told me his name. Since then, over drinks with homicide detectives Terry Chalmers and Rafael Piñero, I had learned Quick's second-in-command was Lester Tolliver, AKA Spider. Never arrested, he'd served with Quick in the first Gulf War and was a suspect in gang-related murders stretching back almost two decades. Now he took a seat by the front window and looked at us as Ileana sat.

Spider.

I wondered why he was there. I wasn't afraid, but I was cautious. A man who had never been connected to any of the murders he was suspected of having committed wasn't sloppy enough to take a shot at me in a restaurant full of people, especially when he had to know I'd be carrying too. Besides, there was no reason to kill me. My last case had nothing to do with his employer, whose illegal enterprises certainly included drug trafficking. Now, however, I wondered if Spider had been following Ileana. Or was he there to keep an eye on someone else at our table? What if he—or, more specifically, Lorenzo Quick—was the one looking for Keisha? Had Spider Tolliver jabbed the needle into her arm on Quick's orders? Of course, maybe he had come in just for lunch and noticed me across the room.

Right.

"Okay, Gideon," Ileana said, snapping me back. "Tell us how we can help."

Unless our table was bugged, Spider would be unable to hear what we said halfway across the dining room. A bug was unlikely unless Cassidy or Yvonne had brought it, which meant Quick's reach was farther than I had imagined. The absence of wires did not preclude Spider from having a wireless earbud. Momentarily, I drummed my fingernails on the wood tabletop and glanced at him for a reaction to the noise. Nothing. Then, taking a deep breath, I explained to Yvonne and Cassidy the idea I had shared with Ileana the night before: Keisha was on the run from someone because she was a witness and marked for murder.

Eyes widening, both women looked at Ileana, who confirmed my story with a nod.

"I think she's always on the move." Again I glanced at Spider for any sign he could hear us. His face remained impassive as a server set a cup of coffee in front of him, but he was still looking at us. "She tries not to be in one place too long," I continued, lowering my voice even more. "Maybe she spends the occasional night in a homeless shelter. Maybe not." I took three large notecards from my shirt pocket and spread them on the table. "Last night Ileana gave me the names and addresses of nine homeless shelters where Keisha might crash for a night. These are the places I need you to watch."

"Three each," Cassidy said. "How are we supposed to be in three places at once?"

"No, five for you and four for Ileana," I said, sliding a card to each.

"What am I supposed to do?" Yvonne asked before the objection could come from Cassidy's parted lips.

"I'll get to that. First, the shelters." I looked from Ileana to Cassidy and back. "I don't want either of you to spend all night anywhere. You're not on a stakeout. Just drive by each place a time or two every night over the next few days and look."

"Just look?" Cassidy asked.

"At the people coming and going," I said. "Stop once or twice and take a peek inside, within an hour of closing time if you can. See if Keisha's there. If she is, don't go to her. If possible, don't even let her see you. Text me, I'll come. I've given each shelter a two-letter code so I'll know exactly where to go. Text the code, period. Talk to Keisha only if she sees you and tries to leave."

"To slow her down," Ileana said, nodding. "Should we follow her?"

I shook my head, mainly for Cassidy's benefit. No matter what I said, Ileana, I knew, would follow Keisha, even if it meant straight into the arms of a killer. "Just remember which direction she was headed when you last saw her."

"What about me?" Yvonne's voice held a note of impatience.

"You're the one on stakeout." I slid the last card to her. "Know where that is?"

"Not far from my apartment." She narrowed her eyes at me and grinned. "But you already knew that, didn't you?"

"I want you to drive by or walk by or sit nearby in your car off and on the next few evenings. Always take a good look up the driveway. I think there's an apartment over the garage in back. There are two upstairs windows. If you see lights in either one, call me."

"Call? Not text?"

"Call, and wait for me to get there."

Just then Mia brought our order and handed Ileana a menu. As we ate, I added all their phone numbers to my cell's contacts list. Then we sent quick texts to each other to establish threads. Cassidy's message was a thumbs-up emoji. Yvonne texted, *Meet LJ?* I replied, *After K found*. Right now LJ was prepping for exams and then working on Keisha's documents. He didn't need an attractive distraction.

When the lunch and small talk ended and the cell phones were back in purses and pockets, I told Cassidy and Yvonne they were free to leave but asked Ileana to stay behind for a minute so we could discuss another matter. The two young women rose and put on their coats. Cassidy shook my hand again and thanked me. Yvonne flashed a smile that made me want to introduce her to LJ. They went out together, laughing after Cassidy said something I couldn't quite hear.

Spider never even glanced in their direction.

I thought about that as I looked at Ileana and shook my head. "What am I going to do with you?"

"What?" she said, a now cold French fry suspended a few inches from her mouth.

"If you see Keisha, you're going to follow her, aren't you?"

She lowered then raised her eyes. "Well, I can't just let her walk away."

"Even if it brings you face to face with whoever wants to kill her?"

She dropped the fry on her plate and let out a long breath. "She's my friend."

"I know," I said. "I know too you can take care of yourself. But if these people are cold-blooded enough to force somebody into a heroin overdose, they won't hesitate to kill you." I watched her face tighten. Good. It meant she was taking me seriously.

"So what should I do?" she asked after a moment.

"Take out your cell phone." I produced my own as she opened her purse. "Now go to your app store and look for a locator program that will let me find your phone." She did so, and moments later we were linked by a friend finder application. "Here's a new two-letter code to tell me you're with Keisha or following her. Easy to remember. BB."

"BB? Like a BB gun?"

"Like Bronco Buster," I said, remembering the story she had told me in her office. "Ride her, cowboy." As she laughed, I was glad to see the tension in her face lessen. "Text that to me and my phone's GPS will lead me right to you."

Two minutes later, when she left, Spider made no move to follow her. He just sat there and continued to stare at me with his cold, flat eyes.

17

L eaving Mia's tip on the placemat, I carried my second iced
tea over to Lester Tolliver's table and sat across from him.

"Hello, Lester," I said. "How's the dry-cleaning business
these days?"

Face blank, he said nothing.

"Or do you prefer Spider?"

"I have no objection to a nickname given to me by my mother."
His unblinking eyes remained unreadable but his soft baritone held a
trace of menace softened by amusement.

"All right, Spider. I'm not in the mood for a swim today. You forgot
to bring Mickey, Donald, and Goofy, so it won't be easy to change my
mind." Lorenzo Quick was so paranoid about being bugged, he held
meetings with people he didn't know in his indoor pool only after
they had undergone a latex-gloved full body search and entered the
water naked. In our October encounter, Spider had brought three
large men, all presumably armed, to discourage my resistance to
getting into their car and to reinforce my appreciation of a midday
swim. "So Mr. Quick will have to call my office for an appointment."

"He doesn't wish to see you, sir." As he had been in our previous
meeting, Spider was unfailingly polite. "At least not today."

"Then why are you here?"

He held up his coffee cup. "For a detective, Mr. Rimes, you are regrettably deficient in your observational skills." His lips twitched for a second. The son of a bitch was enjoying himself, fighting back a smile.

"This blend is so good, I may have a second cup."

I drank some of my iced tea, maybe to dampen the annoyance I was beginning to feel.

Spider set down his cup and leaned toward me half an inch or so. "Lunch with three attractive young women, none of them your regular lover. You must be on the mend."

I said nothing but felt my jaw tighten as annoyance began the climb toward anger.

"How is your shoulder, sir?"

"Who's asking?"

"I am, but I'm certain my employer would want me to. When he learned you had been shot, he told me more than once how much he enjoyed meeting you."

"Because he enjoys scaring naked people in his pool, with those gold-capped vampire fangs and the knife he keeps in the pocket of his swim trunks?"

"Because he enjoys *testing* them."

I leveled my eyes at Spider. "How'd I do?"

"Most people in such a situation feel afraid, or at least vulnerable and intimidated. That you didn't impressed him so much he has wondered aloud more than once what it would take to get you to work for him. I trust you understand how rare such a sentiment is when it comes to my employer."

"I believe I do." I took another sip of tea. "So, you're here to recruit me?"

"Far from it." The salt-and-pepper mustache still threatened to spread into a smile. "Even as he considered it, he remembered how tense you were even in warm water, always ready, calculating your odds. We both reached the same conclusion. It would never work."

"Why not?"

"Ours is a family business—not blood family but chosen family, which means the bonds are stronger. The rugged individual has a hard time finding faith or footing in such a group." He began to raise his cup.

"So I would be a bad fit."

"The worst." Lips pressed tight and cup hovering below his chin, he exhaled through his nostrils. "My employer has known many men like you."

"Rugged individuals?"

"Cynics in search of redemption." His flicker of a smile vanished. "The permanent outsider is the hardest man to divert from his chosen path. He is just too stubborn." He shook his head and downed the last of his coffee. "Stubbornness, I'm afraid, is your fatal flaw."

There it was, the tail end of the warning that had begun with his allusion to Phoenix. Looking into Quick's affairs could get me killed, maybe Phoenix too. Spider would be the one to drop the hammer. Was I being warned because of Keisha? No, I decided. That didn't feel quite right. We regarded each other for several seconds before he spoke again.

"So, how is your shoulder?"

"Fine."

"You traded your nylon rig for a belt-clip. Even under your sweater, it's easy to see your grip is pointed outward, so you can pull with your left hand. Plus, your posture is off. You're sitting in a manner that eases pressure. So I doubt your shoulder is fine."

"Nothing deficient in your observational skills," I said. "You ought to be a detective."

He gave a small shake of his head. "Shitty pay."

"But good enough, especially if you're ambidextrous."

"Ah, you're no slouch with your left hand." Finally, he let himself smile—a small one but a smile just the same. "Glad to know that."

"But dancing too long *does* bother my shoulder, so just tell me why you're interested in my current work." I leaned toward him, lowered my voice. "I doubt you or your people had anything to do with the young woman you know I'm trying to find. So what's up?"

He looked down at his empty cup for a moment, as if contemplating whether to ask for more coffee. Then he took a deep breath and looked up, the flinty look slipping from his eyes. "Do you have any idea why my mother started calling me Spider?"

"No."

"When I was small, I liked to crawl around on my belly. She took my shirt off so grit on the floor and carpet fibers would make me stand up and try to walk. But before I stood I scampered about on my hands and feet. I was pretty quick. She said I looked like a spider running across the floor, and the name stuck."

The faraway look in his eyes surprised me, so I remained silent and let him continue.

"My mother got Alzheimer's some years back," he said. "Broke my fucking heart, especially when she no longer remembered who I was. Toward the end, she thought I was her father or her brother. Some days I was a complete stranger. But before she ended up in the nursing home, one of the people who was especially good to her, who helped her get the support she needed to stay in her own house as long as possible, was a young sister named Simpkins. Dr. Simpkins. The same young sister who had some trouble a while back and disappeared."

"Knowing her as you did, it was your professional opinion she would never do what the newspaper said she did."

"Exactly."

"So your people had nothing to do with—"

"Not our style to force things on civilians, especially good ones. Good business demands a certain purity of product. Success is based on repeat customers, not dead ones." His eyes hardened again. "If I knew somebody who did something like this—"

I nodded my understanding of his unfinished sentence. "You don't know who but you figure it might be a competitor, somebody outside your regular network."

He shrugged. "No shortage of them. You can't make deals with everybody. There's a lot of young fools out there, greedy and impatient."

"Even careless," I said. "Leaving a job unfinished is just unprofessional."

"I appreciate a man who knows the fundamentals."

"How long have you been following me?"

"Since yesterday. When I found out you were the one hired to find her, I thought I'd check on your progress."

"Because you knew that as a cynic in search of redemption, I'd keep looking till I found her."

"Yes."

"Then lead you to whoever hurt her, so you could make a deal or settle a score. It could be business or it could be personal. You're ready to play it either way, as long as I stick to finding my clients' daughter and pay no attention to things that don't concern me."

This time his smile was broader, and the contrast with the emptiness in his eyes was unsettling. "I'm so glad we understand each other."

I sat back and thought for a moment. "Why reveal yourself? Why not just keep tailing me to the end?"

"My employer is not the only one you impressed, Mr. Rimes. Sooner or later you'd have made me. I didn't want you distracted—for both our sakes."

"Since yesterday," I said, resting my chin on my fist. "I remember the company car was a Lexus SUV. Your personal ride wouldn't be a black Navigator, would it?"

"No. Why?"

18

The Erie County Bar Association holiday party was held in the Grand Ballroom of the Hyatt Regency downtown, close enough to Phoenix's loft that we walked. As I hung our coats on one of the stainless steel racks outside the entrances, Phoenix exchanged her boots for shoes and moved to one of the floor plans propped on large easels near the doors to find the table reserved for Landsburgh, Falk, and Trinidad. Then she took my hand and led me inside.

The ballroom was already full of women in gowns and dinner dresses and men in suits and tuxedos. With an open bar set up on either side, most of those in attendance had a drink in hand. A five-piece band near the first door filled the air with soft jazz. It took us a long time to get near our table, in a far corner, because Phoenix, elegant in her off-the-shoulder black dress and ocean blue Larimar necklace, was intercepted every few feet by someone she knew, or by women she didn't, who felt compelled to compliment her. My own suit—my only suit—was a navy pinstripe I so seldom wore its condition was good enough not to embarrass her and basic enough not to draw attention away from her. I shook hands when introduced, smiled, and nodded when greeted in passing by someone I didn't

know. I slipped off to get us drinks when she was drawn into conversation by an old law school classmate.

Holding Phoenix's Malbec and a Captain and Coke—my cocktail
of choice when I had to wear a tie—I turned and nearly collided with
Mayor Ophelia Green. She had replaced her customary glasses and
business pantsuit with contacts and a stylish lavender dress. Antique
gold pendant glittering at her throat, she was on the tuxedo-sheathed
arm of the tall State Supreme Court justice whose relationship with
her had been a secret until after she won a second term last month.

"G!" she said, offering me a cheek to kiss. "What a nice surprise!"

"Looking better, I hope, than the last time you saw me."

For a moment she said nothing, the beauty mark at the corner of
her mouth falling as her smile faltered. Perhaps she was remembering that we had last talked when she came to my hospital room
shortly before the election. Having served in Iraq with her late
husband Danny, I was a family friend hired as an independent investigator to look into matters related to the murder of her personal
driver. I had been shot in the shoulder during that investigation. My
findings, once publicized, had guaranteed her re-election. Perhaps
now she was wrestling with the knowledge that, in essence, I had
taken the bullet for her.

Her bronze cheeks flushed, and she glanced at her companion.
"G, I am so sorry. Gideon Rimes, this is Hal—"

"Judge Chancellor," I said. "I've seen your picture in the paper, sir.
I'd shake your hand but—" I held up the drinks, one in each hand.

"A pleasure to meet you just the same, Mr. Rimes." Hal Chancellor's voice was radio-deep and smooth—James Earl Jones lite. His
dark face looked kind, the eyes behind his horn-rimmed glasses pale
brown and flecked with gold. "This is my sister, Glendora."

I hadn't realized the attractive woman standing to the judge's left
was a third wheel. Clad in a rust-colored dress and matching headwrap, she was a shade or two lighter than her younger brother and an
inch or two shorter. She looked vaguely familiar. When she smiled
and said she was delighted to meet me, the last tumbler fell into
place: the judge had a sister who'd lost a September primary bid to

represent the Ellicott District in the Common Council. A widowed elementary school principal who'd taken early retirement, Glendora Chancellor-Pratt had run on a platform that included limiting the gentrification of her district. Mona and Winslow Simpkins—and Keisha—would have been her constituents.

"Phee's told me a lot about you," Hal said.

"Then let me plead the Fifth before we go any further."

"Oh, everything she said was good," he said. "Right, Glennie."

Eyes never leaving mine, Glendora nodded.

"But the next character witness may be less generous, so I need insurance."

Hal and Glendora both laughed as Ophelia said, "G, you must be here with your lawyer friend. I've heard so much about Miss Trinidad. During the campaign, I spoke with her law partner a few times, and leaders from the Latino community, but I've never made her acquaintance. She wasn't there when I came to your hospital room."

"Our table's in that direction," I said, gesturing with the wine glass. "When I find her, that's where we'll head. Come on over when you get a chance."

Leaving as Ophelia, Hal, and Glendora ordered drinks, I started toward where I'd last seen Phoenix. Of course, she had moved on by then to another conversation in another location. I found her about fifteen feet from where Landsburgh, Falk, and Trinidad were to sit. She thanked me for the wine and introduced me to a stocky blond man in an ill-fitting tux—Rudy something. I shook Rudy's hand and told Phoenix Eileen and Jonah were waving me over so I would see her when she joined us.

Eileen set down her beer and greeted me with a cherry-lipstick smile when I reached the table. A paralegal who doubled as her Uncle Jonah's office manager, she was in her mid-twenties and had thick shoulder-length red hair. Her forest green dress underscored both her emerald eyes and her pallor. She blushed when I bent to kiss her cheek, likely embarrassed that she had told Phoenix more than once she thought I was cute, for an older guy. Before straightening, I noticed that the black quad cane she used because of a spinal disorder had been replaced by a bright green model that sparkled with glitter.

"My party stick," she said. "Good for dancing, if Phoenix doesn't mind."

"She'll tell you to hit me with it if I step on your foot, but I'm in."

Seated on Eileen's left, brandy glass in hand, was Jonah Landsburgh, the founder and senior partner. A rawboned man with a head full of unkempt white hair, he had tired eyes and a face creased by seven decades of experience. On her other side sat Brian Saxby, owner of a storefront gallery on Allen and life partner to the attorney beside him, Cameron Falk. A few years younger than Phoenix, both men had dark hair, average builds, and wore well-tailored suits. Cam's was a midnight blue three-piece. Brian's burnt sienna two-piece was highlighted by a blue, brown, and gold Jerry Garcia tie that was clearly the best neckpiece at the table. Beside Cam and in more basic clothing were his parents—or so I assumed because I had not yet been introduced to them. Phoenix had told me George Falk served at the Berlin Wall and Toshiko was born a few years after her parents were released from the Japanese-American relocation camp near Granada, Colorado. Jonah had offered them the seats left vacant after Bobby, one of his long-time poker buddies and closest friends, had decided to take Kayla to Manhattan for the weekend.

Jonah and Cam both stood, the former to greet me, the latter to make introductions. After shaking hands all around, I set down my drink and sat beside Cam's mother, catching a whiff of apple-scented perfume. Toshiko was thin, a bit round-shouldered, and nursing a cosmopolitan. George was thickset and balding, with a bottle of beer beside his water glass. They were pleasant enough but quiet, directing most of their attention to their son, obviously proud he was a named partner in a feisty law firm. My first real conversation, then, was with Jonah, across the empty chair waiting for Phoenix.

"Heard from Bobby?" He took a sip of brandy. "He and Kayla having a good time?"

"Haven't heard a word, so they must be."

Jonah narrowed his eyes. "He say anything about Kayla retiring from the bench?"

"Not to me." I thought about his question. "Why? Looking for a new law partner?"

"Wouldn't hurt, especially if the New Year brings us the case we're chasing."

"I hear it'll need a lot of investigative hours." It was no surprise Jonah was hinting at what Phoenix had mentioned at dinner the other night. Since returning to work, I had taken two depositions, completed two background investigations, and served four subpoenas for the law firm. They'd had no dedicated investigator for more than a year, and for a major class-action suit they would need at least one. He would have expected her to tell me about it and now was probing my level of interest.

"We're still evaluating, but it has the potential to be our biggest case ever."

"Then count me in. Beats getting shot."

Jonah laughed, but I sensed Toshiko stiffen beside me, which meant Cam likely had told his parents everything about their new investigator. I turned to her and smiled as she took a hefty swallow of her Cosmo. Surprised, she dabbed her mouth with her napkin as I asked a few questions about Cam's childhood. Eventually, I engaged her husband in a then-and-now comparison of army idiocies that made all three of us laugh. By the time Phoenix joined us, brushing her fingers across the back of my neck as she sat beside me, Toshiko had sent her husband for another drink. I was almost sure she would sleep without worrying her son was in danger because he associated with a ruffian people wanted to shoot.

The remainder of the evening was uneventful. The food was better than I expected, the speeches shorter, and the mood lighter once Eileen declared there would be no more shop talk. Because we were walking back to her loft, Phoenix and I both had a third drink, as did Toshiko, who leaned against her husband's shoulder and smiled when the music resumed after dinner. The band shifted from soft sounds to danceable numbers that spanned several decades of popular music. I danced twice with Phoenix, once to a "Harlem Nocturne" that let the tenor saxophonist stand apart from the rest of the band and once to a jazzed-up "Sexual Healing." Later, as Phoenix flashed me a smile, Eileen invited me onto the floor for "Moon River" and left her cane beside her chair. For a slow song, she explained, it would be easier if I just kept an arm around her waist. We had the first extended conversation of our two-month acquaintance during that dance, and I led her back to her seat with a genuine appreciation of her radiance, wit, and drive. As I pulled out her chair, I realized that the man who saw past her cane was in for a wonderful relationship.

Ophelia and the Chancellors never came to our table. I thought nothing more of them—or more specifically, Glendora—until a few days later.

19

On Sunday morning, eyes closed against gradually increasing sunlight and fingers locked behind my head, I lay on my back beside a still sleeping Phoenix. As I listened to forced hot air fans push heat into the loft and the faint noises of Main Street coming to life eleven floors below, I slipped into what I'd once read was the wisest hour of a person's day, the unfocused time just after waking.

My mind pinballed through every step I'd taken in my hunt for Keisha in the hope something I'd missed would announce itself. Winslow and Mona couldn't believe their daughter was a drug user. Neither could Ileana, Carl Williamson, or even Spider Tolliver. Sonny Tyler had sounded genuinely surprised by his ex-girlfriend's disappearance. Despite Loni Markham's suggestion, she had hooked up with the wrong crowd, the threatening text LJ found supported the idea Keisha had run for her life after surviving a forced overdose intended to kill her as well as Odell. I was still uncertain who was the intended target and who was collateral damage, but the embedding of non-medical, non-church text in so many unrelated documents in her hard drive suggested Keisha had stumbled upon something worth hiding. What was it and where had she found it? Humanitas?

Sermon on the Mount? Odell? Or was there another source not yet on my radar?

The paragraphs I'd read were in business-speak, different from the language of the phone text. Were the two linked? How? Had that text made her run, left her trusting almost no one? The impulse to keep her parents and co-workers safe was understandable, but she hadn't even gone to the cop wife of one of her best friends. Had she risked trusting Fatimah, who'd lied to me about how often they were in touch? With LJ assembling what was hidden in the Word files into something that might explain Keisha's actions, three women watching places she might turn up, and two offers to have somebody watch my back, I felt the need to do something myself. But the wisdom of the hour—Melville's maybe?—suggested I could do nothing but wait.

We had fallen asleep almost at once last night. Now Phoenix stirred and stretched, yawning. Then she snuggled against me. "I know you're awake. I can hear you thinking."

I unclasped my hands and slid an arm around her. "Okay, what am I thinking about?"

"That in a little while you'll make me breakfast—a spinach and cheese omelet, toast, bacon, coffee, and grapefruit."

"Sounds like what I put in your fridge yesterday, Miss Cleo."

"Uh-huh." She walked her fingers through my chest hair. "But first you're going to light a fire in the fireplace. Then you'll lead me into the bathroom so we can shower together. After that, you'll lead me back out here to the throw rug in front of the fireplace."

"Damn," I said. "I guess you *can* see into the future."

"If you think my second sight is hot, just wait till I practice my braille on you."

Much later, in our robes and smelling of the grapeseed lotion we had massaged into each other's skin, we ate in front of the gel fireplace. Our plates were on the coffee table, our backs against the couch's seat cushions, and sections of the Sunday *Buffalo News* on the floor between us. This was different from the previous four Sundays we had spent together. The first and third we had awakened in my bed and gone out to breakfast. The second and fourth had been here, but we had eaten at the granite-topped island in the kitchen. After each of those leisurely mornings, we had spent the afternoon out, at stores or movies or last week taking a long car ride. In the evening, after dining in a restaurant or getting take-out, we had come back to one place or another to watch Netflix or HBO. If our relationship continued on its current trajectory, Sunday would likely become both our day and our refuge.

"So what do you want to do today, mister?" Phoenix asked, popping a piece of bacon into her mouth as we swapped the *Viewpoints* and arts sections.

"Whatever you feel like, counselor." I opened the arts insert—called *Gusto*—to the book review pages. "The smartest person in the room should take the lead."

She laughed and covered her mouth to keep the bacon inside. "There's a review on the front page, of a new installation at the Knox."

The Albright-Knox, just a few miles from where we were, had long been considered one of the ten best art galleries on the planet. I went to the *Gusto* front page and located the headline *Sensorium, a full-body experience*. The reviewer described an exhibit for everyone, especially those with one or more sensory impairments. Most of the works were meant to appeal to senses other than sight. There were mosaics, sculptures, and plastic creations to be touched, raised drawings visitors could trace with their fingertips, texture boxes into which they could stick their hands as a recorded story unfolded in surround sound. Also, there were floors that vibrated or crunched, an electric train large enough for adults to ride imaginary beasts inspired by J.K. Rowling, non-musical soundscapes to soothe or stimulate the body, wall jets that in total darkness sprayed mixtures of scents intended to evoke a sea voyage, a forest hike, or a space station. Several corners even had stations where one could experience both food and non-food taste sensations, like variations of popcorn and dry desert air. Of course, among the strictly visual pieces was the Mirrored Room, which had been at the Knox for more than fifty years and was one of the first infinity rooms to be exhibited anywhere.

"Like your braille on steroids," I said. "A good way to spend the afternoon, if I'm able to walk again by then."

Phoenix smiled and shook her head. "Let's not get into who crippled whom. Better if we just share the blame."

"Okay." I took another bite of toast. "We can limp out of here whenever you want."

She bit back a chuckle. "I need to do some legal stuff after we finish here. An hour, maybe two. Are you good till then?"

"I brought my laptop."

But I never booted up the Lenovo. With the dishes in the dishwasher and Phoenix at the desk near her bed, I dressed in jeans and a pullover and stood at the window beside the fireplace. Sipping cold coffee, I looked down at the traffic and Metro trains on Main Street and again reviewed my efforts to find Keisha. In the absence of word from LJ or Ileana and her Humanitas crew, I still had no idea what to do next. That left me feeling increasingly agitated as the afterglow of making love subsided. When I was in my teens and wrestling with impulsivity, Bobby had lectured me now and then about the perils of impatience, often ending with something like, "Son, sometimes you just have to wait for things to happen." However much I hated waiting, I had to accept that this was one of those times.

Early that afternoon, however, something *did* happen. Phoenix and I were at the art gallery, about halfway through Sensorium, when my cell phone buzzed. I saw the call was from Oscar Edgerton and moved out of the hall that held the electric train ride to answer. Oscar was breathless as if he'd been running.

"Rimes, they shot Win's wife!"

My mind was a half-beat behind him, trying to make sense of his words. "What?"

"Somebody shot Mona Simpkins!"

20

We found Winslow Simpkins in the Buffalo General ER waiting room, flanked on a padded bench seat by Oscar and Louisa Edgerton. Clad only in an old suit, Winslow had the empty, bloodless expression of someone still in shock. Standing over him were two uniformed police officers, both men. One took notes on a metal document case clipboard and the other scanned the room. His eyes fixed on us—particularly me—as we drew near.

"I'm their attorney," Phoenix said, leading me into the cluster.

As if confirming her statement, Louisa and Oscar, still in their winter coats, stood to embrace Phoenix. Louisa cried into Phoenix's shoulder as Oscar grasped my hand and pulled me in for a quick man-hug. "Still in surgery," he said. "She took one to the chest."

The older cop, brown-skinned and bulky, held the clipboard. "We're almost done here, ma'am, sir. Then we'll get out of your way." His dark-haired colleague, whose cheeks bore the windburn of a regular skier, stepped aside and continued to watch the room. His right thumb was hooked on his duty belt, near his holster, as if he expected trouble. I thought about that, wondering how likely it was a shooter would storm a hospital ER to finish killing an elderly woman.

Not very, I decided, but I was glad just the same my baby Glock was on my belt beneath my leather jacket.

A light-skinned woman whose bearing normally made her look taller than her five feet, Louisa clung to Phoenix, so I took the seat on Winslow's right when Oscar sat again on his left. Winslow was shaking—shivering, I realized. Oscar put an arm around him.

"Back to the car, Mr. Simpkins," the senior officer said. "Can you describe it?"

"Dark," Winslow said. "Black, maybe blue. Real big I think. I got down so quick."

"Limo big or SUV big?"

"SUV. I don't know what kind. I don't pay much attention to stuff like that anymore."

Black Lincoln Navigator, I thought. But I didn't want to complicate the investigation by speaking, especially if I was wrong, so I said nothing.

As much for Phoenix's benefit as for Winslow's, I realized, the officer reviewed the details of the report form, which gave me a rough picture of what had happened. Winslow and Mona had come home from a late luncheon at church and were about to enter their front door when a dark SUV sped past and someone inside fired several shots at them. They both dropped to the porch floor. Winslow didn't know his wife had been hit until the car was out of sight. He used the old flip phone in her purse to call nine-one-one and covered her with his topcoat. Then he called Oscar, who got there before first responders. Winslow had got only a glimpse of the SUV and had no idea who was inside. They were retired, he had said in closing. For the most part, they divided their time between church and home, with trips to the supermarket and occasional visits to the casino downtown. He had said nothing about Keisha but I knew her name would come up during the investigation and could steer things one way or another.

As Winslow initialed the form to confirm his statement, the blend of cold and fear that had soaked into him on the porch was still strong enough to make his hands shake. "I just don't understand," he said, lower lip quivering as it had a few days ago in my office.

As the senior officer handed the tear-off slip with the case number to Phoenix, Oscar pulled his friend closer.

"I know, Win. It's crazy. No sense to it."

Winslow's eyes teared. "Who does a drive-by on old folks who eat dinner on TV trays while they watch *Wheel of Fortune*?"

21

W hen the police left, I signaled to Oscar that he and I should talk. We surrendered our seats on the sofa-style bench to Louisa and Phoenix and stepped outside as if for air.

Oscar pulled on leather gloves and turned up his coat collar. "This got something to do with Keisha, right?"

I pulled on my own tightly knit gloves, designed for runners, warm but thin enough to let me grasp coins or slip a finger into a trigger guard. "I think she disappeared on purpose because she knew some bad people would come looking for her."

"People bad enough to shoot her folks to smoke her out."

"Yes, but I'm not even sure they wanted to hit anybody."

"How do you shoot a gun at somebody and hit 'em by accident?"

"It wasn't an accident. It was a don't-give-a-fuck-either-way drive-by, as long as it drew Keisha out." I gave him a summary of my investigation, just enough that he would understand what had happened and follow my thinking. "These guys are cold but not pros or they would've made sure Keisha was dead in the first place. Cold *and* professional would've corrected that first mistake by taking the time to shoot both Mona and Winslow dead, to guarantee Keisha would come out of hiding."

"So they woulda kept on you with their Navigator."

"Exactly. Twice they started something and took off before they finished the job, hoping it would have the desired result. Between those events, they followed me but gave up after I made them and they couldn't find me."

Oscar's sigh frosted and hung in the air a bit. "The real deal woulda kept looking."

"But they're like kids who try to clean up a mess before Mommy gets home and just keep making it worse."

"Which makes them young or inexperienced or both."

"Yes. Who but someone young would text a threat?"

"What do you think is next?"

"The mess is still there. And here."

"So they'll come after Win and Mona again."

"Maybe they'll get luckier next time if we don't run interference." I thought for a moment. "The house is a crime scene. Win can't go back there while they're still processing it. The shooting was outside, so they'll probably let him back inside by tomorrow. But he can't stay. I'll go with him, so he can get some clothes."

"He can stay with us, long as he needs to. We got plenty of room."

I nodded. "But you can't tell anybody, not your other friends, or his, or Louisa's. Not your neighbors, or folks from church, or in the shelter, or any other place you go. You never know how people are connected and how an innocent comment could reach the wrong ears."

Oscar was quiet for a time, considering all I had said. Then he nodded. "Okay. But we both know Win ain't going nowhere tonight except up to Mona's room. If she makes it."

"Then you and I'll have to cover that. The cops will check on her, but as far as they're concerned, she's just a random shooting victim. There's nothing in her background that will justify a round-the-clock police guard." Mona would move from surgery to post-op care and finally the ICU. Her greatest initial vulnerability would be the ICU, not easy for an outsider to get in and out of, but not impossible. If we were lucky, things would be settled before she was moved into a regular room. "Oscar, from here on out you're going to be Mona's brother, which means you can be with Win with no trouble. Be sure to refer to her as your sister when you're talking to hospital staff. That'll get them used to you being there to help your brother-in-law through all this."

"What about you?"

"No problem. Pop."

Oscar grinned. "You're big enough to be my kid. A little old though."

I smiled and shrugged. Then I began to think about how word might reach Keisha and the certainty that she would come to the hospital when it did. Mona's name would likely be run through the system before it was released to the press, so the six p.m. newscasts probably wouldn't have it but the one at eleven might. In any case, she'd be in the news by tomorrow.

"I expect Keisha to try to come here by tomorrow," I said.

"How we gonna keep her safe? They could be outside waiting for her to show up. They could put a bullet in her or snatch her up just like that." He snapped his fingers, his gloves dulling the sound.

I closed my eyes and tried to picture every door into the medical center. The ER on East North did not offer non-medical personnel a clear path into the core of the hospital. The main entrance on High Street led straight to a security station and information desk that gave out visitor passes. Older buildings on High were attached to the main tower and must have had their own doors as well but I had no idea how many there were and whether they were secure. Another entrance on Ellicott led to the information desk too but I couldn't remember if there was a stairway someone could use to avoid check-in. The Gates Vascular Institute behind the main building also faced Ellicott but had less foot traffic to its security station. Checkpoints and keypads aside, there were at least six ways into Buffalo General, perhaps more. Also, I had no idea whether the nearest sister facilities —Roswell Park Cancer Center, and The Women and Children's

Hospital—had connecting tunnels underground. Maybe I could call someone for help—Jen Spina, when she wasn't working, maybe even Jimmy, whose wheelchair wouldn't look out of place in the lobby.

Finally, I opened my eyes and sighed. "There are too many ways inside for the two of us to watch alone," I said. "The people I could call wouldn't be able to give us the coverage we'd need." Then I remembered something. "Maybe we need to have some faith here."

"What do you mean?"

"How smart is Keisha?"

The answer came with no hesitation. "Very."

"If she's been visiting homeless shelters kind of in disguise because she knows people are looking for her, why wouldn't she take the same precautions to come here?"

Oscar thought about that a moment. "The best place to wait for her is Mona's room."

"Right, Pop." I gave him a beat to smile. "Let's talk to Mom and Uncle Win."

We went back inside and explained our new kinship without detailing the reasons someone needed to be with Mona at all times. Winslow accepted without question my lie that his house would be tied up by police for at least three days. After a moment of staring across the waiting room at nothing, he asked if they could go to Walmart for clothes and toiletries before going back to Oscar's. Aware of the particulars of my hunt for Keisha, Phoenix shot me a sidelong glance full of concern but said nothing that might agitate Winslow. Louisa, however, put her hands on her hips and scowled at me. "Old as your ass is, I'm supposed to be your *mother*?"

"Stepmother?" I said, shrugging. "Married to a much older man."

She laughed at that, as did Oscar, Phoenix, and, finally, Winslow. Seconds later I tried to estimate how much of that moment of broken tension Dr. Felton Markham had witnessed when he walked through the automatic doors of the ER and I wondered what he had made of it. In any case, the instant he reached us, he began to extract the oxygen from the room.

His brilliant smile only fleeting, he gave momentary hugs to

Oscar and Louisa and embraced Winslow for a long time. Eyes skyward, he called upon God to grant us courage, especially Brother Simpkins, as we struggled on the patch of ground that stretched between good and evil. Then he insisted we all hold hands for a more formal prayer I'd have found too long and too loud on a busier day in the ER. He prayed for more strength, understanding, and God's forgiveness for all our transgressions. He requested everlasting grace be showered upon Mona's soul and the hands of the surgeons striving to save her life. My own hands could have used a drop of grace right about then—at least my left, which Louisa squeezed as if it were the last rung on a helicopter ladder rising away from a burning building. Phoenix's grip on my right was gentler but there was still enough tension to betray her own fear.

When it was over, and blood began to return to my hand, Dr. Markham sat beside Winslow and put an arm around his shoulders. Oscar sat on Win's left, and Louisa took a chair perpendicular to her husband. Phoenix and I sat on a bench directly across from her.

Trying to sound more curious than interrogational, I asked Dr. Markham how he had learned of the shooting.

"We got a phone call—or my wife did." He turned to Winslow. "A neighbor lady of yours heard shots and called nine-one-one. She waited for sirens before looking out the window and seeing police cars stopped in front of your house. When the ambulance came and yellow tape started going up, she called Mother Brody. She said the person put in the ambulance looked a lot like Sister Simpkins, so Mother Brody called us." The minister turned back to me. "Didn't need the scanner in my car to find the nearest emergency room."

Word hadn't come from television or radio, but I was no less relieved. The nameless neighbor and Mother Brody from the church were likely still making phone calls, as were the various people they must have told by now. That meant Keisha would hear before the night was over and would almost certainly come to her mother's bedside. As Dr. Markham shifted his attention to something Louisa mentioned, I whispered to Phoenix, "Bobby and Kayla are coming in on Jet Blue around six-thirty but I need to be here, maybe all night. Can you get them?"

"Of course. But we came in your car. You want me to take it or should I go home and get my own?"

I thought a moment. "I may need my car."

Phoenix nodded. "I can get an Uber."

"Or *she* can drop you off." I angled my head a bit toward Louisa, not wanting her low threshold for hearing her name to draw her out of her conversation with the minister. Nor did I mention Oscar, for the same reason. "He's gonna stay too."

Phoenix hesitated before speaking, looking at Winslow and realizing that however softly we were speaking, one's threshold for the name of a loved one was only slightly higher than for the sound of one's own. "You think *she* might come here?"

"I do."

"You think others could too. Looking—"

"Yes."

"Then you—"

"I will. I promise."

Phoenix squeezed my hand and rested her head against my shoulder. We sat like that for the next twenty minutes or so, mostly quiet and our breathing in synch as Dr. Markham alternated between listening to his congregants and trying to reassure them of the power of God's love.

But everyone was quiet by the time the doctors came out.

Phoenix and I knew them both from my recent stay in Buffalo General. Dr. VanBeek, a prominent trauma surgeon, was a tall man with pouched eyes and blond hair going to gray. The foot-shorter attending physician was Ayodele Ibazebo, a Nigerian woman and former student of Bobby's who had stitched up my head nearly two months ago after a SWAT cop hit me with his rifle stock. Both had been part of the surgical team that extracted the bullet from my shoulder.

Smiling as he moved toward us, the lead surgeon showed no recognition of me, a man he had saved and later spoken to for only a minute. His colleague, however, had told me to change my line of work for the sake of one of her favorite professors. Dr. VanBeek, the residue of a Dutch accent in his voice, explained to Winslow that Mona had survived the removal of the bullet and a wedge resection from her right lung and was now in recovery. But Dr. Ibazebo glared at me the entire time with bright amber eyes that would have reduced me to ash if they had been lasers.

22

The doctors expected Mona to be in recovery for three or four hours.

Winslow and Dr. Markham were allowed to see her for fifteen minutes. After they returned to the waiting room and the minister took his leave, a still worried Winslow sat down and described the tubes and machines connected to his wife. She was groggy and unable to speak with a mask and tube, he said, but perked up at the sound of Dr. Markham's prayer. She was still being monitored and nurses needed to get her up for short walks. It would be a while before anyone could go back and sit with her again.

At five Louisa announced she was ready to drop Phoenix home and take Winslow to Walmart. Phoenix pecked me on the lips and followed the others to the exit. When the doors slid shut behind them, I texted Ileana and Cassidy to say that if they were free, it was a good time to make stops at their assigned shelters. In a separate text, I asked Yvonne to sit on the address I'd given her. Trying to sound urgent but saying nothing of the shooting, I told them to call me at once if they saw Keisha.

An hour after Louisa and Winslow got back with KFC dinners,

Bobby sent me a text. His long weekend of shows, museums, and walking around Manhattan had exhausted him, so he would see me tomorrow—maybe for lunch. I replied *Yes*. Phoenix called to say she was going to watch Netflix but her phone would be right on the coffee table if I needed her. Two hours in, Winslow was permitted to return to recovery to spend the rest of the time there with his wife. Louisa drifted off to sleep with her head against her husband's shoulder. Oscar and I chatted in whispers to keep from waking her.

Around eight Mona was moved to the surgical ICU on the fourth floor.

ICU staff was diligent about limiting the number of visitors to two. Winslow was disappointed to learn he wouldn't be allowed to sleep beside his wife, so he sat at her bedside until visiting hours ended. Oscar, Louisa, and I rotated in and out of the other visitor's chair.

When it was my turn to step past the sliding glass doors, I put a hand on Winslow's shoulder before I sat down next to him. Despite being a combat veteran and having been shot myself, I was stunned at how diminished Mona looked in an elevated hospital bed, with an NG tube in her nose and a trach tube in her mouth. In addition to the susurrating ventilator near her head, there was a ton of other machinery and more wires and tubes than I could count. I remembered that the only other time I had seen this woman, I'd been struck by the contrast between the warmth of her smile and the grief in her eyes. Her smile compromised, her eyes now held an undiluted mixture of grief, pain, and fear that made me silently promise to find the person who had done this to her. She saw I was there and blinked at me. Minutes later, when I stood and shook Winslow's outstretched hand, she blinked at me again. I left Mona's room wanting to believe she had read my mind and given me permission to do whatever I must to get justice for her family.

In the softly lighted waiting room, Louisa was in the recliner we took turns saving for Winslow so he could sleep there through the night. Oscar was on a padded bench seat beside her, their overcoats piled beside him. The only others in the waiting room were three men who had taken turns saving the other recliner—an elderly man now nodding off in it and his two middle-aged sons. They were on a death watch for their wife and mother, two rooms away from Mona. Volume inaudibly low, CNN played on the wall-mounted flat-screen TV.

"Visiting hours are almost over," Oscar said.

"Let him spend his last minutes alone with her," Louisa said to her husband. "Then we can say goodbye and you can get him in the morning. He'll want a real bed by then."

Eyes tired and shoulders slumped, Oscar looked at me.

I said, "Walk with me. I need some coffee. Louisa, you want anything?"

"Lord, no. It's been a long day, and I'm going straight to bed."

Oscar and I rode the elevator to the first floor, where there was a 24/7 Tim Horton's in the corridor that linked the medical center to the vascular institute. As we took our places in a mercifully short coffee line, I said to him, "You're whipped. Go home. Get some rest. I'll stay here tonight. In the morning bring Win a change of clothes and I'll take off. But keep him here till two or so. Then I'll come back to stay with him till you get him in the evening."

"Win'll be safe with us tomorrow night but what about Mona?"

"I'm working on it." I thought again of Jimmy. His motorized wheelchair offered mobility and a chance to blend into the hospital environment. Peggy Ann was a retired nurse practitioner. Both could help monitor the comings and goings of ICU visitors. Also, I thought of Jen Spina. I had no idea how much juice she had with fellow officers, but maybe she could coax a few to spend a *pro bono* off-hour or two sitting on the ICU. I would have to trust her judgment when it came to officer selection. Or maybe I should wait on calling Jen till Mona was in a regular room. She would be more vulnerable there than in the ICU.

"Gotta tell Louisa why we're doing this," Oscar said after a moment.

"Yeah, she needs to know."

"Think I will go home tonight. Last thing my bladder needs is caffeine."

I bought myself a large coffee and Oscar a glazed sour cream donut he said was calling to him. Then I noticed Ayodele Ibazebo seated at a corner table, coffee in hand and reading the same Sunday paper Phoenix and I had finished earlier. Her glasses were low on her nose and her hair, though short, looked mussed. How long had *her* day been? I told Oscar to start back, that I would catch up with him. As he left, I went over to her table.

She looked up before I reached her and pushed her glasses up.

"Dr. Ibazebo, thanks again for saving my friend's wife." I sat across from her without asking. "Her husband was so afraid he would lose her."

She took a deep breath. "Mr. Rimes, I apologize if I seemed rude earlier." Her faintly British accent suggested the history of her upbringing and education. "I was just surprised to see you here. I should not have been." Her eyes moistened, and she wiped them. "Sometimes what I face in this ER is so dispiriting. Not just shooting —often children shooting children—but stabbings and beatings and rapes and husbands hurting wives. It is all part of this country, this culture. I can accept that. But most of the people close to me are so seldom touched by it that it is foreign to my life outside this place. But here you are, three times in two months." She hesitated and bit her lip. "It follows you, violence does. It is part of what you do and who you are, even though your father, Dr. Chance, is one of the gentlest men I have ever known. It is difficult for me to accept that he raised you. He is such a good man."

"He is," I said. "He taught me right from wrong and also taught me to be fearless. The three times you've seen me? I was the one beaten and then the one shot. Now an older couple I know are in some trouble." I shook my head. "My godfather understands that the work I do requires the fearlessness he instilled in me." For a long beat, I looked straight into her amber eyes. "I'm not afraid to do what must be done."

She broke eye contact and glanced down at the newspaper. "I usually get to the news late. After your surgery, I read an article from the day before. It said you caught a murderer." She smiled, sadly. "I know you are some kind of cop, a private cop who tries to help people."

"Yes. Right now I'm trying to help the couple up in the ICU."

"Was that woman shot because of you?"

I drew in a breath to answer but let it out before I spoke. "I don't know."

"Someone must do these things, I know, act as a wall between violence and the rest of us. But the smell of it sticks to you in a way it does not stick to me. When you carry that stink everywhere, you can't help but transfer it to others." She downed the last of her coffee.

"I know you're worried about Dr. Chance, about what will happen because of me."

She turned the now empty cup in her hands and rolled up the rim to see if she had won one of the prizes offered in the current promotional cycle. Her sigh told me the printing on the lip of the cup said PLEASE TRY AGAIN. "I worry about you," she said finally. "*You* are a good man too. I don't wish to be the one to tell your father you died on the table."

WHEN I GOT BACK UPSTAIRS, Winslow was already asleep in the recliner, covered by a light blanket and softly snoring. Oscar stood beside the chair, holding his wife's coat for her.

Louisa slipped her arms into the sleeves. "Win needs to be right here, right now, till Mona's out of the woods." Then she yawned. "Oscar will be back in the morning." She looked at her husband, who nodded and gestured toward the door. "Good to see you again, Mr. Rimes."

When Oscar and Louisa were gone, I took a seat opposite Winslow, near the door-less entryway, positioning myself so I could keep an eye on the corridor that led to the high-tech nursing pod.

Luckily, Mona's room also was visible from where I sat. If some man came up claiming he just got word of his mother's condition and wanted to see her for only a moment, I would have plenty of time to reach him before an unsuspecting staffer led him to her room.

Someone had turned on the TV captions, probably at the request of either Louisa or one of the sons of the man in the other recliner. I quickly fell into a routine of watching the pod and corridor, sipping coffee, and catching snatches of the current mess in Washington. After fifteen or twenty minutes, my phone buzzed in my jacket pocket. The call was from Yvonne, and I stepped into the corridor to take it.

"I never saw any lights over the garage," she said, almost breathless. "All the times I've been here, never. But I just saw Keisha! I saw her come out and get in the van—"

"The flower shop van?"

"Yes! The flower lady is driving."

I had been right about Fatimah sheltering Keisha in the apartment above her garage but the absence of light in the windows meant I hadn't anticipated Keisha was smart enough to cover them. *Damn it!* Now I was angry I hadn't played the hunch myself, days ago. Maybe I could have avoided all this, spared Mona the bullet. Maybe—

"They're heading up Kensington toward Main," Yvonne continued. "Should I try to catch them?"

"No," I said. "They're coming to me."

I broke off and stepped back into the waiting room just in time to hear a nurse speaking softly to the elderly man and his sons: "If you want to say goodbye, it's time."

I stepped out and moved a respectful distance away from the doorway as the three men, one son awkwardly embracing the father and the other carrying their coats, followed the nurse to their loved one's room. If Dr. Markham had been here, he might have tried to pray with them, or at least to send up a prayer in their wake. But I had been agnostic since being orphaned in childhood. Raised by agnostic godparents—now *that* was a term full of irony—I had long believed prayer was unnecessary if an all-knowing God knew your thoughts.

So I thought about the men, and the journey of loss that lay ahead, and wished them well. Then I glanced at Winslow, who seemed comfortable in the recliner after all. Sitting, I picked up my coffee cup from the small table where I'd left it and took a hefty swallow.

Keisha was on her way, and I needed to be alert.

23

Having already seen a larger one on Isaiah Kelly, I recognized the *Flowers by Fatimah* work uniform at once.

About twenty minutes after my phone call from Yvonne, a khaki-clad woman slipped inside the doors at the far end of the corridor that led to the ICU. Carrying a large bouquet whose green cellophane covering obscured her face, she stopped and looked about for a few seconds before tentatively moving forward. I looked long enough to determine it was Fatimah, not Keisha. Then I leaned forward and took a *People* magazine off the table. I began to page through a story about the British Royal Family, absorbing none of it because I forced all my attention to my peripheral vision. How she had got past the security desk was a question I would have to remember to ask—if I didn't spook her into running. As she drew closer to the waiting room doorway, I leaned back and raised the magazine to hide my face. After she moved past where I sat, I stood in the doorway and watched her.

An after-hours flower delivery on a Sunday night to an ICU that barred flowers was certain to get the attention of staff in the nursing pod. Two nurses, a heavyset middle-aged woman and a thinner youngish man, looked up from their computer screens simultaneously and rose to intercept the obviously confused delivery person. They reached Fatimah before she got to the pod and took turns explaining how there must be some mistake. As if short-listed for a Tony Award, Fatimah fiddled with a delivery slip and mumbled something about a special delivery for Mrs. Simpkins. I couldn't see her face but her trembling shoulders and the flutter in her voice made me think maybe she wasn't acting at all.

"Sorry," the man said gently, "but flowers aren't allowed in Intensive Care."

"They said I'm supposed to deliver them tonight." Fatimah's voice held a mixture of confusion and fear that felt real. "My boss—"

"Take them back downstairs," the woman said. "They'll be kept in storage until Mrs. Simpkins is assigned to a regular room."

"But I'm supposed to put them right by her bed so she'll see them in the morning."

"We don't allow flowers in here because they may aggravate a patient's condition," the man said, his patience flagging. "Look, I don't want to call security."

"I think there's still family in the waiting room," the woman said. "Her husband and her nephew." Her oversized red plastic eyeglass frames turned toward the doorway where I stood. "Sir," she said in a stage whisper, "maybe you can help this woman with these flowers for your aunt. Sign whatever she needs and get them back downstairs."

Fatimah turned around and looked at me, eyes widening and mouth falling open in surprise. Then she looked past me.

I spun around just in time to see the corridor door closing behind a slender, salt-and-pepper-haired woman in short-sleeved blue scrubs and a long-sleeved black tee shirt. A metal clipboard was in her hand and a name tag was clipped to the v-neck of her top. But both her smooth face and her reaction at the sight of me belied the wig she wore. Pivoting on one foot, Keisha Simpkins dropped the clipboard, threw a shoulder against the door, and pushed her way back out.

I bolted after her to the slowly closing door and slammed

through. Around the corner, I glimpsed her ducking into a wide entryway. I followed and reached the bank of elevators reserved for hospital staff. It was empty but I'd heard no bell, so I went through and rounded another corner to the elevators reserved for visitors. She had pushed the call button but was already backpedaling away when I got there. I stopped and held up my hands. But she continued to back up until her shoulders were against the nearest door to the stairs. Her left arm snaked behind her so she could grasp the knob. Her right hand produced a butterfly knife from the pocket of her scrubs, and she flicked it open like a pro.

"Dr. Simpkins!" I said. "I'm not here to hurt you. Your parents hired me to find you."

Chest heaving and wig askew, she glared at me and made small circles with the knife. "Come near me and I'll cut you, you lying motherfucker!"

"Didn't Fatimah tell you who—"

"She didn't believe you either. Said you looked like a stone-cold killer." She held the knife toward me, ready for an upward thrust under the rib cage—which meant she knew what she was doing. "Come any closer and you'll bleed out before you hit the ground!"

"I don't doubt it," I said, lowering my hands. "You're holding that knife like a real killer, but only because you've studied gross anatomy. You're shaking too much to have killed before."

"Doesn't mean I can't put you down!"

"No, but I was Army CID and I've done homicide investigations. Wet work is a lot harder in real life than in the movies." I heard footsteps drawing near behind me. Without looking over my shoulder, I reached back and held up a hand to stop whoever was there. I didn't want Keisha to attack or charge into the stairwell in such a state she might fall and hurt herself, even if she didn't land on her own knife. "My name is Gideon Rimes, with Driftglass Investigations. Your parents—"

"Keisha?"

The voice behind me belonged to Winslow Simpkins. I turned

just enough to see who else was with him: Fatimah and both ICU nurses. The woman told the man, "Call security."

"Yes, call security," I said. "Get someone to guard Mrs. Simpkins round the clock, even after she's out of the ICU. I believe bad people are coming for her, but the police don't so they won't post a guard. I can't watch her all by myself."

Neither nurse moved.

"Baby Girl," Winslow continued, "we went to Mr. Rimes for help. He didn't shoot your mama. It was a drive-by."

"They wanted to flush you out, and they did." I held out my hand. "Even now they may be watching the hospital. Let me help you. Please."

Keisha's eyes welled. "I'm sorry, Dad. So sorry. This wasn't supposed to happen. None of it." Tears began to slide down her cheeks and she made no effort to wipe them away—or lower the knife. But her left hand released the doorknob.

The older nurse moved closer and stood beside me. She made her voice as comforting as she could. "You look familiar. Have you ever been on staff here? I know I've seen you before." She smiled. "Your mother must be so proud of you. She's going to be just fine, but I need to get back to her and monitor her. You can come with me if you want to see for yourself." She held out her hand. "But give me the knife first."

Having ditched the flowers somewhere, Fatimah detached herself from the others, which now included a few more people in scrubs of varying colors. She went to Keisha, placed her fingers on her friend's forearm, and eased her knife hand down. "He's right, Kee. That little bulge under his sweater is a gun. Coulda shot us all and been long gone by now."

The nurse took a step away from me and swallowed audibly. I heard someone behind me take a step back.

"Your father says Rimes is legit, fine," Fatimah said. "But we been here too long. Just a peek to check on your folks. Remember? They're okay. It's not safe to stay longer."

Keisha let Fatimah take the knife from her. "Dad, kiss Mom for me and tell her I love her. Both of you." She wiped her eyes. "I can't be near you right now, for your sake."

"No, Keisha!" I could hear in his voice that Winslow was struggling not to cry. "Just come on home." The scrape of a shoe suggested he'd taken a step forward.

Shaking her head slowly, Keisha held up a hand to stop him. "I'll be home when this is over." Her voice cracked. "I'll explain all of it then. Promise."

"Let me go downstairs with you," I said. "Cover you till you get to your van."

Fatimah looked at me and said nothing for a moment, perhaps wondering how I knew they had come in the van. Then she closed the knife and slid it into her back pocket. "We're covered. Tonight." Eyes never leaving us, she opened the door and nudged Keisha into the stairwell. "But I got your card, Mr. PI. We'll call." She stepped into the stairwell herself, her right shoulder holding the door. "Don't try to follow us down. Stay here and look after Keisha's folks. That's all we want you to do right now."

The door closed behind them, and they were gone.

Her nametag flipped around so I couldn't see it, the older nurse let out a sigh as she looked at me and pushed up her red-framed glasses. "So you're *not* the nephew and you carry a gun. Great. Anything else I should know?"

"I'm a retired army cop, licensed to carry." I took a breath. "You're a lot braver than most people."

She snorted. "The ICU is not for the faint of heart."

"Understood. But at least for tonight, it will also have a paladin." I turned and put an arm around Winslow's shaking shoulders. "Ma'am, I can't stop Death from making his rounds, but I *can* keep his earthly disciples from padding the passenger list."

24

At six-thirty the next morning, after Oscar had returned with fresh clothes for Winslow and taken my seat in the waiting room, I found myself waiting for an elevator beside MaryAnn Maclin, the ICU nurse who had tried to talk Keisha down. To my surprise, she had declined to call security the night before. Now, an unzipped, down-filled lavender coat revealing her name tag, she looked at me with a weariness I couldn't help feeling mirrored my own.

"Long shift?" I asked. She'd been on duty when I got there over nine hours ago.

"Twelve hours and change," she said. "Three days a week, staggered. I won't be back here till the day after tomorrow. Thank God."

"Which means I'll have to explain myself to whoever works your station tonight." I let out a long breath. "Unless you'd care to put in a good word for me."

"One of the other nurses remembered you were in here yourself not long ago. She was glad to see you'd recovered." The elevator doors opened. She stepped in first. "Mrs. Simpkins is doing well. She'll probably be in a regular room by this afternoon. I'm sure staff won't mind wheeling in a recliner for her favorite nephew." Then, briefly, she smiled.

I went home, fell into bed, and sank into blissful nothingness. My phone alarm pulled me from a dreamless sleep just before noon. I called Flowers by Fatimah and got a recorded message that the shop was closed because of an out-of-town death in the family. I wondered if Fatimah had locked everything down as a precaution. Or had something happened? The news feeds on my phone were up to date and said nothing of the shop, the Kelly family, or Keisha. I decided I would swing by for a look before returning to Buffalo General.

After a shave and a shower, I went upstairs to my godfather's apartment for lunch.

White cheek stubble, old jeans, and a sweater with threadbare elbows told me Bobby had planned a stay-at-home Monday. While he spent much of his retirement giving guest lectures, mentoring young scholars, and attending non-profit board meetings, a day of rest after a trip was hardly unusual. Sitting at the ceramic-topped dining counter in his stainless steel kitchen, I couldn't help thinking of poor Kayla. Though her weekend must have been just as tiring as his, she was likely in court or working in her chambers. It was probably just as well they kept separate residences.

Glasses slipping down his nose as usual, Bobby put lunch on the counter—chunky tomato soup, tuna melts on multigrain bread, two Coronas—and sat across from me. As we ate, he told me about the three shows they had seen, two of them Tony Award winners, and a museum exhibit that had taken nearly a full day to see. In addition to shopping, they also had ridden elevators to two of the most popular observation decks: the Top of the Rock at 30 Rockefeller Plaza and the One World Observatory at the new World Trade Center. He had promised Kayla they would return to the Empire State Building and the Statue of Liberty, which they had visited a few years earlier, on their next trip. He finished his summary of their getaway with the Sunday brunch they'd had in the impressive Harlem brownstone of a former Buff State colleague who now taught at NYU.

"His wife is one of the top architects in New York," Bobby said, swigging the last of his Corona. He described their home in minute detail, from the woodwork and bay windows to the French doors between rooms and the restored tile floors in the bathrooms. "Their unit alone—two bedrooms—costs more than this whole building."

"What did the judge think of it?" Kayla's condo was on the ninth floor of a ten-year-old high-rise near the marina, with a panoramic living room window that offered a stunning view of Lake Erie and amenities that included a balcony, an in-unit laundry nook, and a community exercise room with a sauna. But I suspected she had found the filigreed ceilings and wainscoting of a Nineteenth-Century brownstone irresistible.

"She loved it, even after she found out how much it cost." He got up and went to the fridge for more Corona. "Want another?"

"No thanks," I said. "I'm working this afternoon, and tonight."

Bobby sat down again and popped the top. "Phoenix told us you were on a case but didn't say much about it."

While I had no trouble keeping a client's confidences, I valued my godfather's grasp of details and his insights into human behavior. Sometimes, as certain of his discretion as I was of nightfall and sunrise, I shared case details without naming those involved. On more than one occasion, his take had put me on the path toward a resolution. Now, as I put away the last of my soup and sandwich, I summarized the Keisha Simpkins affair. He listened without reacting —until I got to the woman's appearance in the hospital last night. Then his eyes widened and he held the Corona without sipping for a long time. I concluded with a recap of where things stood. Finally, he took a swallow.

"So this girl saw something or knows something that put a target on her back."

"Yes."

"Also, the absence of some kind of attack on the place she was staying tells you the people after her don't know about it yet."

"I'm going to stop there before I go back to the hospital. To make sure."

"Which means her parents are still targets to draw her out."

"Yes."

"The friend with them now, you're sure of his ability to protect them?"

"I am," I said. "He's a close friend of theirs and no stranger to security matters."

"The same man who brought the father to you? A guard at the women's shelter?"

"He's career military and a retired prison chaplain."

"So he's older, like the father." Bobby thought for a moment. "You're going to need more help, especially when she's out of the ICU. You haven't tried going to the police?"

"I don't have enough proof yet."

"Then you'll have to find help elsewhere."

"Any suggestions?"

"Me, for one. The dead boy's father for another." He took a pull of Corona. "You said he was in Nam."

I was quiet for a time. Carl Williamson was a possibility worth considering, for his anger if for no other reason. If these were the same people who had murdered his son, he'd want a piece of them. Maybe he deserved one. But I was reluctant to involve Bobby, to expose him to danger. He was an English professor who had never served in the military, much less been in combat. Even as I had the thought, I knew my desire to protect him was irrational.

He smiled as if he had read my mind. "Nice of you to worry about me but you seem to have forgotten who got you your first heavy bag and taught you how to punch it without breaking your wrists. I wasn't always an absent-minded professor. I learned how to handle myself early."

"You've never been an absent-minded professor, Bobby."

"Twice I disarmed students who threatened me or somebody in my class."

I had heard both stories. "All that was a long time ago, and the kids had knives. These are bad people with guns."

"But not that smart, according to you. Sure, they did a drive-by.

The question is, are they dumb enough to shoot up a hospital in the middle of the afternoon?"

"Probably not," I conceded after a moment. "They're looking for my clients' daughter because they want to stay *off* the radar. A shootout would put them *on* and make them a high priority."

"You've always been smart enough to look for help when you needed it." He took a long breath to let that sink in. "So let me help you this afternoon when the hospital is full of people with cell phones who can all dial nine-one-one. I'll follow you in my car. I can sit in the lady's room or outside the door, wherever they prefer. Let your chaplain friend handle the mornings. See if the boy's father can do tomorrow afternoon. Then I'll do the next day. Save the overnights for yourself and sleep till one or even two." He leaned toward me the way he always did when he wanted to drive home his point. "I know, three old men. Maybe we will seem like the Over-the-Hill Gang, but if we take the day watch while this lady gets better, you can do something useful with your afternoons."

"Like checking on the flower shop," I said.

"And finding her daughter before the other guys get lucky."

———————

25

C arl Williamson agreed to sit with Mona the next day, Tuesday, but only if I went with him first to see Winslow so they could apologize to each other. Outside Mona's private room, after I introduced Bobby to them, I described my phone conversation with Carl to Winslow and Oscar. When I finished, Winslow sucked his teeth.

Oscar put a large hand on his friend's shoulder and lowered his face a bit to look him in the eyes. "Win, sounds to me like he knows Keisha didn't give his boy drugs, and after all this you gotta know his boy didn't give 'em to her." He let Winslow consider that a moment. "Think how much better you'll both feel when Rimes gets the bastards who did this to your kids."

Despite what I had let Carl believe during our meeting in his kitchen, I had been hired to find a missing woman, not the thugs who might have hurt her. Having brought Winslow to me, Oscar knew this better than anyone. But without my having said anything, he understood the parameters of my mission had changed. Not only had Keisha, through Fatimah, charged me with protecting her parents, now I was expected to get the bastards too. Winslow gazed at me, eyes red and eyelids so weary his blinking looked slow and deliberate.

Having covered his wounded wife with his coat and seen his daughter flee in fear, he too knew things were different. It took him a moment to find the words to reaffirm his priority was still Keisha.

"Mona's awake," he said, his voice thin. "I didn't say nothing about Keisha being here last night and people looking for her 'cause I don't want her to get all upset. But if you've got folks here to watch over her, that's so you can find Keisha and bring her home. Right?"

"Yes."

Then he nodded, and despite the two-visitor limit, we all went into Mona's room.

She looked much better than when last I had seen her. Still tubed and wired, she was sitting up and talking. Color had come back into her cheeks. Winslow kissed her forehead and said he was heading back to Oscar's because he needed to rest. Then he introduced Bobby as my stepfather. He said Dr. Chance had come to visit because Mr. Rimes had told him so much about the two of them. Instead of shaking her hand, which had a needle taped in place on its back, Bobby nodded toward her in what looked like the beginning of a bow. It was his pleasure to meet her, he said. He hoped she wouldn't mind if he sat with her while her husband and Oscar took a break and Gideon continued doing the job she had hired him to do.

"So you a doctor too?" she asked. Her voice was hoarse, the after-effect of a tube withdrawn earlier.

"Not that kind," my godfather said.

She looked at me and narrowed her eyes at Bobby, the doubt roused by our lack of resemblance suggesting she might have misheard her husband, who, plainly, had misheard me. "You really his daddy?"

"Since he was twelve," Bobby said, with a tone that settled it. He took the chair beside the bed and leaned close to her. "I can tell you all kinds of stories about what he was like as a kid." Then he smiled.

Mona smiled, looking as flirtatious as an elderly gunshot victim could.

Chuckling, Oscar steered Winslow out.

And I went to work.

26

The neon lights were still on in the plate glass windows of Flowers by Fatimah but dark curtains behind them kept the shop interior hidden. The arc window in the upper part of the front door held a CLOSED sign. My hands gloved, I tried the handle anyway, but the door was locked.

I had parked around the corner on Bailey. Now I looked both ways on Kensington before I went up the driveway—which was clear because it had been shoveled in the past day or so and last night's dusting of snow had already melted. The windows were too high to peek into. At the side door, I rang the upper and lower bells and waited. Thirty seconds passed. I pressed both again. Still no response. Glancing at the street a final time, I moved into the back yard. Tall vinyl fences were in the back and on the house side. Thick shrubbery was on the driveway side. The yard felt secluded. No exterior cameras I could see, but I pulled down my watch cap anyway and pulled up the hood of the sweatshirt under my jacket. A mercury vapor light was mounted on the clapboard, near the back porches and out of reach. It had a motion detector sensor angled downward but that mattered little in the middle of the afternoon. If I kept away from the driveway, I would remain unseen.

The lower porch had no stairs and was enclosed by glass as if it were a greenhouse. The upper was open, its awning cranked shut and outdoor furniture covered for the winter. A weathered wooden swing set sat in the middle of the snow-covered lawn. Beyond it was the garage whose upper apartment windows were covered. The entrance was at the corner where the concrete met the lawn. I passed it, crunching through the snow to the garage window. More curtains kept me from seeing inside. Then I returned to the apartment door and listened to my surroundings as I considered which building I would enter first.

The only identifiable sounds came from traffic on Kensington and the whisper of wind. Somewhere in the distance was hammering followed by its echo, too far away to concern me. A bell from a nearby church or maybe the school just off Bailey rang three times, signaling the hour. I continued to listen. No music, no TV, no talk radio chatter. No Christmas carols. But more important to what I was about to do, no voices or sounds of people bustling about. No kids. I tried to remember if Fatimah had said how many children she had. Kids, she had said, and I hadn't asked for information. Daughters, Bianca had said, so there were at least two. That meant that if the bastards had got here ahead of me, I might find five bodies.

Remembering the flower shop's alarm panel and interior security cameras, I decided to check out the garage and its apartment first. It was unlikely that a detached garage would be included in the alarm system. I reached into my jacket pocket for the leather case that held the lock pick gun and tension tool I usually kept in my gun safe. I put the bent end of the tool into the door lock and inserted the pick gun. Exerting pressure on the tool, I squeezed the trigger four or five times, until the lock's pins vibrated into place and the tool turned like a key. Withdrawing the pick gun and the tool, I opened the door and stepped inside.

It was dark, so I clicked on my pocket flashlight. A staircase led to the apartment. To my left was a solid wooden door that opened into the garage. I unlocked it and looked inside. Against the far wall was a tan Dodge van with *Flowers by Fatimah* on the side. Along the front wall were garden tools, a power mower, and boxes of flower shop supplies like plant stands and Styrofoam rings. Oil spots dotted the remainder of the cement floor, suggesting there was a second vehicle. Closing the door and mounting the stairs, I made a mental note to log into IntelliChexx for Ike Kelly's DMV registrations. The apartment was compact—a bedroom, a kitchenette that doubled as a TV room, and a narrow bathroom. The unmade bed and the dishes in the sink suggested the occupant had intended to come back, but there were no clothes, anywhere.

At least there were no bodies, I told myself. Yet.

Going back downstairs, I stopped in the entryway to think about the alarm system. While the garage had not been included, I had seen the security panel inside the flower shop. Ordinarily, such panels at primary entrances had delays of thirty to forty-five seconds to give the person entering with a key time to punch in the security code. Most systems had interior panels in places like the master bedroom, so occupants could activate the alarm at night and deactivate it in the morning. Also, each panel would have two panic buttons that requested immediate police or fire dispatch. The average response time was three to six minutes, but busy days could push that to fifteen or twenty. If someone had broken in, especially with Keisha on high alert, *somebody* would have pushed the panic button, the primary purpose of which was to scare away the intruder. A determined and skillful killer could have taken them all out in the time it took a squad car to reach the house, but that would have meant the place I planned to enter was already a crime scene. The absence of police tape and the empty slot in the garage suggested I would find no bodies, no dead daughters.

But I had to be sure.

Two-family houses, as this one had been before the lower flat was converted into a business, sometimes had two separate alarm systems. The front door to the upstairs, solid steel and pristine, had struck me as seldom used. Perhaps that was intended to keep business and home separate. The side door, then, might serve as the primary access to the second floor. In any case, the interior wall would have one or two panels or none at all. If there were no panels I would know it the instant I opened the door, and I'd have to run. With two or one, I would have just enough time to get inside, peek at the downstairs if there were no additional doors to open, take the steps two at a time to peek at the upstairs, again if there were no doors to open. Locked doors usually meant the person with the keys was gone. While it was not impossible that whoever was after Keisha would lock the doors on the way out, I thought it unlikely they had grown more brain matter so soon after shooting Mona in broad daylight and fleeing.

I left the garage and went to the side door. Once I picked the lock and turned on my flashlight, I held my breath and began to ease the door open. There was no siren shriek, only the musical beep of the entry delay.

Thirty to forty-five seconds.

The hallway had a single panel but no video camera. Nor was there a door to the flower shop workroom, which showed no sign of intrusion. I knew there were cameras in front, and I didn't have much time, so I continued upstairs, the beeping of the alarm timer followed me to a locked door on the second floor. I decided to chance picking the lock, even as I counted off the seconds in my head. *Thirty-four. No alarm yet.* Holding the light and the tension tool in my left hand, I got the door open, darted through the kitchen to the living room, and saw nothing to suggest a struggle or violence. The alarm blew just as I opened the door to the undisturbed second bedroom. Having found nothing in the first either, I skipped the third and raced through the kitchen to the stairs.

At the moment of the first blast, I had forced the count in my head to reset. Now I tried to focus past the rhythmic banshee wail that proclaimed a B&E to the neighborhood. *Five, six, seven.* Ten to fifteen seconds after the alarm started, the security company would call the first number on the contact list, likely the flower shop landline, to make sure the siren hadn't been triggered in error. Getting no answer, they would attempt to reach the property owner's cell phone, or they would dispatch the police, and then try the secondary contact number. Either way, I had very little time. I reached the outside door at the count of twenty-one and charged through the yard to the vinyl fence that led to the next street. As I pulled myself up and over, I figured I had at least three minutes before the police arrived.

I tumbled into crusted-over snow in a large back yard that held an old steel-sided above-ground pool covered for the winter. I scrambled to my feet, cursing because snow had found its way inside my boots and pools were supposed to be surrounded, which meant I'd probably have to go over another fence. But as I rounded the corner of the house, I saw that the gate at the end of the driveway was open. I tucked my hood back inside my jacket and slowed to a walk as I neared the gate. Passing through, I turned south and walked a long block till I got to Collingwood. Then I turned left, continued on a short distance, and turned left again to emerge onto Bailey.

The first sirens sounded in the distance.

My car was half a block away. Moving toward it at a normal pace, I went straight to the liftgate in back and raised the wheel well cover. Once the small leather case with my lock pick gun was under the edge of the compact spare tire, I closed the back, climbed into the driver's seat, and pushed the START button.

An Avenue Pizza shop was a couple of blocks ahead. I decided to go there, to order a cold sub and a bottle of iced tea to take to the hospital later. While I waited, I would use my phone to log onto IntelliChexx. Once I knew the make and plate number of Ike Kelly's car, my trip to Buffalo General would be leisurely and circuitous. I would need time to drive past the flower shop at least twice on the chance that the alarm provider had reached Ike and he had come home to inspect the damage.

I knew it was a longshot, but if he did come, I might be able to follow him back to wherever his family and Keisha were hiding.

Before I pulled away from the curb, however, my ring tone sounded through the car's audio system. The number on the screen was blocked but I pushed the TALK button anyway. The soft, mannered baritone that came through the speakers chilled me.

"Mr. Rimes, there is no reason my employer should know you are accomplished at breaking and entering, so I will say nothing of it. But I felt the need to express my personal admiration. Your speed and professionalism—"

"Not like you to stroke another man's ego," I said. "What do you want, Lester? To let me know you're still back there?"

"I'm so glad you didn't insult me by suggesting I wanted to black-mail you, sir. I am confident you left nothing to support such an effort." He laughed. "As I have told you, my interest in your current situation is entirely personal. I will find my way to your vicinity whenever I have the time. Today I had the time." He paused, perhaps to let the idea of my vulnerability sink in. "But I mean you no harm. Who knows, I may even end up being your guardian angel."

27

When I got back to the hospital, about six-thirty, Mona was asleep, a nasal oxygen tube and an IV in place. Bobby sat at her bedside, reading an old *O Magazine* with a cover that featured a smiling Oprah Winfrey seated in a white wicker chair. On the bedside tray were a *Vanity Fair* and a *People* I expected he had already ripped through. A court reality show was on the TV angled toward the bed but the volume had been muted.

"Want half my sub?" I said softly. "Turkey, cheese, spinach, tomato, oil, no onions."

He shook his head and kept his own voice low. "If you're gonna be here all night, you'll need the whole thing. I'll do a chicken breast on the George Foreman or maybe pull a casserole out of the freezer."

Draping my jacket over the back of the second visitor chair, I sat down and began to unwrap my sandwich. "How is she?"

"Pretty good, considering she was shot. She tires easily, so we talk a while, and then she drifts off. After half an hour or so she wakes up —or they wake her up for something—and we talk again." He closed the magazine and massaged the back of his neck with his left hand. "Nice lady."

"Yes. Any visitors?"

"Some people from her church. Two older women and the minister and his wife."

I thought for a moment. "They come separately or together?"

"Separately. One woman stayed about fifteen minutes. The other was here half an hour before the Markhams came and left a few minutes after that."

"What did you think of the Markhams?"

"I've met him here and there at public functions, but he didn't remember me. He's more or less the same man I saw then and see on the news now, practical and caring but given to making a show of prayer. It was my first time meeting his wife though. For the most part, she was quiet but much more observant than the average person." He chuckled. "She's pretty too. Very pretty. Trust me, she knows it."

I considered his assessment. "She wasn't that quiet when I interviewed them in his office last week." I lowered my voice to a whisper. "She was more concerned about the church being embarrassed by association with a drug user than about Keisha being found."

Bobby nodded. "Gotta keep up appearances. You have any luck at the flower shop?"

Between bites of my sandwich and swallows of iced tea, I gave him an abbreviated account of my afternoon. I told him I had visited the Dorans—who would be joining us at Mira's for Christmas dinner if she hadn't yet told him. I said nothing of Spider Tolliver's call or the GPS tracking device LJ had found and removed when he swept the underside of my Escape. Ike's silver Impala had failed to show after his alarm was triggered, I explained, so LJ would try to unearth credit card usage for Keisha, Ike, or Fatimah. "I think something spooked them and they ran. Be nice to know what it was and where they are."

"Must be staying somewhere." Bobby flipped to another page in the magazine. "If they're riding on plastic, LJ will find them. But what makes you so sure these other people aren't good enough to track cyber footprints, like your friend Mr. Quick?"

The mention of Quick so soon after I'd heard from Spider made me hesitate before answering. Tolliver and his associates had come for me in October because I had run an IntelliChexx search on Lorenzo Quick, whose name had come up in my investigation into another murder. Whoever handled his IT got a search alert that gave them my IP address, which led them straight to me. "If Quick wanted Keisha, she'd have been dead days ago," I said finally. "She'd have died from the overdose and been written off as a useless user."

"Maybe they're staying with family."

"Fatimah's an only child. I don't know if her husband—"

Bobby lowered his magazine at my abrupt silence. "What?"

"Family isn't always blood. Be right back."

I stepped into the corridor and walked to a waiting room adjacent to the elevators. Gazing out the huge plate glass window at the still-new buildings of the Medical Corridor, I called Jen Spina's private cell. It went straight to voice mail.

"Jen, Gideon Rimes. Apparently, Keisha was staying at Fatimah's. They both showed up at the hospital last night but took off when I tried to get close. Now Keisha's gone, along with Fatimah's whole family. If they're staying with you and Bianca—or you know where they are—please tell Keisha I have people looking after her parents. And I haven't forgotten your offer. If you want to sit with Mrs. Simpkins for a few hours, just let me know." I paused and took a breath. "Keisha knows by now I'm being straight with her but she hasn't reached out yet. Please have her call the hospital and ask to be put through to her mother's room. I'll be here tonight myself." I gave the room number and added what I hoped would be too vague to lead to my prosecution for B&E: "Tell Fatimah and Ike I just wanted to make sure nobody had got to them." Then I clicked off and went back to the hospital room.

Mona was still asleep, and Bobby was shrugging into his coat. "All good?"

"I left a message with one of her friends." I sat down again.

"About all you can do if you're here. Something comes up and you need to call..."

"I know. I will."

Squeezing my shoulder, Bobby left, and I opened the *Vanity Fair*.

The room phone trilled ten minutes later, just as I finished the first half of my sub. I got to the nightstand by the second ring, but the first had already startled Mona awake. She was shifting in bed, trying to angle herself to reach the phone.

"I got it, Mona," I said, lifting the handset. "Mrs. Simpkins' room."

"Mr. Rimes?" Her voice was calmer than last night, steadier but still not resolute.

"Yes."

"It's Keisha. Can I talk to my mother?"

"She just woke up. I'll give her the phone but first I need to tell you I know your mishap was unintentional. These people—" I stopped, mindful of Mona, now looking at me expectantly because she had heard her daughter's voice. Uncertain what she knew, how much she could surmise, I half-turned away from her. "What I don't know is why. Whatever it is, I'd like to help. If we can meet somewhere—"

"No, not yet."

"I don't know *who* they are, but I know *what* they are." I let Keisha ponder that for a second or two. "For the sake of your family and friends, please trust me. I can—"

"Not until my mother's fit enough to travel." She let out a long, shaky breath as if struggling to maintain her determination. "Once I get her and Dad out of town, somewhere safe, I'll sit down with you and your lawyer friend. You told Fatimah she would help me. I'll give her that chance when my folks are gone. I'll explain everything. Do whatever you both say." The sound of her swallow came through the handset. "Now, can I talk to my mother? Please."

I passed the phone to Mona, whose hand was up and waiting for it. Her low threshold for her daughter's voice had already pushed tears out of her eyes and made her lower lip tremble. There was fear in her expression as if at last it was clear something external to her daughter was threatening them all. "Keisha? You okay, baby?" Her voice cracked into an almost whisper. "You coming home soon?"

Keisha's voice was not as loud as it would have been coming through a cell phone but the receiver was far enough from Mona's ear that I could still make out her answer: "Not yet, Mom. It's not safe, but I'm okay."

Not wishing to intrude further, I stepped into the corridor and pulled the door shut.

I waited until I could no longer hear the timbre of Mona's voice. Then I went back inside to find her shoulders heaving and her cheeks wet but the sound of crying trapped in a throat still too irritated to permit full release. I moved to the bed and put my arms around her as best I could. She turned her face into the strip of pocket near the bottom of my hoodie and wept freely, her vocalizations reduced to measured hums against pain. Afraid I would dislodge the IV tube under her collarbone if I moved, I remained still, the fingers of my left hand lightly patting her shoulder. I kept my eyes on the vital signs monitor for changes that indicated a problem. Temperature, pulsox, and respiration were steady but her heart rate and her already high blood pressure notched up a bit as I stood there. After a few minutes, as her tears began to lessen, her heart rate went down and her blood pressure dropped back to 138/82. At last, with a long throat-clearing attempt, she pulled away from my hoodie. I let go of her and reached for the small tissue box on the nightstand.

"Hard to talk to her when she's so scared," Mona rasped, wiping her eyes with the tissue I gave her.

"Harder when you're recovering from lung surgery and getting oxygen." I pulled one of the chairs closer to the bed and sat. "Don't try to talk if it's hard."

For a long moment, she looked at me, scowling without speaking. "Somebody forced that drug shit into her, and now they're trying to kill her. That's why she ran." She coughed and pulled another tissue from the box. Then she took a couple steadying breaths before she wiped her lips. "But I guess you knew that already, being a detective and all."

"I suspected it." I put the tissue box back on the nightstand.

"But you didn't tell us."

"Didn't know for sure but I thought she might be trying to lead them away from you."

A swallowed laugh scraped the inside of her throat. She began to cough again, wincing repeatedly. When she finished she said, "They shot me anyway. To make her come out of hiding."

"I'm here to make sure they don't get a second chance."

"She said she was here last night. Winslow never told me." She gave me a sidelong glance and frowned. "You didn't either. Maybe I was too out of it to remember anything but you'da thought somebody woulda wanted me to know my only child was alive and well." Her breathing was more strained now, as if each inhalation had a difficult passage through a nose dried by oxygen and throat raw from coughing. "Sometimes it's like you men don't know how to talk at all."

Winslow was already standing by the bus and didn't need me to kick him under it by putting the choice of silence on him. Blame wasn't the issue but Mona's feeling that she had been left out.

"I'm sorry," I said, leaning forward and resting my forearms on my knees. "Truly. But the way you're breathing now..."

Nodding, she said, "I know you thought it was the right thing to do, to keep me from getting too worked up—*this* worked up—so I thank you." Closing her eyes, she let out a long sigh and took a few more steadying breaths. "Hard to stay mad at a good man. Winslow is a good man. Your daddy said you're good-hearted too."

"I had a good role model."

"Such a smart man. Knows so much about so many things. I could listen to him talk all day."

One corner of my brain began formulating a way to tease Bobby for talking so much that she kept falling asleep. "He is a retired English professor, my godfather."

"I think he told me that." She smiled and her eyes brightened a bit, though her voice was weakening. "He married? I mean, I got a friend who—"

"He's with somebody," I said. "Happily." I had to steer her back to the phone call before she couldn't talk anymore. "Mona, I need to ask you about your conversation with Keisha. To help me protect her."

"Okay."

"She was staying at Fatimah's and then they all left. Did she tell you why?"

"Somebody kept calling the house in the middle of the night and hanging up."

"Did she tell you where she is now?"

"With Bianca. Did you know her wife's a cop?"

"A good cop. She'll be safe with them." I leaned forward again. "Does she know the people who hurt her and killed Odell?"

Mona shook her head. "She'd never seen them before. Two big black men who cut them off and held guns on them and said she was too nosy." Fresh tears pooled in the corners of her eyes. "She tried to tell people at the hospital but nobody would listen."

"Does she know what they meant by nosy?"

"About something she found by accident. She didn't say what it was."

"She tell you anything else?"

"Not to trust anybody. Not to tell anybody what she told me. Except you."

28

After visiting hours ended, things were calmer and quieter, but nursing rounds continued as staff changed IV bags, administered scheduled medication, checked monitors, and tended to personal needs. Mona had two bedside visits, both from women: an aide before nine to help her into the bathroom and a nurse around eleven to check a med line as she slept. The nurse reminded me that coffee and snacks were available from a vending machine near the waiting room. By midnight, with most televisions off and most rooms lit by night lights, the corridor slipped into overnight quietude, with hushed voices at the nursing station and fewer audible squeaks of rubber soles on the floor.

Coffee from the machine sucked but kept me awake, more from a roiling stomach than a caffeine jolt to my nervous system. Having burped enough bitterness as I read through the magazines, I filled two plastic cups with cold water from the bathroom sink and slid my chair to the wall nearest the foot of the bed. There I plugged my charger into an outlet so I could check headlines and play games as my phone juiced up. Seated this way, I sipped water and passed the time, half-obscured by the privacy curtains. The only other light was the dim glow of a plastic panel above the bed

Mona slept on her back, snoring softly.

Shortly after one, a small woman in flowery pink scrubs stepped into the room. She had narrow shoulders and brittle-looking auburn hair. I saw her before she noticed me half behind the curtains. There was something familiar about her. But even after watching nursing station personnel go about their duties over the past few hours, I could not place her face. I thought perhaps she had come on during a shift change or was a floater covering for someone on a break. She stood just inside the door for a second and glanced back over her shoulder. Then she approached the bed with tentative steps, passing the wall-mounted box of nitrile gloves without taking a pair. From her pocket, she took out a hypodermic needle, uncapped it, and pulled the plunger. When I got to my feet, she saw me and stopped, her hand shaking. Her eyes widened enough to register both surprise and what I first thought was discomfort.

"Hello," she said, voice deeper than it should have been in so narrow a frame. "Just some medicine for her SVC line." The tremor still visible in her hand, she offered a nervous smile that, even in the diminished light, revealed blackened, crooked teeth and gaps where other teeth once had been. Then I knew why she looked familiar. This woman wasn't Veronica Surowiec, the fallen physician I had met at Sanctuary Nimbus, but her unsteadiness and dentition suggested she was likely a member of the same methamphetamine sisterhood.

I moved toward her without speaking, and she shifted her hold on the hypodermic. Backing away, lips curling into a snarl that became a throaty laugh, she held up the needle as if it were a dagger, to frighten me into stopping. But I kept coming, grabbing the pink plastic water pitcher off the nightstand, removing the lid, and throwing the contents at her. Stunned by the water, she took another step back before she lunged at me with the needle. I swung the pitcher in an arc as if it were a baton, first connecting with her hand and disarming her and then backhanding her across the face harder than I intended. I heard the plastic crack. She went down, blood pouring from her nose and leaking between the fingers of her right hand as she tried to scoot backward into the corridor with her left. Her eyes glazed over with tears.

When I got to her and began to reach down toward her, she screamed, "Rape!"

In the millisecond that the nursing station five rooms away was completely silent, I unholstered my gun and pointed it at the woman still sliding away. "Don't fucking move!" But she inched backward anyway, so I racked my slide. That stopped her, just as the corridor filled with people in scrubs and lab coats, even a few in hospital gowns. Many crouched or ducked into other rooms once they caught sight of my gun. Others simply froze.

"Call security," someone said above the rising chatter.

A dark-haired young man in a white coat drew near, his hands at chest level, palms out as if to calm me. He stopped when I looked at him. "Sir, I don't know what's going on, but please put down the gun."

"Call security!" someone else said.

"I just did!" came another voice.

"Does anybody know this woman?" I said.

Wet and bloody, the woman on the floor looked at everyone frozen near her, made a quick calculation, and took in a lungful of courage. "This motherfucker tried to rape me!"

"Sir," the man who had drawn near said, "whatever it is—"

"*Does anybody know this woman!*" My shout silenced everyone. Some of them looked at the woman on the floor and then at each other. I heard some ask others who she was and noticed one woman shrug. "Nobody knows her? Then call nine-one-one."

"He tried to rape me," she said again, wiping her eyes. "Fucking bully tried—"

"You just tried to kill Mrs. Simpkins, in the room behind me." After gasps, another millisecond of silence. Then I heard someone say, "The gunshot victim," and someone else, "He's that bodyguard they were talking about." I gave a quick nod to the woman on the floor, to let her know that I too could play to the crowd. Her tears stopped, and her eyes—blue, I now saw, and intelligent—met mine with a fury that felt primal. Then she gazed about, her anger giving way to the same fear I hadn't recognized when I started toward her in the semi-darkness of the room. She angled herself toward the wall so she could sit up.

I looked at the man with his hands still raised as he took another step closer and said, "I'm working here and I told you to call the police, so don't be stupid." He stopped, lowered his hands. "I knocked a syringe out of her hand. She said it was for the SVC line."

"The subclavian vein catheter. That's—"

"Explain it later," I said. "The needle's gotta be on the floor. Why don't you go find it, so police can figure out what's in it? Please. And put on gloves. She didn't grab any when she came into the room. Her fingerprints must be all over the barrel."

He turned to look at a tall, middle-aged woman in a pristine white coat with a stethoscope hanging out of one pocket. A supervising physician, I assumed. She nodded her permission. He went into the room and dialed up the lights. I heard Mona say, "What's going on? Is that Mr. Rimes out there doing all that hollering?" Then the woman in white stepped into the space the man had vacated and looked straight at me.

"The poor thing's soaked and bleeding. Can we do something about that?"

"Toss her a towel. I don't want anybody close if the 'poor thing' has another weapon."

A small white towel made its way to the front of the crowd, and the woman now sitting with her back against the wall put it over her nose just as the man returned with the hypodermic in a blue-gloved hand.

"It's empty," he said.

"Perfect for an air embolism," I said.

29

So, you beating up little girls now?"

Dark hair half-combed and light brown cheeks dotted with stubble, Rafael Piñero sat behind his desk in the homicide squad room, glaring at me in the interview chair across from him. Instead of his customary suit and tie, he wore jeans and a black BPD sweatshirt. It was half-past three, and I had just finished summarizing my investigation. Earlier, I had refused to accompany the responding officers to nearby B District unless a uniformed cop was posted outside Mona's hospital room. While one officer seemed ready for a testosterone spray-off with me, his more experienced partner asked the resident who had found the syringe how it could be used to commit murder. After hearing the explanation, he turned to me and asked if I knew anyone on the force who could vouch for me. I told him detectives Chalmers and Piñero. A few phone calls later, the younger uni sat in a chair in the hospital corridor while I took a ride down to headquarters, not B District, beside his partner. Handcuffed, the woman rode in back. Now she was waiting in an interrogation room.

"She isn't a little girl," I said. "She's a grown woman who tried to stab me with a needle with God knows what on it." I took a breath. "Didn't mean to hit her that hard."

"A little woman, bro, and you broke her goddamn nose. With a water pitcher." Piñero let out a low whistle and sat forward, resting his elbows on the desktop and his chin on his hands. "Okay, so you think she was trying to kill this old lady you were guarding. Who is she again?"

"The mother of the woman I was hired to find."

"The woman who overdosed."

"The woman forced to overdose."

"Okay, forced. But you still haven't figured out why."

"When we find out who this woman is, maybe then we'll know why."

"Takes time. We got no idea what Jane Doe's real name is. She's not talking. Hasn't even lawyered up. We can put her face and prints in the system and wait for hits. But she's gotta be charged with something for anything we do to matter. So far you got nothing. The cops who answered the call found her bloody on the floor because *you* put her there."

"Somebody shot her—the mother, I mean. I was sure they'd try to finish her so I was there." I smiled at him. "Thanks at least for putting in a good word. I'll sleep better knowing Mrs. Simpkins has police protection."

"Hold the fucking phone a minute, okay? I called in a favor and got you brought here instead of B District. To homicide. But nobody died tonight. Your private-eye-who-brought-in-a-cop-killer shit only goes so far, you know? This is probably the last hole-punch for *that* particular card."

I figured it was true and said nothing.

Piñero pursed his lips. "So, we got the lady covered for the moment, but I don't know yet if we can do round-the-clock, especially if that dipshit walks outta here uncharged. That call is above my grade. *You* will have to convince the brass to spend the money. Good luck with that." He leaned back, folded his arms across his chest, and surprised himself with a yawn. "Woke me the fuck up. Woke up my girl when we were both wiped out—and don't even *look* like you want to ask why. Man, they coulda called Terry. He's chickless right now and probably snoring out to the sidewalk."

"Sorry." I spread my hands in a *mea culpa*. "I gave the guy both your names."

"Prick probably turned his phone off 'cause he had a premonition *you* would get into some shit tonight." He drummed his fingers on the desktop. "Why is everything so twisty-turnaround with you?"

"What do you mean?"

"First, that shooting is not my case, and neither was the overdose. Frankly—"

"I know. Survive an overdose or a shooting, your priority drops."

"Not just that. Maybe there is an upstart gang trying to challenge Lorenzo Quick's operations—foolish, you ask me. Maybe these two big black dudes did off this teacher and try to kill his girl on Jefferson. Maybe they shot up her folks in the middle of Orange Street. That doesn't explain why a little white meth mama tries to kill an old black church lady. Until they run in the same circles..." He pushed everything away with a wave of his hand. "Too many hypotheticals. Be easier if the assailant in the hospital was a big black guy." He grinned. "If you broke *her* nose, you probably would've iced *him*."

"Might've had no choice."

"At least I could investigate then. This still isn't a major case. At best you stopped a tweaker from assaulting somebody. But you'd be hard-pressed to prove even that much. The idea someone sent her to do it is a lot to swallow. The narcotics overdose, the shooting—you gotta connect the dots, show this is all one case. Then I can get the guys working each end to share information."

"Can I talk to her? You got her in the box."

"Hell, no! Civilian! Some guys I'd risk my pension for. You ain't one of them. Yet." He shook his head. "Sooner or later she'll get a lawyer. Once he got wind a private citizen did an interrogation—in homicide, no less, when nobody died and his client might've been coming down from a meth binge—he'd think it's his birthday."

"Can I watch?"

"The detective sergeant on duty, the guy who put her in Interview One, is good people. Before you got here I told him what you told me on the phone. You can join him at the window. A professional courtesy. Off the record, of course."

"Of course."

"Never to be fucking mentioned."

"Okay, I got it."

"The whole night will be off the record unless I get something to give the detectives."

"Fair enough."

Piñero stood, stretched. "I'm going to the break room for coffee. Want some?"

"Sure. Black."

He returned with a small cardboard tray that held four Styrofoam cups of coffee. He set one cup in front of me. Then he picked up a legal pad from his desk and motioned for me to follow him. Wrapping tissue from the box on his desk around the hot cup, I sipped as I went.

Fiftyish and weary-looking, in shirtsleeves and loosened tie, Detective Sergeant Pete Kim had a firm handshake and a gravelly voice. Taking his coffee from Piñero's tray, he gestured me into the observation room, dimmed the lights, and opened the curtains. On the other side of the two-way mirror sat Jane Doe, twitching and gazing about. The handcuff chain connecting her to the table ring was long enough to let her chew a thumbnail or scratch her forearms through her sleeves, which she did every few seconds, as if unconsciously. In the overhead light, her bruised nose packed with wadded cotton, she appeared smaller, more fragile than she had on the hospital floor. Despite the blood on the front and puckers left after the fabric dried, her oversized scrubs still bore the fold lines of something recently removed from its packaging.

"The scrubs look new," I said to Kim.

"And too big. Maybe picked up just for tonight, like a prom dress." He turned to me and grinned. "Some date you turned out to be."

I shrugged. "What I get for not signing her dance card."

We both sipped coffee as Piñero stepped into view, the pad under his arm and a cup in each hand.

"I been here fucking forever," the woman said.

"I'm Detective Piñero, ma'am. I brought you some coffee." He slid a cup to her and took a step back as if getting out of range in case she decided to throw it at him.

Chain ratcheting through the ring as she raised the cup to her lips, she took three hefty swallows, despite the steam we could see rising. Then she set the empty cup down, throat apparently intact, and angled her head awkwardly to wipe her mouth on her sleeve.

"Start by giving me your name," Piñero said. "We're video-recording. Okay?"

"Already told that chink cop I got nothing to say 'cause I didn't do nothing. I'm the victim here." Gazing up at a space above the mirror —the camera bubble, I presumed—she poked out her lip and absently dug at her forearm. "Jesus! Can't I talk to somebody white?"

Piñero shook his head. Still standing, he placed the pad on the table and made a show of reviewing his notes on the top sheet as he drank his coffee. "Could be looking at serious charges—criminal trespass, impersonation, disorderly conduct, assault with a deadly weapon, maybe even attempted murder."

"Attempted—*shit!*"

"I want to hear your side."

"I ain't got no side, Paco!" She scowled at him. "That big nigger tried to rape me!" Her voice was even deeper when laden with contempt. "But you won't do jack shit about it 'cause he's a friend of yours. Yeah, I heard that fucker give your name to the cop in the hospital. He didn't believe me either and your asshole buddy got to ride in front."

"Probably to keep you two separated." Moving behind her, he bent close to her ear. "I know him but that doesn't mean we're friends or that I gotta believe everything he tells me." He glanced up at the glass and fought back a smile. "You're right. He can be a real asshole."

Without looking at me, Kim chuckled and shook his head.

She rattled the chain. "Then how come he's not the one locked up in here?"

"What, you think this is our only interview room? He's in another one."

"Cuffed?"

"Standard procedure. He told me his story. Now I want you to tell me yours." He rounded the table and sat across from her so that Kim and I were looking at his back. He set down his cup, flipped to a blank sheet, and took a pen from his shirt pocket. "So he tried to rape you. That's a serious accusation."

"It's true!" She snorted. "You cocksuckers never believe the woman."

"Tell me what happened, as much as you can remember."

She was quiet a moment, eyes blinking rapidly, darting back and forth. Fingernails ragged from chewing disappeared under her sleeves now. "When I came through the door he grabbed me and pulled me to him. Fucker tried to kiss me."

"Tried to kiss you?"

"Stuck his tongue in my mouth."

Still watching her, Kim said softly, "Man, if you want some Listerine, I'm sure we've got a bottle around here somewhere."

"I'm good," I said.

In the box, Piñero jotted something down. "What did you do?"

"What do you mean? You think I came on to him, told him he could have some of this?" She thrust her narrow chest forward. "I fucked niggers before but he ain't my type."

Piñero's snort vibrated through the observation room speaker.

"No. What did you do when he tried to kiss you?"

"What do you think? I pushed him off me and tried to get away."

He wrote something else. "Then what happened?"

"He grabbed my arm and wouldn't let go! I fought but he knocked me down."

"So you fought him and he held on?"

"Yes."

"Tight?"

"Yes! He twisted it and it hurt real bad."

"Which arm did he grab?"

She appeared to think a bit. Then her face brightened, and the chain rattled through the ring again as she held up her left and worked the sleeve down.

Piñero scanned her arm and made another note. "Are those scratches from him?"

"Of course!"

"Then he hit you and you fell down?"

"Yes."

"What did he hit you with?"

"His fist. What else?"

"Not the water pitcher?"

"His fist, Paco!"

"All right. How did you get into the corridor?"

"Crawled 'cause I was still dizzy from being hit."

Piñero was quiet for a five-count. Then he leaned forward. "Why did you go into that particular room in the first place?"

"I was looking for my friend. I went to the wrong room. By mistake."

"Your friend's name?"

"Mary." She nodded as if confirming her memory. "We went to school together."

"Last name?"

"Decker," she said after a moment. As her lie sprouted details, she was beginning to shift more in her seat. "I think that's her name now."

"You know we'll check the name."

She smiled. "Go ahead."

Mary Decker—a shot in the dark or a name she had seen somewhere? I had no idea.

"Okay, so you were there in the hospital to visit your friend Marcy," Piñero said. He paused but she never challenged the name *Marcy*. "You went to the wrong room, and this guy grabbed you."

"Sure did!"

"Want to press charges?"

"Maybe."

"You'll have to give me your name if you want to file a complaint."

A dark tooth clamped over her lower lip. She looked down as if avoiding her interrogator's eyes. "Let me think about that. Maybe it's best not to get involved." Then she looked up. "It's late and I'm tired. I want to go home. What if you just let things go? Tell him to stay away from me or he'll be arrested?"

"We're kind of past that now."

"Why? It's his word against mine. Can't we just drop it? Maybe I misunderstood."

"You misunderstood his tongue in your mouth?"

She said nothing.

"At least help me understand." He leaned back, folded his arms. "Help me understand why you were in the hospital after visiting hours. Why you were dressed like you work there when you don't. Why you had a hypodermic we're gonna find your fingerprints on."

I turned to Kim. "She's playing stupid. Any way I can get a note to Piñero?"

"Sure." He handed me a pad from a small utility table in the corner. "When you're ready I'll knock and hand it to him."

I set down my cup and took out my pen. I wrote *Did she come in early, see "Mary Decker" and change into scrubs? How does she know what an SVC line is?* I was forming my third question when there was a tap on the observation room door. Kim and I exchanged a look before he stepped out. Then I heard a man say the front desk had sent him up. He asked if the woman who had been brought in was in Interview One. When Kim said yes, someone rapped on the interrogation room door and didn't wait for a response to open it.

Clearly, Jane Doe was startled by the knock. Now her eyes widened as a tall, russet-skinned man in an expensive navy suit and charcoal topcoat stepped inside and told her to say nothing more. She didn't seem to recognize him. She nodded anyway.

"This interview is over, detective," the man said. "My client is leaving with me."

Kim stepped back into the observation room. "Harlow Graves for the defense," he said. "Wonder how he got wind of this."

I'd heard of him and seen him on billboards but had never crossed paths with him.

Piñero stood and positioned himself between Graves and the woman. "Just talking, counselor," he said. "Trying to sort something out. She hasn't been charged with anything."

The lawyer stepped around Piñero and leaned close to look at the woman, who shrank away from him as if afraid. He offered her a reassuring smile, and tension left her shoulders.

"Looks like Abu Grhaib up in here," he said. She let him slide her sleeves up one at a time. "The commissioner can expect a notice of intent to file."

"Her face was like that when she got here," Piñero said. "The hospital treated her before she was brought in. Our video will show she's been scratching her arms since she got here. Sometimes, people like her have brittle skin."

"People like—" Graves spun around. "How do people like her get this facial injury?"

"That big—" Having already called me a nigger, the woman appeared to search for a new word to describe me to her black lawyer. "That big cocksucker hit me!"

"What big cocksucker?"

"A PI bodyguarding someone in the hospital. She went into the room, dressed in scrubs and carrying a hypodermic. When he got between her and the patient, she swung the needle at him. He hit her with a water pitcher."

"His fist!"

"Hard enough to cause serious injury," the lawyer said. "I want his name."

Piñero shrugged. "Check with the hospital. He's the one who said to call nine-one-one."

"I went to the wrong room!"

"Who was it you were trying to see?" Piñero said. "Mary? Marcy? Margie?"

"He tried to rape me and I tried to fight him off!"

Graves took the cue. "So my client was trying to defend herself against this thug. Clearly self-defense."

"Funny, but that's what he said to responding officers. She acted like the needle was a dagger." Piñero angled his head at her. "What was it you called him again? He's a big what?"

Instead of announcing that I was somewhere in the building, Jane Doe lifted her hands, links of chain taut in the table ring. "I just want to go home."

Piñero unlocked the cuffs. Harlow Graves led the woman out of Interrogation One. Piñero looked at the mirror and held up a finger. Then he left the room. A minute or two later he joined Kim and me in the observation room.

"They're gone."

"That was some weird shit," Kim said. "He came out of nowhere."

"Pete, you told her to cool her jets while we sorted everything out, right?"

"Yep."

"So she never got to make a phone call?"

"Nope."

"Never lawyered up." Piñero looked at me. "You know what this means?"

"Somebody was watching. They called Graves." I paused as I realized I'd likely seen his face at the bar association holiday party. "Somebody inside General or waiting outside."

"If she can afford Harlow Graves," Kim said, "she should've had a gun in that room."

I thought for a moment. "Do either of you think she knows him?"

Piñero shook his head as Kim said, "No."

"He didn't seem to know her either," I said. "He never called her by name."

Piñero ran a hand through his hair. "So what makes a prominent black attorney rush in to help a woman he doesn't know? A woman with obvious racial bias?"

"A Korean, a Puerto Rican, and an African-American walk into an interrogation room," Kim said. "Feels like for somebody we were a joke waiting to happen."

Piñero let out a long breath. "Rimes, this just got more interesting. I'll push for the round-the-clock. Mrs. Simpkins might be a witness. We'll definitely process that hypo."

30

I got to redeem my fully punched caught-a-cop-killer card after all. Piñero woke up Deputy Commissioner Shallowhorn and explained everything. Also, he reminded her I had done a solid for the department six weeks earlier. She authorized protection until Mona Simpkins was discharged and ordered Piñero to review the notes of the detectives working both cases.

I reached home at six and called Oscar's cell to tell him to sleep in because Mona now had police protection. To my surprise, Louisa answered. Oscar was in the shower, she said, and Winslow was still asleep. But they had told her everything so I didn't need to try leaving a message in some kind of silly man code. Sorry, she couldn't see my smile, I told her what happened at the hospital and downtown. "Glad it was you there, not Oscar and Win," she said. "My husband is more than ready to help, but he's not as young as he thinks he is."

"Thank him for me," I said. "I'll talk to all of you soon."

Next, I sent separate text messages to Carl Williamson and Jen Spina. I gave Carl Oscar's phone number, in case he wanted to reach out to Win, and Mona's room number, if he wanted to visit. Jen's message included a reassurance to Keisha that her parents were now safe and a request that she call me some time that afternoon. A subsequent text went to Ileana, Cassidy, and Yvonne, telling them to stand down because I now knew where Keisha was. I thanked them all for their help, giving extra praise to Yvonne for pointing me in the right direction. Then I fell into bed without waiting for replies.

I woke at ten past one and had a fried egg sandwich and apple juice before showering. As I ate, I checked my phone. Three responses, one missed call. At eight Carl had thanked me for letting him know and said he'd take Rhonda to visit Mona soon. Shortly before nine and fifteen minutes later, respectively, Cassidy and Yvonne both typed *You're welcome.* Yvonne reminded me I had promised to introduce her to LJ. I texted back that it was exam week but that I would keep my promise by the weekend. The missed call had come from Ileana just before noon. No message. I was just about to return her call when the phone vibrated in my hand.

LJ.

"Hey, G! I got your stuff done." He sounded cheerful. Probably the thought of the check I would send him.

"Already?"

"I had it last night. I woulda called this morning but I had an exam" He chuckled. "It was simple, once I unmasked every section and printed it all out. Kinda like a jigsaw puzzle with sentences and paragraphs. I'll email it to you after this call."

"So what was it?" I asked. "The short version."

"It was actually three documents, all about taking over some low-cost apartments and renovating them into upscale condos—*very* upscale places. It was a company I never heard of, FBF Development, Flame Bright Fame. Know anything about them?"

"No."

"They're not super-rich—in fact, just a few years old. But they've got projects going in a handful of cities. Detroit, Cleveland, Pittsburgh. Now Buffalo, soon Rochester."

"Nothing in Chicago? New York or Philly?"

"No."

I thought about that for a moment. Rust Belt cities with populations well under a million. I wondered what, if anything, that meant. "Any other information about them?"

"I'll put some links in the email to the company website and a couple articles. Also, my bill. It'll cover the two new first-person-shooters I want to get, so thank you *very* much."

"Would it be enough for a night on the town with a nice young lady?"

LJ snorted. "Yeah, if I had one."

I laughed and said, "I know somebody who wants to meet you. Who's dying to meet you. She works with Keisha Simpkins." Then I told him about Yvonne, that she had finished the program right before he started so she had maybe four or five years on him. Something she read about him in a newsletter made her want to meet him. I described her in detail and said I found her strikingly attractive.

"So she's about my height, older, and *bald*?" He was quiet a moment. "She have cancer or something?"

"I don't think so. I think it's just a choice. Is bald a problem?"

"No!" he said quickly. "I'm just trying to picture her. So far I'm seeing the women in *Black Panther*, and they're hot. But I'm wondering why she wants to meet *me*."

"She said the newsletter made you sound like a genius and your picture was cute." I thought of quoting Oscar Wilde—*the only thing worse than being talked about*—but leveled with him instead. "Maybe she wants to pick your brain for something because you both speak Geek. But she could want more." I heard him take a deep breath. "Never know if you don't take a chance."

After we clicked off, I texted Yvonne and told her I had talked to LJ and she should expect a call or text from him in a few days.

Once the dishwasher was loaded, I opened my laptop, logged into IntelliChexx, and entered Harlow Graves. Born in Rochester. A string of addresses from Monroe County to New York City, where he had completed Columbia Law School, to suburban Buffalo, where he now lived. No liens. No bankruptcies. No criminal record. No bar association censures. Married to Rosalind Morrow-Graves, a Buffalo native and Williamsville elementary school teacher. Two girls in their teens. In addition to their sprawling home in suburban Amherst, the family owned a summer cottage on Lake Ontario in the Niagara County town of Barker, which had very few persons of color. Facebook showed Morrow-Graves was a light-skinned woman with long hair and daughters of similar complexion. Google revealed Graves was the type of lawyer who navigated the intersection of corporate law, personal injury litigation, and criminal defense. He had represented several area companies in a variety of capacities, from mergers to complex lawsuits, and won six and seven-figure personal injury settlements. He had defended Greater Buffalo Oncology Solutions in a Medicare fraud case and, in a drunk driving case tailor-made for local news rivalries, a prominent TV anchor who had struck and killed a college student bicyclist. In his more than two-decade career, Graves had received numerous professional and service awards, served on a *very* long list of not-for-profit boards, and handled many cases *pro bono*. Nothing in his resume suggested connections to any kind of organized crime.

So why had he come for the woman who tried to kill Mona?

I let that question settle into the back of my mind where parts of myself that I didn't understand would work on finding an answer. Opening my email, I retrieved the documents LJ had promised and skimmed through them. Two of the reconstructed files were investment pitches. Flame Bright Fame invited investors to partner in the purchase of two properties adjacent to Buffalo's growing medical corridor, for development as high-end residences for medical professionals. The language was a touch overdone, as was sometimes the case for educated people who thought fancy words equaled good writing. The third document was an internal memo that discussed successful techniques employed in other regions for getting reluctant owners to sell at low prices that made them feel they had outsmarted the buyers. Among these were aggressive intervention with assessors, which I took to mean bribes, and a suggestion that RoofRaiser, an experimental customer relationship management real estate database I had never heard of, could lower property values to favorable levels. All three documents carried the name QC Griffin, board chair —someone I would look for when I clicked the links from LJ.

Apart from the obvious manipulation, nothing stood out to me then—except that poor people would be sacrificed in another round of feeding the rich while they were still at the trough. Then I thought of the woman I had met the other night at the bar association dinner, whose brother, Judge Chancellor, was the new man in Mayor Ophelia Green's life. Glendora Chancellor-Pratt. Gentrification had been a central concern in her failed Common Council campaign. Perhaps she knew something about FBF. I made a note to contact her.

My phone buzzed. A text from Jen: *No meet til parents out of town. She'll call u.*

Before I could key in a reply, the phone vibrated again with an incoming call. Ileana.

"Gideon? It's great news you found Keisha!" She sounded breathless, but not quite with excitement. "Have you talked to her yet?"

"Still working on the details," I said. "But she's safe for now." I paused. "Thanks again for all you've done."

"Can't wait to see her." Something in her voice caught. "But that's not why I called."

"What is it, Ileana?"

"Veronica. She called me at the office this morning."

"She did?"

"She called out of the blue and said they had made her do something she didn't want to and now they were after her so she had to get away."

"After her? Who are *they*? What did they make her do?"

"She wouldn't say, but she sounded scared. She asked me for money so she could get a bus ticket."

I fought the sigh that wanted to follow the breath I took in. "Intercity bus companies require photo ID these days. Does she have one?"

"I don't know." Ileana was quiet for a moment. "Even if she does, after all she's been through, she doesn't look the same. Nobody will ever think she's a doctor or even a driver. She presents as a substance abuser or someone with mental health issues."

"Or both," I said.

"The way she smells, they won't even let her in the bus station much less on the bus."

I agreed with Ileana's take on the invisible cloud that enveloped her friend but kept that thought to myself. "Could she want the money for drugs?"

"Maybe." She paused to consider, and when she spoke the hesitation left her voice. "She's always on the make for drug money, but she never asked for a bus ticket before."

"She never asked you," I said. "Could have asked somebody else." I waited for a response. When none came, I added, "You're going to give it to her, aren't you?"

"That's just it. I was supposed to meet her twenty minutes ago at the Walgreens down the street and give her a hundred bucks for food and a ticket to her sister's in Syracuse. She didn't show."

31

D r. Glendora Chancellor-Pratt lived in a modern home on Carlton Street, a few blocks away from the school where she had taught for eighteen years and served as assistant principal and later principal for nine. Her study was a paneled room to the left of the front entrance. The shelves were full of books and trophies. The walls held framed citations that included her doctorate. In casual brown slacks and a matching headwrap, with a loose-fitting white top between, she sat behind an antique wooden desk. Closed laptop pushed aside, she held a mug of herbal tea in both hands. I sat opposite her, my notebook open, my mug on a coaster. I asked her to explain gentrification to me as if I were ten.

"I hardly think such simplification is necessary, Mr. Rimes," she said. "Gideon—if you'll call me Glennie. After decades of teaching, I have a theory—unproven scientifically, of course—that the eyes are as much a window to the intellect as they are to the soul. What I see in your eyes tells me you already grasp the concept."

Her manner was calm but authoritative, her voice strong but pleasant. She was clearly someone who had talked for a living and was accustomed to adjusting tone and word choice to the responses she got. She reminded me of Bobby. I liked her.

"Shakespeare would agree, Glennie, but he might make an exception in my case."

She laughed. "All right. Let's start with this house. We had it built, Will Henry and I, twenty-five years ago, after our first home, which sat on this very lot for almost a century, burned down from faulty wiring—which was the fire investigator's way of saying our fuse box was so damn old it melted."

"You decided to rebuild instead of relocating."

"We could have left, gone to the suburbs," she said. "But we both believed it was important to maintain a stable middle class presence in this community." She sipped her tea. "Fortunately, it was during one of those periodic waves of urban renewal. Our insurance was supplemented by federal funds so we could do more than just replace what we had lost. The end product was something that looked very suburban, right in the heart of the Fruit Belt. The year it was finished we began the tradition of having my last-day-of-school class picnic in the back yard. When I was principal, I made it an end-of-the-year staff cookout. Students and teachers alike who have moved on or moved away drop by when they're in the neighborhood or in town, just to see how I'm doing. They remember this place fondly."

"It's a lovely house," I said.

"And a loved house," she said. "Will Henry was an engineer and helped design it. He was very proud of his work, especially this study and the solarium out back."

Because the lot next door was vacant, I had noticed the oval-shaped solarium when I walked from my car to the house. In the snow-covered yard, it resembled a transparent igloo. "I'm sure you'll get a good price if you sell, but somehow I don't think you will."

Glennie shook her head, sadly. "He had rheumatic fever as a child. His heart gave out nine years ago, in the bedroom right above us. But I still feel it beating in every room. I know it's very Poe, but I hope you don't find it *too* creepy."

"Not at all," I said. "I was raised by an English teacher."

She laughed again, harder this time. Then she said nothing for a few seconds. "I've had offers, even without a FOR SALE sign out front. That was one reason I ran for the Council seat. Will Henry and I were big proponents of *economic* integration. Like many black folks back in the red-lining days, we grew up in neighborhoods shared by white-collar and blue-collar workers and a handful of welfare recipients. Kids with fathers and mothers who worked factory jobs to provide a middle class life played and went to school and church with the children of black office workers, doctors, lawyers, people who owned corner stores, beauty parlors, and barbershops. Even the poorest kids saw examples of the fruits of hard work. Then came the civil rights movement and later race riots and so-called *unrest*. Lots of folks who *could* afford to move *did*. Housing equality was important but the poverty left in its wake grew more and more concentrated."

"Which made upward mobility harder." I sipped my tea, a berry blend.

"Exactly. Then factories began to close. Unions began to die. The entire middle class, not just black folk, started backsliding, even before jobs and businesses fled to the suburbs. For blacks, what could no longer be done by law was now done by wage suppression and limited public transportation. If you don't have a car, how do you get to a job where the busses don't run? How can you move up to the middle class if you can't even get to the interview?"

"You can't," I said.

"The saving grace for the minimum wage worker, and the retiree with a piece of a pension, was always a poor neighborhood where they could pay the rent, even if they had to buy overpriced food from corner stores run by new immigrants who hand-painted their signs. That's what this area became. But when you have economic development without economic integration, things change again. Once you build a high-tech medical corridor with jobs most neighborhood people just don't qualify for and then convert empty factories and warehouses to expensive lofts and condos and upscale markets, poor folk and even the immigrant store owners get pushed out and have nowhere to go." She set her mug down and leaned forward, looking straight at me. "The politicians, bankers, and developers tell us this is urban renewal, but it's urban displacement fueled by greed. When there's money to be made dead ahead, poor people are like a road-block made of helium balloons. That's why I ran, with the support of several neighborhood associations. But I lost to the incumbent. I didn't know Ophelia then and had no idea she was the woman Hal had begun to see. Maybe her endorsement would have made a difference."

"You don't see Mayor Green as part of the local political network?"

"Not entirely. She broke through the Buffalo Boys' Club to become mayor, even if she does work hand-in-glove with some of those threatening our neighborhoods. I could have provided a balance and helped keep her responsive to the people." Recitation finished, she leaned back. "Does my explanation meet your simplicity requirements, or were you testing me?"

"It tells me you're the one to ask about efforts to gentrify. Are you familiar with any of the developers?"

"The usual suspects. Benderson, Ellicott, McGuire, a few smaller companies, like Onyx Global Group. Merlotta dropped their proposal just a few weeks ago, right after the old man lost his run for mayor. Uniland submitted a new one the next day. So many projects and proposals are floating around nobody can say for sure what's going to happen."

Now I leaned toward her. "Ever hear of FBF, Flame Bright Fame? I know, a strange tag for a developer. The board chair is one QC Griffin? Male? Female?"

"A small outfit," she said, thoughtfully rotating her mug as it sat on its coaster. "An upstart out of Detroit. Looking for investors and hoping to get a foothold somewhere as pay-to-play practices collapse under public pressure. Griffin is a man, I think, but I don't know much about him. A college kid doing research for our neighborhood groups found another name, somebody who actually runs the company but keeps a low profile. Dante Cuthbert."

I wrote *Dante Cuthbert* in my notebook, right beside *QC Griffin*.

We talked a bit more as we finished our tea. After she answered all my questions about gentrification, we drifted onto other topics, including my friendship with Ophelia and her late husband Danny. But when Glennie pointed to an award and recited its backstory, and then did the same with a citation, I figured it was time to leave. I pocketed my notebook, stood, and thanked her for the tea.

She stood too, accepting my outstretched hand and holding it a few seconds too long.

"Gideon," Dr. Glendora Chancellor-Pratt said, "I know I'm somewhat older than you and I know from Ophelia you have a lady friend, a lawyer. Now, I don't wish to embarrass you or in any way make you uncomfortable, but I like you. I get the feeling you like me too."

"You're very likable, Glennie," I said. "But I—"

She leaned across the desk and silenced me with two fingertips pressed to my lips. "I just want you to know if things don't work out with your friend, I'm available, for occasional comfort. I'm not interested in another marriage or keeping house with another man. But there are things I miss, things I don't want to give up just yet." She withdrew her fingers, put them to her lips for a moment, and smiled. "I can be very adventurous."

I returned the smile. "Even with Will Henry's heart beating in every room?"

Glennie shrugged. "It's been a while, but I've been known to tell him to close his eyes or go wait in the solarium."

We both laughed but her face grew serious again almost instantly.

"When you tell your lover about this—and if you're the man I think you are, you will—please promise me that you'll be kind. That you'll both laugh with me and not at me."

"Promise," I said.

32

On Thursday morning, Veronica Surowiec was found face down in the Black Rock Canal. Tangled in submerged tree roots along the east bank and bobbing amid chunks of ice, she was spotted at dawn by an employee of the nearby Buffalo Sewage Treatment Plant and recovered from the water by eight. But the body went unidentified until late afternoon. A fingerprint check led to an earlier drug arrest and, finally, to the Humanitas Institute.

Ileana called me around four and told me, tearfully, that detectives were on their way to take her to view a body they thought was Veronica. She asked me to accompany her inside for the formal identification. I agreed to meet her outside the building.

The Erie County medical examiner's office was located at the rear of ECMC, the county medical center. I got there before Ileana, parked in the lot some distance away, and walked to the entrance. Five or six minutes later, a gray unmarked police car rolled into the parking lot and stopped near my Escape. To my surprise, Terry Chalmers climbed out of the driver's seat. Wearing his brown fedora, Rafael Piñero got out on the passenger side and opened the door to the back. He offered a hand to Ileana, who got out and waved to me from across the lot.

Chalmers walked toward me, bald head covered by a knit watch cap and dark face wearing a scowl. His hands were jammed in the pockets of his long leather coat. It was obvious they were balled into fists. Even at a normal pace, his long legs would have covered the distance more quickly than Ileana's. But he strode faster today, bearing down on me with an urgency I had not seen in the couple months I'd known him.

"Imagine my surprise," he said when he reached me, voice deeper than usual, "when that nice lady told me if we got here early, she would have to wait for her friend Mr. Rimes before going inside. I only know one guy named Rimes, so this shit's gotta be complicated."

"You and Rafael aren't my only pals, Terry," I said. "I may not be in George Bailey territory, but my friendship portfolio is pretty healthy."

"Fuck this guy Bailey and your portfolio! I want to know if this is related to the mess downtown the other night. You know, that missing overdose survivor whose mother caught a drive-by bullet and would've caught an air bubble in the heart or lungs if you hadn't clocked a meth head with a water pitcher to keep her from sticking a needle into Mama's vein."

"Good summary."

"Rafael's report was good enough to get Shallowhorn to authorize protection for your client and for us to review two other investigations, which means serious attention to detail."

"I don't know if it's related," I said as Piñero and Ileana joined us. I moved to Ileana, whose eyes were red-rimmed, and put an arm around her shoulders. "Ms. Tassiopulos works with Dr. Simpkins, the woman whose parents hired me. Ileana's been helping me, giving me background details, introducing me to other colleagues and acquaintances."

Ileana confirmed what I said with a nod.

"I understand you found Dr. Simpkins," Chalmers said. "If somebody popped her mother to draw her out, she must know something we need to know. Where is she?"

"Moving around and communicating by phone," I said.

"Got a number?" Piñero said, the tips of his ears reddening from the cold.

"Different numbers." I shrugged. "Borrowed phones, burners maybe. When her mom is released and her folks are safely out of town, she'll come to me. Talk to me then, okay?" I looked at Ileana and squeezed her shoulder. "Right now, there's another matter."

"They said she was found near the goddamn sewage treatment plant," Ileana said, her voice cracking. "She deserved better than that."

Chalmers led us through the Family and Visitors Entrance into a corridor with mint green walls. I unzipped my jacket and pocketed my watch cap. As we passed the dry-erase on-duty board, I noticed that Mira was listed as working. She knew Chalmers and Piñero and had high opinions of them, but neither she nor I had ever disclosed to them we were foster siblings, raised in the same home and as close as any biological brother and sister. Their awareness of that would have compromised their professional relationship with her and our relationship with each other, especially when she bent the rules to help me on a case. On the way to the viewing window, a balding, white-coated staffer named Kevin led us past a closed office door that bore the nameplate MIRA POPURI, M.D. I did not expect to see my sister because she spent so much time in the autopsy room. But I listened anyway for the sounds of U2, whom she often listened to while doing paperwork. The office was quiet.

We stopped at the end of the corridor. Kevin explained what would happen and then opened a dark curtain. He stepped aside as we gathered at the rectangular window. A bony-looking body lay on a stainless steel table, beneath a sheet that didn't quite cover the matted blonde hair. An autopsy technician on the other side of the glass folded back the sheet an inch or two below the shoulders. Already the clothing had been removed and cataloged, the body likely weighed and measured. But no incision had yet been made.

Ileana caught her breath at the sight of her emaciated friend. "That's her," she said, swallowing hard. "That's Veronica Surowiec." Then she buried her face in my sweater and began to cry.

The corpse's face should have been a puffy pinkish-blue, blood having settled there as she floated face down. Her upper lip was split, rotting teeth visible behind it. One cheek was gashed, the other swollen, and her jaw dislocated. None of that had been caused by her position in the water. The upper surface of the skin we could see was a bloodless white, with puckered sores visible on the shoulders and scapulae. If she had died soon after speaking with Ileana, she might have been in icy water for nearly two days before being transferred to refrigerated storage. The absence of signs of decay was to be expected, but I was certain drowning was not the cause of death. Nor was the bluish-gray discoloration on the back of the shoulder facing the glass, the right color to suggest hypothermia. Veronica had taken her last breath well before immersion and exposure to the cold. She had been struck in the face—at least three or four times—and had lain on her back long enough for *livor mortis* to set in. Whatever the COD, somebody had dumped her in the canal. Gazing over Ileana's head, I exchanged looks with Chalmers and Piñero. Their expressions said they had reached the same conclusion, even before I had.

Homicide.

"Like she was sewage," Ileana said, shuddering against me and gripping my sweater with her fist. "Just another piece of shit to flush away."

So much for Nasty Nica, I thought.

After closing the curtain, Kevin extended his sympathy and offered to direct Ileana to a grief counselor located elsewhere in the hospital. She declined. Then he led us around a corner to a well-furnished office where she signed several forms, including one that indicated she would claim the body when it was released. Once the copies were in separate wire letter baskets, he handed Chalmers a chain of custody form and an itemized list of what had been collected from or near the body. Everything had been transferred to Central Police Services on Elm Street for processing in the forensics lab. After scanning the list, Chalmers passed it to Piñero, who studied it before handing it to me.

One yellow wool coat, torn and dirty.

Remembering the filthy coat she had worn at Sanctuary Nimbus, I held the list so Ileana and I could read it together. There wasn't much. Coat. Cap. Three shirts, two pairs of leggings, and two pairs of socks, all worn in layers and cut from the corpse with blunt-tipped scissors, along seams where possible. Fingerless gloves inside knitted mittens. Split sneakers. Scarves. Plant debris and trash had been collected from the fabrics, rips and stains noted, pockets emptied. A few coins and two wet dollars. No jewelry. No underwear. No bra. No—

"She carried bags, didn't she?" I said to Ileana. "Cloth shopping bags, I think."

"Probably stolen," she said. "More than half a million people sleep on the streets every night in this country. They're robbed, raped, assaulted, murdered—and nobody cares. The richest fucking country in the world and nobody gives a shit!"

None of us said anything as fresh tears rolled down Ileana's cheeks. After a moment she wiped her eyes and accepted the arm I offered. I handed the list back to Piñero. Kevin guided us back to the corridor that would take us to the exit. Chalmers took the lead once more. We passed Mira's office again. This time she stepped out, gowned and gloved, face covered by a protective plastic shield—as if she had been present for the removal of clothing and collection of trace evidence and was ready to resume the procedure as soon as we left.

Our eyes met for barely a second before she turned to Chalmers and Piñero.

"Detective sergeant. Detective." She nodded to each. "Nice to see you."

"Dr. Popuri," Chalmers said, as Piñero returned the nod. "We're done with the personal identification." He angled his head toward Ileana, who still held my arm.

"Of course." Then Mira looked at me as if she had never seen me before. The dark eyes behind her splash shield twinkled with momentary mischief but held only respectful sympathy when she looked at Ileana. "You're the family? I'm so sorry for your loss."

"Only a friend," Ileana said. "She doesn't—didn't—have family." She looked up at me. "He's not my husband or boyfriend, just somebody kind enough to help me through this."

"Mr. Rimes is a private investigator," Piñero explained.

"I don't see many Sam Spade types in here," Mira said, eyeing me up and down.

She was enjoying herself so much she had chanced an in-joke. I had to bite my lip to keep from smiling. I would have to do my Bogart impression for her later, somewhere more appropriate, like Christmas dinner. As teenagers, we both had followed Bobby's suggestion that we read *The Maltese Falcon* before watching his VHS copy.

"Rimes, this is Dr. Popuri," Piñero continued. "Assistant medical examiner."

"Gideon Rimes," I said, nodding rather than reaching for a gloved hand. "Pleased to meet you, doctor. This is Ms. Tassiopulos."

"The pleasure is mine, Mr. Rimes." Mira's smile vanished when she turned back to Ileana. "Ms. Tassiopulos, I want you to know I will take great care with your friend."

"Thank you," Ileana said. She wiped her eyes with the back of her hand.

Mira excused herself and disappeared around a corner as I zipped my jacket.

Outside, Piñero to my left, I walked Ileana to the unmarked sedan. She sank into the back seat as he held the passenger side door. Chalmers looked at me over the top of the car.

"Thank you, Gideon," Ileana said. "I hope we can talk soon."

"You're welcome," I said. "We will,"

Then Piñero shut the door. He sighed, shook his head. "From the look of things, the body on that table was in terrible shape before she died." He kept his voice low so Ileana wouldn't hear through the safety glass. "I'd say she was a heavy user as well as a heavy bag."

"Truth undisputed," Chalmers said softly. "A toe tag waiting to happen."

"She was a doctor," I said, letting that fact sink in a moment. "She lost her way."

"She was still a user, and abused," Piñero said. "What is it with you and druggies anyway? That's two in just a couple of days."

"Three, if the other doctor he's talking to is a user too," Chalmers said.

"By the way." Piñero snapped his gloved fingers—which made a small thump. "Got your girlfriend's prints back from the other night." He took a notebook from his coat pocket and thumbed it open. "Felicity Sillers." He spelled the surname. "An arrest record from here to Pittsburgh, mostly Southern Tier, mostly petty. Drug use. Solicitation. Public lewdness. Public intoxication. On the way here I half expected her to be the one under the sheet."

"Guess she lost her way too," Chalmers said.

"Easy to do mixing it up with Rimes," Piñero said.

I ignored the dig. "Either of you ever hear of a guy named Dante Cuthbert?"

Both detectives shook their heads.

"He got something to do with this?" Piñero asked.

"I don't know yet. I just came across the name in my investigation."

Chalmers threw up his hands. "Course you did. Local boy?"

"I think he's out of Detroit."

"Is he even here?"

"Maybe," I said.

Piñero laughed. "This just gets better and better, Terry."

"Maybe we just came across another murder that could have been prevented if you weren't stumbling through your investigation like a kid in a cookie factory," Chalmers said. "You gotta talk to us, Rimes. Plus, we gotta sit down with Dr. Simpkins."

"Soon as I get something you can use, I'll bring her in," I said.

"Fine, but I want to see *you* tomorrow. Let's say noon."

"I'll provide the cookies and milk," Piñero said.

Without waiting for my confirmation, Chalmers opened the door, sank behind the wheel, and keyed the ignition.

Piñero opened the front passenger door as the car rumbled to life but stopped before climbing inside. "Man, I think that pathologist likes you. The way she looked at you, she was seriously flirting. Hey, if Phoenix comes to her senses and dumps your sorry ass, you got options. Very pretty options."

I shook my head. "Dr. Popuri looks too smart to hang out with a guy like me."

Piñero laughed and said, "Truth undisputed."

I gave him my most innocent grin as he got in the car. "Besides, she reminds me of my sister."

33

After reading Mira's text—*Fun not knowing you. Talk tomorrow*—I spent more than three hours on IntelliChexx and other restricted search engines that evening. I copied and pasted into separate files every bit of information I could find on Dante Cuthbert, QC Griffin, and Flame Bright Fame. By ten-thirty I had more than twenty pages to print and add to the envelope that held Keisha's files.

Just before I went to bed, I got a text from Jen Spina: *Mom out in a.m. We're taking everyone to family out of state. Back by tomorrow night. Keisha will call early Saturday.*

In the morning I joined Bobby for breakfast.

As he stirred sausage, eggs, tomatoes, mushrooms, and peppers in his favorite cast iron skillet and sprinkled in shredded cheddar, I set plates, utensils, and coffee mugs on the counter. While we ate the frittata, I summarized my investigation. Having sat with Mona, he already knew several names of those involved, so I saw no need to withhold new names and new developments. It was as if I were rehearsing what I would say to Chalmers and Piñero.

I told him about the attempted break-in at the Simpkins home, the Navigator that followed me, my interviews with Reverend and

Mrs. Markham, Ileana and her co-workers, Keisha's oldest friends and her ex-boyfriend, Carl Williamson, even Glendora Chancellor-Pratt, though I kept her proposition to myself. I described the trip to Sanctuary Nimbus, the hospital fight with Felicity Sillers, her rescue from Interview One by Harlow Graves, and Veronica Surowiec before her autopsy. Finally, I showed him Keisha's documents from Flame Bright Fame.

"Do you think it's some kind of hostile take-over?" he asked after skimming several pages. "Hostile enough to kill for?"

"Maybe," I said. After a swallow of coffee, I continued. Dante Cuthbert and QC Griffin were also names Bobby had not heard before. Now he listened attentively as I recounted what I had learned of them and even held off interrupting me until I finished my recitation.

Both had been born in Detroit, forty-six years ago, five months apart. Dante was the oldest of four children and the only boy born to Rod and Lizzy Cuthbert, both auto workers. Dante's cousin Quentin Cuthbert Griffin was an only child born to Rod's sister Paula, who died in childbirth, and her husband Archie, who signed over care of his newborn son to his brother-in-law and sank into an alcoholism so intense cirrhosis claimed his life less than a decade later. Dante and Quentin were raised as brothers. When they were thirteen, Quentin was hit and killed by a car as the two crossed a street. For a time Dante was in and out of trouble but he straightened up by tenth grade and attended Eastern Michigan on a scholarship. After graduation, he took a job in a finance company. Ten years later, he established FBF to buy, rehabilitate, and sell abandoned houses in the inner city, many of which had sat empty for decades. Unlike other developers, FBF prospered during the subprime mortgage crisis, because their homes were affordable even as the market collapsed. Dante began a slow expansion during the economic recovery. The company was still small enough to avoid the scrutiny invited by larger organizations but apparently successful enough to establish a presence in mid-sized cities eager to attract young professionals with new developments.

"The question," Bobby said, "is how a dead boy got to be chairman of the board."

"Probably the same way he worked part-time jobs in his teens and twenties and even earned a GED," I said. "I have a theory."

"But I thought you said he finished high school and went to EMU."

"*Dante* did," I said. "*Quentin* got the GED. Dante had access to his dead cousin's birth certificate and social security card. Both have driver's licenses, employment histories, tax returns. Quentin wears glasses while Dante doesn't, but their faces in DMV photos look the same. For years they shared an address, but now they live in different places, twenty miles apart, Dante in a Brush Park condo with a wife and Quentin in a studio apartment on Woodward Avenue near Pontiac. Neither one, by the way, has ever been arrested."

"Of course not," Bobby said. "Dante probably had to be finger-printed and bonded to work in finance. Quentin's getting arrested would ruin that." He ate another forkful of the frittata. "What about the parents? Do they know all this?"

"Can't say. Rod died when Dante was still in high school, Lizzy three years ago."

"So he established a separate identity because he anticipated it would be useful—lower taxes if total income isn't lumped together, a wife in a condo and maybe a girlfriend in the studio. There are prob-ably other angles we don't know yet. That's pretty calculating." Bobby thought for a moment. "But why bring them together? Why make your dead cousin board chair? Won't other board members notice a resemblance?"

"If there are other board members. It could all be a front for something else."

Bobby excused himself and went into his living room, which had floor-to-ceiling bookcases and even a rolling library ladder. Several minutes later he returned with a thick paperback and took his stool again.

"I remembered something," he said. "One of my hobbies is etymology."

"Everything is one of your hobbies if it involves reading," I said. "Word origins?"

He smiled. "Yes. Take window. It's from the Old Norse *vind*, for wind, and *auga*, for eye. Thus window means *wind eye*. Sometimes in a child's drawing of a house—"

"The windows look like eyes," I said. "You just can't stop teaching, can you?"

"True, but I think you'll find this one interesting." He opened the book and turned it around so I could see the page. "Given names and surnames have meanings too." He pointed to my name on the page. "Gideon, for example, means *destroyer* or *warrior*."

"From the Old Testament."

"My name, Robert, means *bright glory*. The *-bert* names are all related because the *-bert* root means *bright*. Robert. Herbert. Norbert. Albert." He flipped to another page and tapped. "Cuthbert. It means *bright fame*."

"Cuthbert gave a form of his surname to his company?"

"What does that tell you about him?"

I thought for a moment. "He's a narcissist who plasters his name on things, in code. Add to that a second identity and you've got a secretive narcissist." I shrugged. "Educated enough to know the etymology. Clever enough to have a back-up identity if something goes wrong. That means he's formidable. He's—" I whispered the name Dante Cuthbert and the company name once more. Then it hit me, and I looked across the counter at my godfather. "Dante."

Bobby's smile widened. "What's the best-known part of *The Divine Comedy*?"

"Dante's *Inferno*," I said. "Flame Bright Fame. He named the whole damn company after himself as if he shares his identity with it."

My phone vibrated. I took it from the pocket of my jeans and looked at the screen.

Mira.

34

I don't see any cookies and milk," I said.

In dark slacks and a heavy green sweater, Terry Chalmers sat behind his desk in the squad room, which was busier than it had been the other night—voices, ringing telephones, clicking computer keyboards. Tan suit jacket unbuttoned and a round toothpick in his mouth, Rafael Piñero straddled a steel folding chair beside the desk, his arms resting atop the back. As I took the chair across from Chalmers, and put my manila envelope on the desk, they looked at each other for a few seconds. Then Chalmers sighed and leaned forward to pull a wallet out of his back pocket. He took out a ten and gave it to his partner, who pocketed it.

"A bet whether we'd have to go get you," Piñero said. "My faith was not misplaced." He took out the toothpick and made a sad face. "But I hear Cookie Monster got busted last night trying to pick up a hooker on Genesee Street. Means you're shit outta luck on snacks."

Chalmers stood, several file folders in hand. "Too noisy here. Interview Two is free."

Picking up my envelope, I followed them to the same windowless, pale green interrogation room where I'd spent a Sunday morning back in October. This time, however, I was dressed in more than shorts and a T-shirt. Nor would I be cuffed to the table ring. I pulled a chair to one end of the rectangular table and sat. Piñero took the opposite end, and Chalmers sat on the interrogator's side, tapping his file folders with a ballpoint pen.

"Two city homicide cops, one retired CID investigator, and nobody wants to sit in the suspect chair," I said, putting my envelope on the table. "Interesting."

"Okay, Rimes, no smart-assedness from here on out," Chalmers said. "You too, Raf."

"All right," Piñero said.

Chalmers sighed. "We got enough work to do on a normal day—if there is such a thing around here—without having to waste time on every crazy idea you get, G. But I spent part of last night and most of this morning going over that overdose case and the old lady's shooting." He made a clicking sound with his tongue. "Shit doesn't add up."

"You've been a cop a long time," I said. "What stinks to you?"

Chalmers crossed his arms and let out a long breath. "First, the autopsy report on the dead teacher. Height, weight, skin condition, teeth, general appearance of health—there was nothing in there to suggest *any* drug habit. Good veins, no tracks or needle marks. No sneaky injection sites, like between the toes. No damaged nasal tissue. No lung or heart damage. All that's not to say he couldn't overdose his first time riding the horse, but it feels wrong."

"Narcotics buttoned it up quick because it was just another tragic opioid death," Piñero said. "The ME says the COD was an overdose. The tox screen says heroin and China Girl. If folks off themselves by accident and the evidence supports it, the case is closed quickly."

"Right," Chalmers said. "The detectives saw no bruising to suggest either one had been held down and injected by force. Williamson's prints were on the hypo they both used."

"A gun," I said. "Somebody puts a gun to your head or points it at somebody you love and says swallow this or inject that, what do you do? You take it because lots of people get high without dying but not too many come back from a double-tap to the head." I paused. "How are you supposed to know it's laced with enough fentanyl to kill you?"

"That brings us to the second thing," Chalmers said, thumbing his pen button. "Why? I don't mean why go to the trouble of making this look like an overdose. That's easy. It won't be the same kind of investigation. But why do it at all? What's the motive?"

"Not robbery," Piñero said. "They both had money on them when they were found, not enough to suggest dealing, but amounts that fit their jobs. Maybe payback?"

"For what?" I said. "I haven't found a single person who thinks either one of them was using. Or hung around users. Or suppliers. But before we go there, what about the guys who said Odell was dealing? There were supposed to be three informants."

"Weren't ours," Chalmers said. "Somebody fed that straight to a reporter at the *News*. Everybody ran with it, even the DA by not charging the survivor. How's that for fake news?"

"The finest kind," I said. "The little lie that doesn't get a lot of attention. No tweets. No deflections. It just sits there, without controversy, doing its job, day after day."

"Then there's shooting at the parents," Chalmers said. "The detectives on that haven't found anything solid but some brass in the street, 9mm casings with no usable prints. They looked into Mr. and Mrs. Simpkins. He's retired from the goddamn gas company. She gets social security from a lifetime of jobs in retail stores. Solid salt-of-the-earth church folk. Fixed income, a paid-off house in the inner city. These kinds of people aren't targeted unless it's for robbery. They're collateral damage, waiting to be caught in a crossfire. Except there was nobody else out on the street that day."

"Then the other night, this meth mama tries to cap the mother," Piñero said. "But you just happen to be there because none of this makes sense to you either. So you break her nose in self-defense. With no witnesses, it's a he-said-she-said, hard to make a charge stick. But then Harlow Fucking Graves comes to get her out and he doesn't even know her name."

"Which brings us back to the why." Chalmers slid a hand under his sweater to scratch an itch. "With something this elaborate, there's gotta be money at stake."

"Big money," Piñero said. "Maybe big enough to justify an interdivisional operation, like homicide and narcotics, or interagency, like BPD and DEA."

"Add to that a dead meth head," Chalmers said, opening one of his file folders and sliding it across to me. "The preliminary autopsy report. No ligature marks. No gunshot or stab wounds. No canal water in the lungs—not that we expected any. Vomit traces along the esophagus but she didn't choke on it. This Dr. Surowiec died from blunt force trauma."

I spent a few seconds skimming the report Mira had summarized in our telephone conversation earlier. Then I looked at the photos, arranged in the order in which they were taken. Between the close-ups of Veronica's face tipped forward by a headrest and the step-by-step record of the Y incision and removal of organs were pictures of a wrinkled, skeletal body. She had lost considerable muscle mass during her addiction and time on the streets. Despite an abundance of sores and various patches of skin that looked rough as sandpaper, what stood out most was the damage to her chest and abdomen, multiple bruises, two of them shaped like figure eights, and small, round-edged gashes likely caused by a ring. "Beaten to death," I said finally. "Apparently with fists. Her body was too frail to take it."

"A shitload of blows to the midsection," Piñero said. "Broken ribs, ruptured spleen, collapsed lung. A real sick fucker did this."

"We knew about the beating beforehand from seeing the body," Chalmers said. "But the extent of injury surprised even us. You'd have seen it for what it was yourself if they had lowered the sheet more."

"Fortunately, somebody was thinking of the poor woman there to confirm the identity of the victim," I said. "Her friend. You had prints and already knew there was no family. The dislocated jaw distorted the face enough to make photo ID trickier but there was no need to show Ileana the worst of it."

"Exactly," Piñero said.

Chalmers put down his pen and leveled his eyes at me. "So give us your take, G."

"Got a question first," I said.

"Sure," Chalmers said.

"You guys dug so far into this, enough that you have your own doubts, and still made a bet I wouldn't show?"

They looked at each other, and Piñero laughed. "The real bet was whether you'd remember the cookies and milk," he said. "I had faith in you, bro."

"We smart-asses have to stick together," I said.

I opened my notebook and recounted the past week, from the moment Oscar Edgerton brought Winslow Simpkins to my office to what I discovered in my second last IntelliChexx search. I shared every detail I had noted and as many additional points as I could remember, at least for things I was willing to tell them. I said nothing of Glendora's offer of sex or my breaking into the Kelly home. Nor did I mention LJ's cracking into Keisha's devices because there was no need for him to be on their radar, just as there was no need for them to know one of Keisha's best friends was married to a cop. Though I told them about the Navigator, I did not reveal that Spider Tolliver had followed me into the Towne Restaurant. Before I produced and went through all the FBF papers, I said that I had heard from Keisha and expected to meet with her tomorrow.

After reviewing them, Chalmers thought the papers Keisha had taken great pains to hide were not evidence of a crime but evidence of intent to force the sale of two properties that had the potential to become more valuable. Much of the language, he agreed, sounded as if it had come from a prospectus intended to attract investors, but none of that was criminal. Even the memo that discussed ways to manipulate sales was hardly suggestive of illegality. "Shitty business practices aren't in and of themselves against the law," he said. "This is a weak motive for forcing an overdose or beating a druggie to death."

"What if you don't want the targets of those shitty practices to get a heads-up they're in your crosshairs?"

Chalmers and Piñero looked at each other and shrugged.

"I'm still not buying it," Chalmers said. "People have the option to sell or not sell. Nothing here talks about putting a gun to somebody's head. What else you got?"

Next, we went through what I had learned about Dante Cuthbert —minus Bobby's etymology lesson—and QC Griffin. That proved more intriguing, at least to Piñero. "You know, federal witness protection has been known to make mistakes, like giving families in hiding sequential social security numbers. If this is on the level, and he actually is maintaining two working identities, this Cuthbert guy is good. Yes, it's fraud but out of our jurisdiction and tied up with a lot of real estate crap. Still no evidence of a crime *we* can investigate."

"Real estate can be useful for lots of things," I said. "Buy for a song. Rehab cheap. Sell at a modest price with a solid profit margin. Repeat. This company flips like a gymnast, especially in places ready for upscale development. Like Rafael said, big money."

"Where are those properties this outfit wants to buy?" Chalmers asked, finally.

"One is a low-income family housing complex on Best Street," I said. "The other is a senior citizens apartment building on Virginia. Both are in the Medical Park Neighborhood and both are owned by the Sermon on the Mount Community Development Foundation."

"Wait a minute." Chalmers sat forward. "That's the church where Dr. Simpkins was the secretary."

"Yes."

"So you're saying Cuthbert and his company wants to force this church to sell so those properties can be turned into upscale condos for high-income medical professionals?"

"Yes."

"That'll put a lot of people on the street," Piñero said. "Poor people. Snatch even an empty purse, it's a crime. But snatch a home away from the poor, it's just business."

I took a deep breath. "Imagine the people running the church and foundation know nothing of efforts to force a sale. Imagine they're cornered somehow and have no choice. FBF squeezes them out and sells everything to a big developer without even having to rehab the properties themselves. But forewarned is forearmed. With good legal advice, the minister and his wife might be able to block the effort and save affordable housing for people in the neighborhood. Maybe Keisha was threatened to keep her from alerting them."

"Speculation," Chalmers said. "Still, seems like there'd be a ton of bad press."

"Maybe bad enough to scuttle the project," I said.

"Maybe so much it'd cost somebody a lot of money," Piñero added.

Chalmers made a clicking sound again. "How did Dr. Simpkins get this information?"

"I'll ask her tomorrow," I said.

For a time we were all quiet as the two detectives paged through and traded sections of the documents I had brought. They were studying everything, trying to make sense of my admittedly imperfect conclusions. Now and then Chalmers scratched notes on a pad he had carried in with the folders or used his cell phone to get online and verify something he had read on one page or another. Piñero alternated between rereading a page and then staring off as if in thought. Eventually, he got up to stretch and carried a few sheets with him as he paced from one side of the interrogation room to the other. I just sat there. I sensed I was missing something but I was confident I was in the vicinity of the truth.

Finally, Chalmers broke the silence. "So, without a speck of evidence, you believe Dante Cuthbert is here in Buffalo. That he's threatened and killed people and will kill again to swing a deal that could put a lot of money in his pocket."

"I'm sure of it."

"Why?" Piñero said.

"This."

From the inside pocket of my jacket, I took out the page I had chosen not to put it in the envelope with the other documents. Now I unfolded it—a printout from an IntelliChexx search of the Michigan

DMV—and handed it to Chalmers. Piñero came over to read it over his shoulder.

"It didn't matter that I couldn't see a front plate at Delta Sonic that night because Michigan doesn't require one," I said. "Dante Cuthbert owns a black Lincoln Navigator."

35

That evening Phoenix and I dined at her favorite Italian restaurant. Vino's was on Elmwood in North Buffalo, diagonally across the avenue from a building complex that once produced the luxury Pierce-Arrows driven by Golden Age Hollywood stars and international royalty. Now it housed artist studios, drafting firms, martial arts dojos, independent social service agencies, and not-for-profit dance and theater companies. Presently, one section was being renovated into upscale condominiums—more urban development fever, but at least no poor people would be displaced by this project.

It was brisk outside, and the restaurant's steamed windows promised warmth. Having done legal work for the owners, Phoenix explained as she led me past the small statues of lions that flanked the entrance, she was always given the same quiet corner table when she made a reservation, whether she was alone or with a client. Inside, however, was anything but quiet. The front room was a crowded dining area with white tablecloths, white walls full of black and white photographs, and a dozen conversations crisscrossing in warm air that carried traces of garlic, oil, and marinara. There was a bar on one side. The slender blonde woman behind it brightened as

Phoenix waved to her and leaned across for an embrace when we were close enough.

"Theresa, *this* is Gideon," Phoenix said.

"*You're* the one she told me about!" Theresa reached across the bar and pumped my hand. "So happy to meet you, Gideon. Any friend of Phoenix is welcome here at any time. If we're full, we can always find you a seat at the bar."

"Thanks," I said. "I'm glad to meet you too." I took in a deep breath through my nose. "But if your food's as good as it smells, I'd eat it while standing in the corner."

"Oh, it is," Phoenix said to me. Turning to Theresa, she added, "He would too."

Laughing and giving Phoenix a subtle nod of approval, Theresa signaled a young red-haired woman in black—her nameplate said Amy—and asked her to lead us to our table.

We followed Amy into the second dining area, where our table was indeed in a corner. When we were seated, she placed menus in front of us, lit the votive candle inside a small glass in the center of the table, and recited the evening's specials. When she returned with our bread and a bottle of Malbec, Phoenix ordered garlic oil pasta. I chose spaghetti with pesto. We both asked for Italian sausage on the side.

"Hope you don't mind the garlic," Phoenix said when Amy left to place our order. "If it's too strong and coming through my pores, I can always stay at my place tonight."

"I'll take you any way I can get you," I said. "Besides, mine has garlic too, so I'm not defenseless. But if the night goes the way I imagine it, the garlic will be sweet as rosewater."

"You can be so corny sometimes," she said. Still, she smiled as she dipped bread into a mixture of oil and balsamic vinegar and took a bite. After the first slice was gone, she was quiet for a minute or two, sipping wine and thinking, I hoped, of what would happen later. But then she said, "What time do you expect Keisha to call in the morning?"

"The text said early. I don't know if she'll try the apartment, the cell, or my office. The office automatically bounces incoming calls to my cell. I gave her my apartment phone number. She'll have no trouble getting through. We'll decide where to meet when she does."

"Will we take her to eat?"

"Sure, if she's hungry." I dipped my second piece of bread and chewed. "At the very least I think we'll get some coffee. Somewhere we can talk."

"I can promise to be with you both when she tells her story to Rafael and Terry, if she can bring herself to trust me."

"You're better at inspiring confidence than I am. Just ask your partners."

Phoenix laughed. "If you saw the knock-down, drag-outs we have in the office—"

"No matter. Since we've been together, I haven't met anybody who dislikes you."

"Those are all people who know me. Keisha doesn't know me."

"She doesn't know me either, but people who love her convinced her to trust me," I said. "Trusting you will come easier to her. She already told me she'll do whatever we say. We just need to say the right thing."

"With all she's gone through, I'm afraid of saying exactly the *wrong* thing."

When our salads came, Phoenix steered the conversation back to Dante Cuthbert, whom we had discussed on the drive over. Because the driver's license photos I had found were old, she had used her phone in an attempt to retrieve recent pictures of Cuthbert and his alter ego through Google and social media sites. A white Dante Cuthbert in England looked to be in the British army. A brown-skinned Cuthbert in India wore a lot of superhero t-shirts. A black Dante Cuthbert in LA was clearly too young. Frustrated then, she had changed her search parameters to approach the problem from another angle. Now she took the phone from her purse and showed me several pictures of Lincoln Navigators. "Which one?"

I pointed to a newer model. "Remember these LED running lights. That's what I'll be looking for in the rearview mirror. If you see a configuration like this around the headlights and I seem not to notice, just tell me. Then get down and stay there."

She paused a few seconds before asking, "You think he'll make a run at you?"

"Frankly, it's a longshot. The office is my only public address. Very few people know where I live." Quick and Tolliver did but I hoped she had forgotten that.

"You have LJ. Maybe he's got somebody smart too. Maybe a man clever enough to have two working identities is just as good himself at digging up information."

I reached across the table with my left hand to cover her right, casually placing my fingertips near her radial artery. "His prime target is still Keisha." I spoke soothingly, all the while shifting my gaze from her eyes to the seconds display on my watch and counting in my head. "At some point, I might see him somewhere." Pulse normal so far. "But I doubt it'll be tonight." The breathing I had grown accustomed to in the past several weeks sounded even and unstressed. "Tonight is ours." Still, there was tension between us.

Releasing her hand, I speared a grape tomato with my fork and popped it into my mouth. I chewed it slowly. "So good," I said, making one silly pleasure face after another—until, finally, she cracked a smile and said how attractive chewing made me look. The next moment ended in a laugh when I recalled yesterday and told her Piñero had thought Mira was flirting with me.

We talked about other things after that. One of the great pleasures of our relationship was that we never ran out of things to discuss. That evening we covered three or four current events before our entrees came. Then Phoenix smiled at me again and said, "Eat up. You're going to need your strength."

36

On Saturday morning we showered separately so someone could answer the phone. The call came in at nine when I was toweling off. Phoenix stepped into the bathroom and handed me my cell. Then she pecked me on the lips, hung up her bathrobe, and said, "I hope you left me some hot water."

"Keisha?" I said, taking the phone into the next room as I pulled on my own robe.

"Mr. Rimes?"

"Yes."

"Was that your lawyer friend? The one you sent flowers?"

"Yes. Phoenix Trinidad." I heard the shower turn on.

"She sounds nice. It sounded so sweet, the two of you together. So normal." Her voice caught. "I want normal again."

"If your folks are safe, Keisha, we're almost there."

"They're safe."

"Good."

"So are Fatimah and her family. All out of state."

"I won't ask where." Robe soaking up the water on my back, I sat on a bistro chair at my kitchen counter and shifted the phone from my right hand to my left. A pad and pen were already there, waiting. I picked up the pen. "How and where should we meet?"

"Not here. Bianca and Jen have been so good to me I don't want them to risk anything else."

"They don't have to."

"Jen even took a couple of sick days to stay home with me in case —in case somebody showed up here."

"Is Jen with you now?"

"Yes. They both are."

"I don't need to know where they live, just where you want to meet."

"How about Tim Horton's?"

"Which one? Feels like there's one every three blocks."

She must have lowered the phone. Her voice sounded far away when she said, "He wants to know which one."

"Pick one with a single door," I said, raising my voice so they would hear me.

A knocking sound indicated the phone had changed hands.

"Rimes? It's Jen."

"Hi, Jen. Pick a Timmy Ho's with one door. That way I can watch it as we talk."

"I'll be there with my off-duty piece to cover your six," Jen said. "But I'd rather watch one door than two or three. I spent time in E District. You know the Tim's across from UB Main Street?"

"Yes. One door."

"Meet us there in forty-five minutes."

"I've got friends in homicide. My lawyer and I will take her to them afterward. She have any evidence?"

"Not that I've seen but I believe her."

"Thanks, Jen."

"Listen to her and then thank me by fixing this."

37

Keisha and company got to Tim Horton's ahead of us. In jeans and a purple down jacket that covered her gun, Jen was already seated across from the door when Phoenix and I walked in. Bianca, in a hooded green tracksuit, and Keisha, in a brown headwrap and bulky Christmas sweater, sat in cushioned armchairs near the decorative electric fireplace. Their coats held the remaining two armchairs for us. Bianca paid no attention to Jen, who seemed to be watching a soundless but captioned MSNBC program on the TV above the fireplace.

I counted six other customers seated with coffee cups and donuts or breakfast meals: three young women at the table farthest from the door, a man of grad student age typing on a laptop, a thirtysomething man in dark work clothes, and an elderly woman two tables away from Jen. A young couple stood at the counter, looking up at the lighted menu and discussing what they should order. Behind the counter were five employees—three filling orders, one working the cash register, and the last at the drive-thru window. If we kept our voices low, we could have a private conversation.

We sat. I introduced Phoenix to Keisha and Bianca. They already had coffee, as did Jen, so Bianca got in line to get a medium for each of us.

It was hard to reconcile the Keisha who sat across from me with the pretty, cheerful-looking woman I had seen in photos on her parents' mantel. The night her clumsy disguise to get into the ICU failed, her face had become a mask of terror. Now, with no make-up and her body in a hideous sweater too large to be hers, this Keisha looked more tired than afraid, more resigned than hopeful. But when our gazes met, I remembered Glendora Chancellor-Pratt's theory that the eyes were a window to the intellect. However tired the skin around them made her seem, the eyes behind Keisha's glasses were sharp and calculating.

"Being on the run is hell," I said softly, trying to set the right speaking level for all of us. "Even when you have good friends to help."

"Worse when you put your loved ones in danger." Keisha matched my volume. Good.

"But they're safe right now, so you can think past worrying about them to ending the threat to all of you." I leaned toward her. "I want to hear what happened, but how you share that is up to you. I can ask questions, you can tell your story without interruption, or we can make it a conversation. Your choice. Phoenix will clarify any legal questions. When we're done, I'll call a friend in homicide. He'll advise us what to do next. Officially."

"What about unofficially? Jen says I don't have much evidence."

Unofficially, she had a fan who would solve her problem happily if she identified the people after her. But the price of getting into bed with Spider Tolliver—and, by extension, Lorenzo Quick—was likely too high.

"We'll worry about all that later," I said. "How would you like to start?"

"I've smoked weed three times," she said. Her voice was steady and her eyes drilled into me. "I can tell you the month and year but not the day, except for that Christmas Eve party sophomore year of college. Apart from that, I've never used illegal drugs in my life."

So, it was going to be a conversation, which was fine with me.

"I believe you. Everything I know about you says I should. What about Odell?"

Keisha bit her lip and looked off for a moment. "Odell was a good man. Smart, kind, playful but gentle. His parents and friends and students all loved him. I loved him too." Her eyes moistened. She took off her glasses and wiped her eyes. "Odell didn't use drugs either, not even weed. That stuff in the paper about him being a dealer was one hundred percent Grade A Angus bullshit. He was so high on life he said he might try weed if he came down. But he never came down. Even if he did use, he didn't deserve to die like that."

Phoenix leaned forward and took Keisha's hand. "Nobody deserves to die like that."

"Tell me about that night," I said.

Bianca returned just then and set our coffees on the low table around which the chairs had been arranged. Seeing the tears, she sat and took hold of the hand Phoenix had released.

"Odell proposed at dinner that night." Smiling faintly, Keisha didn't even try to wipe her eyes. "I'd been suspecting it was coming soon. We had been talking about maybe moving in together, getting a house near apartments where our parents could live." She sniffled, and Bianca handed her a napkin. "He took me to Panorama on Seven at the Marriott downtown," she said after wiping her nose. "We sat at a table by one of those giant windows overlooking the harbor. No clouds, the lights and moon reflecting on the water—it was beautiful!"

I heard Phoenix swallow beside me as if clearing her throat. I made no move to take her hand, for fear the gesture would distract Keisha. Neither one of us had sipped coffee yet.

"He was nervous as all get-out," Keisha said. "He was so cute like that I just wanted to pinch his cheeks. He couldn't wait for the meal. He took out the box right after we ordered the wine and opened it. The ring inside was wrapped in paper, which confused me at first. He gave it to me. When I unwrapped it, I saw it wasn't a diamond ring at all. The stone was red, and the paper had been cut out of a Bible, part of a page from Proverbs."

"A price above rubies," I said. "That's what you were to him."

Blinking as more tears came, she nodded. It was apparent she needed a moment. Bianca put a hand on her shoulder and leaned as close to her as she could.

In the silence that followed, Phoenix and I both reached for our coffees and drank a little. I gave her hand a quick squeeze.

"What happened to the ring?" I asked when Keisha seemed ready to go on. I feared I already knew the answer.

"I guess they took it."

"Who took it?"

"The men who stopped us. The men who—" Shuddering, she covered her mouth with the back of her hand.

"Take your time," I said after a couple of seconds. "There's no good way to tell it. No easy way. Maybe you should start with how you got to Jefferson and Best."

She nodded again, removed her hand, and reached for Bianca's. "We took a ride after dinner. A nice long ride, just to talk, because I said yes. We drove up Main all the way out to Williamsville and then we took Union Road to the Kensington Expressway. We got off at Best because we were going back to my house. The basic route is left on Jefferson, right on High, right on Orange. But a car pulled alongside us and wouldn't let Odell get in the left lane for the turn. They forced us across the intersection, and Odell cut into the Wiley parking lot. They followed us in and pulled ahead and slammed on the brakes right in front of us. Odell tried to back up but hit a high curb. Before he could shift again two men jumped out and pointed guns at the car. Odell locked the doors but one of them put his gun right next to the driver's side window and told us to get out or get shot. We—we got out."

Keisha was squeezing Bianca's fingers bloodless, to what must have been a point of pain. But Bianca remained silent.

"Can you describe the men? Did you know them?"

"No. Both medium brown-skin, one a shade darker than the

other. Both big, the biggest one maybe your size. They looked enough alike I thought they were brothers."

"What about their car? Make? Color?"

"Big SUV. Dark, I think black. It looked black in Odell's headlights."

"You know the make?"

"No. Sorry."

"You think the car was following you all along?"

"I don't know. Must have been."

"What happened next?"

Keisha released Bianca's fingers and shifted uneasily. "They turned off our headlights and made us stand in front of the car. Between the streetlights and stadium night lights, we could see just enough. They made us take off our coats and roll up our sleeves. I still wasn't sure what was happening. At first, I thought they just wanted to rob us. But when they took out this little case that held a needle, I got really scared. I took a step back like I was gonna run. The bigger one—he was on my side of the car—he pointed his gun at me and kinda giggled. A creepy giggle, so I froze, too scared to cry. The other one, the one in charge, put the case on the hood of the car and told Odell to pick up the needle. His voice sounded familiar, but I still wanted to believe this was random bad luck. Odell picked it up and said, 'Now what?' The guy said, 'You're gonna send nosy Miss Sugar Notch here up in the elevator.' Felt like a kick in the belly, like there was no chance we could survive now. Odell said hell no, even if it meant getting shot. The guy said, 'What if you're not the one shot?' Next thing I knew I had *two* guns at my head. From then on Odell did whatever they said, right down to choosing which arm and wrapping his tie around it. He plucked the needle, squirted some out, and they said not too much. Then Odell injected some into me. They said to give me half. But I think he gave me less and saved for more himself. He gave his life to give me half a chance."

"My God," Phoenix said, so softly it was almost to herself.

"They made him leave his prints on the syringe," I said. "Do you remember anything else?"

"Everything for the first few seconds. The bigger guy told Odell, 'Your turn.' I was terrified as Odell wrapped his tie around his own arm but I never saw the needle go in. All of a sudden there was this wave of pleasure all over. Warm and tingly everywhere." Her voice dropped to a whisper. "Kind of like coming and coming and coming but without sex and without sound. Then I felt happy, drifting, peaceful, kind of like after sex when you're falling asleep."

"Do you remember the paramedics reviving you?"

"The memory is vague. I can't be sure if what I remember is real or imagined because of what I know from pharmacology class. I remember gagging, coughing. I'm pretty sure I was cold because I was shivering, but I'm not sure why. Was it because of the drug or the time of year? I kind of remember being in the car with Odell next to me, but maybe all that's from what I read in the newspaper or saw on the Eyewitness News website. I wasn't fully myself till I woke up in the hospital the next day."

We were all quiet for a time. Bianca excused herself to use the restroom. Phoenix took a deep breath, sank back in her chair, and took a hefty swallow. I heard her whisper, "Wow."

Keisha sank back in her chair also, seeming lighter somehow. Sipping what was now warm coffee, I was glad Jen was there because I had become so caught up in Keisha's story I lost all track of my surroundings, something I was unaccustomed to doing. I looked about, chiding myself for not having seen or heard the changes. There were more people now, all the previous diners except the man with the laptop having been replaced. Two were reading newspapers. Several were engaged in their own conversations.

I drank a bit more and set down my cup when Bianca returned.

"Keisha, are you good for a few more questions?" I asked.

She put her glasses back on and leaned toward me. "Yes."

"Did the police question you when you woke up?"

"Not much. I tried to tell the hospital staff what happened and was told rehab required me to take responsibility. They said I was lucky not to be charged. So when a detective came to see me later that day, he asked questions that fit the narrative, and I kept the truth to myself."

"Do you know why this happened to you and Odell?"

"Yes, I do."

"Tell us about it."

"For many years I was the secretary at my church. I took minutes at various meetings, handled basic correspondence, did the newsletter, and maintained the church's Facebook page. All pretty routine stuff because I can write and type fast. I'm good with computers and know my way around the web."

"Does the church have much of a web presence beyond Facebook?"

"There's a website but it hasn't been updated for a long time. Mostly, we used the domain and space from the provider for email and cloud storage." No longer speaking of the night her fiancé was murdered, Keisha seemed almost relaxed, matter-of-fact. "The church has a general email in its domain, which I managed as part of my duties. Dr. Markham has a personal email. So did I. Also his wife, the deacon, and deaconess board chairs, the building committee chair, the youth group mentor, the congregation president, and the treasurer."

"Sounds like a lot of bureaucracy for a church with, what, five hundred members?"

"More or less, but Dr. Markham has visions of getting bigger and branching out. He'd like to have a megachurch, not in the Texas sense with five thousand members, but enough to have two morning services and one evening service on Sunday and eventually open a branch up in Niagara Falls. He said we needed a solid administrative structure to do that."

"How could he manage three services in Buffalo and one or two in the Falls?"

"Oh, Mrs. Markham is ordained too. She would handle Niagara County."

Neither of the Markhams had mentioned that she was a minister too. I thought about that for a moment. "All that in addition to her work at the Sermon on the Mount Community Development Foundation?"

"Oh, she's dynamic. She preaches once every couple of months. She's the deputy choirmaster, back-up organist, and a community leader. When I was young I wanted to be just like her." Keisha sighed. "But it's funny you should mention the foundation. That's where all this started. Two months ago we got an email I thought was from a church member. It was a forward with documents attached. Sometimes when things needed a response I'd save them to a flash drive and take them home to work on them later. I did that with these files. When I opened them I skimmed paragraphs about selling foundation properties for huge profits. I didn't know what it was about but I figured the sender had been spoofed."

"Who was the sender?"

"Raheem Harris. He's only fourteen and addicted to PlayStation. His mother is a friend of mine." She shrugged. "The spoofing was no accident but I figured the real sender had posted it to the wrong church account. So I read through the docs more closely. This time I recognized the addresses on Best and Virginia and realized some-body was planning to force the foundation out of the benevolent landlord business. It was some company named—"

"FBF, Flame Bright Fame," I said.

"Yes. I'd never heard of them. I couldn't find much about them on the web other than they were in Detroit, which made no sense for something small in Buffalo." Her own coffee was now cold enough for her to finish it in a long swallow. She set the empty cup back on the table. "I made back-up copies of all the files because I didn't know what was going on and wanted a record. Then I went back into the church email and saw the message was gone."

"Who had access to that email?"

"The Markhams, the board chairs, the treasurer, and a couple of committee chairs."

"Did you check the log-in history to see who deleted the original?"

"I tried but the whole thing had been wiped, going back weeks."

"Whoever did it had to have seen *you* opened the email too. Did you tell the Markhams?"

"Not at first, but then I started getting calls on my cell saying I'd better not tell anybody what I knew. Different men. No voices I recognized, then. One of them said I couldn't possibly understand what I was reading. Another told me this business proposal could fall apart and bankrupt the church if it got out early so if I loved my church I'd keep it to myself. Somebody else said, 'It would be a shame, Sugar Notch, if your folks got hurt.'"

"Sugar Notch," I said. "So you knew at Wylie's it was the same man."

"Yes. I was insulted and mad but didn't take it seriously until the Sunday my purse disappeared at the monthly church luncheon and later turned up in the men's room. The only things missing were the two flash drives I kept in it. That's when I went to Mrs. Markham. I told her about the threats and the theft. I thought the foundation was in trouble. I resigned as church secretary. I knew it couldn't be everybody but the idea that somebody in my worship family could harm me or my folks was like acid poured on my faith. Once I got home, I did my best to hide the other files. If somebody got in and stole my computer, they wouldn't find any reason to hurt us. The next Sunday, during announcements, Dr. Markham told everybody I was retiring from my post as secretary because the demands of my job were so great. They gave me a standing ovation. I thought that was the end of it."

"Until you and Odell were forced into the stadium lot."

"Yes. More threats came after I got out, from the same man, so I ran." Lips pressed together, she closed her eyes, squeezing out more tears. "I tried to get off the grid. I was homeless for a week or so, roaming the streets, going from one shelter to another because I was afraid if I used a card somebody could track me. I couldn't put my family or friends in danger. But after a while—" She wiped her eyes. "It was too hard, so I called Fatimah. But even after I was in the room over her garage, I went back to homeless shelters now and then to toughen myself up, in case I brought heat on Fatimah's family and had to leave."

I took out my notebook and pen and slid them across the table to her. "Give me the names—not the titles or boards—but the names of everyone with access to that account." As she wrote, I gave her the two-minute summary of FBF's business model and expansion to other cities. She slid my notebook back across the table just as I began telling her about Dante Cuthbert. The list had seven names. I recognized only two: Custodian Tito Glenroy and attorney Harlow Graves, the church treasurer. I was forming my first question about Tito when I looked up and saw astonishment spreading across Keisha's face.

"Dante?" she said. "The guy pointing the gun at me called the man in charge Dante." She hesitated, narrowing her eyes, perhaps processing what I had said or resisting an immediate conclusion. "Cuthbert is Mrs. Markham's maiden name."

38

I should have seen it," I said again, checking my rearview mirror once more as I pulled onto the Kensington Expressway toward downtown and police headquarters. "I should have put it all together long before now. Damn it, I'm slipping in my old age."

Back in the coffee shop, Keisha had been stunned by the possibility that the man who had tried to kill her was related to the minister's wife she admired. She had said nothing as I flipped back through my notebook for all I had on Dante Cuthbert. When I found the name Melony listed as the fourth-born child of Rod and Lizzy Cuthbert, I realized I had invested so much thought in my theory Dante and Quentin were the same person that I never considered his siblings or where Loni Markham had come from. Now, with Keisha in the back seat, we were in my car and headed toward Chalmers and Piñero.

"It wasn't obvious," Phoenix said. "You were looking at two different names in two separate places. Melony Cuthbert in Detroit, Loni Markham here."

"It's not just that," I said. "It's Harlow Graves too. I skimmed some church bulletins early on but I didn't remember H. Graves, treasurer, so I never connected him to the lawyer who got Felicity Sillers out."

"*I* don't know every lawyer in town and we all belong to the same Bar Association," Phoenix said. "Why should you?"

"I don't blame you, Mr. Rimes," Keisha said. "You came looking for me and took care of my parents. You even kept that Sillers bitch from killing my mother. I'd rather you did that than sit still and think of everything."

Can't afford to sit still, I thought but did not say. *Sitting still gets you caught.*

"Listen to her, Gideon," Phoenix said. "Stop beating yourself up." She half-turned toward the back. "Keisha, I know you're disappointed, but maybe Mrs. Markham has nothing to do with her brother's business. He could be going after her foundation because he saw a weakness, a chance to score big. But the fact they're related might get somebody interested enough to look into your case deeply enough to get justice for Odell."

"I didn't deny Odell and I shot up together. What happens when I change my story?"

"You gave your statement under duress. You can recant it."

I had noticed the vintage blue Cadillac DeVille behind me on Grider a block or two before I turned onto the expressway ramp. I had noticed the broad grille in my rear-view mirror because the Cadillac emblem above it sat inside a widened V, which meant the car was decades old, though it appeared to be in excellent condition. When it turned onto the entrance ramp behind me, it ceased being a curiosity, probably driven by an elderly man who just couldn't part with it, and became a concern.

It was late Saturday morning and sunny. Last night's snow had been cleared from the expressway. Light traffic was heading deeper into the city. At first, the Caddy kept pace with me, six or so car lengths back. Now, as we passed under the Delavan Avenue overpass and emerged in the center lane on a straight shot to downtown, it began to speed up. Five car lengths. Four. Three.

The expressway began its descent below street level, to stretch nearly two miles long that had high walls at first and then sloping greenery. Over the years planners had proposed covering the walled section to make a tunnel below a restored Humboldt Parkway. A few years earlier, an elaborate action sequence for a Mutant Ninja Turtles movie had been filmed in this section. But the Caddy closing the distance between us to less than two car lengths was likely not being driven by a trained stunt man. A tap the wrong way risked forcing either car into a concrete wall or abutment. Still, the Caddy swung into the left lane and began to pull alongside us.

Just before it entered my side mirror's blind spot, the passenger window slid down.

And time began to slow.

"Get down!" I shouted, lowering my head as much as I could without taking my eyes off the road. The instant I heard the shot, *both* rear passenger windows exploded. What the hell was he shooting? A second shot punched through my door, and I felt it tear through the width of my seatback. Phoenix and Keisha both let out full-throated screams, which I prayed meant neither had been hit. If this had been a movie, I might have reached for my gun and fired back with my left hand—after I lowered the window, of course. But it wasn't a movie, and as someone who remembered how hard it had been to get a cell phone out of a pocket before Bluetooth technology was standard in cars, I knew I had no choice but to drive.

Phoenix shouted to Keisha, who answered yes, she was okay. I jammed my foot to the floor. But my four cylinders were as much a match for the Caddy's eight as my Glock was for whatever gun they had. The Caddy kept up with me effortlessly. A quick look told me the big man in the passenger seat was white, with close-cropped hair and a dark beard that posed no threat to ZZ Top but seemed more than menacing enough in its own right. I glanced again but couldn't see past him to the driver, mainly because he was steadying himself for another shot. He took aim with a large revolver.

I swerved left slightly, hoping to nudge the Caddy into the concrete Jersey barrier that divided the highway. Yes, I had seen too many movies but I couldn't think of anything else to try at that moment. When the cars touched, however, the squeal and scrape of my middleweight SUV shuddering against an old tank vibrated through every tire and bolt, into the steering wheel, and right up my arms to my shoulders. I pulled away, fearing I'd lose control, almost doing so. I dropped off the gas a bit and slowed just enough to regain control as the Caddy pulled ahead.

"Son of a bitch!" I said.

Having prevented one shot, I had set up another. Now the passenger turned and stuck his gun out the window. The angle was awkward, an over-the-shoulder left-handed effort that might have been hampered by his seatbelt or his size. His attempt to adjust himself gave me the time I needed to shift lanes and get behind them.

I shot a sidelong glance at Phoenix, who hunkered as low as she could with her seatbelt still fastened.

"I'm okay!" The combination of speed and shattered back windows gave us a noise level that required her to shout. "Drive!"

The Best Street exit was up ahead, the same exit Odell and Keisha had taken the night they were intercepted. We were in the far left lane. There was not enough time to get over to the right lane to take it. Maybe at Jefferson, the next exit, but that meant passing a car whose shooter had time to reorient himself and his hand cannon for a shot through my windshield or into the engine block. If there had been no Jersey barrier on my left, I might have risked riding the shoulder because surely the gunman would not try shooting past the driver.

The Caddy began to slow. I got close enough to see the big man trying to get over the front seat into the back. Without his seatbelt, he could lean out a rear window and take careful aim with his left hand. With a heavier car and no passengers, I might have tried a PIT maneuver right about then, even without a PIT bumper. But it had been too many years since my law enforcement pursuit intervention training, and the car I would attempt to spin around from behind might have a thousand pounds on mine.

Promising myself my next vehicle would have a PIT bumper, I hoped the shooter wasn't left-handed.

We passed Best Street.

"Phoenix, can you reach my gun! My belt, on the right!"

She sat up a bit. I felt her fingers groping for my Glock. I shifted a bit, hiking my right side an inch or so, and felt the gun pulled free.

"I haven't fired one in a long time!"

"Give it to Keisha!"

"Keisha! Here! Take it!"

I couldn't quite hear Keisha's response, so I raised my voice. "Both hands! Short barrel so brace it on the window frame! Shoot when we're close!"

I checked my passenger side mirror, relieved to see other cars had slowed and fallen far back. I made the only move I thought I could. I shifted into the center lane again and put the pedal to the floor. Trying to pull alongside the Caddy, I made no attempt to hit it. I hoped to keep my car close enough to it that the shooter inside would be reluctant to stick his arm out.

Keisha didn't need me to tell her when to pull the trigger. As soon as we drew even with the Caddy and I caught sight of the driver because the shooter was in the back seat, she let loose, squeezing off four shots before we passed. The explosions were loud inside the car, but I managed to stay focused on my driving as I counted. Six left in the magazine.

The Cadillac dropped back just as we passed the Jefferson exit and entered the stretch of highway that gradually rose to street level. Ten or twelve car lengths behind us, the Caddy kept coming. We had bought ourselves breathing room, nothing more. Locust then, maybe Goodell—I hoped to get to one of those exits before they caught up to us, swing onto a street, and scramble out of the car for a last stand. I also hoped Keisha hadn't dropped my Glock out the window. But that fear vanished when my peripheral vision caught sight of a shaking hand coming over the back of the seat and returning the gun to Phoenix. The relief I felt at the sight of the gun let me process the other information I had taken in.

Tito Glenroy, the church custodian, was driving the Cadillac—which, I remembered, he had inherited from his father, an elderly man who probably couldn't bring himself to part with it.

We reached the Locust Street exit.

I took the off-ramp at full speed because Tito had gained on me and I needed time to angle the car into a defensive position when I stopped. But while the expressway had been plowed already, the access street parallel to this section of it had not. Hitting a patch of snow-covered ice, I lost control as I tried to make the near-hairpin turn onto Locust. Despite all-wheel drive, the Escape spun out. I turned into the skid but was going too fast to keep the car on the street. Both back tires blew out when we swung into and past the curb. The back end slammed into the street sign and one-way sign on the corner, shearing off the thin posts that held them. The explosion stunned us. We stopped in a snowbank.

The front airbags hadn't deployed. But the left side impact had caused the driver's side airbags to go off like mortar shells. My hearing gone, time seemed to slow even more, seconds stretching forward until the numbness in my body began to recede and my vision to sharpen. I felt pain in both shoulders. Brushing off bits of safety glass and fumbling with my seatbelt, I saw my gun was not in Phoenix's hand or on the seat beside her. Somewhere on the floor? Panic set in that I would not find the Glock in time. I looked up, saw the Caddy barreling down the access road straight toward us, picking up speed, fishtailing as it came.

"Get out!" But even as I screamed I knew there wouldn't be enough time.

Tito must not have anticipated that this adventure would damage his automotive inheritance. I had no way of knowing just then whether his car was badly scraped by our contact with it or how many bullets had struck it. But he must have decided his classic had suffered enough insult and injury for one day. Rather than ram us, he turned the wheel slightly to avoid us—planning, I was sure, to stop so the shooter could get out and finish us. But the Caddy hit more ice, at a faster speed than I had reached. The rear-wheel-drive must have thrown Tito off just enough that in attempting to straighten out the car he jumped the curb and shot straight into the abutment of the pedestrian bridge past the corner.

The crash was deafening.

Gun or no gun, I had to move fast if I wanted to stop them from killing us. I got out and stumbled through the snowbank and then through the Caddy's tracks to the wreck. The driver's side back door was jammed shut. The shooter was in a heap, his legs up and his head in the footwell. He was still. The front end was crumpled against the concrete, steam rising from within, the hood now shaped like a tent, antifreeze melting snow near the flat left front tire. There were no flames. The windshield had rained inward, leaving bits of safety glass everywhere. The side window had disintegrated, its door hanging by a hinge. Tito was inside, unmoving, covered with glass, his large body enveloping the steering wheel as if shielding it. His head was still attached to his neck but at a sickeningly unnatural angle.

Presently, pounding drew my attention back to the rear. The door began to move with each thump as if the shooter had righted himself and was trying to kick his way out. An instant later the door squealed open wide enough for him to begin to work himself free. I didn't know whether he had his gun, but I knew I didn't have mine, so I threw myself against the door when his legs were halfway out. He howled and swore at me. I slammed the door against him again. Then I jerked it open and grabbed him by the front of his studded leather jacket. He was even bigger up close, and heavy. With both shoulders hurting, I had a tough time dragging him out. When, finally, his huge head cleared the door, I let him go. He slumped onto his back in the snow, blinking, chest heaving. Blood streamed down one cheek from a gash in his forehead.

I glanced into the Caddy and saw no gun.

Intending to pat him down for the gun, I dropped a knee into his chest. That knocked wind out of him but not enough to keep him from swinging on me with his left fist, weakly. If he hadn't just been pulled from a totaled car after being battered by the door, he might have knocked me cold. His glancing blow to my chin had enough behind it to rattle my brain. Something cut me at the point of contact. Twisting my head away, I pushed his arm down across his belly and held it there with my left as I poked him in the eyes with my right. He screamed, whipping his head from side to side, free arm flailing as he tried to grab me. Then he began to buck as adrenalin kicked in, but he couldn't throw me off. Calling me a cocksucker and threatening to rip my balls off, now he tried to work his free right hand down his side—maybe in search of his gun or a knife. When I reached for that arm, he wrenched his pinned arm free. I pushed myself up just enough to drop my knee into his chest a second time. Then I snatched a handful of beard and punched him squarely in the face. Again. Again, cracking his nose. Still, he struggled, snarling, spitting blood at me. His rage seemed to grow with each inhalation. Both arms now free, he went for my neck.

Just then a leather boot came down hard against his cheek and a 9mm muzzle pressed into his temple. Breath ragged and eyes wet as she bent over him, Phoenix held my Glock with both hands, the left gripping and steadying the right. "Sneeze," she said in a hollow whisper, "and I swear to God your brains will decorate the snow!"

Sliding off the shooter, I stood and took the gun from her, carefully.

39

A re we gonna find bullets from your baby Glock when we go through this wreck?" Piñero asked as we walked away from the Caddy. Tito's body had been removed from the car but not the scene. Having been examined and photographed *in situ*, it was now in one of the ambulances on the other side of the yellow police tape that cordoned off the entire corner. Soon Tito would head to the ME's office. I wondered if Mira would catch his postmortem.

"You might," I said, shrugging. "Can't say for sure where they went because I was driving. These weren't exactly range conditions, you know."

"No. This SOB's old school, straight-up Dirty Harry." Piñero held up the plastic evidence bag containing the long-barreled Smith & Wesson .44 Magnum he had found under the front passenger seat. "Least you didn't shoot him when you had him on the ground."

"The temptation was fierce," I said. "If I had, maybe Keisha wouldn't have run off."

"Well, you did break his nose." Piñero smiled. "You've been doing a lot of that lately."

We had to duck under the crime scene tape to reach Locust, which was blocked by a fire truck, two ambulances, two police cruisers with lights still flashing, and Chalmers and Piñero's unmarked car. A uniformed officer stood beside one of the cruisers, directing traffic exiting the expressway to the next available right turn, two blocks ahead on Maple. Cuffed and bandaged, the man whose wallet identified him as Delano 'Butch' Madden was in the back of the other cruiser, a short distance away. Phoenix sat on the rear step of the other ambulance, talking to Chalmers as a paramedic finished wrapping her right arm in bandages.

Passing what was left of my Ford Escape, Piñero and I went to the ambulance first.

"You okay?" I asked Phoenix.

"Scrapes, nothing deep." Her voice was strangely flat, detached. I wondered if she was in shock. She stared at me before speaking again. "You're the one still bleeding."

The paramedic turned to me. A tall Latina with threads of gray in hair pulled back into a ponytail, she had put Betadine and a fabric bandage on my chin when her unit first reached the scene. Now she looked at me for a moment. Then she pulled on a fresh pair of nitrile gloves and removed the bandage, which I had bled through. "You may need a stitch after all."

"Let's try another bandage," I said. "Maybe surgical glue if you have it. I don't have ER time today."

She scowled at me, a look that clearly rebuked me for telling her how to do her job. "What is it with you two? Too busy and important to get checked out by a full-fledged doctor?" But she got to work.

Chalmers and Piñero moved away from us. Presumably, they were comparing notes. Chalmers had decided to interview Phoenix himself because of her prior brief relationship with Piñero, who had talked to me. Both men knew Phoenix and I had plenty of time before their arrival to coordinate our stories if we had been inclined to lie. But we had told the truth about the Caddy's pursuit and gunfire—omitting, as we agreed, that Phoenix and Keisha had both handled my gun. While we focused on Madden, Keisha apparently took off on foot.

"They must have been on us for a while," I said.

"On you, probably."

"Maybe using cell phones to hand us off from one car to another. Waiting for Keisha to make contact." I remembered how cocky I'd felt after we located Spider Tolliver's GPS tracker. Maybe I'd have to start sweeping for trackers every day. "Something else I missed."

"It's not your fault," Phoenix said. But she sounded uncertain.

"Now I have to find Keisha again," I said as the paramedic smoothed a new bandage over my cut. "Home's just blocks away. If Terry sends a car, I doubt she'll open the door."

"Someone tried to kill her." Phoenix's voice was so matter-of-fact it almost made me shiver. "They might think she's hurt. Exigent circumstances."

"If Terry orders them to go in, she might run again. I don't want her to run."

"She's run enough. She needs to be somewhere she feels safe."

"Okay," the paramedic said. "A drop of glue and a different type of bandage, but if it keeps bleeding you're gonna need a stitch unless you *want* a scar."

"Thanks," I said. "Sorry to be a pain in the ass."

"Early afternoon on a twelve-hour shift," the woman said. "If I let every asshole get to me, I wouldn't make dinner without killing somebody." Smiling, she stepped up into the back of the ambulance and started securing the supply storage compartments for departure.

Phoenix stood, slowly and deliberately, her silence and faraway look unsettling. I took her arm and led her away from the ambulance. Before I could ask her what was wrong, Chalmers and Piñero walked over to us.

"You both declined transport to a hospital," Chalmers said. "But I still need you to come downtown and make a statement. Afterward, we'll see that you get home."

"Sure, but I need some things from my car first," I said. "Nothing relevant to your investigation. Just some personal things and tools I don't want to disappear between here and the collision shop."

"Make it quick," Chalmers said.

I ducked under the yellow tape and walked around my Escape

before gathering things from inside. At the time of the crash, I had given no thought to the extent of damage or cost of repairs. Now that the threat of being shot was gone, I could scarcely believe what I saw. Yes, a bullet had obliterated both rear passenger windows, but the collision had cracked or shattered other windows as well, in ways that would take an expert to explain. The liftgate window was gone. The front passenger window held only jagged chunks of safety glass—likely the source of Phoenix's abrasions. The windshield was buckled outward, a maze of cracks. Other external damage was easier to decipher. From its contact with the Caddy, the driver's side had a thick strip of scratched, peeled paint that ran almost the full length of the car. The corner signposts were not round but stainless steel U-lines that gouged the roofline, the rear door, and the rocker panel as they were sheared off. I knelt to examine the underside. In addition to causing two side-wall blowouts, slamming into and over the curb had bent the rear axle. I had a sinking feeling my insurance company would cut its losses.

"Shit," I said, getting to my feet and brushing snow off my knees. "Totaled."

"That's no way for a lucky guy to sound," Piñero said. He had come under the tape and was standing by the open driver's side door. "Let me show you something."

I joined him.

"Check this out." He pointed to a large bullet hole in the edge of the front door. Then he opened the door and pointed to the next leg on the bullet's journey, a semicircle in the front edge of the post between the front and rear doors. Finally, he popped my seat forward and put a fingertip into a hole in the edge of the seatback.

"I felt it go in," I said. "I didn't have time to stop and think about it."

He leaned in and felt the other edge of the seatback. "No exit, so it's still in there and will send this SOB away for a long time." He withdrew and straightened up. "Which means a .44 Magnum slug passed within inches of your spine. A little bit this way or that—and you're pissed about the *car*? Shit, bro, you're alive and walking on two legs, so fuck the car."

"Fuck the car," I said, without enthusiasm.

Just then the ambulance with Tito's body started moving up Locust, no lights, no siren. It was followed a moment later by the second ambulance, also running silent.

"Okay," Piñero said. "Get your stuff so we can go downtown. Then maybe we can talk about how all this fits together."

I kept a reusable grocery bag in the glove compartment. I filled it with insurance and registration papers, loose coins, maps, and a zipper pouch that held spare eyeglasses. Then I went to the rear compartment and dug out my auto tool kit, a plug-in compressor, an auto battery charger, and the leather case that held my lock pick gun. Apart from the soft-sided tool satchel, everything went into the grocery bag, with the lock pick gun near the very bottom.

I walked over to Chalmers, Piñero, and Phoenix. Chalmers was speaking on his cell phone. He ended the call and put the phone in his pocket a few seconds after I set down my bag and the tool satchel.

"Everything you've told us is consistent with what we've been able to determine so far," Chalmers said. "The shootout matches what dispatch heard from drivers behind you who got off and called nine-one-one. One guy said it was like the OK Corral."

"It was nothing like the OK Corral," I said. "Except that asshole had a revolver."

"Which didn't hit your ungrateful ass," Piñero said. "All you got was a cut that *might* leave a scar."

I thought about my cut for a moment and looked across the street at the squad car in which the shooter sat. Then I remembered yesterday's photos. "Something I'd like to know."

"Who sent him?" Chalmers said. "Gotta wait for that till we get him in the box."

I took a breath. "Can I sit in on the interview?"

"No," Piñero said. "You're a civilian."

After a moment, I walked across to the squad car and jerked open the back door. "Okay, asshole, who the fuck sent you after me?"

Hearing footsteps rushing toward me, I reached inside and pushed Butch Madden down on the seat with my left hand, as if I were going to hit him again with my right. His hands, cuffed behind him, came into view. "Who was it, Butch? Dante Cuthbert?"

Just as the young uni seated in front climbed out to intervene, Piñero reached me, grabbed my right arm, and pulled me out of the car. "G, don't do something stupid to get him kicked on a technicality! Especially when you're not even on the force."

I offered no resistance as he pulled me away. He let me go when we were back across the street. I took Phoenix's hand, which felt strangely limp.

"He's wearing a ring on his left hand," I said to both detectives. "I think I've seen it before and I think it's what cut me."

"You've seen his ring but not him," Chalmers said.

"A ring like it," I said. "Check it against those gashes on Veronica Surowiec's body."

40

To my relief, the statement took less than half an hour to dictate and sign. Then Piñero drove us the few blocks to Phoenix's condo. He promised to call me after Madden's interrogation.

"Well, I need to go sit in a chair and open a bottle of wine," Phoenix said, shaking her head as we stood in the foyer of her building. She sounded exhausted, maybe exasperated. Maybe afraid. "If I know you, you'll want my car to look for Keisha."

"And to drop this stuff off at home," I said, gesturing toward the grocery bag and tool satchel at my feet. "I'll try to bring it back tonight."

She took the Toyota fob off her key ring and handed it to me. "Keep it tonight. I think I'll crash early if you don't mind. I need some time alone."

"All right." Something caught in my chest but I tried not to let it show.

"In fact, it's okay if you keep it a couple of days. I'm close enough to the office and the courts it won't break me to use Uber. Just try not to get it shot to pieces." She did not smile.

"Thank you." I hesitated. "I *am* sorry about all this."

"No need to be sorry." She gave me a quick kiss as the elevator doors chimed open. "You didn't start it. But do whatever you have to do to finish it." Then she stepped inside, and the doors closed behind her.

For a long time, I just stood there, wondering if events of the past couple of hours would comprise the straw that snapped the spine of our relationship. All relationships carried risk, but most such risks did not involve gunplay. Since we'd been together, I had been shot and now Phoenix herself had been shot at. How long would it be before she decided the physical and emotional hazards of being with me outweighed the physical and emotional delights of our being a couple? But none of that could be sorted out just yet. She was right. I had to finish things.

Taking a deep breath and picking up my belongings, I took the elevator down to the parking garage under the building. I opened the back of Phoenix's RAV4 and put everything inside, except the lock pick gun.

I didn't need the lock pick to get into the Simpkins home. I still had the key Keisha's parents had given me. I went through the house quickly. Keisha was neither downstairs nor up, but the stoppered malbec bottle on her counter and the glass tumbler in her sink, rinsed but still holding a splash of water tinged with crimson, suggested she had been there not long ago. Stoppered wine was also a sign she hoped to return.

Synching my phone with the car's Bluetooth, I called Jen on the way to my next stop.

"We haven't heard from her yet," she said when I gave her a synopsis of what had taken place. "But we know all about the shooting on the expressway. Burned up my scanner for a while. Now it's on the department's telephone gossip tree. I understand the driver died in a crash and they got the guy who pulled the trigger on you."

"Yes," I said. "The driver was Tito, the janitor from your wife's old church."

"Jesus!" She hesitated. "Are you and your lady friend okay?"

"We weren't hit so—"

"That's not what I meant," Jen said. "I could tell by the way she looked at you in Tim Horton's, she's *so* into you. I could see you're gone on her too. Bianca could too. But bullets hitting the car you're in can change things. Civilians—"

"Her father was a cop," I said. "She knows."

"Knowing and handling are two different things." She paused. "You've gone over and above for my wife's best friend—and her family—when technically you're not even on the job. That means a lot to us. If you and—Phoenix, is it? If you need somebody to talk to, a sounding board like a couple where one partner has to worry whether the other one will come home, we're here for you, Rimes."

For a few seconds, I said nothing. "Thanks, Jen. You've got good instincts and good intuition. There's a detective shield in your future."

"Kind of you to think so," she said. "I'll let you know if we hear from Keisha. Now I have to go tell Bianca about this guy Tito."

We broke the connection just before I reached my destination on Masten Avenue.

41

The house was a small single-family dwelling, with white clapboard, brown trim, and leaded glass in the front door. The old F-150 sat in the driveway. With no parking spaces left on that stretch of Masten, I turned the next corner and found a spot on Edna Place. Climbing out, I ducked into a yard and hopped two fences. With Tito dead and having no family, I figured it was as good a time as any to look through his place for something useful.

Watch cap pulled down and driving gloves still on, I gazed about to make sure I was not being observed. Then I went to the side door. A small window likely over a kitchen sink was to the right, the front of the house to the left. Through the sheer curtain covering the leaded glass in that door, I saw a short flight of stairs just inside the entrance.

The pick gun made quick work of the lock. I slipped inside, closed the door behind me and pocketed the pick. I heard the chime alert of an alarm panel but not the beep of an entry code countdown. Either Tito had not set his alarm or someone was here. For several seconds I just listened, waiting for any sound of movement. Hearing nothing, I went up the steps and into the living room. Afternoon sunlight streamed through the sheer curtains over the windows in the sun porch and the glass in the front door. The alarm panel was beside the door, its green light indicating it was in READY mode.

The place was clean but belonged to another time. The wall beside the stairs showed Tito had inherited not only his parents' home but also their ancient plastic-covered furniture and faux-antique lamp tables. The opposite wall was his concession to modernity. A seventy-inch flat screen was mounted above a glass-doored media cabinet that held an assortment of electronic devices, including a closed laptop. Rocker-style gaming chairs flanked the cabinet, with X-Box and PlayStation controllers on the floor between them. No shelves or books, no desk or file cabinets. I had come in with only vague ideas of what I was looking for. Now I had no idea where to start. I turned toward the dining room, thinking it might hold something with drawers that needed searching. I went into it, stepping off the worn carpet onto a wide-planked hardwood floor. On my third step, a board squeaked under my weight.

"Is that you, baby?"

I froze.

The voice, a woman's, had come from above. Upstairs. Next, there was a yawn, followed by shuffling footsteps.

"I got so tired waiting for you I fell asleep. If we're gonna fuck at all today, you better get up here and get busy. I'm horny as hell but we gotta go soon."

I said nothing. Having recognized the voice, I drew my gun. Had I overlooked her car outside? Or had she parked on a different side street?

"Tito?"

She started down the stairs, her bare feet and legs coming into view just below the upper landing, the hem of a blue man's bathrobe flapping about the knees. She came down two more steps, the landing blocking everything above her torso. Then she stopped.

"Tito? If that's you, say something."

I said nothing.

She began to crouch, to peek—perhaps, I thought, questioning whether she had heard anything after all. Her face came into view and her eyes widened with surprise when she saw me, the gun in my left hand trained on her.

"Don't even try to go back upstairs," I said.

Loni Markham came the rest of the way down the stairs, resting her hand on the finial atop the railing post at the bottom. The robe she wore was loose enough for the swell of her breasts to be visible but tied enough to hide the specifics of the nudity beneath the terrycloth. She did not try to close or remove the robe. She just stood there, looking at me, hazel eyes dancing, calculating.

"Mr. Rimes, you're the last person I expected to see here today." Briefly, she looked down, offering a nervous smile. "I guess I'm the last person you expected to find." She hugged herself then, peach-colored nails standing out against the blue of the robe. But the gesture came across as pure performance, as did her subsequent attempt to smooth her hair. "I should be embarrassed by all this, but I can't help feeling a little relieved. Sneaking around isn't really my thing." She looked at the nearby sofa. "Do you mind if I sit?"

"Go ahead."

Now tightening the robe, she sank onto the sofa. The plastic made a burping sound, followed by the brief hiss of air forced out of the cover encasing the cushion. She scooted back against the upright cushion and stretched her arms across the top. The seat hissed again as she made a point of crossing her long legs. She had peach-colored toenails too.

"Mind putting that gun away?" she said. "It's obvious I'm unarmed."

"Not just yet," I said.

"If you're looking for Tito—"

"Tito's dead."

"Oh." Her eyebrows went up as if she had just heard a neighbor's dog died and she wasn't sure how she felt about the dog, or the neighbor. Several seconds passed before she asked the question that would have come to most people the minute they heard the news. "What happened?"

"A car accident."

"Did he—did he suffer much?"

"I'm pretty sure he died instantly."

She nodded but still showed no emotion for a man she apparently had been waiting to screw senseless, not even relief that he had been spared pain. "At first I thought maybe you killed him."

"Why would I do that?"

"I don't know. But you're here, in his house, uninvited and holding a gun on me." She lowered her hands to her sides, palms down, and leaned forward. "Did somebody tell you about Tito and me? A couple of my friends knew. They encouraged me. They understood when I told them what it's like to be married to a man so wrapped up in the needs of the spirit that he forgets the needs of the flesh and misses most of the hints."

"While Tito was so good at catching passes," I said.

Loni's smile seemed genuine this time, as radiant as the one I had first seen in her husband's study. But her eyes were still weighing, assessing, planning. "It seems we've come to the point where you must decide what to do. Tell my husband or walk away. You have no authority to do anything else. Either you want money for your silence —or maybe sex. I'm willing to offer either to get back to my life without trouble. Maybe I'd even offer both."

"This isn't about your husband." I sat in a wing chair perpendicular to the sofa. More hissing from plastic. Resting my left arm on my knee, I kept the gun pointed at her.

"Then maybe you're here to rob the place and I surprised you."

"Or maybe I'm here to find out why Tito tried to kill me. Why he and Butch Madden were trying so hard to kill Keisha Simpkins when they had a fatal accident." I made a mental note that Loni's face showed no surprise at the mention of Keisha's name, no curiosity at the mention of Butch Madden. "Truth is, you're far from the last person I expected to find here."

She shrugged.

"I tell you Tito and Butch tried to kill Keisha and you don't even blink.

"So?"

"You don't even ask who this Butch character was."

She uncrossed her legs. "Maybe I don't care who he was."

"Maybe I should call the police. Have them take you in as a material witness."

"Go ahead. You're the one who broke in. You're not a cop. You don't have a warrant. I have a reason for being here. Clothes in a closet upstairs, toiletries in the bathroom, even a toothbrush with my DNA. What do you have?"

"Your motive for murder."

"Whatever Tito did or didn't do has got nothing to do with me."

"Does it have something to do with your brother Dante?"

Loni's lips parted in surprise, another glimmer of truth. But she caught herself and closed her mouth quickly. Her brow furrowed and she narrowed her eyes at me.

"Keisha told me one of the men who tried to kill her called the other one Dante."

"I don't recall saying I have a brother named Dante," Loni said. "Even if I do, he can't be the only one in the world."

"Murder and attempted murder," I said. "Your brother forced a heroin overdose on Keisha Simpkins and Odell Williamson because Keisha figured out your foundation was being used as a scheme to make money in real estate development while putting low-income people on the street. Somehow she got hold of documents that laid everything out and she brought them to you, thinking you were the victim. She admired you so much. How could she know then you were behind it all, with a direct connection to FBF Development?"

"So now I'm Donna Corleone?" Loni chuckled. "You don't know shit."

"I know it wasn't enough just to recover the files in a high-tech age. It wasn't enough to threaten her parents to keep her from talking. To make sure no one got wind of your plan, Keisha had to die. When people die today, most of their documents die with them, on hard drives that are obsolete before their funerals. Sure, they're on Facebook forever, but those are just digital headstones in a cyber cemetery on the information highway. Nobody pays them much attention."

"So that's it? An admitted drug user gives you a name, one you probably gave her first, and that makes me a murderer." Loni let out a long sigh. "Gideon Rimes, ace private eye. More like Ace Ventura, pet detective."

"Dante Cuthbert is your brother, Melony. You might as well admit it."

Instead of replying, she undid the robe and opened it so I could see her fully naked. She sat perfectly still—breasts full, stomach taut, legs parted enough to show me what I was missing—her hazel gaze fixed on mine as if daring me not to look. "I would have given you a couple thousand bucks and the fuck of a lifetime to avoid complicating my marriage." Then she retied the robe and sat forward, forearms resting on her knees. "But not for a horseshit soufflé like this. Even if I had some big money deal in the works, how do you know the plan didn't include relocating residents to better housing? Nothing illegal in that. No motive for murder, especially one as sketchy as forcing an overdose. Yes, Dante Cuthbert is my brother. FBF is his company. So what? Think all this is more than wheeling and dealing? Prove it." She sat back, crossed her arms, and smiled. "Negro, please!"

She was right. There had to be more than controversy and potential embarrassment to make them kill, to make Keisha run and Dante use a second identity. There were stakes I hadn't seen, hadn't imagined. If there was interstate criminality, the money would have to exceed the profits from a local real estate venture. The operation that produced that kind of money had to be bigger than a development company but off the books. Under the radar but labyrinthine, with supply chains and loyal soldiers. Drugs. It had to be drugs. Was FBF some kind of shadow company using development projects to legitimize drug money? If so, where did people like Felicity Sillers and Butch Madden fit in?

"How about this," I said. "Your brother's company is quiet enough to avoid too much attention. It has projects in several smaller cities trying to revitalize. Suppose FBF is actually a laundromat."

She said nothing.

"Suppose your foundation is too, and gentrification is just part of the spin cycle. What if the kind of bad publicity that comes with putting poor people out in the cold would shine a light where the cockroaches wanted to hide? Maybe a government agency or the press would get curious enough to dig down and ruin the whole thing." I watched the peach fingertips of her right hand ease toward the gap between the two-seat cushions. "If Tito was enough of a player to try to kill Keisha, maybe he also kept a gun stashed in his couch. For situations just like this." I shrugged. "Could be wrong about that, but if I think there's a gun down there and you're reaching for it, I'll put a bullet in your chest."

Her fingers froze, as did her breathing. When next she exhaled, she folded her hands in her lap.

"There's Butch too. I can't figure exactly where he fits."

"Never heard of any Butch," she said. "I don't know all Tito's friends. Our thing was strictly fucking, once or twice a week. Anything else is on him."

I smiled. "Good. If you don't know Butch, you don't need to worry he'll flip on you now that he's in custody." I let that sink in, pleased she had to struggle to mask her surprise. "No, he didn't die. You haven't had a chance to call Harlow Graves yet either. But it doesn't matter. Unlike Felicity Sillers, Butch will be charged with something. Attempted murder. A high-speed shootout on the Kensington? Bail is going to be steep if it's granted at all."

"I still don't know Butch," she said. "Or this Felicity."

"Probably why Harlow Graves didn't know her name the other night," I said. "But I bet Butch and Felicity know somebody who knows somebody who knows you. All a good investigator or forensic accountant needs is a thread to pull." I shook my head. "Sooner or later even Graves will have to answer for his role in this mess."

That remark was a stab in the dark, but Loni Markham offered no reaction, nothing to confirm or deny the lawyer's complicity. She was quiet for a long time, so still it was hard now to tell if she was breathing. She stared at me, almost unblinking, as if uncertain what to say.

Finally, the hands clasped in her lap pulled apart. She flexed her fingers.

"Nothing you've said proves anything illegal on my part or the foundation's," she said. "If you walk out of here today, you've got nothing that can harm us. So I'll be at church tomorrow with my clueless husband, who'll never believe you if you go to him with this. I'll attend all my meetings next week and the week after. Utter one word about me in public and I will own you." She leaned forward, fixing me with the coldest stare I had ever seen. "But my brother is going to kill you for this. No matter what." Her eyes hardened as she continued, the hatred in them crystallizing. "No matter what happens out there, remember what I'm telling you in here, right now." Her voice went lower, to a venomous whisper. "My brother will kill you. The first time he killed, it was for me. He's much better at it now."

"Which brother would that be?" I said. "Dante or QC?"

"I have one brother. You'll meet him soon enough but you'll never see him coming."

"Because your brother has two identities, and I don't know either one."

"What?"

"Your family had all the documents after your cousin Quentin was killed by a car. Dante Cuthbert and QC Griffin are the same person."

Loni burst into laughter that went on for several seconds. When she stopped, she let out a long breath and smiled her priceless smile again. "Oh, Rimes, for a while there you had it all figured out, even without proof. But not the family part." Her smile disappeared and her jaw tightened. "What you don't know, couldn't know, is that we all hated Quentin Cuthbert Griffin, especially Mama. He was a snotty, cowardly, selfish little bastard who thought the sun rose and set on his narcissistic little ass. Quentin Cuthbert Griffin—he used to introduce himself just like that, like he belonged in Fuckingham Palace. The oldest child, so everything had to be his way. Right? A bully who hit us whenever he felt like it. Took our stuff because it was there. That psycho even took tooth money from under our pillows. One day when I was about nine, he punched me right in the mouth, just to see how much I would bleed."

"Where were your parents through all this?"

"Mama would have done something but our daddy woulda beat her. We didn't learn the whole story until after he was dead, after he drank himself into his grave from grief. Pop, you see, fussed over Quentin because the little shit reminded him so much of the dead sister he loved." She paused, closing her eyes and taking a long breath before she continued. "The dead sister whose bed he shared when they were teenagers, whose bed he visited now and then even after they were married to other people." Loni smiled again, icily. "That's right, Rimes. I *had* two brothers, but the day after Quentin Cuthbert Griffin knocked out my tooth, my Dante pushed the fat bastard in front of a car. Now I have only one."

Just then I heard a car engine shut off and heavy doors slam shut. I sprang to my feet and looked toward the sunporch. Through the sheers, I saw an SUV had parked behind Tito's F-150—large enough and dark enough to be Dante's Navigator. I spun back to Loni just as she plunged her hand between the cushions. Lunging, I grabbed her right wrist before she could pull the .38 revolver from its hiding place and wrenched it out of her hand,

It was a camo-colored Charter Arms Tiger II. I pointed it at her. "Upstairs," I whispered.

Clutching the banister, she pulled herself up just as heavy footsteps hit the porch. Two large men in winter coats appeared through the sheer curtains covering the door glass. I heard a key slide into the lock.

Already at the landing, Loni screamed, "Dante, QC, he's got a gun!" and ran the rest of the way up.

I didn't hesitate to press the advantage of surprise. My first shot, from the .38, took out the leaded glass. I heard somebody cry out, "The *fuck*, man!" That left ten bullets, four in the .38, six still in my Glock. A gun in each hand, I went toward the front door at an angle, firing steadily, calmly at the billowing sheers, forcing the men to scramble off down the steps. I knew at any moment they would return fire—or Loni might come downstairs with another gun. But I needed all of them off balance for just a few seconds, long enough for me to reach the door.

And the alarm panel.

When I jabbed the panic button that made the alarm service connect directly to the police, the Tiger II was empty so I dropped it on the carpet. I had two rounds left in my Glock. One for each of them if they ignored the otherworldly screech of the alarm siren and waited for me to come out the side door.

42

P eeking through the partly opened side door, I waited as Dante Cuthbert and whoever was using the QC Griffin iden- tity backed the Navigator out of the driveway and took off. Then I pushed open the door and ran through the snow in the back yard. The second alarm I tripped in less than a week shut off just after I made it over the first fence. Having assumed the men on Tito's porch would run from the siren, I was not surprised his lover had the password and could silence the system. But I had got what I needed, a way out.

After the second fence, I paused to look around before emerging from another driveway. No Navigator. I went out to the street and climbed inside Phoenix's RAV4. I started it and took off before it could warm up. Knowing what I knew, my next step would be alerting Chalmers and Piñero. They would know whom to push for an official investigation. All I had to do was watch my own back because Dante Cuthbert was coming for me. It would have helped if I had got a good enough look at him to recognize him later.

But first things first.

When my phone rang through the car's sound system, I was crossing Main on my way to Elmwood and my apartment building.

"Hey, G, it's Raf."

"You at your desk? I'm heading your way after I make a stop. Give me thirty."

"Good, because shit is starting to pile up in front of the fan. Hey, wait a minute. You sound like you're in a car. Your ride was totaled. What are you driving?"

"Phoenix's RAV4."

"Okay, turns out you were right. We checked Surowiec's autopsy pictures. The senior criminalist and the ME himself both say those gashes and weird figure-eight bruises coulda come from the ring. It's being processed right now. But Butch says he didn't do it."

"Course he does," I said. "Why would he lie?"

Piñero laughed. "He might be telling the truth. That ring? It's custom made for a biker gang outside Jamestown. The Immortals. That stretched out eight is—"

"An infinity symbol," I said.

"With a tiny inscription. *Ride free. Die free. Forever free.* Dennis Quinell at the *News* did a piece on them last year. Protection. Prostitution. Gunrunning. Murder for hire."

"Drugs?"

"Of course. Licit and illicit. The meth mama whose nose you broke?"

"Felicity Sillers."

"She used to be Butchy boy's bitch."

Now I laughed. "Bet you can't say *that* five times fast."

"You're the one broke both their noses." He cleared his throat. "He got her into meth because of the hyped-up sex but she went farther down the tubes than he did and got lost. He still taps her now and then but says he doesn't love her anymore."

"You getting all this from him?"

"Yep. We sorta hinted that under New York law he could get the needle for killing a doctor, even if she was a meth head. Butch isn't the brightest guy you'll ever meet."

"That was cold, man, even for you."

Piñero chuckled. "I know, right? But it worked. He turned out to be a choir boy waiting for the right song to sing. He already spent time in the joint, two different pens in the state system. He says that was enough for him."

"But he started shooting in public. He's gotta go back."

"We explained that but he wants witness protection. 'I have enemies,' he says like he's in a fucking comic book. He *might* talk if he can be put somewhere he's never been."

"Not much of a poker player."

"But he can give up a lot on the Immortals. The right people are interested. An ADA is with him right now. Somebody from the state's WITSEC is on the way, to evaluate."

"He got a lawyer?"

"A public defender who gave me shit about the needle nap I promised him, but he wants to roll over and she's walking him through it."

"Don't you wish they were all this easy?"

"Absolutely. Anyway, he says somebody else in the gang mighta done Surowiec but not him. Oh, get this. The guy killed in the Cadillac, Titus Glenroy?"

"Yeah?"

"Butch says they played college ball together."

"Jamestown!" I said as something moved from the back of my mind to the front and I pulled up outside my apartment building.

"No, Jamestown doesn't have an NCAA school."

"No, *they* played at Eastern Michigan," I said. "But Jamestown— shit! I know where I've seen the ring. Maybe why Surowiec was killed. Can I call you back in a few? Put me on speaker when I do."

"Sure but later you gotta tell how you knew they played at EMU." Piñero hung up.

I parked half a block from my building. I carried my bag and tool satchel upstairs to my apartment, reloaded my Glock, and was back in the RAV4 in five minutes. Once I had turned around for a straight shot down Elmwood, I called back. The phone rang once.

"Rimes, it's Terry," Chalmers said. "Raf is with me and the door is closed."

"I can't tell you how I got some of what I'm gonna say," I began, "but maybe it's enough to keep the Butch thing going. I'll be there in fifteen minutes, so save your questions. Oh, and I'd appreciate it if you can send down a parking pass for Phoenix's car."

"Will do," Chalmers said. "I'll send Raf down with it when we finish the call."

I had been wrong about Cuthbert's dual identity, I explained. Without revealing where and how, or my shooting through Tito's door, I summarized my conversation with Loni Markham. Crossing Virginia Street, I ended with her daring me to find proof FBF and the church foundation were both laundering drug money. Then I shifted gears to my earlier visit to Sanctuary Nimbus.

Ileana and I, I explained, had found Veronica Surowiec there during our search for Keisha. It was that evening I noticed an infinity ring on the hand of Brother Jeremiah Grace, who had grown up in the village of Celoron, right next to Jamestown. I repeated what Ileana had told me she heard from Veronica just before her disappearance: *"She called out of the blue and said they had made her do something she didn't want to and now they were after her so she had to get away."* My theory was that Veronica may have refused to do it herself but had been forced to coach Felicity Sillers on how to inject an air bubble into an SVC line. Having tried to get away, she was beaten to death to keep her from talking.

Skirting the Niagara Square traffic circle in front of City Hall, I told them I would be there in less than two minutes. "One more thing," I said. "I owe you an apology."

"For what?" Chalmers asked.

"For not remembering sooner that the Sanctuary's business manager, a guy I never met, has something in common with Butch. His name is Marco Madden."

"Damn. All right. Get up here and make another statement so I can get a warrant."

43

The warrant to go to Sanctuary Nimbus for the infinity ring took nearly two hours. There was much discussion about how to proceed. Given that the Sanctuary was a quasi-public shelter beginning to receive drop-ins for dinner, a no-knock warrant and caravan of squad cars would likely complicate matters more than necessary. Evidence and lives could both be lost amid chaos in a crowd that included drug users, petty criminals, the mentally ill, and people guilty of nothing other than being born poor or losing a job. In the end, the brass decided one unmarked car and one tactical SUV would go to the Sanctuary.

I was not party to official discussions but learned the specifics later. While Chalmers and Piñero were in a meeting to finalize details, I sat in front of Piñero's desk in the homicide squad. I was on my phone, giving information to my car insurance company when Harlow Graves appeared in the doorway. He strode over to the desk, briefcase in hand. He wore the same charcoal topcoat he was in the other night, but the suit beneath it was black, not navy.

"You're not Detective Piñero," he said.

"Very observant," I said.

He stared at me for a moment. "No, you're that private detective, Gideon Rimes."

I ignored him and finished my call. Then I stood to face him, not to intimidate him because I had only an inch or so on him, but to keep him from trying to intimidate me.

"Sir, I don't recall ever meeting you. Yet you know who I am. I find that curious."

"I really don't care what you find curious, Mr. Rimes." He threw his shoulders back a bit and took a breath. "I'm here to see my client. I want to know where he's being held."

"Does your client have a name this time, Mr. Graves?"

He said nothing. I was unable to read him. Was he stunned I knew his name and that he hadn't known Felicity's? Was he pleased his billboards all over town were working? Or maybe he was pissed off I had told Loni he would pay for associating with her.

"Do *you* find something curious, Mr. Graves?" I asked.

"Where is Detective Piñero?"

"Not at his desk," I said. "But you must have noticed that already, the observant lawyer that you are. If you'd like to leave a message, I'm sure you have something to write with inside that fancy double-buckle briefcase." I sat back down and returned to my cell phone.

Setting down his briefcase, Graves parked half his butt on the corner of the desk and glared down at me.

"You know, Rimes, you may think you're a tough guy, wearing a bandage on your face like it's a medal. But you're going to be in a lot of trouble before I'm through with you."

I wanted to offer him the opportunity to wear a bandage, but I held my tongue.

"You assaulted at least two people, a man and a woman," Graves continued. "You broke both their noses, I imagine with some signature martial arts move. The woman says you tried to rape her. You discharged a gun on a public highway, causing a fatal crash. Add to that breaking into and entering a private home. All this without a shred of legal authority."

"You already know about the broken nose and the expressway

shootout," I said. "She didn't when I left the house, so somebody must have talked to her before she talked to you."

Graves snorted. "When this whole affair is over—"

"What affair? Loni and Tito's? Or are you screwing Loni too? Does Rosalind know?"

Graves stood, fists clenched at his sides. Loni had given him enough to identify me but not enough to let him know he couldn't frighten me. Now he was unsure what to do. I hoped he would take a swing at me. But he stood there seething, cheeks darkening and flaring nostrils the only part of his body that moved.

"Whatever this affair is, my part is finished," I said. "I found my clients' daughter and got my car shot up and totaled in the process. I did my civic duty and gave police information I thought was evidence of a criminal enterprise. They don't need me anymore." I brushed my hands together a couple of times as if ridding myself of dirt. "You want to push the B&E thing, go ahead. With him dead, cops are gonna search Tito's house sooner or later. They'll find more than I did unless you give your client time to clear it out. If you think you can bring it up without implicating yourself—" I sat back and folded my arms. "You should tell Loni Markham the puzzle pieces are falling into place. She and her brother should get out while they can."

"Her brother?" Graves looked confused. "Since when does she have a brother?"

"It was something she kept need-to-know," I said. "Apparently, you weren't on the list. So sorry, old man. But thanks for confirming she's the one who sent you."

"You're not as clever as you think, Rimes."

Just then a cluster of suits and uniforms emerged from a conference room across the hall. They stood near the squad room door, talking, shaking hands. A Buffalo police captain the size of a fullback and four other officers were in uniform. Three men and two women wore suits and carried briefcases. Chalmers, Piñero, Pete Kim, a man with a badge on his belt, and a woman with a badge on a neck chain rounded out the group. The captain, two of the uniformed officers, and the mix I thought must be lawyers and city officials moved out of sight down the hall. The detectives and two remaining uniforms came toward Graves and me. Having shared time on the other side of a two-way mirror, Kim and I exchanged nods.

"Detective Piñero," Graves said. "I'm here to see my client, Delano Madden."

Chalmers and Piñero exchanged looks.

"Didn't Madden have counsel?" Chalmers asked.

"I thought so," Piñero said. "Sarah Dockery, right?"

"Yes. She's the one negotiating his...proposed deal."

"If she wasn't his lawyer, then who the hell was she?" Piñero feigned shock. "She sure seemed to know an awful lot about the law. My God, we've been fooled again!"

"Don't quit your day jobs," Graves said. "I'd like to see Mr. Madden, now."

"You must not have heard us." Chalmers leaned close to Graves for a moment. "Mr. Madden *has* an attorney."

"Dockery is a public defender. She was simply holding a chair until I could get here."

"Did she know that?" Piñero said. "Let me ask her. She might still be at the elevator."

"Ask her if she told him about Madden's nose," I said. "Somebody did."

"No shit?" Chalmers said. "He knew?"

"Knew *I* did it."

"Damn." Chalmers leaned close again. "Who told you about Madden's nose?"

Graves sputtered something unintelligible but full of pomp and indignity.

"Ask him who sent him to claim the client," I said. "Ask him if he even knows Madden. Something tells me this guy couldn't pick Butch out of a crowd of two."

"Have you ever met Mr. Madden, counselor?" Chalmers asked.

"Well..."

"A yes or no answer."

Graves hissed and turned to me again. "When I lodge my

complaint with your superiors," he said over his shoulder to Chalmers, "I'll be sure to include that you're now taking orders from a civilian with a PI license. That is certainly a breach—"

"Not a civilian," Piñero said. "A retired investigator turned independent contractor. He's on retainer with the mayor's office. He works with us from time to time, when we need his special expertise. We have a letter to that effect from the city's corporation counsel."

"That's right," Chalmers said. "He's a consultant."

"That tired TV cliché?" Graves said. "Does the PBA know about this?"

"I'm a rep," Chalmers said. "How could they not? Does the ABA know you're trying to poach another lawyer's client?"

Graves ignored the question. "His special expertise?"

"Is not your concern." Chalmers gestured to those gathered around. "We're busy right now, working on a case we're not at liberty to divulge. So if you don't mind—"

After Graves pushed his way through the crowd and stomped out, Chalmers turned to one of the detectives. "Marczak, see if Kirk Wiggins is working the front desk again. He got reprimanded last year for loose-lipping arrest details. If it's not him, we need to be on the lookout for somebody else who might be trading info for money."

A middle-aged man in a pin-striped blue shirt and wearing his badge clipped to his belt, Marczak nodded and left the room. But I doubted it was Wiggins. I expected that through the foundation, Loni had lots of sources who didn't know what she was.

I looked at Piñero. "You guys have a copy of my letter? When I showed it to you a couple of months ago, you wanted to tear it up."

"We had a copy even then," Chalmers said. "Faxed over from the mayor's office before you showed it to us. We were pissed at her, not you. Contract talks were in the toilet and here she was saddling us with you."

"Now that we know you, G, we get pissed at you for being you," Piñero said. "But if you're coming with us to Sanctuary Nimbus, your letter's gotta be in play."

44

It was half-past six and dark when we got to Sanctuary Nimbus on Bidwell Parkway, with two officers in the SUV and Pete Kim in a winter trench coat, sitting beside me in the back of Chalmers's car. The two uniformed cops took up positions outside two different exits. With Kim waiting outside the main entrance, Chalmers, Piñero, and I got in line to go inside.

Eyes ever distant and voice fragile, Pastor Paul was at the door that opened onto the softly lit, repurposed church interior. Beside him was one of his volunteers, a middle-aged woman in a knit sweater and long woolen skirt. She seemed to be there as much to look after the old man in monk's robes as to greet entrants. As he shook hands with each person who entered, Pastor Paul smiled with a satisfaction reminiscent of the afterglow of a holiday meal, as if contact with another person in and of itself was enough to nourish him. He seemed not to hear the sounds around him: scraping feet, low-volume music from a handful of small players, the squeak of cots being shifted or sat upon, voices and occasional laughter. I had given his backstory to Chalmers, Piñero, and Kim on the way over. Because I had already met Pastor Paul and Brother Grace, Chalmers said, I would take the lead.

When we reached him, I took hold of his dry, cold hand and shook it gently. "Good to see you again, Pastor Paul. I'm Gideon Rimes, Ileana's friend. I met you last week."

"Ah." The upward tilt of his head suggested recognition but may have masked doubt.

"These are my friends, Terry and Rafael," I continued, as Chalmers and Piñero stepped forward to shake his hand. "I was telling them what a wonderful job Brother Grace does for you. Is he here tonight?"

Pastor Paul looked confused, his lower lip quivering. The woman beside him smiled and shook our hands. "I'm Camille," she said. "Brother Grace is either downstairs in the dining hall or carrying supplies down there from the bell tower." She pointed toward a nearby staircase, which had age-darkened steps winding in both directions. We thanked her and went toward it. So far, I noticed, about a third of the cots on the main floor had been claimed. Too many people if something went wrong.

The sound of voices from below pulled us downstairs. The church basement had a low ceiling and cold gray walls, with a large room on either side of the staircase. To the left was the main dining hall, which had fifteen rectangular banquet tables and a kitchen with a serving counter at the far end. Ten more tables were set up to the right, in a space that once held Sunday school classrooms, if the faded construction paper crosses and cut-outs of Jesus holding lambs or children were any indications. Only the main dining room had people in it, taking up fewer than half the seats.

Brother Grace was near the counter in the same pile-lined suede jacket he'd worn last week. He was talking to a winsome young blonde woman, probably a volunteer. She seemed to hang on his every word. I realized the Sanctuary was a perfect place for someone like him to seduce an attractive college student fulfilling volunteer requirements for a course. He would smile whenever he saw her and talk to her whenever he could. He would thank her for volunteering and look embarrassed when she said she admired his compassion. Then one night when the lights were out and the industrial snoring of the chronically lung-impaired began, he would invite her to stay up with him after the other volunteers turned in or left. He would take her somewhere they could be alone, probably not his room in the parsonage when he was on duty. But what about the bell tower he had said was unsafe but was somehow sound enough to hold supplies? Would he take her there, or elsewhere because the bell tower held things she shouldn't see?

"That's him," I said to the detectives. "Give me a little room."

I walked across the room quickly, smiling, holding out my hand, weaving around chattering people and empty chairs. "Brother Grace! Hey, man, it's good to see you again!" His eyes narrowed. He took my hand when I reached him and let me pump it, but clearly I had startled him. "Friend of Miss Tassiopulos. I met you last week."

"Mr. Rimes, right?" he said, pretending he had just recognized me. "What brings you back?" He crossed his arms over his chest. I saw the ring on his right hand.

"Who's your friend?" I said as Chalmers and Piñero closed the distance between us. "My name is Gideon Rimes." I took the woman's hand and held it as if I might be interested.

"Brigid Blake," she said, blushing a bit. "Are you a friend of Brother Grace?"

I smiled. "I said I met him just last week."

Her blush deepened as I released her hand. "Right." Then she smiled. Giggled.

"So, Rimes, what brings you back?"

The question was gratuitous. If Brother Grace had thought I carried myself like a cop when I was an ex-cop, surely he would recognize the two men behind me, broad-shouldered and clad in long overcoats, were still on the job.

"My friends Terry and Rafael," I said to Brigid and Brother Grace as I cocked my head toward the detectives. "We were just upstairs and Camille said you needed help getting supplies down from the bell tower. So here we are."

Brigid giggled again. "You said it was hard to get help. I think these guys can carry a lot more than I can. But I'll be here later if you want to talk some more." Waving at Brother Grace and giggling again, Brigid went over to an old woman whose hands shook so badly she couldn't steady the spoon she was trying to dip into her soup.

"Okay," Brother Grace said. "You're cops. What do you want?"

"I take it you heard about Veronica Surowiec," I said. "She was found dead recently."

"Who? Oh, you mean Nasty Nica." He nodded, sighing a bit. "Yeah, I heard. Damn shame. Wasn't she in the river or something? Drowned?"

"The Black Rock Canal," Chalmers said, eyes shifting from Brother Grace to his ring.

"These detectives are friends of mine," I said, leaning close to Brother Grace as if we were old friends. "When they heard I had seen Veronica here, they wanted all the particulars, which is why I'm back. They have some questions that I couldn't answer but they don't want to ask them out here in front of everybody."

"Hey, bro, why don't we go get that stuff you need from the bell tower," Piñero said. "We all got strong backs. Kill two birds, you know."

Brother Grace looked from one to the other of us, hesitated, and then shrugged. "Sure, why not. Let me show you where it is."

He sidled past us and mounted the spiral stairs, his work boots thumping a steady pace. We followed, with Chalmers in the lead and Piñero behind me.

"So when did you last see—what did you call her? Nasty Nica?" Chalmers said.

"Her street name," Brother Grace said. "I last saw her the night Mr. Rimes talked to her. She left in the morning and I never saw her again."

"Did she drop in here often?"

"I guess once or twice a week." There was no stress in his voice. "You get to know a lot of the regulars, but Nica stood out. She had a real foul mouth, cussed like a sailor. And..."

"And?"

"Her smile." He stopped and looked back at us. "Musta been a nice smile at one time, you know? Kinda smile that makes guys hold open doors and wish they'd get lucky. But with her teeth all gross and shit, that smile just made her look pathetic. Even scary."

"Did you know she was a doctor?"

"I heard that a couple of times. I remember thinking, Damn. Life's a bitch."

We resumed climbing the stairs. I half expected Brother Grace to bolt when we hit the main floor. I wasn't worried because we had the doors covered. But he reached the first floor and kept moving up, the three of us in his wake.

"I know people thought Dr. Surowiec drowned," Chalmers said. "But we didn't find any water in her lungs, which meant she was dead when she went into the canal."

"No shit? Huh."

"Somebody beat her to death, bro," Piñero said.

"That's terrible," Brother Grace said.

"The killer wore a ring," Chalmers said.

Three steps below the small landing at the top of the stairs and the dark wooden door that led to the bell tower, we came to a shadowy split-level tile floor that held a disused choir loft. Inside were cracked benches, broken folding chairs, parts of music stands— all dimly lit by a flickering sconce on the outside wall, just above a bookcase full of old programs, paper church fans, and hymnals that smelled of mold. Brother Grace stepped onto the tiles.

"That's far enough," Chalmers said.

I was behind him, still on the steps. Piñero was behind me.

"But the keys to the bell tower are on that hook." Brother Grace pointed to a brass coat hook beside the sconce. On it was a large key hoop.

"We don't need to go in the bell tower," Chalmers said. He withdrew a folded blue paper from his inside pocket and handed it to Brother Grace. "We have a search warrant here for an infinity ring. Since you're wearing one, we'll start with yours. Then you can tell us if any more are in the building."

Brother Grace opened the warrant and leaned close to the sconce to read it.

His forehead nudged the fixture, and the light went out.

Something cut through the sudden darkness with a whipping sound that connected with flesh. I heard Chalmers cry out. He stumbled backward into me, forcing me to flail for the handrail. I caught it before my eyes began to adjust and strained to hold on as Chalmers's weight forced me backward into Piñero. As we tried to keep ourselves from tumbling down the stairs, something clattered to the floor. Now a shadow, Brother Grace pounded up the last steps, jerked open the door, and disappeared into the bell tower like a bat into the night.

"Son of a bitch!" The light came back on, Chalmers having reached the sconce and jiggled it. Blood dripped out of a gash in his left cheek. He pulled tissue from his pocket and pressed it against his wound. "Bastard knew the wiring was shaky."

"Jesus." Piñero pointed to a tubular steel rod that lay on the floor. It looked as if it had come from a music stand. One end was wet. In the dimness, the color was uncertain to the eye but we knew it was red.

I pushed past Chalmers and opened the bell tower door, but he came right behind me and caught my arm.

"His advantage," he said. "You're lit. He's not. If he's got something up there—"

As if on cue, I heard the unmistakable sound of a slide racked on a semiautomatic pistol. The first shot boomed down through the darkness, tearing a hole between us in the wooden floor of the bell tower landing. The gun was at least .40 caliber.

Chalmers and I pressed our backs against the walls as much as possible. A second shot just missed my foot. The landing was too narrow. Sooner or later Brother Grace would hit one of us. Chalmers and I both unholstered and fired back, two shots each. It didn't matter that his standard-issue Glock 22 S&W.40 was louder than my baby Glock. Each explosion in so tight a space must have hurt everyone else's ears as much as it did mine. Backing down the stairs to give us room to retreat, Piñero screamed, "Shots fired! Shots fired!" into the handy-talky he pulled off his belt but his words sounded distant to my ringing ears. "Get in here and get these people out of the building!"

The ringing faded. I heard screaming. "Out the back!" I shouted. "Not the front!"

"Active shooter in the bell tower! Shooter in the tower!" Piñero said. "Get people out the back so he can't pick 'em off! Call for back-up!"

Chalmers pushed me past him down the stairs. "You got nowhere to go!" he shouted up to Brother Grace, who answered with another shot. Chalmers grunted and clutched his upper chest, toppling into me. We both hit the tile floor outside the choir loft, me on my side, Chalmers on his back. Fedora askew, Piñero pulled his partner to one side, while I skittered backward to the bookcase beside the loft.

"Shit," Chalmers said through clenched teeth. "Shit. Shit. Shit."

"Officer down! Officer down!" Piñero said into his handy-talky. "We need EMTs in the bell tower *now*." Then he tried to peel open Chalmers's leather coat. "Lemme see. Lemme see." Chalmers choked back his pain as Piñero worked the ruined leather over his shoulder.

"How bad?" Chalmers and I said, almost in unison.

"Upper chest, just under the clavicle, maybe two inches from his left shoulder."

Piñero wadded a handkerchief with tissue and pressed it into the wound. I heard feet thudding up the stairs and spun my gun toward the sound just as a rifle came into view.

"Whoa, man! Just me!" Pete Kim said. "My heart's too old for shocks." He held up an AR-15. "From the SUV. The officers are clearing out the church. SWAT is on the way."

"Fucked up my face and shot me," Chalmers said, his breathing labored. "The bastard fucked up my face—"

"You're a tough SOB, Terry," Piñero said. "All that time in the gym, you got this *pendejo* trying to shoot through rhino hide. We'll bring him down so you can spit in his eye."

Three EMTs reached us in less than ten minutes. Piñero, Kim, and I kept our guns trained on the bell tower landing as two men and a woman stabilized Chalmers in the choir loft and got him down-stairs. We followed them part of the way down and held our position to keep Brother Grace in check. After a few minutes the SWAT commander, a big man named Stoll, stepped in to take charge.

"I'm going to the ER," Piñero said when we reached street level and went outside, where the ambulance was just closing its doors. "Pete, you run point till the brass get here."

"Got it, Raf," Kim said as SWAT team members hurried past in various directions.

A few minutes after Piñero took off, Stoll came back down with one of his officers and pulled Kim out of earshot. The three of them spoke for a few minutes. Then the SWAT men moved off and Kim returned to where I stood.

"Standard breach?" I said.

He nodded. "It'll take a bit to set up. Once they establish a perimeter and get some shooters on nearby roofs, we'll all have to knock on doors to evacuate the nearest homes and get other people to their basements. We know he's got at least one piece up there, probably a pistol."

"Sounded like a handgun," I said.

Kim looked at the AR-15 still in his hands and shook his head. "I sure hope he doesn't have any long guns. The last thing a residential neighborhood needs is bullets whizzing every which way."

"This your first SWAT op?" I asked.

He sighed and looked down. "My first was a long time ago, when I was on patrol. A guy with a warrant out on him took his own kids hostage. Didn't end well." He swallowed. "Twenty-three years on the job, ten in a suit, I have a reputation for taking everything in stride. People still ask where I'm from. Or why I'm not in computer science or medicine. I tell them I'm as bad at math as every other kid born here, and my Korean is even worse. Good old Pete, reliable smartass. But I still think about those two little boys and wonder what might have happened if I'd just let the guy jump that stop sign and didn't follow him home."

"Whatever you can't let go makes you a better cop," I said.

"Thanks." He smiled. "At least there are no hostages in play this time. They might be able to talk him out."

I doubted Brother Grace would surrender but kept the thought to myself.

Later, when several captains were on the scene and everything was in place, the SWAT team geared up and went inside. Kim and I crouched behind a cruiser as Commander Stoll made his final megaphone appeal to Brother Grace, which was answered by a single gunshot. Half a minute passed before we heard wood shattering, followed by the *whoompf* of tear gas canisters. No other shots were fired, which made me wonder if Brother Grace had put one through the roof of his mouth.

Presently, the cruiser's radio crackled with Stoll's scream: "Everybody pull back *now!*"

Kim and I stood up and looked at the bell tower. At first we saw nothing. Then, between the louvers, there was an orange glow. Within minutes the tower was engulfed in flames and gunfire filled the night.

What the SWAT team had not known—and no one would know with certainty for almost a week—was that the tower was full of decades-old newspapers, German Bibles, and hymnals from the church's Nineteenth-Century immigrant founders, all ignited by hot tear gas canisters fired up into the darkness. There were also assorted firearms and enough drugs of various kinds to get half the city high. Boxes of ammunition cooked off during the blaze. Bullets bounced and zinged within the stone walls for fifteen or twenty minutes, but no one outside was hurt. The air grew heavy with a burning smell—a mixture of antiseptics, ammonia, other cleaning agents, melting plastic, pungent weed, and something sickening that made a WIVB reporter in a live TV report describe the air as a "cacophony of olfactory horrors."

Pete Kim and I watched the wooden cross atop the tower burst into flames, light up the neighborhood sky, and fall to the street below. Soon the charred frame could no longer support the stone. The building began to fall in upon itself, shattering the few elegant stained glass windows that had not yet blown out and sending up clouds of debris to join the billowing smoke. Covering our mouths and noses as best we could, we choked and coughed and spat as we began to back away from a blossoming hazmat nightmare. I recognized one odor I had not experienced since Iraq and had never wanted to encounter again.

Part of me hoped Brother Grace was already dead when the fire reached his flesh. But another part of me remembered the autopsy photos of Veronica Surowiec and imagined that even in her morgue drawer across town, Nasty Nica must be smiling her scary smile one last time.

45

Having heard from Piñero that Chalmers was in recovery and would be in the ICU by nine or ten that morning, I went home after the Sanctuary Nimbus fire, showered off the smell of smoke, and climbed into bed when most people were having breakfast. I slept till one-fifteen.

Coffee in hand and rereading the account of the Sanctuary Nimbus fire in the Sunday *Buffalo News*, I was still in my robe when my doorbell surprised me. There was no name label in the slot above my doorbell, and all my mail went straight to my office a quarter-mile away. Few people knew my actual address. Most friends would call ahead before coming. Bobby used his landlord key whenever he felt the need to check on me, and Phoenix had her own key—which I hoped she would want to use again. My bell rarely rang, even by accident.

I went to the intercom by the door and pressed the TALK button. "Yes?"

"Rimes?" a woman's voice crackled. "It's Jen. Me and Bianca are downstairs."

The one hitch in my need for privacy. Law enforcement could always find an address.

"We have to talk to you," another voice crackled, tearful and unsteady. Bianca.

I pressed TALK. "Okay." I buzzed them up and tightened my robe. Then I opened my door and watched them climb the stairs.

Both wore jeans and ski jackets. Jen's knit watch cap was a lighter purple than her ski jacket. With a blue hoodie under a puffy red jacket, Bianca looked less elegant than when I first met her at the Galleria, and her face looked more tired.

I gestured them into my living room. Despite tired eyes and an arm around her wife, Jen, the cop, took in everything—the arched windows above the built-in bookcases, the flat-screen TV and sound system, the prints of Henry Ossawa Tanner's *Banjo Lesson* and *The Thankful Poor* and Faith Ringgold's *Echoes of Harlem*, the free weights, push-up disks, and heavy bag in my workout corner. Then she noticed the bandage on my chin and looked away. My assessment of her had been right. One day she would make a fine detective. On the other hand, her eyes wet and haunted-looking, Bianca seemed to notice nothing. Both women sat on the black leather couch, as I dropped into the leather armchair I used to watch television.

"How can I help you?" I asked.

Jen helped Bianca out of her ski jacket. "I thought she was heading to the Rowhouse around the corner to get pastries to go with our coffee." Then she removed her own jacket, revealing a heavy beige sweater, and put both coats on the far end of the couch. "But she went to see Keisha and now she's scared."

"Keisha's got a gun," Bianca said, her voice low and her face looking distant and taut in the hoodie. "She's going after Mrs. Markham."

I sat forward. "You know this how?"

"I saw it." She pushed her hoodie back. "I—" Her face fell then, tears beginning to trickle down her cheeks. She turned into Jen's shoulder and cried.

"Keisha sent her a text this morning," Jen said, matter-of-factly, as she had been trained. "She asked if they could meet at the bakery near our apartment, without me so she could give Bianca something private. It was this." From her back pocket, she took a folded piece of lined spiral notebook paper and handed it to me.

I opened it and sat back. I recognized the tight, precise handwriting.

Dear Mom & Dad, Bianca (+ Jen) & Fatimah (+ your family),

First, I love you all. Before, if you asked me if there was a hell, I'd have said it doesn't matter. If what the church says is true and you live a good life, you don't have to worry. If it's all just myth and you live a good life, you still don't have to worry. You did the right thing, doing more good than bad, helping more people than you hurt. A good life lived can be its own reward. I tried to live a good life. But then I went to hell. Dr. Markham likes to say we're born in the crossfire between heaven and hell and we remain there until the end. Which way we're pushed is not always up to us. That's why our faith must be strong. But I saw the man I loved murdered. I nearly died myself. This left me on the run and afraid.

This hell was created by a woman I admired, maybe even loved. At first, I thought she couldn't possibly be involved. She must be as much a victim as I was. Then I looked out the back window of a car and saw one of my former Sunday school students trying to kill me. That's when I knew the suspicions I had denied were true. His crush on her was never a secret. He would do anything she asked.

But that all ends today. If you're reading this, I am dead. At least I died knowing I put an end to the woman who destroyed me.

Thank you for loving me. Please remember me to Ileana and all my friends at work, and to Odell's parents, who deserved better. Don't forget Mr. Rimes and Ms. Trinidad for saving my life so I can complete what I think God may have put me on this earth to do.

Love always,

Keisha

"What time was this?" I asked, folding the note and handing it back to Jen.

"About eight-thirty," Bianca said, sniffling. "She gave me that because she said she was going to take the fight to Mrs. Markham and finish it. Today. There was a good chance she might not make it out, so she wanted me to have this for her parents and friends. If she called me tonight, that meant she was okay and I should rip it up or burn it. If not—"

"May I see the text?"

Bianca took an iPhone from her hoodie pocket, tapped the screen, and passed it to me. I read the cell number and the message, which matched Jen's summary. For a moment I thought about all of it. Then I handed back the phone.

"You saw the gun," I said.

"Yes, it was in her purse."

"A handgun then. Any idea where she got it?"

"No."

"Describe it."

"She didn't take it out. I saw it when she opened her bag to give me the note." Bianca looked at Jen. "It kinda looked like your guns, baby, smaller than the one you take to work, a little bigger than the one you let me shoot in the woods." She turned back to me. "Black, with a split trigger thingy."

"So maybe a Glock, probably 9mm," Jen said.

"I saw the letters PPQ on it," Bianca said.

"A Walther?" Jen said. "Who does she think she is, Jane Bond?"

I let out a breath. "What kind of purse?" I asked.

"Medium size, brown with a shoulder strap."

"What is she wearing?"

"A black jacket with a fur collar. Black pants. Brown boots."

I vaguely remembered the jacket from Keisha's coat tree the first time I saw it. I was certain she hadn't slept in her own bed last night because Loni and Dante knew where she lived, but clearly she had gone home to dress for her mission. Had drunk a glass of wine.

Jen looked at me and bit her lip. "People who don't know what they're doing can have accidents with safety triggers."

I nodded. "This is something you could take to your department."

"Bianca asked me not to."

"I'm afraid *angry black woman with gun* will mean *shoot on sight*."

Bianca squeezed Jen's hand. "I know it's not always like that, baby, but this is my sister we're talking about."

"I know," Jen said, closing her eyes

"I don't want to take the chance."

"I know."

"So, back to my original question," I said. "How can I help?" I needed them to say it.

Bianca released Jen's hand and used the back of her own to wipe her eyes. Then she gazed straight into my eyes. "I want to hire you to find her before she does this and bring her in alive. I'll pay."

"No need," I said. "Unfinished business I already promised Jen I'd fix. But you have to know where things stand. Keisha still thinks they tried to kill her over a real estate deal."

I stood and went to my kitchen counter to get two sections of the Sunday paper I had already read. I took them to the living room and put them on the coffee table in front of the couch. Then I summarized the articles for Jen and Bianca.

The front page reported the Sanctuary Nimbus fire, with a full-color above-the-fold picture of the church engulfed in flames and an erroneous detail, perhaps provided by shelter staff. The lone fatality was an as yet unidentified man who had shot a police officer, fled into the Sanctuary, and locked himself in the bell tower. Tear gas canisters from the responding SWAT team were theorized to have started the fire by igniting stored papers. The unnamed officer was recovering after surgery.

The local news section reported a two-car accident near the end of the Kensington Expressway that claimed the life of one driver and saw his passenger arrested for possession and discharge of a firearm, which numerous drivers had reported by cell phone. The driver and passenger of the second vehicle were treated at the scene and released. Police were investigating whether criminal recklessness or icy conditions had caused the mishap. The article carried all our names except Tito's, whose identity was being withheld, pending notification of next of kin. Nothing connected the accident to the fire.

"I knew about the crash, and you told me about Tito," Jen said. "I heard the fire was a SWAT op gone wrong but we haven't seen the paper till now."

"We were outside the church all morning," Bianca said. "Watching for Keisha but she never came. The ten-thirty service ended a little while ago, and we came straight here."

"You thought Keisha would try to shoot Mrs. Markham at the church?" I asked.

"She told me she would settle things today, where everybody could learn the truth." Bianca spread her hands. "If she goes to their house, nobody will see what happens. It has to be at church."

"Is there another service or event today?"

"The monthly luncheon was last Sunday when Keisha's mom got shot. But there's a brief service every Sunday night at seven—a welcome, a sermonette, some songs of praise."

"Are there fewer worshippers in the evening?"

"Usually, as I recall."

"Fewer bystanders but enough witnesses to report whatever Keisha says." Jen shifted her gaze back to the newspaper pages. "So how does this fire relate to the crash and Keisha?"

"The guy who burned was the one who tried to have Keisha's mom killed. He and Butch, Tito's shooter, had rings from the same gang. Things went off the rails when police went to the shelter with a warrant for his ring for testing in another murder. Also, Tito and Butch played ball together at EMU."

"What does all that mean?" Bianca asked.

"Long story short, a white biker gang from the Southern Tier and a black drug gang out of Detroit are working together, using a development company, a church foundation, and a charity to cover money laundering and drug distribution. The newspaper doesn't say what caused that smell last night, but my nose told me a lot of drugs burned up."

"You were there?" Bianca said.

"Course you were," Jen said, smiling. "I can still smell smoke on you. But that's an off-the-wall partnership. Mrs. Minister is tangled up in a lot more than we thought."

"Including sleeping with Tito." I saw the surprise on Jen's face but not Bianca's.

"Kids started teasing him about his crush on her when he was twelve," she said. "He would just look at her and his eyes would glaze over."

"I guess Loni Markham didn't have to look far for devoted help." I shook my head and sighed. "I better get dressed."

"You've got a little time," Bianca said. "The service doesn't start till seven."

"Any idea why Keisha didn't show outside church?" I asked.

"No car. It was a long walk. Or maybe Jen's right and she wants fewer bystanders."

"Could be," I said. "But I think it's because she met you at Rowhouse earlier and couldn't get to the church fast enough to hide. With Sunday school and service right after that, it was too busy for her to slip in unseen. Everybody knows she's missing. Wouldn't being seen cause excitement and make it harder for her to take a shot?"

"So you think she'll try to get inside some time *before* vespers," Jen said.

Bianca scrunched her face in doubt. "I'm sure the church is locked between services."

"But until a few months ago, Keisha was the church secretary," I said.

Then Bianca's face lit up with understanding. "She still has her key."

46

I made Jen and Bianca leave before I got dressed. "From this point on, for the sake of your career, you can't know how or when I got into the church," I said to Jen. Then I looked at Bianca. "But I wouldn't mind if you wanted to show your off-duty police officer wife the church you grew up in and brought her to the evening service."

Bianca went up on her toes to kiss my cheek. "Thank you."

After making a necessary phone call, I shaved and decided the surgical glue had made replacing the bandage on my chin unnecessary. I dressed in a sweatshirt, jeans, and rubber-soled boots. My shoulder and right arm felt ready, so I swapped the cross-draw holster for my nylon shoulder rig and pulled on the black utility jacket I used for the occasional bounty hunting job. It had a hood and pockets everywhere for plasticuffs, a short baton, Gorilla tape, a tactical knife, and a tactical flashlight that doubled as a stun gun. I added the lock pick gun.

Before going to the church, I stopped by Buffalo General to see Chalmers in the ICU.

MaryAnn Maclin, who had tried to calm Keisha the night she tried to see her mother, was on duty at the high-tech nursing pod, overseeing other patients but not Chalmers. She shook her head sadly and said, in a lowered voice, "Please tell me you are *not* here to see the man in Number Six, the detective who got shot."

"Sorry," I said. "I guess he'll be known by the company he keeps."

"I heard what happened after Mrs. Simpkins left us." She kept her voice low but she smiled. "The whole hospital was talking about a PI who prevented a murder. I knew it was my paladin even before I heard the patient's name. You know, I had to look that word up."

"Then if I'm ever known by the company I keep, talking to you will bump me up several notches."

"Oh, I do know a bullshitter when I hear one." She laughed, softly. "I *am* married to a man who sells cars."

Chalmers was alone, sitting up in his bed, trying with one arm immobilized to read a newspaper amid tubes and wires. The sutures in his right cheek were small enough to make them seem a steroid-fueled advance team for the rest of the stubble on his face. He looked up and half-grinned when he saw me. "Can't smile too much 'cause it hurts." His voice sounded groggy.

"I see you made it through your post-surgical hangover," I said. "How you feeling?"

"Okay. Luckily it wasn't a full slug, just a chunk from a ricochet. They're pumping in pain meds every so often. It makes me loopy. I think I got the last one a few minutes ago."

"Hope it helps,"

"They said I'd be in a regular room by tonight. That's good, but I'll be off at least six weeks. Gonna need PT for my arm—just like you. I won't know what to do with myself."

"That'll take you past the holiday season. How about a ski trip when the rates drop?"

"Damn you, G," he said, biting his lip. "I'm not much of a laugher, man. I *smile* at jokes. If I smile too much and tear these stitches, it's all your fault."

"Sorry," I said. "If it's any consolation, the PT they'll send you to is very good."

He eased his head back against the pillow, took a deep breath.

"Maybe I could spend time trying to patch things up with Diana. You know, she dumped me a couple of weeks ago."

"I heard. Sorry about that too."

"That's all right. A special ed professor is out of my league anyway, like Phoenix is out of yours. Inevitable for guys like us."

I said nothing as I thought about Phoenix. Was it inevitable that she would leave? I pushed the thought aside. I would have my answer soon enough.

"Maybe I should talk to that doctor who checked on me this morning. African lady from my surgical team. She was pretty. Can't remember her name though. Too out of it."

"Dr. Ibazebo," I said. "I know her. She's one of Bobby's old students."

"Is she single?"

"I don't know, but if Diana is out of your league, Ayodele's a champ in a completely different sport."

"Ayodele. What a pretty name." Then Chalmers nodded toward the paper open in his lap. "By the way, did you see that shit? He shot me and *ran into the shelter*?" He clicked his tongue in disgust. "Pastor Paul's got some nerve trying to distance himself from *Brother* Grace."

"I don't think it was Pastor Paul. An ambulance took him away after the building came down. Looked to me like he was having a heart attack. I don't know whether he ended up here or in another CCU but I heard on the radio he didn't make it."

He tapped the paper. "This just says people were taken to hospitals for exposure and firefighters for exhaustion."

"Hey, they gotta put the best face on it. The stuff about Brother Grace probably came from one of Pastor Paul's guys trying to run interference," I said. "Maybe Marco Madden."

"Raf stopped by about an hour ago. After the fire and what folks on the scene thought must be drugs burning up, this investigation can only grow. So far nobody's been able to find Marco. Be nice if we could connect him to that damn church lady you keep talking about. The threads are still too loose for me." He put his head against the pillow again, and the rhythm of his breathing changed. "So how are you spending this fine December Sunday?"

"I'm gonna try to tighten some of those threads and keep my clients' daughter alive."

"You can't tell me more, can you?"

"Not yet." I smiled. "I think I'll let you rest a bit."

"Yeah. Feels like that stuff is kicking in."

He closed his eyes, and I left.

47

Sermon on the Mount was a short walk from Buffalo General, so I considered leaving the car where it was. Once I got outside, however, I realized I couldn't break into the church if there was a car in the lot, especially Dr. Markham's Town Car or Loni's Camry. I would need a place to wait for whoever was inside to leave. It was too cold to wait outside. I drove past the lot and was glad to find it empty. Light afternoon traffic on Sunday made a U-turn on Main Street easier then than any other time of the week. I parked across the street from the lot and got out.

I crossed Main and walked around the outside of the church, noting the exits. There were three for the public: the front door at the top of a stone staircase, a side door at ground level near the front, and the parking lot door Dr. Markham had opened for me on my first visit. A wide garage-style door in the very back seemed to be for deliveries.

I ended up at the parking door, climbed the three steps, and pressed the electronic doorbell, just to be sure. As I waited to see if anyone would answer, I looked back at the RAV4, at the apartments and storefronts across the street. Seeing no curious faces, and getting no answer, I took out the lock pick gun and turned my back toward the sidewalk so anyone passing would process the scene as someone using a key.

The corridor I stepped into was dark but warm. I wiped my boots on the commercial-sized mat and listened for any indication of movement. The only sound I heard was a radiator hissing. I thought about that. Maintaining the heat had been Tito's job. As far as I knew, his body was still unclaimed and unidentified. The newspaper article had carried no details about his car, no request for information. His name would not be made public until the next of kin came to identify him. Because he had no next of kin, there was a chance the congregation did not yet know he was gone. Who knew? Certainly Loni Markham and Harlow Graves. She had no reason to claim the body yet, no reason to draw police attention to the home church of a would-be murderer while she tried to figure out her next move. Graves took his cues from her. One of them—or someone else, like Dante or QC—had come in to adjust the thermostat.

I took out my Taclight and moved along the hallway with the beam held low.

Most older Christian churches had the same basic cruciform layout—the front door at the back of the sanctuary, the narthex opening onto the nave where worshippers sat, a wide aisle between rows of pews, a narrow aisle along either wall lit by stained glass windows, a transept or wide area in front leading to a raised chancel for the altar and the pulpit. Sermon on the Mount was no different. But passing Dr. Markham's office, I decided to explore the areas outside the sanctuary first. Keisha would need somewhere to hide before her ambush. It would help to anticipate where.

I went down the middle staircase to a basement lit by EXIT signs. It had classrooms with accordion doors on either side of a Sunday school chapel, a dining hall and kitchen, a choir changing room, and a steel-doored room that had the boiler, breaker boxes, and delivery door. Hiding in bathrooms was impractical, so I checked storage closets, none of which offered much room to stay out of sight, at least not for someone my size. Maybe Keisha could pull it off, but there was no place to sit, and breathing for a long time amid boxes and dust would be difficult. She would likely need a more comfortable spot.

I climbed the back stairs to a corridor that bracketed the sanctuary, with a door on either end to permit entry on either side of the chancel during a service. The only locked rooms I found were the minister's office and an anteroom for storage of collection plates, a box of hymn board numbers, communion supplies, and other paraphernalia. As I stepped inside the nave on the right, I saw the left front had two rows of metal folding chairs arranged around an upright piano in the transept, with a drum kit off to one side. The Markhams had said something about the choir singing down in front because there was a problem with the loft.

Not up to code? New organ? Something.

I shone my beam toward the narthex. A traditional choir loft was above it. I went to the front of the building and pushed open one of the amber-glassed swinging doors. To my left, I saw stairs to the side door heading down and stairs to the loft heading up. Yellow tape with *Danger* in black letters made an X across the archway to the loft. I removed one leg of the X and squeezed past it to go up. If the loft had been ready to collapse, I reasoned, there would have been more than tape. At the top, I put a foot in front of a pew and pushed down on the floorboards. No give. Maybe it couldn't support an entire choir, but the loft would hold me. When I sat on the floor, I realized I was behind a solid front panel and could not be seen from below. Shining my light around, I saw a large vacant space on the other side. Pipes were still in place, but the organ itself was gone, which explained the folding chairs. Up here the choir would be too far away from the piano. Likely having died from old age and neglect, the organ must have been disassembled and removed in pieces, some too heavy to get across the loft to the stairs. I sidled between pews to the edge of the cavity, looked down, and saw no framework to support the narthex ceiling panel below. No one would risk coming up here. It wasn't the best place to set up a handgun shot but a perfect spot to hide.

I went down to reattach the tape. Then I returned to the loft and sat on the floor.

The doorbell rang an hour or so later. I didn't have to strain to hear it. It wasn't the bell on the parking lot door but the bell beside the front door, right below me. It rang for a long time. After half a minute or so of silence, it rang again. When no one answered, I heard the scrape of a key in the lock and the squeak of a heavy door. It closed and the bolt shot back into place. Whoever was there took time to listen before wiping boots on the narthex floormat. A moment later came the sound of painter's tape being peeled away then smoothed back down, followed by footsteps on the stairs. The weak beam of a penlight came into view.

I took out my Taclight, cupped one hand over the front, and pushed the button three times. When she rounded the corner to step into the loft, I hit Keisha full in the face with the 1200 lumen strobe beam. She dropped her penlight and covered her eyes with her left hand as her right plunged into the bag hanging from her left shoulder.

I saw the gun come out. "It's Gideon Rimes," I said. "Don't shoot, Keisha." I clicked to the standard beam and lowered the light. "This is one of my favorite jackets."

She lowered the gun. "What are you doing here!" Her voice was a harsh whisper, though we were alone in the building.

"Waiting for you." I angled the Taclight so we could see each other. "No glasses. Must mean contacts. When you go to shoot, you have to make sure you can see your target."

Keisha stood there looking at me, saying nothing.

"Jen and Bianca came to me," I said. "They showed me your text and told me everything. Bianca's worried sick about you."

"Shit." Keisha plopped onto the first pew. "I told her not to tell Jen."

"Jen's her wife." I picked up her penlight from the floor and handed it to her. Then I rose and sat in the pew beside her. "Jen's a cop and Bianca's worried about her sister. How did you think this would play out?"

She was quiet as I braced the Taclight between two hymnals on the bench between us. We were half in shadow but could still see each other.

"All relationships have secrets. Believe me, I know. You can't know everything about someone. Maybe you're not even supposed to." I paused to let her consider that. She looked at me with uncertainty. "But if you died tonight and Bianca did nothing to stop it, *this* secret would have killed them as a couple. Bianca would have blamed herself and transferred her misery to Jen until it broke them apart." I paused. "I like them a lot, your friends, just the way they are."

"They showed you the text. What about—"

"Was Bianca the only one you told what you planned to do?"

"Yes."

"Then it doesn't matter."

She was quiet a moment. "I have to do this, for Odell. For Mom and Dad. Sometimes you have to be willing to make the sacrifice." She shook her head, eyes moistening. "If I don't, Odell died for nothing." She started to stand. "I'm going to clear his name."

"You'll die," I said, taking her arm and gently pulling her back into her seat. "If Dante is anywhere in this building tonight, he *will* try to kill you."

She wrenched her arm free. "I told you, I'm willing to make the sacrifice."

"He wants to kill me too but I'm not ready to go." I offered her tissue from one of my pockets and waited for her to dab her eyes. "Now, I think I know what you want to do. This loft is too far away."

"I wasn't going to shoot from here!"

"Course not," I said. "I think your plan is to sneak downstairs, go through the basement, and come up near the front. Then you'll step in and make your move. Right?"

She said nothing.

"The trouble with your plan is that Loni expects you."

"So?"

"So, her brother and at least one of his men are in town. There may be more. She'll have *somebody* at each door. They'll have guns, maybe with silencers, or cord to strangle you—while people are singing gospel songs on the other side of the wall. You'll never get close enough by trying to go around."

She looked at her gun before returning it to her bag. "I still won't let you stop me."

"I'm not here to stop you. I'm here to keep you alive."

"How are you going to do that? By walking me right down the aisle?"

"Yes." I took her hand in mine and looked into her eyes. "If we think it through, you can finish this tonight. You can get justice for Odell, and we can both walk out of here alive."

48

L oni must have entered through the parking lot door. The first sign we had anyone else in the building, about thirty minutes before the start of service, was the squeak of the side door being opened from the inside, followed by Loni's voice saying, "Come inside, quick!"

Then there were men's voices greeting her and the scrape of feet, first on a doormat and then hitting the stairs that led to the narthex.

Keisha and I were still sitting on the floor in the dark in the choir loft. During the previous half-hour, I had made a phone call and sent two text messages before I explained to her all I had learned since our meeting in Tim Horton's. Now, left index finger pressed to her lips, I held her right hand with my own. My fingertips felt her pulse racing. For a moment I was afraid the tension might cause her to exhale too loudly and set things in motion before we were ready. Someone switched on the narthex ceiling fixtures, which threw muted light up to us, enough for me to see her eyes widen with fear. I took a few deep but quiet breaths, calming myself. Then I raised my eyebrows as if to ask if she understood what I wanted her to do. When she nodded, I removed my finger. She caught her lower lip between her teeth.

We waited. Listened.

"I told you before I wished you'd brought more people, D," Loni said. "Least two."

"Told you, QC and I could handle things." The voice was deep and melodious as if the vocal cords had been cut off an upright bass and sewn into his throat with angel hair filament. "Holiday time keeps my people busy organizing for the new year."

I raised my eyebrows toward Keisha again. She nodded. Dante.

"Problems here might mean problems everywhere. Local cops get on to something interesting and hook up with the feds—Jesus, all it takes is a thread. This shoulda been simple. Follow the guy hired to look for her and take her out when he finds her—him too if necessary."

"He made us the first day."

"So you rented other SUVs. Gave him room to do his job. Passed him back and forth by cell phone when you saw him. One morning you followed him home from the hospital, so you started watching his place. Good plan. Sooner or later he'd lead you to her, and he did."

"Damn it, Loni. Once we saw they were together in the coffee shop, we passed them like we were supposed to. I mean, we coulda gone in and made a massacre out of it, but the idea was to keep a low profile. Nobody told Tito and that dumb biker hillbilly to make a run at a moving car. They were just supposed to follow and pass them back to us for the kill."

"Maybe Grizzly Man was pissed Rimes beat up his bitch in the hospital," Loni said. "I don't know these clowns on the flip side. A wall of protection, deniability—that's the whole point of compartmentalization. They fucked up the hospital hit and ended up killing some meth addict, which led to the fire. God knows how much we lost in product and cover in that mess. I hope there's nothing to connect those fools to us. They're your responsibility."

"Tito was yours. He fucked up just as much as the white boys. He was supposed to shoot *at* the bitch's parents, not hit them. Like we needed another investigation."

"Don't go blaming Tito! You liked him just fine when he made this business hook-up possible. There woulda been no investigation at all if you'd got it right the first time."

For a few seconds, no one said anything.

"Nobody knew Tito was gonna clock out either. Sorry." More silence. "But the real pain in the ass here is this guy Rimes. All up in our shit and not even a real badge."

"Right. If anything has stretched this out, it's him. He's always a beat behind us but unwilling to just step off. We underestimated how persistent he would be."

Keisha smiled at me and mouthed *Thank you.*

"All the years it took us to build this up, and he almost tanks it in a week? He got off the *if necessary* list a long time ago. That mother-fucker has got to die. He's mine."

"Chill, Dante. You gonna get your shot." This was a new voice. "So you really think she'll come here tonight?" Higher, reedier, a bit too cheerful. "She that stupid?"

I looked at Keisha. She nodded again. QC.

"No, I'm not sure, QC." Loni sounded exasperated. "If I was, I wouldn'ta had you watching her house all day and Dante watching mine. I woulda just had you come here. If you'd brought more people, I wouldn'ta had a pinch hitter burning a tank of gas shuttling back and forth between Rimes's office and his apartment building."

Then there came a giggle, high and almost a cackle as if Macbeth's witches were laughing through waxed paper. "I'm just sayin', maybe she's smart enough to get out of town with her folks. So they're in Cleveland?"

"Sister Simpkins called one of her friends, who told me after church this morning when I mentioned how surprised I was they weren't there. I said it like I was hoping they had good news about Keisha. But they're not important right now."

I looked at Keisha. Looking horrified, she shook her head and mouthed *Sorry.*

"Always amazes me how much you know," Dante said. "It's like a sixth sense."

"All people love to talk, Dante. Church ladies and cab drivers. Hospital aides and janitors. Counter clerks and food servers. Everybody wants to confess or impress. That's why nobody can keep a secret. I learned a long time ago to just listen and piece things together. I'm still surprised I could keep the news about Tito a secret."

"Yeah, how'd you pull that off?" QC asked.

"Two people in the congregation know. I bought us a little time by convincing them the police told us not to say anything until the investigation is complete. Talking about it could get all of us charged with obstruction of justice. Then I called the police on a burner and said I was Tito's Aunt Susie. I'd be back from California Monday night to identify him."

"You're sure good old Felton doesn't know?" Dante asked.

"Good old Felton doesn't even know I have a brother," Loni said. "When I last saw him, about an hour ago, he didn't know about Tito either. He was gonna make a couple of hospital stops and then come straight here." She paused. "Okay, here's how we're gonna do this. QC, I want you by the side door, there. Just hold the door for folks and smile. Anybody asks you're just visiting from out of town and saw we were having a service. Dante, I want you between the parking lot door and the right side door near the altar, across from where I'll be, at the piano. You've seen Felton on TV. See him here, same story. You're just visiting and thought you'd drop in. Ask how to get to the men's room."

"Who got the front door?" QC asked.

"You, until my pinch hitter gets here. Then it's his."

"Who is it?"

"No one you know and no one who knows you," Loni said. "Compartmentalization, remember? Okay, if either of you see Keisha or Rimes, move on them, even if they come in with the crowd. Silencers or not, do not shoot inside this church, in front of all these people. Just get them outside with the threat of shooting. If Rimes shows, make sure you get his gun. Get them around back where nobody can see. Then you can drop them. Put them behind that row of blue garbage totes until things are over and we can clean up."

"Your pinch hitter up to all that?" Dante asked.

"No. He'll call QC from the side door if either one shows. *All that* is up to you two."

There was a knock.

Footsteps crossed the narthex and went down the stairs. The door squeaked open.

"About time."

Two sets of footsteps returned to the narthex.

"Sorry I'm late," Harlow Graves said. "Had to drop Ros and the kids at a movie."

Keisha's eyes widened and she mouthed *Harlow Graves?* I nodded.

Loni made introductions without explaining her relationship to any of the men, except to say that Graves was a church VIP who would greet worshippers at the front door. Then she summarized the plan for Graves and told them in a few minutes they would take their places while she went to the piano. She would begin playing ten minutes before the service started. The choir would come up the side stairs to the narthex and walk in step with the music down the center aisle, followed by several deaconesses who would greet those in attendance, and finally her husband.

Fifteen minutes later the music began.

49

P eeking over the solid front of the loft, I saw Loni at the piano and watched the last of the choir take their seats, followed by a boy maybe fourteen who sat at the drums. Deaconesses moved from pew to pew, shaking hands and exchanging pleasantries with worshippers. There was a jubilance to the exchanges filling the air—rapid talk, chuckles, outright laughter. I could see smiles, hands on shoulders, heads bobbing up and down, women kissing cheeks and giving hugs. But gradually the conversations trailed off to an expectant silence. Dr. Markham had not yet come in. I ducked down as heads began to swivel in search of him.

A moment later I heard an almost collective sigh of relief. Footsteps hurried down the center aisle. A finger tapped a microphone, and the speaker above us in the loft thumped.

"Brothers and sisters, after pleasant hospital visits with Mother Carlyle and Brother Fisher—both coming along nicely, praise God —it was my intention to simply close this day of worship with a joyful noise that would lift our spirits as we went back to work this week." Dr. Markham's customary authoritative tone seemed unsettled. "But—" His voice cracked, and I knew he had listened to my message on his office answering machine. "But the unexpected compels me to change the order of service tonight. Would you mind if I did that, if I changed the order of service, in the name of the Lord?"

As one, the congregation said, "No!"

"Thank you, brothers and sisters. I reached the church only a short time ago and checked the messages in my office when I came in." He hesitated. "Somebody from the police left a sad message about one of our own and a number to call back. I didn't want to believe what I'd been told because the man didn't leave his name, but I called back. Now I can confirm that a son of this church, our custodian, Tito Glenroy, is dead."

The gasps were almost in unison, followed by chatter, questions, crying. I couldn't see it as I kept out of sight but I pictured Dr. Markham holding up his hand to calm everyone.

"They said he was killed in an accident on the expressway yesterday afternoon but went unclaimed all night because there was no one to identify him. They couldn't give me details because they're still investigating. I imagine him there, cold and lonely, sad nobody came, wanting nothing more than to go home. Funny thing though. The man I spoke to said a note clipped to his file said his Aunt Susie was coming from California on Monday to claim the body. As far as I know, Tito doesn't have an Aunt Susie. If any of you know differently, please tell us now." He paused, waiting in vain for confirmation of Aunt Susie. Then he swallowed audibly. "If Tito died yesterday, that means he didn't come in to turn up the heat this morning. It means —" Dr. Markham began to cry. "I told that boy time and again not to leave the heat so high when nobody was here, and he was good about it because he knew what our heating bills are. But this one time he must have left it on when he went about his Saturday chores—like he knew he was gonna die and didn't want us to be cold. Should I forgive him?"

"Yes, forgive him!" a woman said, and the congregation echoed her sentiment.

"I forgive you, Tito," the minister said. "I forgive you in the name of Jesus and for all your service to this faith community. I forgive you, and I ask that my dear wife lead the choir and all of you in 'I'll Praise His Name.' For poor Tito."

The first few notes were shaky—because, I suspected, Loni was calculating how this revelation would impact her plans. But that mattered little to me because I had plans of my own. As the tempo picked up and the sound of the gospel number filled the sanctuary, I sent another text message. Then I crept downstairs as far as I could, pulled down the tape, and peeked around the archway. A minute later Oscar Edgerton, overcoat unbuttoned, pushed through one of the swinging doors and went to the front door. Music muffled his exchange with Harlow Graves, but a rush of cold air told me Graves had agreed to Oscar's request they step outside for a moment to discuss a matter of importance to the church.

Which was what I'd told him to say in my most recent text.

I had called Oscar from home earlier, before heading to the hospital. I laid out the case as I understood it. Though he found it hard to believe Loni Markham was behind everything, he had read about the crash and the fire and even knew a woman had been found dead in the Black Rock Canal. He hadn't known about Tito and agreed to tell no one, not even Louisa, until the news was official. Giving me the benefit of the doubt, he'd promised to attend the evening service and keep his phone on vibrate so I could tell him what help I needed. My first text had told him to sit near the back. My second told him to get Harlow Graves outside.

Now that Graves was gone, I peeked as far as I dared around the other side of the archway. I couldn't see all of QC, just a thick arm and shoulder stuffed into a wide-striped tan suit jacket. I clicked on the penlight I'd got from Keisha and rolled it hard toward the stairs. With the singing, drumming, and piano playing in the sanctuary so loud, I couldn't hear the penlight bounce down the stairs toward him. I couldn't hear whether he called out to Graves. But I knew he would come up the steps to see what was going on.

I readied myself.

Right arm inside his jacket, QC moved into view as he began to pass the arch. He was big, a bit shorter than I but heavier, with medium brown skin and a broad back. He turned, as if peripherally aware the Danger tape was missing, a mouth between fat cheeks beginning to open, beady eyes beginning to widen.

I grabbed his right arm with my left hand, jammed the glass breakpoints of my Taclight into the soft flesh of his neck, and pressed the stun button. QC jerked and made a strange hiccupping motion with his mouth. The music covered whatever sound he made, as well as the *phfft* of his silencer. But I felt his gun, still in its holster, jerk when the shock made him seize and squeeze the trigger. I saw the blood soaking through his pants and lowered him to the steps but kept hold of his right arm.

He looked up at me, blinking, mouth moving without saying anything, gun hand trembling. Then he started to giggle, an unnerving sound even amid loud music.

With my free hand, I stuffed the pocket square from his suit jacket into his mouth and pushed it deeper as he tried to speak. Then I removed his gun from the cross-draw holster on his left hip, unscrewed the still warm suppressor, and tossed it aside. The gun and his cell phone went into one of my pockets and plasticuffs came out of another. Rolling him onto his right side, I cuffed his hands behind him and then his feet at the ankles.

"You shot yourself, QC," I said. "If you need a tourniquet, all I've got is your tie. But if you try to scream, I'll tie it around your mouth, and you might bleed out. Should I use it to stop the bleeding?"

Still on his side against the edges of the stairs, he nodded, hard.

With my tactical knife, I cut away enough of his pants to show me the bullet was likely lodged in his meaty left hip. The rate of blood flow did not indicate arterial damage or the need for a tourniquet. I cut a long strip off his pants and tied it around the entry wound just tight enough to make a temporary bandage. Then I rolled him back as far as both sets of cuffs would allow. His angle was awkward against the stairs. He looked uncomfortable.

"The good news is, you won't bleed out and you still have your dick," I said, undoing his brown and gold tie and pulling it from around his neck. "The bad news? I don't trust you to keep quiet." I wrapped the tie around his mouth twice and knotted it between his teeth. Flaring nostrils told me he could breathe. Then his beady eyes became discs full of fear.

Keisha had come down the steps and now stood behind me, gun in hand. "Hello, QC. The bitch is back."

"Keisha, eyes on the main course," I said. "Yes, it's personal but this idiot's only the appetizer."

"I know." She slipped the gun back into her shoulder bag. "I just want to see him sweat." Moving from behind me, she put one boot heel against the makeshift bandage and pressed down with all her weight.

QC's eyes grew so wide his irises were ringed by white. He shook and jittered and made a horrible muffled trumpeting in his throat, cheeks filling like a bellows. When she stepped back, he was puffing hard, his forehead slick. His eyes were still fearful but now wet.

"There," she said, as I stood. "That was for Odell."

Just then the front door opened, letting in another blast of cold air. Harlow Graves walked in, his face twisted in apparent disgust, and said something I couldn't hear over his shoulder to Oscar, who was behind him. Graves saw me and stopped in mid-sentence as I leveled my Glock at him. Then he saw Keisha and QC. He started to turn as if to head back outside, but Oscar caught his arm and twisted it into a hammerlock that kept him angled to one side. Graves muttered something about making us pay—until I motioned them over, placed the barrel against his forehead, and told him one word or wrong move would make Rosalind a widow.

Oscar looked at Keisha and smiled. "Girl, your daddy is sure gonna be thrilled to see you. Soon as I can, I'll hug you for him." Then he looked at QC, who had slid down to the floor in front of the stairs. "Which one is he?"

"The fake cousin," I said. "He shot himself when I shocked him." I looked at Graves. "I take it he denied any involvement."

"Denied every word," Oscar said. "Told me he was just a lawyer who didn't know anything about FBF."

"Yet here he is sharing guard duty with FBF's chairman of the board, and the CEO, both of them cold-blooded killers." I gestured to Graves's tie. "We need to truss him up the same way, so we can finish this without interference."

Nodding, Oscar removed Graves's tie as I pulled out more plasticuffs. It took less than a minute to immobilize and silence Graves, whom we left on the floor near QC.

Despite the lessening of fervor and the slowing of the drumming that meant the song was winding down, I gave Oscar and Keisha a moment to embrace. I took that time to type and send my final text message of the night. Afterward, I asked if they were ready. Both nodded, tears in their eyes. Then, with Keisha on my left and Oscar on the other side of her, each of us with an arm around her, we pushed open the door and started down the aisle. I kept my right hand inside my jacket, near my shoulder holster.

In a billowing white surplice with a kente cloth stole bracketing the cross that hung from his neck, Dr. Markham had just returned to the wooden lectern. When he saw us, his mouth fell open. "Oh, my God!" he said after a heartbeat or two, so close to the microphone his words reverberated. "Even as the good Lord takes one of our children from us, he sends another one home!" He pointed to us. "Praise the might of our Lord!"

Seated at the piano with her back to the congregation, Loni spun around on the bench and froze, clerical collar bobbling with her swallows, her white surplice and black underskirt twisting and riding up to reveal too much thigh, which would have been considered indecent if anyone had been paying attention to her.

But as far as I could tell, all eyes were on us as we made our way through the center of the assembly. I saw mouths hanging open, smiles, looks of disbelief, confusion on the faces of children and a few of the elderly—and Jen, in her purple ski jacket and rising from an end seat beside Bianca. Following my texted instructions, she moved near the entrance Dante was supposed to secure. I heard gasps, voices, utterances of gratitude for God's mercy and goodness. We moved slowly, as I had said we must. To observers it looked as if Keisha had difficulty walking, forcing us to go at her pace. This gave

Oscar and me a chance to assess our surroundings, to see what might unfold. As I expected, we commanded so much attention that people rose and came to us, surrounding us and obscuring Keisha as a target.

When we reached the front, Dr. Markham came down the chancery's two steps and embraced Keisha as if she were his own daughter. Tears squeezed out of his closed eyes and for a moment I felt sorry about what he would soon learn about his wife. Then he shooed the bustling, chattering congregants back to their seats, saying, "We're gonna let this child tell her story!" and "Hush now!" and "God's given us this chance, so we must listen!" He put his hand in the small of Keisha's back, to steer her up to the lectern, but she twisted away from him with a fluid motion that nearly upset his balance, pulled the pistol from her shoulder bag, and pointed it right between Loni Markham's eyes.

This time the collective gasp and subsequent babbling were so loud I was sure no one heard Keisha say, "Up!" But everyone saw the gun. Everyone saw Loni stand and watched as Keisha twisted her arm in a hammerlock and forced her up the chancery steps—keeping Loni between herself and the door I expected Dante to use, as I had instructed. In the silence that followed, all anyone heard was Dr. Markham say, "Keisha?"

Now Jen was by the closed right side door, hand in her coat, waiting. Oscar moved to the opposite door, his hand holding the closed pocket baton he sometimes used to discourage abusive husbands from trying to see their wives sheltered at Hope's Haven. I stayed near Keisha but gave her enough room to position Loni up at the lectern.

"Keisha," Dr. Markham said again. "Child, what has come over you?" He clearly wanted to take a step toward her but dared not move. "What have they done to you?" He looked at me with an uncertainty that was trying to become anger but kept dissolving into fear. "Mr. Rimes, what is this—"

"Must be drugs!" Loni shouted. "She's on drugs again! Somebody help me!"

"Liar!" Keisha screamed, pushing the gun barrel into the side of Loni's head, hard.

The door near Jen began to open but stopped partway. She pulled her gun and flashed her badge to the handful of people looking at her. Several crouched down in their pews.

"You're going to tell them everything," Keisha said, "or you're going to die."

"Keisha, please," Dr. Markham begged. He looked at Jen and then at me with my hand still inside my jacket. "Please put down your guns. All of you. This is the house of God."

"If God's given us this chance to listen, Dr. Markham," I said, "I think we should."

The door near Jen eased shut.

Exerting pressure on Loni's right arm and putting the PPQ against her ribs, Keisha nudged her sideways just enough to put herself behind the lectern's microphone.

"All of you know me," she said. "A lot of you have known me since I was a baby. A few weeks ago some of you comforted my folks when I was in the hospital for an overdose. You said you couldn't believe I was doing drugs. The truth is, I wasn't. My boyfriend—" Her voice faltered as tears began. "My *fiancé* Odell and I were cut off by two men and forced to inject heroin at gunpoint." She paused and took a deep breath. "The person behind it all was a woman I trusted, a woman I looked up to and loved, a woman who was nothing but a she-wolf in clergy clothing. Now Loni Markham is going to tell you why she's been trying to kill me since I got out of the hospital." Amid the congregation's gasps and utterances of denial, Keisha sidestepped enough to jerk Loni to the microphone. "Tell them."

Loni's gulp sounded over the public address system. "This is all a misunderstanding."

"Tell them, you bitch!" Keisha said. "Tell them about the drugs and the money laundering and your brother."

"Brother?" Dr. Markham's surprise was underscored by the murmurs that rippled through the crowd. "We've been together over twenty years. You said you were an only child."

"Tell them!" Keisha screamed. "You think I won't shoot? Remember, I still love the man I saw die." She released Loni's arm and stepped back, keeping the gun leveled at her.

I looked at Jen and then at Oscar. So far, no additional movement from either door. Where the hell was Dante? Had he retreated because he couldn't see the situation? Had he gone through the basement to the front of the building and found QC? Were they starting his Navigator even now?

As the congregation listened in stunned silence and her husband sank onto the piano bench in horror, Loni confirmed the basic details of her foundation's entanglement with FBF Development, a company headed by a brother she had left behind in Detroit years ago, along with the rest of her dysfunctional family. He had found her some years back, she said, and blackmailed her into cooperating with him. She spun the story with a sincerity that made her an unwitting pawn in a Faustian bargain to increase the wealth and good works of Sermon on the Mount and its foundation. Even as she spoke, however, I saw doubt, disappointment, and anger on enough faces to know she had lost the congregation. Loni too must have seen that any sympathy she hoped to rouse evaporated with each sentence. After saying the decision to kill Keisha had been her brother's, she stopped speaking and dropped her mask.

If this were Salem in 1692, I thought, *she'd already be on her way to Gallows Hill.*

Seething, Loni turned to Keisha. "There. Happy now?"

"No," Keisha said. She pulled the trigger twice, hitting Loni squarely in the chest.

For a moment there was a perfect stillness in the church.

There had been no explosions, nothing to make anyone cower in fear of a third shot. Those who ducked had done so reflexively, but the absence of sonic booms was confusing. The snap of the PPQ was not unlike the *phfft* of a suppressor, but there was no extension on the barrel. As if surprised she was still standing, Loni looked down at her chest and saw the huge splotch of blue staining her robe. Then she looked at Keisha, who fired again and again, each snap of the CO_2

cartridge adding yellow, green, more blue, and purple to the swirl of color on her vestments.

"A paintball gun!" Loni screamed. "A fucking paintball gun!" Hands curled into claws, she lunged for Keisha.

Just then there was a distant *phfft* and a chunk of the lectern blew off. A second shot whizzed past me and hit something as I screamed, "Everybody down!" and dropped. A third shot hit the piano as I tried to get a fix on the shooter. It just missed Dr. Markham, still on the bench. But I saw the flash that time. Though it had been minimized by the silencer, it came from a silhouette standing behind the front panel of the choir loft. "Jen, the loft!"

We both fired two shots at the loft, our gunfire loud enough to elicit screams as the silhouette ducked out of sight.

I charged up the center aisle, yelling "Stay down! Stay down!" and Jen raced along the wall, shouting "Police officer! Call nine-one-one!" We reached the narthex doors at the same time and stood on either side of the center, straining to see movement through the beveled amber glass. Nothing. I signaled I would go through on a three-count, and Jen nodded. Then I kicked open one of the doors and plunged through.

The narthex was empty, save for Harlow Graves, still tied and gagged but now dead, a scorched bullet hole in the center of his forehead. QC's cuffs had been cut and left on the floor. With Jen on the other side, gun ready, I eased open the front door, expecting a shot. Instead, through a light snowfall, I saw a body sprawled on his belly halfway down the stairs.

Jen covered me as I went down. I didn't need to turn him over to see who it was. The split left leg of his pants told me it was QC. The blood pooled around the hole at the base of his skull told me he was dead.

"That the guy?" Jen said when I returned to the top. "Did we hit him?"

I shook my head. "His partner."

"What happened?"

"I guess he couldn't keep up."

We heard the sirens before we pulled the front door shut.

"This is gonna be a real shit show," Jen said while we were still alone in the narthex. "Better give me your gun and we both better wipe our texts. I was just here to visit my wife's childhood church and got caught up in a shootout. You good with that?"

"Absolutely," I said. I handed her my Glock and QC's gun, both of which she pocketed, and then my lock pick gun.

"Jesus, Rimes. Are you gonna hire me if I lose my job?"

"They'll process my gun as part of this scene and get it back to me. But burglary tools—"

"Yeah, yeah." She pocketed the lock pick gun too. "What about your friend? He carrying?"

"A pocket baton. He works security."

Jen nodded. "I don't know his name yet, so don't tell me. And don't tell me any more about your plan with Keisha. Did you know the whole time her gun wasn't real?"

"Odell got her into paintball. A PPQ replica was one of the things I found in her closet when her parents let me go through her home."

"All right then. I got up when the gun came out but I couldn't announce myself or take a shot when I thought doing so would endanger lives."

"Makes sense to me," I said.

We pushed through to the sanctuary and walked down the aisle. There was turmoil on both sides as people asked whether it was safe to leave or if we had caught the shooter. There were also tears and prayers and people still in shock.

Reaching the center, Jen took charge. She called for quiet and again announced that she was a cop, off-duty. "Police are on their way. Get comfortable and stay exactly where you are. It's going to be a long night with a lot of questions. When you're asked what happened, just tell what you saw. Now, is anyone hurt or in need of medical attention?"

"Here," came a trembling, tearful voice. It was Dr. Markham, seated on the steps with his wife's head in his lap. A few choir members were gathered around him, crying and holding onto each other.

As Jen and I walked toward Dr. Markham and the choir members, we saw Keisha and Bianca some distance away from them, holding each other and crying.

"Hurt but long past medical attention," Dr. Markham said. "She's with the healer of all healers now."

50

Just before the detectives arrived, I called Phoenix and said, "It's finished. As soon as the police are done with me, I'll drop off your car and leave the key on one of the hooks just inside your door. It'll probably be late so don't bother waiting up." I said nothing then about all that had happened since Piñero had dropped us off yesterday afternoon. She knew nothing of my breaking into Tito's home. Having read the paper, she might have guessed that the Sanctuary Nimbus fire had something to do with my case but wouldn't know for sure. She couldn't know Loni Markham had died from a bullet likely intended for Keisha Simpkins or that Dante Cuthbert had silenced two liabilities before fleeing into the night. She didn't ask how the case ended or if I was all right. She said, "Okay," and nothing more.

Of course, there were things I didn't know either.

Much would emerge over the next several days as the investigation continued. Fingerprints led to the unsealing of a juvie record that showed QC Griffin was actually Alton Kimbrough, whose resemblance to Dante Cuthbert made people assume they were related. Kimbrough and Dante had shared a cell in juvie when Dante spent time there for pushing the real Quentin Cuthbert Griffin in front of a car. Marco Madden would be found in Wilkes-Barre, Pennsylvania, and would eventually explain the intricacies of the relationship among Flame Bright Fame, the Sermon on the Mount Community Development Foundation, Sanctuary Nimbus, and the Immortals. Within weeks the investigation would expand to include the New York State Police, the Chautauqua County Police, the Detroit Police, the FBI, the DEA, the ATF, and the Department of the Treasury.

As Jen had said, a real shit show.

Also, I had no idea that despite a nationwide BOLO that included his description and his Navigator, Dante Cuthbert would not be caught that week. Nor did I imagine that facing down a killer with a paintball gun would be the stuff of national news or that appearing on camera for all four of Buffalo's network affiliates for the next couple days would make Jen Spina emerge as the hero of the evening. Having gone to the church with her wife, who felt the need to pray for her missing childhood friend, Jen had been there when Keisha came in with a family friend to confront the woman who had tried to kill her. No one mentioned my name in the media that night or any time during the next week. I was happy about that.

What I did know when I sat down with Rafael Piñero and Pete Kim that night was that I was tired, overfed turtle tired, so I answered their questions as accurately as I could in the fewest possible words, omitting my interactions with Jen. Then I left.

It was almost two when I parked in Phoenix's slot in the underground garage and rode the elevator to the eleventh floor. Letting myself in with my key, I slid the Toyota key over one of the hooks near the door. Then I noticed the flickering glow from the interior of the loft. I went inside and passed the kitchenette island.

Her robe wrapped around her, Phoenix sat on her steel-framed sofa in the living-dining area, in the light of an alcohol gel fire crackling in her ventless fireplace. Electric light from other buildings came in through her tall, uncovered windows.

"My second fire tonight," she said. "These canisters only last about three hours."

"I said it would be late, not to wait up."

"I figured you might want to talk." She was quiet a moment, staring into the fire, not looking at me. "If you didn't, I knew I'd want to. I need to."

"All right."

I went over to the sofa and sat beside her. There was a pillow against the armrest, not a sofa pillow but a bed pillow. I pulled it onto my lap.

Phoenix turned to me, light dancing on the left side of her face. "Is there anything you want to ask before I start?"

I held up the pillow. "Is this where Keisha slept last night?"

"Yes." She bit her lip.

"You don't need to worry about her tonight. She's sleeping in her own bed now."

"Good." A few seconds passed. "How did you know?"

"Jen and Bianca showed me Keisha's text this morning. The number was yours. Want to tell me about it?"

Phoenix tightened her arms around herself and sank down a bit, crossing her bare feet on a throw pillow on the coffee table. "After the crash, after you got out, she started to cry. She said they would never leave her in peace unless she did something about it herself. She swore she would and asked me to be her lawyer." Phoenix smiled in the firelight. "She even did the old TV thing of giving me a dollar as a retainer. I gave her my spare key and one of the special business cards I keep for client emergencies. It's coded to tell building security the woman holding the card is at risk and has my key with my permission."

"You've done this with women you've represented from Hope's Haven," I said.

"Yes, five or six times. But this is the first time I gave anybody my cell to get an Uber." She shifted a bit, continuing to stare into the fire. "I didn't tell you because—well, these people were pretty good at following you. I thought I could give her a chance you couldn't then. Sorry if I seemed odd or off. I'm not used to keeping things from you."

I swallowed and took a breath. "Is that all?"

"No."

"I thought not." I put the pillow behind my head and leaned back. "I thought being shot at—I mean, it's bad enough I got shot a few weeks back. Now *you* almost got shot."

"That's part of it, but it isn't just that. It isn't just that I could lose you." She pulled my left hand into her lap and held it with both of hers. "It's that I could lose me."

"No, *I* could lose you," I said. "If something happened—Look, I understand why you could be having second thoughts, why you'd want out of the danger zone. Getting shot at—"

"You're not hearing me, Gideon," she said, turning to me. "Just listen. Please." She turned back to the fire. "Until you, I was a loner, a hyperactive attorney working myself into the grave. No family but Tia Rosita. Few friends. Figured I was living on borrowed time. Preventive mastectomies or not, I figured it was only a matter of calendar and clock before the cancer that took out the women on my mother's side would take me too. So there I was, driven, with a good income, clients who loved the energy I gave them, and devil may care certainty I had only myself to live for. The occasional one night stand? What did it matter? Better to break a heart early than succumb to hope. Two or three days without sleep? So what? Soon enough I would sleep forever. You get the idea." She brought my hand up to her lips and kissed it. "But then I met you, and things were different."

Having been told to listen, I waited for her to continue.

"Yesterday, after Keisha ran and I found your gun, I almost killed that man," she said, finally. "I wanted to. Something I never thought I'd want to do. I know you've killed in self-defense, and I get that. But when I saw him on the ground, self-defense was the last thing on my mind, even as he tried to fight you. Even after he was still, I wanted to make him pay for what he did to us. If you hadn't taken the gun, I know I would have pulled the trigger. That's what I meant by losing me. I don't want to lose me, but I don't want to lose you either."

Still, I said nothing.

She moved her head to my shoulder and reached over to touch my chest. Her fingers moved over the bumps and edges of the various supplies in the pockets of my utility jacket. "Jesus. Who gave you this thing? Bruce Wayne?"

"I'll take it off," I said, standing. "It's kind of warm in here anyway."

She remained quiet as I slipped off my jacket and lowered it to the floor but she snuggled against me when I sat back down.

"I think I'm afraid," she said a few seconds later. "Of us. Of having feelings so intense so fast."

"I'll understand if you need time. Or space..."

"I don't want time." She took hold of my hand and squeezed. "I especially don't want space. What I want you to understand is how it messes with my head that I was ready to kill for you."

"I think I do." I hoped she would take my word for it because I hated talking about the emotional firestorm of combat.

"I don't like that feeling but I'm ready to feel it again. Does that make any sense?"

"Yes. It's one thing to feel, another to enjoy what you felt." I hesitated. "You're a survivor, Phoenix. That's why you do so well in court, why you had pre-emptive surgery. You're determined to live. When circumstances demand it, that part of your nature kicks in, but you don't find any pleasure in it. You just do what must be done."

"Like you." She chuckled. "Maybe it kicks in harder because I finally have a reason to outrun the calendar."

"Hm."

We stared at each other for several beats and the air shifted, going from emotion to awareness. She stood and slowly pulled me toward the bed in the corner.

The sex started gradually, then became more feverish than ever—all arms and legs and sweat, all hands and nails and clashing tongues. Desperation, heat, whimpers and finally surrender—through it all she clung to me more intensely than I would have thought possible. Her tears hit my chest when she was astride me, hit my face when she leaned down to kiss me, zigzagged down the sides of my face into my ears. Whispers of something she said for the first time echoed in my dizzy brain long after we had stopped: *"I love you. I love you. I love you."*

Afterward, as I drifted toward sleep while lying on my belly, my head resting on a pillow encircled by my forearms, she half stretched herself atop me.

"Too heavy?" she said.

"Never," I said.

"So now you know."

"I do."

"I didn't intend to tell you like this. I just couldn't keep it in anymore, not after yesterday." She was quiet a moment, her head between my shoulder blades, a hand lightly holding my shoulder. "You don't have to say it back, you know." Her breath was warm on my back. "If you're not there yet, I understand."

"But I am there," I said. "I love you too. A thousand kisses deep."

"Quoting Leonard Cohen? You're full of surprises."

"I think that's my last surprise for tonight. You take no prisoners in bed, baby. I'm too beat down to do anything but fall asleep."

"It was a good beat down, though. Right?"

"Finest kind."

51

Mid-afternoon on Christmas Day, Phoenix and I kept a promise to stop by the Simpkins home before we went to Mira's for dinner.

Mona answered the door, wearing a godawful holiday sweater with elves and candy canes, a pair of fuzzy reindeer slippers with red noses, and a pair of felt antlers with little bells attached. As she was still recovering from her chest wound, her breathing was a bit shallow when she invited us inside. But in my brief acquaintance with her, she had never looked happier.

She smiled as I introduced her to Phoenix. "Win told me you were a real nice lady, and Keisha told me what you did for her. I can't thank you enough."

"No thanks necessary," Phoenix said.

"Just the same, God'll bless you both for being so good to us."

Then she ushered us into the living room. A crowd of thirty or so, most in sweaters, stretched from the decorated tree by the front window to the back of the dining room. Red plastic cups in hand, they stood or sat on good furniture, folding chairs, and even the floor, engaged in conversation. Many faces I recognized like Winslow, Louisa and Oscar (who was interim minister at the church), Ike Kelly,

Carl Williamson, Ileana Tassiopulos, a few Humanitas staffers, and faces from the church. Deeper in the dining room, amid faces I had never seen before, I noticed a tall, dark-skinned man in an army dress uniform. Nearby, Keisha stood laughing with Fatimah and Bianca, as Jen rested her head on Bianca's shoulder.

Mona shushed them all and introduced us in a loud voice. "Everybody, this is Mr. Rimes and Miss Trinidad, the ones who helped bring our Keisha home."

Whether standing or seated, they all applauded us and did so for a long time.

Her smile matching the one I first saw in her photos, Keisha pushed her way through the gathering until she reached us and threw an arm around each of us, hugging us so tight I thought she had invented a new sleeper hold. When she stepped back, happy tears brimmed her eyes. "Thank you so much for coming."

"Wouldn't miss it," I said. "I hear you're going back to work in January."

"Thanks to Ms. Trinidad," she said, high-fiving Phoenix.

"Now they can't stay with us long, baby," Mona said. "They've got somewhere else to be. With family, right?"

Before I could answer, Phoenix said, "Yes, with family."

"They can't stay for dinner," Mona announced to all, "but we can't let 'em outta here without a piece of my Christmas cake, now can we?"

For a moment, the resounding "No!" made me feel as if I were back in the church.

So, for us, they had dessert before the Christmas dinner. The cake had buttercream filling, green and red frosting, candy cane shavings, and green and red maraschino cherries. As we ate off paper dessert plates, I had a chance to talk with several guests. Carl Williamson patted my back and thanked me for getting his son's killers. "I hear you kicked some serious ass," he said. Rhonda Williamson kissed me on the cheek and wiped her eyes. Ike introduced me to his daughters, telling them I was the guy who brought Aunt Keisha back to them.

Jen said that in a just world I would have shared in her service commendation and told me to look for my lock pick gun in the mail sometime soon. Any time you need help with something, you call me," she said. I thanked her. I also thanked Ileana for helping me understand the world of the homeless, to which she replied, "You couldn't save Veronica but you damn sure pulled Keisha out of the fire and iced the bastards who put her there. I'm the one who should thank you."

The tall man in dress greens had a neatly trimmed mustache and the green and yellow trimmings of an MP. He came to me and introduced himself as Sonny Tyler, Keisha's ex-boyfriend, on leave from Stuttgart. "Heading back before New Year's," he said. "Had to see for myself she was okay. We're just friends now. I don't hope for more, especially so soon after what happened to Odell. But I wanted her to know I was a phone call away if she ever needed to talk. Thank you for passing on my message." Then he saluted me, and I saluted back.

When it was time to go, Winslow and Mona walked us to the door, with Oscar and Louisa behind them. Mona and Louisa hugged us both, and Winslow shook our hands. Oscar walked us out to Phoenix's car.

"Thanks for putting me back in the real game for a quick minute," he said. "You're both welcome any time, in our home, or the church." Before I could say anything, he held up his hand. "I already know you're not much of a believer. But I think I told you before, you don't have to believe in God for God to believe in you. He believes in you, Brother Rimes. You should feel blessed."

"I do," I said. "You gotta be cold in just that sweater." I embraced him. "Thanks for having my back."

"They're nice people," Phoenix said, as she pulled away from the curb. "All of them."

"Good people," I said. "They didn't deserve to be caught up in something so bad."

"Feeling philosophical, are we?"

"Maybe a bit Dickensian."

"Oh, God, if you're gonna go all Tiny Tim on me—"

"No, not that one," I said. "This was a tale of two churches, two gangs, and double identities. Ultimately, it was a tale of two women, one bad and willing to do anything to hide her true self and one good, willing to sacrifice herself for those she loved."

"What was in that red punch we drank anyway?" Phoenix said, laughing. "Seriously, honey, one of the things I love about you is your need to make sense of a world that proves chaotic with every breath it takes. Sometimes things are what they are, but you see patterns that give you hope. You claim to be a cynic but you're the most optimistic person I know."

"No need to be insulting," I said.

"That was nothing. Wait till we start looking for your new car. I looked up that special bumper thing you want to put on the front. Ugly as sin!"

Because it was Christmas and traffic was light, we took Main Street toward Mira's Williamsville home rather than get on the highway. The sun was still bright. The city was beautiful as we drove through the center of it, just enough fresh snow to make the streets look sparkling and clean, just enough lights, decorations, and closed businesses up Main and into the suburbs to make us feel the holiday spirit had not been sacrificed on the altar of commercialism. Things would be different by February, of course, when the snow was dirty slush and Presidents' Day sales tried to draw people out of their winter doldrums. But right now, on Christmas, winter in Buffalo was breathtaking.

Just as we reached the edge of the Village of Williamsville, my phone buzzed. Pulling it from my pocket, I saw I had a text from a number designated UNKNOWN. I opened the text function and saw a link. I didn't have to click the link to understand what it meant and who had sent it to me. The tiny headline and subheadline told the whole story: *Suspect in Buffalo Triple Murder Found Dead in Detroit River. Cuthbert shot once in head.*

"Dante Cuthbert's dead," I said.

"Good," Phoenix said, turning onto Mira's street. "That means he won't be coming after you. Who sent the message? Your psycho acquaintance?"

Before I could reply, the phone buzzed again, a call from UNKNOWN but I knew who it was before I answered.

"Mr. Rimes, sir, I just wanted to wish you the merriest of holiday seasons." The voice was cold as ever and unfailingly polite. Spider Tolliver, amiable psychopath.

"Merry Christmas to you too, Lester," I said.

"It's a fine day for celebrating the things and people that matter. I just wanted to make sure you got the link I sent. I thought it might be of interest to you."

"I got it. Thank you."

"It reflects a circumstance completely free of obligation or expectation, so please, put your mind at ease. Merry Christmas to Ms. Trinidad. Goodbye."

"Spider?" Phoenix said.

"He killed Cuthbert, no strings attached. He said to tell you Merry Christmas."

"You just bring out the best in people, don't you," she said. "A regular elf."

As we neared the end of my sister's street and her home, I saw the cars that told me Phoenix and I were the last to arrive: Bobby's Camry, the Dorans' wheelchair van, Julie Yang's VW Beetle, the red Sentra that Jimmy told me LJ had climbed out of after three all-night dates.

"So how many of us will there be?" Phoenix said, parking a few doors away. "The house is so small."

"A dozen. Bobby and Kayla, Jimmy and Peggy Ann, LJ and his new girlfriend."

"The one Peggy Ann says is rocking his world something fierce?"

I couldn't help smiling at the picture of LJ and Yvonne. If he survived, he would thank me for the introduction.

"Yes," I said. "Also Julie and her new boyfriend Brett, a grad student in physics. Mira and Shakti. Us. A tight fit in the dining room but we'll make it work."

We climbed out and went to the back of the RAV4 to retrieve the bags of gifts.

Phoenix looked at me as I reached inside. "You know, I worry about the day you might have to face this Spider character. You have scruples. He doesn't."

"It won't be today," I said, handing her a large bag and taking the other two myself in one hand. I lowered the liftgate with my free hand. "Oscar was right. Today I feel blessed."

Phoenix pressed the LOCK button on her fob. "You?"

"Yes," I said. "How often do I have all the people I love in the world under one roof?"

ABOUT THE AUTHOR

Photo Credit: Tamara Alsace

Retired University at Buffalo professor Gary Earl Ross is a multiple award-winning playwright and novelist. His plays include *The Scavenger's Daughter, The Mark of Cain, The Guns of Christmas, The Trial of Trayvon Martin*, and the Edgar Award-winning *Matter of Intent*. Both *The Scavenger's Daughter* and *Matter of Intent* have been made into culturally transliterated films by CITOC Productions of Mumbai, India. His books include *The Wheel of Desire, Shimmerville, Beneath the Ice, Blackbird Rising*, and *Nickel City Blues*, the first Gideon Rimes novel. For more information, visit him at www.garyearlross.net

ACKNOWLEDGMENTS

Novels are not written in a vacuum. Knowingly or unknowingly, others help in too many ways to count. I am indebted to the following: My much better half Tammy, my sister Renee, my cousin Bobby, my friends Dennis Hollins, Duane Crockett, Scott Williams, Mitch Maxick, Gunilla Theander Kester, Susan Lynn Solomon (author of the Emlyn Goode mysteries); my brothers Steve and Rob and my son David for professional perspectives on the criminal justice system and law enforcement; artist and high school classmate Gary L. Wolfe and Karen Carman for perspectives on homelessness; Kelsey Jackson-Ross, no relation, whose performance in my creative writing class tells me she will find her way into print and whose picture of me is part of this book; Nancy Alsace, for insights on nursing practices; Satya Popuri, for insights on a life in science; Amherst Alarm, for tolerating a long-time customer's questions about alarm systems; the Buffalo and Erie County Public Library; and the following eateries you must try on your next trip to the Nickel City: Betty's, the Towne, EM Tea Coffee Cup (Cat and Will), Spot Coffee, Tim Horton's, Panorama on Seven, LaNova, Bocce, Avenue, Just Pizza, and the gone but fondly remembered Vino's (Kathleen Cangianello) and Gigi's (Darryl Harvin).

GIDEON RIMES SERIES

Nickel City Blues
Nickel City Crossfire
Nickel City Storm Warning

SEG Publishing invites you to visit our site!
Join our newsletter and receive a free short story in the Gideon Rimes
Series

Made in United States
North Haven, CT
18 April 2023

35552948R10200